IN THE WORLD of hospitals and doctors the fatal mistake is usually buried with the victim. There is a special kind of silence that nourishes this evil. First it corrupts, then it destroys. It unleashes an arrogance of power that is murderous.

Surgery and sudden death had become a hallmark of the Hatch Clinic. Everybody knew why. No one dared to talk.

Until now . . .

"CHILLING EVOCATION OF A HOSPITAL ATMOSPHERE. . . . THE CLIMACTIC COURT SCENE . . . IS AS DEFINITIVE AS ANY EVER DRAWN."

—Los Angeles Times

THE CLINIC

By JAMES KERR

A FAWCETT CREST BOOK
Fawcett Publications, Inc., Greenwich, Conn.

PRINCIPLES OF MEDICAL ETHICS
AMERICAN MEDICAL ASSOCIATION

SECTION 4.—The medical profession should safeguard the public and itself against physicians deficient in moral character or professional competence. Physicians should observe all laws, uphold the dignity and honor of the profession, and accept its self-imposed disciplines. They should expose, without hesitation, illegal or unethical conduct of fellow members of the profession.

To my wife

THIS BOOK CONTAINS THE COMPLETE TEXT OF THE ORIGINAL HARDCOVER EDITION.

A Fawcett Crest Book reprinted by arrangement with Coward-McCann, Inc.

Library of Congress Catalog Card Number: 68-13322

Printed in the United States of America

PART ONE

1

"WE'RE two hundred miles from San Francisco and beginning our descent," the pilot announced, shaking Peter de Haan out of his thoughts. He looked at his watch. One fifty. They would be ten minutes late in landing. Peter pushed back his blond hair and took a briefcase from under the seat before fastening his safety belt.

The airliner came down slowly through Sacramento Valley clouds to the beauty of San Francisco on a clear day. The travelers looked out at the sun-flashed waters of the Bay, at Telegraph Hill and the matchstick wharves of the Embarcadero, and the Pacific Ocean beyond the Gate. They stared at the bridge as they circled, and then the green stalk of the Peninsula, before they skidded to touchdown.

Peter nodded to the smiling hostess as he stepped out the cabin door. Starting down the long corridors of the International Airport, the tall, uncommonly straight young man frowned to cover his excitement.

In the waiting room he looked around carefully for his new employer's prominent figure. As his luggage finally appeared, he heard over the loudspeakers, "Dr. Peter de Haan, Dr. Peter de Haan, please report to the information booth."

"I was being paged," he told the man at the information desk.

"Yes, sir. The lady right here was trying to contact you."

Peter turned in surprise to see a slim woman with red hair looking at him with a smile. As he stepped toward her, she put out a green-gloved hand.

"You are Dr. de Haan?" she asked. Peter nodded. "I'm Mrs. Hatch, Rosalie Hatch. Dr. Hatch couldn't get here after all. He was very sorry. I know he looked forward to the chance for a visit, but emergency surgery came up, so I'm the substitute." She shook his hand firmly and briefly. "I'll get my car and pick you up in front by the loading sign," she said.

Peter watched Mrs. Hatch's black Cadillac, this year's model, glide up to the curb for him. They accelerated smoothly into the line of traffic, away from the terminal and onto the Bayshore Freeway. He looked around at the rich interior of the automobile. "I like your car."

Peter glanced at her profile, her small nose and delicate chin. She must be in her early forties, because Dr. Hatch was nearer fifty than forty and had talked about children close to college age, but she certainly didn't look it.

"Usually I get the old car and Matthew takes the new one. This year, though, I got the new one and I haven't figured out why. There's a catch somewhere. Probably Matthew wants to go hunting jaguars in Guatemala and hasn't told me yet, or something." She made a face as Peter laughed, noticing to himself how easily she handled the large sedan.

"Matthew said you were from Baltimore. Have you lived there, or did you just go to school there?" she asked.

"I was born there *and* went to school there . . . graduated from John Biddle Med. School a year ago, and just finished my internship at Biddle Medical Center last Thursday. It seems a month already, though."

"Your father's a doctor, is he?"

"He was a general practitioner until he had a stroke eight years ago. He's been pretty well incapacitated since then, at least physically."

"I'm sorry to hear that."

They drove past Candlestick Park and started through the San Francisco Mission District. Mrs. Hatch pointed out views and identified landmarks. As they came over Potrero Hill, the skyline of the city became visible.

"Your apartment is all ready," Rosalie Hatch said, "and my husband said to tell you the first month's rent is paid, so don't be concerned about that. It's on Valleyview Drive, about ten minutes from downtown and fifteen minutes from the clinic."

"That's wonderful of him. I've been worrying about a place to stay."

"You may not like it, but it gives you a few months to look around and find something else, anyway."

Peter was absorbed in the scenes from the Bay Bridge as they crossed it, the steamers and sailboats below, and off to the left Treasure Island. All his life he had heard of the hills and the bay of San Francisco, and they were as unique and beautiful as he had imagined.

After circling Oakland on the Nimitz Freeway, the landscape gradually tapered into rural countryside. Thirty miles from the Bay Bridge, they turned off the freeway into the low hills which formed a rim for the Cima Valley, Mrs. Hatch explained. These flattened out and then they sped through the fertile fields and tiny towns of the valley at seventy-five miles per hour. Peter was impressed with the noiseless, effortless performance of the car. Maybe he should get a Cadillac some day, after all, instead of the Jaguar or Mercedes-Benz he had sometimes imagined.

They went on for a while in the windless hush of the car's speed before she asked, "You're not married, are you, Dr. de Haan?"

"No, not yet."

"Someone in mind?"

"No, I didn't mean that."

"You're not leaving a girl friend behind in Baltimore then?"

"No."

She smiled, for a moment Peter thought provocatively, showing evenly faceted white teeth and smooth full lips. "We're starting into the outskirts of San Marcial now," she said, still looking at him, and that was his last clear recollection of the day. Neither one of them saw the dump truck coming in from a side road before it hit them.

2

PETER wakened in a room that was dark except for light slipping under the door. He could hear breathing near him, apparently in another bed. He must be home, but what would the breathing be? No, this wasn't his room. Why it must be—must be what? No image would form. It wasn't his college room. Where was he? He could see the bed next to him dimly now and the head of an old man in it, but it wasn't his father—the head was bald.

He started through the usual testing procedures. What day it was, where he was born, and so forth. Of course, he knew he was born in Maryland. But then he couldn't remember just where in Maryland. That should frighten him, he decided, but he didn't feel frightened either. Something must have happened to him. What, though? Now really, what day was it, what month and year? It was—no, he couldn't say them after all.

The door opened with a bright flush of illumination onto his face. "Hello, Doctor. Well now, are you coming around?" He could see it was a nurse. Then he was in a hospital.

"I guess so." Now he remembered he was a doctor. He thought he was a doctor. Strange he could not be sure of something that important.

"Do you know where you are?" she asked, as she briskly straightened his bedcover.

"No, I don't."

The nurse said, "I'm Miss Bledsoe, the charge nurse on this floor, which is the A Ward of the Hatch Hospital."

"Where is the hospital?"

"In San Marcial. San Marcial, California. Dr. Hatch's hospital. You know Dr. Hatch, of course."

"Yes," Peter answered uncertainly.

The light was switched on and a broad-shouldered giant clomped into the room, hard heels clicking on the asphalt tiles, a great smile on his face as he came up to the bed. Smothering Peter's hand in his, he asked, "How are you doing there, boy? Heck of an introduction to the city."

Peter looked at the oversized head, the shocking blue eyes, still not fitting this face into his cast of knowns.

"Don't you know me, Peter?"

"I'm really hazy, sir. I have a heck of a headache." Peter realized the man was a doctor. Was he Dr. Hatch?

"Whereabouts?"

"In back here," Peter said, pointing to his right neck.

"Your skull X-rays are all right." The doctor put his left hand, large and warm, on the back of Peter's head. "The egg there on your occiput is getting bigger, though. I'm Matthew Hatch, you know. You flew out this morning to California from Baltimore to start working with us. My wife picked you up at San Francisco International Airport and damned if some goof of a truck driver working for Jerry Hodgens' cement company didn't run into the side of the car just as you hit the city limits."

"Now, I remember!" Peter said. "I was almost remembering, but I couldn't quite."

"Good." Dr. Hatch pounded his fist in his palm. "I guess we'd better get you something to eat. This is the first sense you've made all afternoon and evening. I didn't want to put food in you until you at least came halfway to."

Holding his head from the pain that came with the exertion of talking, Peter asked, "How is Mrs. Hatch? Was she hurt?"

"A little, Peter. She broke two ribs and cut the side of her face. I sent her on home, though, after a few sutures and some tape on her chest. The truck driver didn't even get a scratch."

"I am sorry. And your Cadillac?"

"Totaled. Completely demolished. We can get another one, though, believe me. General Motors makes lots of them. People aren't so easy to replace. Glad to see you're doing all right, Dr. Peter. We'll leave you in overnight if you promise not to chase the nurses." He waved an energetic arm, laughed, and was gone.

Peter lay back in his bed, and the throbbing of his head eased. Now suddenly he remembered everything; he recalled giving his paper at the great Atlantic City auditorium three months before, the one he and Dr. Cunningham had prepared, then meeting Dr. Hatch afterward. He had spent that evening in the physician's suite in the Bart-Patterson Hotel. "I've had trouble deciding what to do," he had told Dr. Hatch. "I could stay at Biddle but I can't make up my mind whether to go into internal medicine or general surgery, which is a pretty fundamental decision. Partly for this reason, plus the fact money's been short in my family since my father's stroke, I've decided to take off one or two years in general practice someplace. Maybe you wouldn't be interested in me on that basis, though."

"Oh, I think so," Dr. Hatch had said quietly, but with the assurance of someone who was used to the attention of others. "I caught your paper today and it was most enjoyable. You did some independent thinking and came up with your own ideas which hold water. You're the kind of young person I want. I think my clinic might be quite the place for you."

Peter had looked at the physician then, at the well-tailored brown suit that covered his oversize frame, at the pale and exceptionally clear blue of his irises, at the large head heavily thatched with brown hair graying at its borders. His appearance was somehow more vivid than life, like that of a celebrity from the films seen at close hand. "It is your clinic, then?" Peter had said. "I mean, you do own it? I didn't quite understand that."

"Yes, I started it over fifteen years ago. And in operating it I've found that if you get a good doctor and give him a chance to work without having to worry about the business details of practice, you have an enormously productive as well as happy man nine times out of ten. So my clinic manager and I handle all the hiring, firing, ordering, what have you."

"That is a different setup."

"There are so many things to tell you about San Marcial and the clinic that it would take all night," Dr. Hatch had replied, but he had gone on talking pleasantly and in a mild-mannered if intense way about his hospital and clinic for several more hours. Ten days later Peter had decided to accept his offer, and now he was here, in this city of 100,000 which he had never seen, lying in a hospital bed in the middle of it, with a headache that didn't seem to want to stop.

And feeling surprised at the change in Dr. Hatch. In Atlantic City the doctor had been shy and earnest, now he seemed no longer diffident, much louder, much heartier.

Turning on the light over his head, Peter looked around the room. It had modern furnishings and fresh paint. In the slanting light from the bed, though, his surroundings were eerie, especially as he could hear the old man in the bed next to him gargling on saliva. The man began to moan and Peter pushed the partitioning curtain back farther to look at him. He was completely hairless, white-bearded and gaunt, and restless now, murmuring incoherently between moans.

"Is something wrong?" Peter called to him loudly. "Do you want the nurse?"

The man nodded and grabbed the side rail. "I'm sick to my stomach," he said, and immediately began vomiting. Peter found his call button and pressed it. The old fellow hung over his metal side rail, moaning and gagging.

Miss Bledsoe came hurrying in. "Yes, Doctor, what is it?"

"My friend here is feeling bad."

"Oh, dear, I guess we're going to have to put a Levine down." An aide came in to clean up the bed. The old man was given a shot, and then Miss Bledsoe passed a tube into his stomach. "Now don't pull on that, Mr. Erlanger," she warned him as she taped it on his nose, "or Dr. Hatch will be very angry at you."

Peter dozed off, the old man quiet at his side again, and then his arm was being tugged. "Here's a tray for you, Doctor. Just custard and tea and broth, and some milk of magnesia."

"I don't need any milk of magnesia, for heaven's sake," Peter said, looking at the nurse closely. "Did Dr. Hatch order that?"

"I've been working with Dr. Matthew for thirteen years now, and I know what he likes. After a head injury, a good cleaning out is always a help to the patient."

"No, thank you."

She shrugged her shoulders, and Peter grinned at her. He knew her type, the caustic, dried-up, old-maid nurse who always knew what was good for everybody.

"What's wrong with the old gentleman here, anyway?"

"He had an emergency operation this afternoon for intestinal obstruction. They put him here because there was no room on the surgery floor."

He must be the one who had prevented Dr. Hatch from meeting him at the airport, Peter thought. He smiled at the coincidence, and then at his own strange and dramatic entrance into the California world, before going to sleep, comfortable, excited again, anxious to get a look at his new environment.

3

PETER awakened early the next morning to the starting up noises of the hospital. He sat on the edge of his bed first, and then stepped down to the floor, happy to feel better. Mr. Erlanger looked gray-pale in the next bed, sweating and pulling at the leather restraints that had been put on him during the night.

Peter was suddenly dizzy walking for the open bathroom

door, and grabbed for the jamb. Later back in bed, though, his head was clear, and he swallowed his breakfast hungrily.

When the young A.M. nurse come in to check Mr. Erlanger's pulse and blood pressure, she shyly introduced herself to Peter as Miss Winters. She was not over twenty-one, Peter estimated, with large brown eyes set in a childish, pimpled face, but she seemed pleasant and conscientious. Peter asked her, "Who is Mr. Erlanger, my roommate? I mean, is he from San Marcial?"

She came close to the bedside, flushing as she bent over and whispered, "He has a little jewelry store downtown, John's Time Shop, and his wife died here two years ago after a cancer operation, I understand. That's all I know about him." Straightening up, she in turn asked, "Aren't you going to be on the staff here, Dr. de Haan?"

"Yes, and I'd love to get out of this room and look around the place."

"Oh, you're on absolute bed rest, Doctor."

"I am? Well, I've already been up to the bathroom."

"You're not supposed to be. No orders." She smiled, made a face, and slipped out the door. Almost at once Mr. Erlanger started coughing heavily and Miss Winters came back to sit him up and pound his back. A tall, older nurse, who had a slight Southern slur to her voice, followed her in soon. "I'm Mrs. Steffan, Dr. de Haan," she said, "the charge nurse on this ward." She reached out a cool hand for him to shake. "I've decided we'll move Mr. Erlanger into a private room that will be open in a few hours. I'm sure it wasn't much fun in here with him last night. He's been so sick since surgery."

"He really hasn't bothered me, Mrs. Steffan, but do what you think best. Practically every minute I feel better anyway. I don't plan to be here long."

"Well, at least stay where you are until Dr. Hatch comes. He'd probably fire us if he found you out of bed. Take advantage of the time to rest while you can. Believe me there'll be plenty to do soon enough."

There were two early visitors in the room, a man and a woman who were apparently relatives of John Erlanger. The old fellow made some sense at first, talking to them, but soon he was off on misty pathways of his own, then drowsing.

The elderly woman, with hennaed hair, spoke to Peter. "I'm John's sister, Doctor, and this is his brother from Los Angeles."

"Hello."

"You're certainly looking better. You were groaning and rolling around yesterday when they brought you in; you worried me. But I don't suppose you want to hear the gruesome details."

"Not especially." Peter laughed at her candor.

"I understand you're going to be in the clinic here," she said, taking off a worn green coat to expose a tiger-striped black-and-tan dress.

"That's right. I'm Dr. de Haan." That sounded too formal to Peter. Away from the Biddle University Hospital he was not quite used to being Dr. de Haan.

"We're so glad to hear that. Dr. Hatch is a wonderful man. He's been my doctor ever since he first went into practice in San Marcial. I got John to go to him yesterday morning, after he'd been sick for a month with pains. He was seeing another doctor who just took his blood pressure and gave him pills, but the pains kept coming back. Dr. Hatch seemed to know right away that he had an intestinal block and had him in surgery within three hours."

"That's too bad he had to operate."

"Dr. Hatch found a real marked obstruction. He said it would be hard to know for a few days if he would make it. You would have thought the other doctor could have found it sooner."

Peter sat up in bed. "Did the nurse tell you they were going to move your brother to a private room?" he asked.

"That's what I heard. He must be worse. I hope he didn't bother you too much."

"Not at all, really."

Dr. Hatch was in a short time later, resplendent in a bright plaid jacket with a red rose in its buttonhole. "I understand from Miss Winters you're doing fine, Peter." The nurse followed immediately behind Dr. Hatch with a bandage cart. "She tells me that you haven't even made a pass at her yet, so maybe you're not doing as well as she thinks." Miss Winters' blushing face appeared at the side of Dr. Hatch's torso as he winked at Peter.

"Oh, Dr. Hatch," she said.

"I think you can be up some today, Peter," Dr. Hatch added more seriously.

"Don't I get out today?"

"Oh, not yet."

"I feel fine."

"You need more time after a shaking up like yesterday."

"Of course whatever you say, but I'm anxious to get going."

Dr. Hatch felt the beat of Peter's artery at the wrist for a half-minute. "Ninety. A little fast for being in bed. Yes, I think you need more rest." He took a couple of steps back as if to appraise the young doctor, his bed, the practice of medicine, life in general. "What are you going to do with a young galoot like this, Miss Winters? Knocked out for six hours last night and wants to walk out of the hospital this morning. What do you think of that? I believe you better give him a little loving today, Miss Winters. That'll take care of some of his energy. Just crawl in the bed and treat him nice. All right?" He smiled at the shrinking young nurse who was looking straight ahead at the wall of the room.

"Please, Dr. Hatch."

"Actually, Peter, it's that curly blond hair on your chest that kills them dead, I think." He laughed out loud now. "Oh, come on, Miss Winters. I'll be good. I'm not trying to embarrass you. Just consider the source, my dear. Peter, we'll keep you here until tomorrow morning and then I'll get somebody to take you over to your apartment. Tuesday evening I want you to come to my house for dinner if you're up to it and we can talk then about business arrangements, what you can expect of us, what we might ask of you. Your office isn't quite ready, yet, anyway, but we have some space you can get by with for the next week or two."

"Fine. I've got to get an old car, too, before I go to work."

"Peter, see Harry Newhart for that, downtown on Poplar Street. Don't talk to anyone there but Harry, and tell him I sent you."

"Let me put that down, and—may I get up then?"

"All right." Dr. Hatch shook hands vigorously, looking Gargantuan to Peter as he leaned over the bed, then disappeared behind Mr. Erlanger's curtain for a minute, and waved cheerfully as he left the room.

Peter still could not get Matthew Hatch in focus. Perhaps it was the sudden unexpected assumption of the patient-doctor relationship between them that had changed him for Peter. Possibly when he got up and around and they were professional colleagues again his personality would shift back to the soft-voiced man of Atlantic City.

In mid-morning Peter got out of bed to shower, having successfully put off a bed bath. Glancing at Mr. Erlanger on his way into the bathroom, he saw the old man's face was chalk-white while his hair was soaked with perspiration. Peter stepped up to him and touched his hands, which were icy, and then noticed the center of his bed showed a spreading red stain. He reached for the signal cord and pushed its buzzer twice, then walked to the door and put his head out, looking down the wide hallway. A stooped janitor was up the corridor erasing smudges on the asphalt tile with his buffer. Peter called to him, "Get the nurse quick!" The old man looked up startled, uncomprehending. "Get the nurse, please, will you?"

The man understood now. "Oh, shurr, I get nurse."

Miss Winters rushed down the hall, pink when she got to Peter's door. "What's the matter, Dr. de Haan, are you sick?" she asked.

"It's Mr. Erlanger. I think he's eviscerated."

Miss Winters was in the room and out again, running back up the hall as she called to a man, apparently a physician, who stood by the nurses' station now. The man nodded as he passed Peter and went in the room. Peter stayed in the hall, enjoying his first moment of emergence. As the doctor came out, Miss Winters introduced him. "Dr. de Haan, this is Dr. Frank Lewicki."

They shook hands and Dr. Lewicki said to Miss Winters, "Go ahead and call Dr. Hatch right away. Tell him what happened. You'd better call the anesthesiologist too."

He turned back to Peter then, a dark, sturdy man with a round dimple in his strong chin. "I'm sorry. Small emergency here. I'm happy to meet you. I'm one of the two internists here. Have you met any of the other doctors in the clinic?" As he talked Peter noticed traces of a Brooklyn inflection.

"Only Dr. Hatch. It seems as I was coming into town—"

"Believe me, I know. I heard all about it. It's been on radio, television, and in the papers, so everyone in this metropolis who isn't deaf and blind knows it." Frank Lewicki laughed. "No doctor ever made such a dramatic appearance in San Marcial, I'm sure. Yes, I'd say I predict great things for you."

Peter laughed with him, liking him at once.

"You haven't met Harry Lawson then. He's right up by the nurses' station, or was." Turning, he called up the hall, "Hey, Harry. Come here." Harry waved back.

"The mother of one of those babies gets him on the phone and you'd think they were talking about buying a thousand shares of Christiana Securities. Harry's the pediatrician here."

"What's going on with Mr. Erlanger, anyway, Dr. Lewicki?" Peter asked.

"Frank. Call me Frank. I think Mr. Erlanger's going to be another triumph of modern surgery where the patient comes out dead. He just had a dehiscence of his abdominal wound and he'll have to go back to the O.R. right away. He was bad to start with and now he's shocky and looks worse."

"I thought that must be it."

Harry Lawson came up to them and said cheerily, "You're Dr. de Haan, aren't you? Don't let this Lewicki character dump all his crocks and emergency room calls on you, that's my first advice." He was entirely gray, short and plump, near middle age, with a beaver face including a low forehead, puffy cheeks, and prominent teeth. "It's nice to meet you, Peter. I heard about your crash."

"I'm feeling good, but Dr. Hatch doesn't want to let me out until tomorrow."

"You ought to have somebody take you around the place today, just to get oriented," Harry Lawson said.

"Characteristically, Matt just got the workmen started renovating the room for your office, even though he's known you were coming for over two months," Frank Lewicki put in. "Until the new place is ready you'll have to share Harry's and my place, so we'll all go nuts together."

"Our building connects with Matt's office by a corridor," Harry added, "which is a good thing, easy for the patients because you'll be taking some of his overflow for a while. At least that's what happened to me when I first came. I started out in general practice and gravitated into pediatrics, though I still assist Matt with his surgery."

"I guess Mrs. Steffan told you about Mr. Erlanger," Frank said to Dr. Lawson.

"Erlanger?"

"Matt did him yesterday afternoon for intestinal obstruction and he just eviscerated."

"Oh, hell, there goes my Sunday morning. Did you talk to Matt?"

"He knows about it."

"I was supposed to take the two oldest kids to mass, so I'll have to get Carol to do that. I better get on my horse before he starts in. Thanks, Frank. I'll be seeing you, Peter." Harry Lawson chugged away on his heavy legs.

"He's so sincere, he practically has bloody tears over his sick kids, the ones with leukemia and fibrocystic disease and that sort of thing. Damned fine pediatrician, too, even though he never had board training," Frank said, looking after him. "If you go to his house you'll get children between your legs and hanging from your earlobes, but some real Swiss cooking. His wife's from a Swiss-Italian family here in San Marcial County. We'd like to have you over sometime, ourselves. Gloria will call you up after you're settled."

"That would be nice."

"If you'd really like a tour of the place today, I'll get old Steve, the janitor, to push you around."

"I'd enjoy that."

"Matthew built the hospital first, then tore down the old places next door to put up the three clinic buildings. Year before last he added a hospital wing in back."

"I'm ready to tour anytime," Peter said.

"Okay, I'll look up Steve," Frank Lewicki said smiling.

Soon Peter was being pushed down the hospital alley by the old janitor and then at the middle of the block, he was suddenly turned forward to what was Archer Street. The janitor pointed to the front of the first white building with its red tile Spanish roof. "Dokator Leslie and Dokator Silvan'." The physicians' names were on a sign in front which showed this was Hatch Clinic Suite #3. Peter glanced over at the next building up the street, and then as they came to it, his heart pounded proudly in its cage to see the sign in front that read, "Hatch Clinic Suite #2, Frank Lewicki, M.D., Internal Medicine; Harry Lawson, M.D., Pediatrics; Peter de Haan, M.D., General Practice."

He had Steve stop the wheelchair. While he pretended to inspect the curved tile of the roof and the stucco front of the structure, he read through the roster several extra times. He reacted to each reading with a sense of unreality and pleasant disbelief.

As they started up again, Peter breathed the fresh white air of the outdoors, conscious of passersby staring at his pajamas and robe and the large bandages on his forehead. He thought about the two doctors he had just met. Frank seemed tough and capable, but friendly; Harry Lawson appeared competent, sincere, of good stock.

They rolled past the larger Hatch Clinic Suite #1 and up the inclining ramp alongside the front steps of the hospital, through the lobby, and turned down the hall of A Ward to stop by Room 22.

"Thanks, Steve, that was a wonderful trip. I enjoyed it."

"Doka-tor de Haa', I can tell you very nice man. Anything I do for you, you let me know, I do it."

"Thank you, I appreciate it."

As he lay back in bed again Peter felt eager to see more of San Marcial and to start work. He wanted to meet the others in the clinic, nurses and doctors, get into his office and prove himself with his own first patients.

Peter looked over at Mr. Erlanger's bed, freshly made up for its next occupant. He wondered how the old jeweler was getting along in surgery. His outlook seemed grim. Of course, the old man was in his sixties, alone, his wife dead . . .

Peter's thoughts were interrupted by Frank Lewicki's arrival in the room. His forehead was moist with sweat and he was in shirtsleeves, carrying his coat.

"Dammit!" Frank said, sitting down and letting out a loud sigh. Peter looked at him, waiting for the next words. "We lost the old man."

"Mr. Erlanger? I thought you would. Didn't you?"

"One whiff of the anesthetic and he was gone. We were going to do it under local. Then he perked up for a while before surgery with plasma and saline and Aramine and we decided to try a light general. But the anesthesia induction was just started and whoof, he was geflommoxed. I've been pumping his chest for twenty minutes, trying to get his heart going, but no use."

"That's too bad."

"Well, hell. Look, if you get out in the morning, let me know. Here's my home phone number, or get the message to my office, and Gloria can pick you up, give you a lift to your apartment. I understand Rosie Hatch has it fixed up for you already."

"Dr. Hatch said somebody here would drive me over, I think Steve. If I need help, I'll let you know, though. I appreciate the offer."

"All right, fellow," Frank said, and walked out.

4

FOUR days later, on Tuesday evening, coming up Sharpe Avenue to Santa Rita Road, Peter saw the Hatch property on the far right corner of the intersection. A high fence stretched for half a city block up Santa Rita Road and another three hundred feet down Sharpe Avenue to outline the small estate. At its entrance was a wrought-iron gate with shingled canopy overhead. An old English sign by the gate read: Hatch—1100 Santa Rita Road. Peter turned into the drive, curving past a great variety of shrubs and young trees. Rows of tall thin Italian cypresses waving in the wind enclosed the house itself and its flowerbeds. A breezeway set off a large garage from the white two-story residence of painted brick.

Peter carefully parked his new acquisition, a five-year-old but shiny green Ford sedan, directly beside a red Triumph convertible, and got out. Going up the stone walk, Peter noticed the size and classic beauty of the house. He enjoyed the idea of visiting, of having dinner in such a luxurious place.

As he rang the bell he saw there were beautiful old carriage lamps on either side of the entrance. Though the day was still hot, dusk was near and a scented breeze from the garden picked at his nostrils, tart with eucalyptus odor and sweet from citrus trees.

An older woman in a maid's uniform opened the door.

"I'm Dr. de Haan," he said.

"Yes, Doctor. You're right on time. Everybody's in the swimming pool, even Dr. Matthew. He just got home from the hospital."

He followed her through the entrance hall and living room, then out the sliding glass doors of the family room, onto the Hatches' broad back patio.

A boy and a girl were slicing the water busily far down the pool. Dr. Hatch was just stepping on the diving board. He turned to see Peter, waving hello to him before he spun through a smooth half-gainer. Peter saw Rosalie Hatch at the poolside in a white suit with a beach jacket over her shoulders. She was relaxed on a steel-and-fiber chaise, a pink bathing cap dangling from her hand.

"Hello, Mrs. Hatch," he said, stopping beside her. He noticed the full curves of her suit, the trim legs beneath, smoothly browned.

"Oh, Dr. de Haan, hello. I didn't see you come out. I was watching Cindy's strokes." She stood up and put out her hand, smiling. "How does your head feel?"

"Just fine." Peter returned her smile, remembering her better than he had since the wreck. "You know, it comes back to me, right this minute, that when I first saw you at the airport you were wearing a green suit, weren't you?"

"Yes, that's right. Really, I never have been so upset. Out here for an hour and in a car wreck. I suppose your family will now believe everything they have ever heard about California drivers."

"I only told them in a letter Monday what had happened, and then I made it mild. I feel good now, anyway. Do you?"

"I thought I might try a swim, but I guess not. I'd been wearing my rib belt all week until I came out here to the pool. I can't move quickly, but otherwise I'm all right."

The boy and girl climbed out of the pool and came up to be introduced. "This is Dr. de Haan, Cindy Hatch, and Matthew, junior."

The tall, fair boy of about seventeen, muscular and with a large head like his father's, offered a dripping hand to Peter. He had the raw, unfinished look of adolescence, but also an added sullenness. The girl was a year or two younger, pleasantly figured on a small frame. She smiled at Peter nicely.

Dr. Hatch pulled himself out of the water at their feet, scrambling nimbly upright to tower benignly over everyone. "Nice to see you," he said, grabbing Peter's upper arm and squeezing it firmly. Peter noticed the thick masses of gray hair curling on his chest, as well as the fullness at the belt line.

"All right, you kids," Dr. Hatch said, "go on in and get dressed. I want Matthew, junior, to help with the barbecue." His son looked expressionlessly at his father, sighed and dived into the pool, swimming across to the opposite side. He pulled himself out and without a backward glance walked into the house through a rear entrance.

"Kids! You'd think I had asked him to paint the house," Dr. Hatch said blandly, pointing to a small cabana against the fence. "We have suits in there, Peter, all sizes. Put one on and have a swim before dinner. It's going to be forty-five minutes before the steaks are cooked, anyway."

In the dressing room, Peter stripped quickly and found a pair of red trunks to fit him. He walked outside, pulling in his stomach, happy for the ten pounds he had gained on internship food to bring him up to 180.

"By George, you've got some muscle there, boy," Dr. Hatch said.

Peter dove in, feeling the delicious rush of warm liquidity against him. He enjoyed the immediate weightless isolation of the cool green water at the bottom of the pool. Coming up, he swam the length and back and then hung, bobbing, at the edge, happily puffing and energetically shaking the water from his hair. He thought how wonderful it would be to earn his way to a fine house like this with a pool and magnificent grounds, a lovely wife, everything. Of course, he wanted more than that from life, he knew, more purpose than that. He wanted to be of service in the world, contribute something, accomplish something medically.

"Enjoy yourself," Dr. Hatch called from the patio, pulling a robe around his shoulders. "We're going in to get dressed."

Peter practiced diving for a while, then swam four more lengths. Finally, he pulled out of the pool, tired. Toweling off in the bathhouse he found himself whistling "Jellyroll Blues." He felt as he had the first day of college, pleasantly nervous and terribly eager to explore every dimension of his new life.

At dinner Peter noticed the quiet but obvious way in which Dr. Hatch dominated the setting. Even young Matthew's protestations to his mother about the chattering of his sister stopped in mid-flight when his father murmured, "That's all."

After dinner the children excused themselves, and when coffee was served, Dr. Hatch began telling Peter about a patient he had seen that day with a mass in his neck near the branching of the carotid artery. "I think it must be a carotid body tumor. I've had several of them and operated with good luck."

"Is that right?" Peter said. "They're not very common."

"You'll see everything here in San Marcial. I think you'll be surprised at the variety of pathology we pick up. I've been trying for a long time to get one of the men going on some papers about our clinical experience in different fields. It would be fine if you could."

"I'd like to very much."

"You'll have to do that then. I like my doctors to feel free to branch out into research of any kind they want to. Also, we give you several weeks off a year for meetings. They're important for keeping up. I take in all the big surgical forums I can, and it may surprise you to know that I find my experience is up to the speaker's in most instances."

When they finished their coffee Dr. Hatch took Peter into his study, and while they talked a bit of medical journals and books, Peter was thinking of his friends who had warned him of his foolishness at not signing a contract before he got out to California. "He says he'll give you twelve hundred and fifty dollars a month, but you ought to have it in writing." Peter had stuck to his point of believing Dr. Hatch would not back down on his proposal, but now that the moment had come to get into the business of his contract, he was suddenly nervous. Determined not to show it, though, he listened with all outward calm to what Dr. Hatch had to say.

"Peter," he began, "it's fine to have you with me. I want you to know you are welcome, and that we're happy about you. I find my wife liked you at once and that means a lot to me. Women have good judgment of people. I was happy, very pleased, too, to get a fine letter from the dean of your school a few weeks ago, agreeing completely with my feeling that you were an outstanding young man."

So he had checked on him, Peter noted, surprised and yet approving.

"If problems arise while you're here—and I say this first of all so you'll remember it—don't ever hesitate to bring them right to me."

"I understand, Dr. Hatch."

"Did you want to smoke?"

"I thought I would, but it doesn't matter. I don't see an ashtray."

"You won't find any here because none of us smoke, but I can get one for you from the kitchen."

"That's all right."

He did seem rather odd about some things, Peter decided. His tone in offering to get an ashtray had been definitely irritable. Why the devil should he care whether *I* smoke or not? Peter thought. It was probably the surgical personality that liked to control other people.

Dr. Hatch settled back in his chair, stretching his imposing physique for a moment, clothed now in a raw silk sport shirt and herringbone slacks. "Looking over the clinic's schedules I find that Thursday seems the best time for your afternoon off."

"Good," said Peter, "it doesn't really matter to me."

"About call systems for our twenty-four-hour emergency room, you should check with Frank Lewicki and George Carr in internal medicine. Les Leslie, our orthopedist, Norman Silvana, our other general surgeon, and I cover the accidents, but you could help us there, too, with some of the minor suturing and the smaller problems. Being the new man you have to expect a little more call than later on. I warn you they'll probably try to dump everything on you they can, so if you need help, roust them out or get me. I'm glad to come over at any time."

"I expect to be an Indian and not a chief for a while."

Dr. Hatch raised his eyebrows and laughed. "All right, good for you. Before we start talking about salary there are a few other things I should tell you." Peter's heart thumped. Money, it was thumping about money, he realized. How dumb.

"We pay for everything but your car. Any examining equipment you should have you can get from us. You get two to three weeks a year for vacation and two weeks a year for meetings, or thereabouts. These things are pretty much up to the individual as to details. I've always found three or four weeks at one time enough to do almost *anything* a person might want these days, hunt elk in Canada, tour South America, or go around the world."

Peter nodded, thinking as he did, that he was beginning to get small but revealing flashes from the inside of the *real* Dr. Matthew Hatch, who was not the same as the one he had met in Atlantic City.

"About salary, I believe we agreed on twelve hundred fifty a month to start, and this can be raised before the year's up. Remember this contract is only for the first year. After that it's a question of a handshake and a gentleman's agreement."

Dr. Hatch's manner became intimate and dedicated now as he began to sketch the picture of their futures together, the future of the clinic with all its doctors. In a while though, he returned to details of clinic operation again.

"The finances are so complicated now with the hospital and clinic that I've hated to have the men get into ownership, too. My own income is enough to cover up the rough spots and smooth out the edges and I'm happy to do that for the sake of good medical practice. That's my incentive in this whole thing and I'm glad to do anything for that. I've always found that if people know, and I believe they do here, that you are practicing first-class medicine with all the advantages of our times, you have no trouble keeping busy, being successful."

"It certainly makes sense to me," Peter said.

"I tell you all this because I don't ever want you to think that you're being deprived of any income by your lack of ownership. I go out of my way to keep the men's income up to what any comparably active practitioner in the community is making. And as I say, it often means a little out of my own income, but I'm happy to do it."

"I understand."

"However, my tax men are working hard on means of setting up a fine profit-sharing arrangement for everyone that may be coming up early next year. I'd appreciate it if you wouldn't mention this, though, as it isn't anything official yet."

"Surely," Peter answered, pleased if surprised at his rapid access to Dr. Hatch's confidence.

"I know you'll like it with us. I feel there are great things ahead." He reached out and took Peter's hand and shook it vigorously. "Take this contract form home with you tonight to read over. After you do, and if it's satisfactory, sign it and give it to Josie, my secretary. Or you can read it and sign it now, if you like. Then you're officially started."

Peter looked it over quickly. It was a simple document mainly stating that he agreed to practice with Dr. Hatch for the coming year at a salary of $1,250 a month. "I'd just as soon do it right now."

"Go ahead." Peter took the large golden pen offered him and signed.

"It's official then," Dr. Hatch said. "Congratulations." He shook his hand again.

As they came back in the living room to join Rosalie Hatch for coffee, the ring of a telephone interrupted their conversation.

"Don't bother, Rosie," said Matthew Hatch. "I'll get it."

"Telephones are my nemesis," Rosalie said. "I feel sorry for you, Dr. de Haan, for what you will have to go through."

She sighed as Dr. Hatch said more loudly, "I can't understand you. Will you please talk louder? Mrs. who?"

In a moment he hung up. "As long as you're signed and

sealed, how would you like to start working tonight instead of tomorrow, Peter?"

"It's fine with me. Are you serious?"

"Yes, I have a call here. Miss West got you your bag fixed up, didn't she?"

"It's in my trunk."

"I don't think that's very nice, to ask someone over to dinner and then send them out on a house call, Matt," Rosalie said.

Matthew grasped her hand. "Can't you see this young man is dying to do it, Rosie?" He smiled. "This call is about a young boy, last name Aragon, about fifteen, the mother said. If it's the family I'm thinking of, I know the father's an alcoholic and the family's on welfare—Aid to Needy Children. I may be wrong, though. Anyway, the boy has passed out, they think he had a convulsion. They live on Bigelow Street." He gave rapid directions on how to find the house.

As Peter got into his car, he took a deep, stimulating breath of the cool night air. When he was nine he decided to be a doctor, now tonight, nearly two decades later, he was at last truly becoming one. It seemed fine and he was happy as he swung out through the Hatches' grillwork gates onto Santa Rita Road.

5

BIGELOW Street was in an obviously poor section of the city. The illumination from the small high streetlights was skimpy and the house number hard to find. Then there was no bell, so Peter pounded on the glass of the door. It was quickly opened.

"The boy's in the back room, Doc," a fat Mexican woman said without expression. She was wearing a shapeless dress and dilapidated tennis shoes, Peter noticed as she led the way to the rear of the house.

Lying quietly there on a bed lacking head and footboard was an obese dark-skinned boy, large but not mature. The room was badly lighted and Peter quickly found there was no way to improve the visibility.

Kneeling at the bedside, he felt the grit of the floor through the knees of his new suit. He fumbled through the unfamiliar interior of his bag for examining tools, but then remembered his pen flashlight and pulled it from his pocket. As he looked at the boy he asked the woman a few questions. Her answers were brief and to the point. The boy's name was Jerry, he had suddenly said his head hurt, left the table and gone to the bathroom where he had vomited and then passed out. She had heard him fall. Half an hour after getting him into bed he was still complaining about a headache and she had called Dr. Hatch.

Peter spoke to the boy, who was sweating profusely but cold to the touch, asking what his age was and how the headache had started. Jerry said he was fifteen, that the pain had begun in the back of his neck as if something had popped there and then spread all over.

Examining him, Peter quickly found a stiff neck and a left eye which turned out and would not track a finger moved in front of it. The pupil was dilated and did not contract when light was shined on it. After ten minutes of checking the boy, Peter arose, his knees painful on being re-stretched.

"What's the matter with him?" the woman asked.

"I don't want a shot, Doc. Are you going to give me a shot?" the boy called out.

"I'll be back in a minute, Jerry."

Peter took the woman back down the narrow hallway to what he saw was a small kitchen.

"Mrs. Aragon," he said, "I think your son is very ill and needs to be in the hospital."

"I'm not his mother. I'm his aunt. He's my sister's boy."

"Oh. What's his last name?"

"He's Jerry Lopez."

"Are you his guardian?"

"No. His folks went away for a few days down to Los Angeles to visit and he's just staying with me."

"He's not going to any goddam hospital!" Peter turned in amazement at a deep croaking voice directly behind him. A gaunt and red-faced man stepped into the kitchen, smelling of alcohol.

The woman ignored him. "What's wrong with Jerry?" she asked.

"I think he's very sick."

"Where's Dr. Hatch?" the man asked loudly. "Is he afraid to come over here himself?"

"Dr. Hatch had me come over for him," Peter said. "Are you Mr. Aragon?"

"Never mind who I am."

"He's my husband," Mrs. Aragon said.

Peter turned back toward her. "Can you get hold of the boy's father and mother? I think he needs to be in the hospital."

"Now listen, Annie," said her husband, looking drunk but speaking clearly. "I told you you shouldn't have called a doctor. Especially that goddam Hatch after what he done to you. Four operations and you've been sick ever since. They'll get that boy in there and open him up and there won't be no more boy. Wait till Ramon comes home. Let him decide what to do."

His words were thrown out at his wife like fighter's jabs. She listened to them, but turned back to Peter when he was done, unimpressed. "You think he's got some virus bug, Doc?"

"I think he may have some bleeding in his brain, Mrs. Aragon. He needs to go to the hospital and have more tests done. For instance, he should have spinal fluid taken from his back for examination."

"You see," Mr. Aragon said. "They'll want to operate on his head!"

"No, no, sir. I couldn't really tell you what is going to be done. Surgery, no, I wouldn't think so."

"What's your name?" Mrs. Aragon asked, suspicious herself now, it seemed.

"I'm Dr. de Haan. I'm new with the clinic."

"The boy has a headache is all and his father will be here tonight and can take care of him," Mr. Aragon put in.

Peter rubbed his forehead in momentary disbelief. As his first case, middle or last, this would be one he would never forget. "I must tell both you people I believe the boy could die if he doesn't get treated. He's very sick and he needs to go immediately to the hospital by ambulance."

"Ambulance," screamed Mr. Aragon. "Ambulance!"

"Shut up!" yelled his wife.

"Ambulance, what the hell."

"Carlos, don't talk like that to the doctor. I wouldn't have called a doctor if I didn't know Jerry's real sick. I don't hold no grudge against Hatch. He done the best he could for me."

"That no-good s.o.b. Money is all he's got in his head."

With practiced grace, Mrs. Aragon hit her husband broadside across his face. He fell back against the door jamb, rubbing his jaw.

"That's no way to speak. It's that damned wine of yours talking, anyway," she said. "Now shut up!"

Mr. Aragon straightened up, scowling, and then vanished from the room. In a moment the front door slammed behind him.

"You can't talk to him when he's drinking, Doc."

"I think we should get the boy to the hospital right away, Mrs. Aragon," Peter said, looking around for a telephone. "Can his folks pay for hospital care?"

"His dad works at the American Airplane Company. He's got good insurance."

"Are they definitely coming back tonight?"

"They should be here pretty soon, unless something happened."

"Somebody's got to sign for him at the hospital."

"I'll drive over to their place. They might come there first."

"Will you go tell him what we're going to do?" Peter asked. "And I'll use your phone to call the ambulance."

Driving in the back lot of the hospital ten minutes later the brilliant sweep of Peter's headlights caught a sign before a parking space that read, "Peter de Haan, M.D." He smiled at his own pleasure as he hurried inside to the front office.

"Doctor," the white-haired switchboard operator said, "I think you need Miss Bledsoe. She's the P.M. supervisor and is at A Ward nurses' station."

"I'll go there." Peter cut back through the lobby's swinging doors to the nearby station.

"You're at work already, Dr. de Haan?" Miss Bledsoe asked.

Peter nodded and told her about the boy.

"You can't admit him here, Doctor. You can't do anything for him or to him without the parents' permission. You understand that, don't you?"

"The boy is very sick and needs care at once whether his folks can be reached or not."

"He should go to the County. They can stand the lawsuit better than a private hospital like this."

"Well, put him in the emergency room when he comes and I'll look at him and see if we can get hold of the family then." He felt annoyed with her. She seemed unpleasant with her authority, not susceptible to reason, coercive and irritating. In short, a typical night supervisor.

The boy arrived surprisingly soon, brought in by the ambulance crew to the emergency room. Peter, waiting in the kitchen over a cup of coffee, had heard the failing wail of the siren and the crunch of the ambulance's tires in the driveway.

Miss Bledsoe directed the gurney into position by the examining table and stood back with fishy-eyed suspicion as Peter came in the room. Jerry Lopez was paler now, his breathing deeper, abnormally deeper, Peter thought. The boy answered simple questions but moaned between times and complained continuously of his headache.

Peter raised an eyebrow and said to Miss Bledsoe, "Would you be kind enough to call Dr. Lewicki? I'd like to have him here, or at least talk to him on the phone."

"I think he ought to go to County, frankly, Doctor," Miss Bledsoe countered, white and dried-up in her anger.

One of the ambulance attendants, a middle-aged man with a midwestern twang, said, "If you want us to move him to County, okay, if you don't, okay, but the boy's aunt said she didn't want him to go to County. She said for sure not to let him go there."

"Thanks," Peter answered.

"Dr. Lewicki's not on call," Miss Bledsoe said.

"What?"

"Dr. Carr's on call for medicine. Do you want me to get him?"

"I guess so. Yes."

In a minute she held up the telephone.

"May I take it outside? And will you set up for a spinal tap, please?"

"There's a phone in the hall." She turned away.

Peter found the telephone and had the call switched. "Hello, Dr. Carr, this is Peter de Haan, Dr. Peter de Haan. I start work here officially tomorrow, but Dr. Hatch asked me to see a patient tonight, a fifteen-year-old boy, and he's turned out to be a real problem. Named Jerry Lopez."

"What's the trouble?"

"He began having a severe headache suddenly at dinner, vomited and nearly passed out." He went on to give his medical findings and ended, "I feel as if I could use some help. It might be a subarachnoid hemorrhage or even meningitis."

"I see. He could have epilepsy, too. Well, I'd say do a spinal puncture. See what that shows."

"I'm worried about taking care of the boy. His aunt says the family does have hospital insurance, but his parents are out of town. I don't know whether I should go ahead with a spinal without their permission, or admit him to the hospital or what."

"Use your own judgment," George Carr said. Peter noticed the words in his final phrase seemed slurred, and he wondered if he had been drinking. When he went back to the boy he found him stiffened with the start of a convulsion and he stayed rigid for several minutes before finally relaxing. His pressure was lower now and he did not respond to questions.

"I'm going to do that spinal right now," he said to the grim nurse, and then he smiled at her. "Don't worry, Miss Bledsoe. It's my neck, not yours."

She stood blankly for a moment. Then as if she did not understand herself what she was doing, she half-smiled back and obediently began opening up the spinal tray. The boy started moaning as he was turned on his side for the procedure. As Peter rubbed his back, feeling for the spines of the vertebrae to position the needle entrance, the ambulance man put his head back in. "Hey, Doc," he said, "the kid's folks are here."

"Miss Bledsoe, do you want to—oh, hell, I'll talk to them." Peter pulled off his rubber gloves and walked out into the corridor.

The father was a small neat Mexican, more Spanish than Indian in his features, and controlled in manner as he spoke. "What's going on with the boy, Doctor?"

"Mr. Lopez, I'm glad to see you. Jerry's very sick."

"With what?"

"I think he may be bleeding from a blood vessel at the base of his brain, though it could be infection, too."

"Is it polio, my wife wants to know?"

"I would say no. It doesn't seem anything like that."

"We want to see him."

Peter looked at Mrs. Lopez. She was taller than her husband and stood oddly with her left hip bent. She had broad smooth lips, goldrimmed glasses, and a dark scarf over her head.

"I want to see Jerry," she said almost inaudibly.

"Of course. Why don't you come in? He may not know you, though."

"He's unconscious?" She burst into tears.

"He hasn't made sense always here, but he does respond," Peter said. "However, I believe he should have a spinal tap done right away. I mean, I should put a needle in his back to take out spinal fluid to see if there's blood or infection in it."

"Did you know my wife had polio?" Mr. Lopez asked.

"No, I didn't," Peter said with comprehension now of the way Mrs. Lopez stood and moved.

"That's what made my wife so bad," he went on, "because they did a spinal tap. She wouldn't have been paralyzed if they hadn't."

"Jerry hates needles. He faints every time someone tries to give him a shot," Mrs. Lopez whispered.

Peter hesitated, unsure how to put the problem to these people now. He wanted to help their boy, if possible, and was worried now as to how to proceed so they would understand the urgency. Mrs. Lopez assisted him.

"Ramon," she said, "I don't think the spinal made me paralyzed. I know you always thought so, but the doctors said it was just the polio and that the spinal didn't have nothing to do with it." She faced Peter de Haan. "Can we see him? Then we could say better."

She looked at her husband, who waited calmly for a moment to show that he was in charge, then nodded.

When Mrs. Lopez entered the emergency room she grabbed Jerry's hand at once and rubbed it between hers, calling his name softly and crying. The boy turned his head toward her, his eyes closed, moaning, not talking. Her husband looked over the room coolly, then put his hand on his son's shoulder. In a minute he pulled his wife away from the boy. "Vera, come on," he said. "We'll be outside, Jerry. Everything's going to be all right." Then in a quieter voice at the door he added, "Doctor, you go ahead."

"We want you to sign this hospital admission paper, Mr. Lopez. Will you give it to them, Miss Bledsoe?"

"Should we send for the priest?" Mrs. Lopez asked.

"Yes, I would," Peter answered.

After they left the emergency room, with Mr. Lopez supporting his wife tightly around her shoulders, the tap took ten minutes. The fluid was grossly bloody and the pressure was far up, nearly 400 millimeters. The boy's body was more relaxed after the procedure, and his headache seemed less painful.

Peter went out to the parents and explained to them that

he had found blood. This probably meant there was a ruptured aneurysmal blister on one of the arteries at the base of the brain. The blood was a strong irritant and more bleeding could cause death.

"What is going to happen to him then? We have no other child. He must get all right," Mrs. Lopez said. In a sense, Peter had enjoyed meeting the challenge of the situation, but now he wished nothing more than that this mother, in such clear grief, should get her son back home again.

"I think a neurologist or neurosurgeon, a nerve doctor or a brain surgeon, should examine him."

Mr. Lopez spoke to his wife in Spanish for a moment, then said, "We want Dr. Hatch to see Jerry."

"Yes, all right, I'll call him. I think I can get him."

"My wife thinks he is going to be all right."

"I don't know, of course. I'm very worried about him."

"You'll get Dr. Hatch to see him?"

"I'll try right now."

Rosalie Hatch answered the telephone. It seemed at least two weeks since he had been in her luxurious house.

"Yes, Dr. de Haan," she said cheerfully, "I'll get Matt." It was a feminine voice, one of those with an enduring ingenue quality.

"Hello, Peter." Dr. Hatch's telephone voice was soft, but there was an aggressiveness, almost an impertinence to its softness. You damned well better hear what I have to say, at whatever volume I choose to say it, was its implication.

"Dr. Hatch, the young boy I went out to see, Jerry Lopez, is here in the hospital and the family would like very much for you to look at him." Peter sketched the boy's problem.

"I'd be glad to come down, Peter. Only take me a few minutes."

By the time Matthew strode briskly in, the boy was in a bed in A Ward. His examination was cursory. "How do you feel, boy?" he asked.

"I got a headache and I'm sick to my stomach."

"He's better now and talking more since the tap," Peter explained.

"Well, Jerry, we've got to get you going. I want to have you out by the weekend so you can go fishing with me."

"I don't like to fish."

"Okay, Dr. de Haan's taking good care of you. We'll have you up there on the river Sunday." He winked at the boy whose eyes shut at that moment in another doze.

"Let's go see the family, Peter. I think you have everything in hand here in fine fashion."

"I'm certainly worried about him, Dr. Hatch."

"Sure, I know you are, Peter."

Mrs. Lopez sat on a couch and her husband was at the pay telephone in the lobby. He hung up immediately as he saw Dr. Hatch push through the swinging doors.

"Hello, Mrs. Lopez, Ramon. I thought it was one of Mrs. Aragon's boys when she called me. I didn't know it was your boy. She was excited, I guess."

"Dr. Hatch, what do you think about Jerry?" Mrs. Lopez asked.

"Frankly, it looks bad. I don't think he's going to make it. Dr. de Haan has done everything right for him so far, but he hardly talks at all. If he gets through the night we'll call the neurosurgeon, the brain surgeon, in the morning and see what he has to say."

"Do everything you can," Mrs. Lopez said. "We want you to take care of Jerry."

"Yes, certainly. You know I'm mostly a surgeon, Mrs. Lopez, but Dr. de Haan and I will take care of him. There's very little hope for him, though, I'm afraid."

"Thank you for coming, Doctor. God bless you."

"Vera, I think you had better go home," Dr. Hatch said to Mrs. Lopez. "I'm going to have the nurse give you a sedative, and you go home and go to bed. If there's any change we'll let you know." Mr. Lopez shrugged his shoulders, looking tired and impassive, but Peter saw there were tears in his eyes.

Walking back down the corridor to the nurses' station, Peter asked, "You don't give the boy any chance, then, Dr. Hatch?"

"I wouldn't say his chances are good, Peter, but he might fool us. I've always found, though, it's best to talk to parents the way I did if there's doubt about what's going to happen. Put it straight to them and make it bad. Gets you out of lots of jams and it doesn't hurt you any if the patient lives."

"The family seems to want you to take care of him," Peter said.

Dr. Hatch put his hand inside his jacket and rubbed his chest in what Peter was learning was a characteristic gesture. "I know that's what it might have seemed they meant, but I've always found that I have to rely on myself to do what's best for patients. I can't let them decide for me. If I want someone else to see them in consultation, or follow them, I tell them or I just do it and they find it out. And they don't object. My patients understand whatever I do is for their own good and there's no trouble about it."

"Of course."

"I'll come in and see the boy right along, but you be the boss. Tomorrow call Dr. T. E. Harman in Oakland, he's better than our neurosurgeon here, and tell him about Jerry, get his reaction."

Jerry seemed quieter when Peter checked again, though he had vomited again or tried to, the hospital aide said. A dark-haired nurse came in with a hypodermic syringe in her hand as Peter started to take the boy's pulse.

"Hello, Dr. de Haan," she said.

"Hello. I'm afraid I don't remember your name," Peter said.

"I'm Mrs. Beauprey, Doctor."

"Oh, yes. Who is the hypodermic for?"

"For Jerry here."

"For Jerry? What is it?"

"A quarter grain of m.s."

"Morphine? I didn't order any morphine."

"Dr. Hatch just did."

"Are you sure? I mean . . ."

"Yes, Dr. de Haan, he did. It's written down on the chart."

"Well, let me check it, will you please, Mrs. Beauprey?" She came back to the chart rack with him. The order was clearly there, both for an immediate dose and then one dose every four hours as needed for pain or restlessness.

"Perhaps I had better call him. I don't think Dr. Hatch knew the boy had already had fifty milligrams of Demerol for pain and twenty-five milligrams of Sparine for vomiting."

"Yes, Dr. de Haan, he did know that. I told him. He said he thought you'd agree Jerry should have a good night's sleep."

"I see he ordered half-normal saline and glucose."

"He said he thought the boy could use the sugar and that he had probably lost some electrolytes from his vomiting."

"Well, all right."

"I'm going to start the I.V. right away, Doctor."

"All right, Mrs. Beauprey. I'll sit here and write up the history and physical."

Peter sat thinking for a while before he wrote anything.

He felt disturbed at Dr. Hatch's orders. From his own training morphine seemed contraindicated here, because it might bring about excessive depression of a brain already injured. He had been taught never to give a patient morphine after possible brain damage.

Mrs. Beauprey came back in ten minutes to say the intravenous fluids were running well. "The boy seems more comfortable."

Peter stood up. "I wonder if there's a bed here I could use."

"Up on the O.B. floor they have one."

"Any place is all right."

Peter went in the room again. Jerry Lopez was on his back now, breathing deeply, but otherwise quiet and pale. "How do you feel, Jerry?"

There was no reponse at all.

"Jerry!" No movement. Peter opened the eyelids and found the right pupil tightly closed, pinpoint, from the Demerol and morphine. The left pupil was large and round as a saucer from third nerve irritation and the eye was turned out as before. His neck could not be bent. The intravenous fluid dripped briskly and Peter slowed it down before he left the room, hurrying a little on his way back to the nurses' station and the telephone.

"This is Dr. de Haan. I wanted to call a Dr. Harman, I think it's Dr. T. E. Harman in Oakland. He's a neurosurgeon. Do you have his number?"

"Just a minute, please. Yes, here it is. I'll try to get him and call you back." In a few minutes she rang to say Dr. Harman was doing emergency surgery in Oakland and would finish at about midnight. He would call back then if Dr. de Haan wanted him to. Peter said he did.

He waited over a cup of coffee in the small diet kitchen. Mrs. Beauprey sat next to him finishing the narcotic check for her shift. They talked a bit. She told him she had a husband and three children.

"Have you worked in many hospitals, Mrs. Beauprey?" he asked.

"Quite a few."

"Do you like it here at the Hatch Hospital?"

"It's fine. There are a few things that bother me. They're too lax about visitors and visiting hours. They even let little children in. I don't approve."

"Do you keep busy here?"

"My goodness, yes. I think Dr. Hatch does more surgery than any man I ever knew or heard of. He must have twenty or thirty patients in this hospital all the time."

"Is he considered a good surgeon?"

"Why do you ask me that?"

"I'm sorry. I really didn't mean to put you on the spot."

Mrs. Beauprey looked at him. "I understand Dr. Hatch is a fine surgeon, very fast and skillful. He has a tremendous practice and works very hard, though there are many people in town who don't like him at all. The other two hospitals in San Marcial, beside the County, are the Cabrillo and the Valley. They get nearly all the doctors who aren't with the clinic. I know some of those outside the clinic feel his prices here are too high, for one thing."

She carried out her records, then put her head back in to say, "Good night. I hope your boy comes through."

"Me too. Thank you."

At eleven Peter found Jerry still unresponsive, looking whiter and poorer. The night nurse showed Peter the small doctors' room upstairs. Before he got stretched out comfortably on the bed the telephone rang. It was the operator.

"Hello, have you got Dr. Harman?" Peter asked.

"No, it's A Ward on the line."

The nurse came on. "Dr. de Haan, the Lopez boy is having a convulsion."

Peter ran downstairs, but when he got to the room the convulsion was already over. He could see continuing minor contractions of the muscles on the left side of his face though.

"Now what to do?" Peter said softly. The night nurse looked over at him questioningly as he glanced back at her. "What I mean is, I'm afraid he's oversedated already, but I suppose we have to give him some phenobarbital. And oxygen. Will you get him one of those plastic mouthpieces for the oxygen, please, Miss . . . ?"

"Mrs. Sawyer."

"Yes, Mrs. Sawyer, and two grains of phenobarbital I. M. He did get the last rites, didn't he?"

"Mrs. Beauprey said he did. He has the scapular on, too."

"He's still cyanotic and the convulsion must have been over a minute or two ago. You had better start the oxygen right away."

"Yes, Doctor."

"And somebody ought to call the family and tell them he's having more trouble."

"Do you think they should come in?"

"If they want to." Peter and the nurse looked at Jerry as he suddenly took two deep gasps.

"Doctor, he's not breathing at all now," she whispered in a moment.

"Mrs. Sawyer, get the oxygen in here, and then find an anesthesiologist who can come over right away."

The nurse ran as Peter listened to Jerry's chest, heard heartbeats, and started mouth-to-mouth breathing. She came back quickly with the oxygen and a plastic breathing tube for Peter to use. The boy began to take occasional breaths on his own as Peter intermittently stopped the artificial respiration, but after no more than three increasingly shallow breaths he would stop entirely again. His right pupil as well as his left was broadly dilated now.

In ten minutes the anesthesiologist was there dragging a gas machine with him. He sleepily introduced himself as Marshall Wormser while putting a tube quickly down Jerry's throat and on into his trachea. Dr. Wormser talked through thin, blue lips, settling his sizable buttocks, much broader than his shoulders, on a stool he had a nurse bring in for him. He began to breathe the patient with the rubber bag of the gas machine. "Is his heart beating, Doc? I'd say he's already gone. What's supposed to be wrong with the kid?"

"A subarachnoid hemorrhage. A convulsion started about twenty minutes ago, and then he suddenly stopped breathing right after it."

The door opened and an aide put her head in. "Dr. de Haan, there's a telephone call for you."

Peter looked at his watch. It was ten to twelve. "That must be Dr. Harman."

"You mean the neuro man from Oakland?" Dr. Wormser asked. Peter noticed now that besides seeming perfectly unpleasant in manner the anesthesiologist had a small, ghastly goatee.

"Yes. Dr. Hatch suggested I call him."

"There's a better man in town, but anyway I can tell you no surgeon's going to touch this boy with a ten-foot scalpel."

At the telephone on the nurses' desk Peter said, "Hello. This is Dr. de Haan."

"Yes, Dr. Harman in Oakland. You were calling me?"

"Yes, sir. I'm a new doctor here in San Marcial with Dr.

Hatch's group. My first night on I've run into some real trouble." Peter went on to tell him the clinical details about young Jerry.

"You gave him morphine, you say?" Dr. Harman put in two-thirds through Peter's narrative. "I would be cautious about it. Central nervous system depression, you know. Might knock out the respiratory center if they have another bleed, that is." He sounded vaguely British. "Try to give them just enough to relieve the vomiting and take the edge off the pain and let it go at that."

"I understand." Peter was embarrassed. "Dr. Hatch suggested some I.V. glucose and Isolyte, too, so we've had that running. Just a few minutes ago he had a convulsion and stopped breathing, though. I gave him mouth-to-mouth and got the anesthesiologist over. He's got him on the bag now."

"Well, you're in real trouble there, aren't you? I don't know what help I could be at this time, Dr. de Haan," Dr. Harman said with slow politeness. "I would be glad to come over to see him if you think the family wants me to. Medically, I would have nothing to offer at the moment. Surgery is out of the question, I would say, and you probably have lost him already, from what you describe. Just plain watchful care is all you can do."

Peter hung up with a sigh, sick at the way his first case was going. When he got back to the room things were no different with Jerry and they did not change in the next three hours. The family came and Peter put his arm around the weeping mother's shoulders as she walked in the room. They stayed for an hour before going home again, assured they could do nothing, and Peter had to tell them it seemed only a question of time.

Dr. Wormser continued to leak and spray hostility around the room. At two thirty A.M. he muttered to Peter, "You might as well accept the fact that all you've got now is a heart-lung preparation, buddy."

At three thirty the boy's heart began to falter badly and he slipped over the last technical hurdle to death at four o'clock in the morning. Peter sadly called the family, talking for a while in explanation and then asking for permission for an autopsy. Mr. Lopez said they would have to discuss it and let him know.

Lying in bed in his small apartment, which still seemed unfamiliar and lonely, Peter felt restless, tired but unable to sleep. He finally got up to take a Seconal capsule. Back in bed he kept thinking about Jerry, his first patient, already dead before his own official starting day at the clinic. He was disturbed about the morphine. Was it right to give it? Could that have affected the boy adversely? Peter knew the boy had died primarily because of the broken blood vessel in his brain and he almost certainly would have died with or without the morphine, but its use still worried him.

The sleeping capsule began to warm him, gradually the knots of fretting inside relaxed, and his thoughts vanished without demarcation into the vacuum of sleep.

6

IN the morning he got to his new job at eight thirty, too early to do anything useful the first day, but still later than he, racked by promptness, had intended. As he was parking, an older man on a racing bicycle pulled into the slot marked "Karl Koepff, M.D." He was dressed in a hounds-tooth sports jacket with a bow tie, and to Peter's mild astonishment, wore a beret on his balding head.

"I'm Dr. Koepff, ear, nose and throat here. You must be de Haan."

As they shook hands, Peter explained it was his first day.

"Ah-ha. Well, come along with me. We'll have a cup of coffee together and you can meet some of the others. Myself, I'm not too interesting. They call me that crazy German who tries to get people to stop blowing their noses. And that I do. Don't ever let any patients blow their noses."

The coffee room was a nook next to the kitchen with small tables in it and wooden-backed chairs. Dr. Koepff poured Peter some coffee and introduced him to Norman Silvana, George Carr, and Les Leslie. Dr. Silvana's name brought back to Peter what Frank Lewicki had said, "He's a damned fine surgeon, but of course, like all surgeons—and unlike internal medicine men, naturally—he's got a few quirks. Such as being obstinate and bullheaded. And hard to get over to the emergency room at night." He was a dark-haired and handsome young man who shook hands with Peter solemnly.

When Dr. Carr was introduced, Dr Koepff pointed out that he was the oldest man in length of clinic service next to Dr. Hatch. George Carr in turn asked Peter, "How did the young boy get along last night?" as he filled a coffee cup with an obvious tremor.

"He died about four A.M."

"What, you lost a patient already? It took me two days to do that when I got here," Dr. Leslie said loudly. "Welcome aboard, Peter. Nice to have you here." Peter smiled at Dr. Theodore Leslie, who was the orthopedic surgeon of the Hatch Medical Clinic.

"Les is the number-one scavenger system of San Marcial. Stay with him on eating and you'll double your weight within a year, Peter," George Carr said, his hand steadier and his eyes brighter with his second cup of coffee. George went on to ask Peter his basic statistics as the others listened until the entry of Marshall Wormser into the room broke up the group into several smaller circles of conversation.

Marshall turned to Peter after some noisy sips of coffee and asked, "How much sleep did you get last night, ten minutes?"

"More like three hours, Dr. Wormser."

"Call me Marsh, for Christ's sake."

"I hope I can get an autopsy on him today, Marsh."

"Hell, man, you can make that a coroner's case. Not can, should. He wasn't in the hospital twenty-four hours, and you don't know what he died from. No question it *should* be a coroner's case."

Les Leslie, overhearing them, said to Marshall Wormser, "Thank you, Dr. Wonderful. Any time you want to know anything, Peter, just ask Marsh here, from the way you should have treated the patient that went sour post-op to where to drop the next bomb."

"Go to blue blazes, Les," said Marsh without a trace of a smile, but still not seriously. "Actually, you should have seen how young de Haan here handled himself last night. First thing you know, we'll be calling it the de Haan Hospital and Clinic."

At that moment Matthew Hatch strode in. "Sounds like a good name, Marsh," he said, as he poured black coffee for himself in a soup bowl.

"I was saying, Matt, that after the way young Peter de Haan had A Ward organized last night I predict he'll be running this clinic inside of ten years."

"Believe me, Marsh, I would sell the place ten cents on the dollar today to anyone." He sipped his coffee again. "The boy died early this morning, Peter?"

"About four, Dr. Hatch."

"I figured he wasn't going to make it. It's hard to lose any case, and I guess especially your first." His hand dived under his jacket's breast pocket to grasp at the left chest beneath the floating white handkerchief points. "You look tired, boy. Take a nap at noontime up in the O.B. room. If Al Humphers is there when you go up, kick him out. I happen to know he got a good sleep last night." He put his cup down and left as quickly as he had come, not saying good-bye but smiling to himself, perhaps at the picture of Dr. Humphers being pulled out of the obstetrical floor daybed.

After coffee, Frank Lewicki took Peter over to their building. As they entered Clinic Suite #2, Frank said, "There are several others around you haven't run into yet. For one, the pathologist, Joe Parmelee. He's really our odd one here. I mean, he's just not as good as he ought to be. Why Matt keeps him on I can't understand. Actually, I suspect Matt doesn't think too much of Joe himself, but he can never fire anybody. If anybody does get fired, Mack, the clinic manager, does it."

"Frank, do you go over to the Cabrillo Hospital at all?" Peter asked as they reached their offices, "or to the other hospital, what is it, Cima Valley Community?"

"Not often. Just too inconvenient. Nothing wrong with them. They're newer, and well run, but I think you may get a little more personal attention in this hospital. Miss West, who's in charge here, works her tail off, nine A.M. every day until all hours. How she even keeps her uniforms clean and pressed is a mystery to me. She is devoted to this place and to Dr. Hatch, and it shows. Still and all, she plays the indispensable part too much, doesn't delegate enough authority, and this shows up in messiness and faultiness of operation. The nurses' chart notes aren't watched, for example, and at times get very bad."

"I understand not many of the other doctors come here to the Hatch Hospital."

"That's right, except some of the doctors from outside the city do send us patients. Jimmy Heints out in Woodfield is an example. Matt Hatch does his surgical stuff, and George Carr or I do his internal medicine. There are three or four others like that, and then there are a few bums who use the hospital, too, guys like Dr. Ed Delaney and Hans Coneff and Susack. When they get around to sending a patient in, you usually need to run, not walk, to the ambulance entrance to beat out the undertaker."

Frank Lewicki lit up one of his frequent cigarettes. White vapors curled acridly around the black hairs of his striking Roman nose. "Medical practice is quite an experience, Peter. You're going to lose a few thousand illusions."

Only one patient had been scheduled to see Peter the first morning, a man for an insurance physical, and he attacked the new, complex form with enthusiasm. At eleven Les Leslie had a patient come in with a severe foot injury. Peter was called over to assist him. He found he enjoyed Les' casual way, and his speediness in the operating room, too.

Frank Lewicki had told him he could get soup and sandwiches, or a hot lunch if he preferred, in the coffee room, so Peter joined the clinic pharmacist, Dean Mason, and the clinic Adonis, Norman Silvana, for the meal. Norman, even with his good looks, had no aura of narcissism, being interested only in medicine and his two children, it seemed. He behaved rather primly, humorless and without passion, Peter thought, almost asexual. Yet excitement glinted in his eye when he mentioned a new suture material, the freshest wrinkle in surgery for breast cancer, or the latest advance in improving stomach suction.

After a brief noontime nap, Peter did a pre-employment physical for the city's largest aircraft plant, then saw several "walk-ins" with colds and stomach pains. Late in the afternoon a young woman came in with vaginitis and showed a trace of sugar in her urine. He made arrangements for her and two others to come back in a week, pleased to be having return appointments already.

The first few days and evenings went by and soon the beginning weeks had passed. Peter's tempo of work picked up by the third week. The main desk began to send him over more emergencies besides new patients who could not wait for one of the other doctors. There was also some overflow from Dr. Hatch.

Peter was surprised at the number of people who told him they were happy to find a doctor "who could handle everything," a doctor who would take a whole family. They also seemed pleased that he was willing to spend time with them to get to know them.

By the end of his first month he had received a dollar

present from an elderly welfare patient, a large bag of walnuts from a farmer in the Cima Valley, and a cigar from the father of the one baby he had brought into the world when the clinic's obstetrician, Al Humphers, had been caught in another simultaneous delivery at the Cima Valley Hospital. He had assisted at four or five varied operations, mostly emergencies. Two of these were with Dr. Hatch, and Peter was amazed at the blinding operative speed of the man.

Peter found the other clinic doctors all too eager to hand him house calls and emergency room calls in the evenings and on weekends. There were enough of these to keep him running. By the last of July he was so exhausted he had the clinic secretary clearly place his name on the schedule for call only every other night and weekend.

Even after that he still got some extra calls on nights when he was officially "off" and most of these he took good-naturedly. He had found out quickly that George Carr simply would not respond to off-hour summonings, nor would some of the other doctors, except in situations that were patently the most serious of emergencies. George and the others seemed to label immediately any off-hour call as either the work of a neurotic patient who wanted help before there was any need, or contrariwise felt the sick person had waited so ridiculously long with a complaint as to deserve no real consideration. It seemed the patients could not win either way.

Peter began to get a few admissions in the hospital, often people that he had seen in the emergency room. Frank or one of the other doctors often worked with him on them at first, but moving into the rush of an active practice he began to handle more and more cases completely on his own. He felt himself emerging from the chrysalis state into real medical life and was thoroughly happy most days.

7

THE second Saturday in August Peter took the north road out of town to the rolling greens and wooded hills of the country club. It was the annual summer party of the San Marcial County Medical Society, and Frank and Gloria Lewicki were waiting for him at the front door.

"That's a beautiful dress, Gloria," Peter said. "Is it new?"

"Yes, but I'm surprised it's so obvious. Did I miss a price tag?"

"No," Peter laughed back at her. As they walked inside, Frank leaned to whisper to him, "I'll take you over to the president, and then he can introduce you around at first, though I'm afraid there won't be anything attractive in the female line here, I mean anybody single."

"I don't care."

"I'm beginning to worry about you. You haven't even had a date since you got here, have you?"

"Come on now, Frank. Besides, I have had a date with Betty Winters, you know, the little nurse on day shift."

"Oh, sure, why she's practically a probie. I imagine you scared her to death," Frank said, laughing.

"It wasn't exactly a passionate evening, I can tell you."

"Well, let me get you over to El Presidente, if I can disentangle Gloria from Dr. Kramer's wife."

After an hour of cocktails and introductions, Frank grabbed Peter's arm again and took him in to their table. It was a large one and the Lawsons and the Condons were already seated there.

"Peter, you know our radiologist, Lew Condon, and this is his wife, Lila."

"Hello, there, Dr. de Haan," Mrs. Condon said in a pleasant New England twang, patting her white-rinsed hair before she put out a hand in greeting.

"And I don't think you've met Doris Lawson." She was round-faced and plump with extremely short boyish hair and a flushed neck.

"Of course, her husband is with her, too, unfortunately." Harry Lawson laughed and put down his giant-sized martini glass to shake hands with Peter.

Al and Maxine Humphers joined them soon, and also a young urologist, Dick Caspari, and his wife.

"The Hatches should be here before long," Gloria Lewicki said. "They're always late to these affairs, I guess because Matthew doesn't really want to come."

Just then Peter saw them coming across the dance floor. Dr. Hatch had on a dinner jacket with a maroon tie and cummerbund, and Rosalie was in a low-cut blue chiffon dress with a deep blue necklace at her throat. Peter wondered at her breastline. If it was real, he was impressed. He decided that she was the most attractive woman at the party as she sat down next to him and at once ordered a Gibson.

"How are you doing, young man?" Dr. Hatch said to him, gripping his wrist as he sat on Peter's other side.

During dinner Dr. Hatch was quiet again here, seemingly uninterested and uneasy except when he talked in soft tones to Peter now and again about a patient or the clinic. California champagne was served with the roast beef, but he refused it, turning his wineglass up. When someone else stopped by the table to say hello or joke for a minute, he fidgeted, not caring to talk, slipping his hand under his coat nervously as he listened to the visitor before ending the conversation with a brief nod or just a quick smile.

The band played a few numbers for dancing during the meal. Just after the dinner plates were cleared away, the band leader stepped off the podium, looked around the room, then came over to Peter's table and whispered something to Dr. Hatch, who nodded and walked off to the front of the club.

"Now what in the world's Matthew doing?" Rosalie Hatch asked, bending toward Harry Lawson. Peter was conscious of the exposure of her breast in the move, and almost pinched himself. What foolishness, getting interested in the chief's wife.

"Do you want some more wine, Peter?" Rosalie asked. He nodded. Even with the food he was getting tight. Perhaps it was the best thing, though. A little purgation might be beneficial after his long stint of work.

Matthew Hatch came back to his seat at the table, and Frank Lewicki asked, "What's the matter, Matt, is the band getting sick at the spectacle here?"

"No, Frank," Dr. Hatch laughed, "it was just a call from Susack in the north county. He's sending an emergency down, so I'll have to go into town in half an hour."

"Oh, no, Matt," Rosalie said. "Really?"

"Now Rosie, you stay here. No reason for you to leave. The Condons can bring you home."

After dessert, Peter danced with Gloria Lewicki. She was small and feminine and smooth-moving on the floor. "You're an excellent dancer," she said.

"Thank you. I wish they'd play some rock-and-roll, though. That's what I really enjoy."

"Oh, I can't do that."

"I'll show you." She laughed hard at her own attempts to learn the frug.

After Gloria, he danced with Lila Condon. She was large and gay, and talked and joked with him, hummed and sang, but paid little attention to their dancing. Next he went silently around the floor with a tired and abstracted Maxine Humphers. Her husband had disappeared for a while, too, but when they came back to the table he was in the midst of a fierce political argument with another doctor.

"Are the Lewickis gone?" Peter asked Rosalie.

"Yes, that damned emergency of Matt's. Frank had to go, too," she said frowning. Peter realized suddenly that she was rather tight. He finished off his glass in two big swallows and asked her to dance.

She talked little on the floor, dancing very close to him. After two sets, she pulled back from him and smiled. "I'd like to have another drink at the table," she said.

"I think we'd have better luck at the bar," Peter answered. "The waitresses have about abandoned us in here."

Sitting at the bar, Peter said, "You know, you fooled me tonight. I thought you probably didn't drink at all."

"I enjoy a cocktail once in a while. Matt doesn't like it in the house, and he never takes a drink anyplace. But I do. Especially champagne. I love champagne."

The doctor next to Peter leaned over and asked him for the time.

"It's ten to twelve."

"I guess my watch *is* right," the doctor said. "No wonder everybody's leaving. I couldn't believe it was that late."

Harry Lawson put his hand on Peter's shoulder then. "Good night, you two. Momma's waiting for me outside, so I've gotta go. At least I managed to get George Carr and his wife into a taxi. Boy, were they loaded."

"Good night, Harry," Peter said.

Walking back to the table, they met Al Humphers. "I've got a woman going into labor, so we're leaving, too, Rosalie. Can we take you home?" he said.

"Oh, the Condons said they would. Thanks, Al."

"I'd like to dance once more. Would you?" Peter asked.

She looked at him, touching the red hair at her neck. "Yes, I would."

A moment later on the floor she said, "I'm sort of high, do you know it?"

"Are you?"

"Yes, it makes me feel dizzy."

"Would you like me to drive you home? I'd be glad to."

"The Condons always want to stay all night. Maybe it would be better. Let me go talk to them."

There was no one at the table, but Rosalie found the Condons on the dance floor, and then came back to Peter. "All right, let's go. They do want to stay until the band stops at one, so I told them you'd take me. I'll get my coat."

Outside, Rosalie held onto his arm and breathed deeply. "It feels good out here where it's cool. Maybe it will help clear my head."

Peter swung the car around and headed down the long, wooded drive to the highway. A plane passed overhead, its motor roaring in their ears for a moment.

"Gee, that fellow was low," Peter said.

"He must be taking off from the airport, which is just south of here."

"Wouldn't it be beautiful flying tonight?" Peter asked.

He pulled out onto the highway, looking ahead to the lights of the airfield.

"Why don't you go right at the next turnoff and drive past the airport?" Rosalie said.

"You mean where the lighted arrow is?"

"Yes."

Peter took the frontage road she pointed out and stopped on a small hill at the end of the field. They looked out at the foreshortened crisscross of the landing strips, their pavement ghost-white in the moonlight. A plane with blinking red and green lights came in before them, flaps down, to drop smoothly on the runway.

She took his hand and squeezed it. It was dark in the car, but Peter could see her earrings glistening.

"It looks so unreal," she said.

"I know. The moonlight does it."

"Will you stay in San Marcial?" she asked.

"I want to start a residency, maybe in surgery, in a year or two. I like it here. I might come back after that. I don't know."

She spoke more softly now. "I think you *should* specialize from what Matt tells me of your abilities. He's certainly impressed." She squeezed his hand again. "And so am I." They looked at each other.

"You know, you are so very pretty."

"You're a sweet boy to say that." She moved her head infinitesimally closer to Peter. He put his arm around her and kissed her. Her lips were soft, her perfume smell strong, suited to her, probably expensive as everything else about her was. And she was really kissing him back, firmly, with lips parting.

"You *are* a sweet boy," she said again when he drew away. "Did you want to kiss me?"

"Of course."

She touched his chin. "You have a cleft there."

"Everyone does in my mother's family."

"Is she Irish?"

"Partly." He pulled her shoulders to him and kissed her once more. She was tight-lipped at first now, resisting, then she relaxed, put her left hand in back of his neck and stroked it as she kissed back.

Peter put his hand on her right breast, feeling its firmness as her wrap dropped off. He let her gown strap down and found her nipple as she shivered under his hand.

"Are you cold?" he asked.

"No."

He let her other strap down and kissed her breasts, felt her nipples harden against his lips. Rosalie began to breathe hard, catching her breath with each inhalation.

"Peter, what are you doing?"

He kissed her on the mouth again, and then she drew away, breathing hard. "Wait a minute," she said. She looked at him, then put her hand on his groin. "You are excited, too, aren't you?" she said. "I can feel you."

"Yes, of course."

She sat up, silent for a moment. "Peter, I think we'd better start home," she said finally. "Don't you?"

Peter straightened up and breathed deeply. "I guess so."

He started the Ford again as Rosalie drew her mink stole over her, and lay silently against his shoulder.

Driving into San Marcial, a car passed them, going very fast. Peter thought it looked like the Casparis. The night was getting cooler, and the wind blew sharply in on his face as they drove. His forehead fixed into a frown as they passed the aircraft plant.

As they came to the north edge of the city, Peter turned east on Santa Rita Boulevard, which skirted San Marcial here. Rosalie asked him then, "Did you think of taking me to your apartment?"

"How did you know?"
"I wondered if you hadn't."
"Would you have gone?"
She sat up now and moved to her side of the front seat. "I honestly don't know. I can't explain what I did tonight. I've never done anything like this before."
Peter said slowly, "I know you'd be sorry and I'd be sorry to go on with it."
"Of course you're right. There's a reason on my side for doing what I did. Maybe I'll tell you some day. But of course there's no sense to it. You're just too damned attractive, I guess."
Peter slowed at the Hatch corner, and then accelerated going through their gate. When he stopped in front of her house, she said, "Don't worry, Peter. I was foolish, we were both foolish, and there won't be any repetition."
She touched his cheek with her hand and whispered good night, then the door slammed and she was gone before he could get out on his side.

8

THE following Monday morning, Peter stopped to see Miss West, the chief nurse of the Hatch Hospital and Clinic, in her small office by Dr. Hatch's in the clinic.
"Did that pill case for me come yet?" he asked her.
"Dr. de Haan, it's on order and I'll let you know as soon as it gets here. You don't have to worry about that." The slender spinster was still abrupt with him. She had shown him around at first very much in the manner of the factory manager with the new apprentice. He had been introduced everywhere as Dr. Hatch's new assistant, and through their original tour, Dr. Hatch's name had come up a hundred times.
Frank Lewicki had told Peter at dinner at his house one night that Miss West had been in love with Matthew for years, and that love was blind. He had not implied anything improper, but just that Matthew Hatch and his hospital and clinic had possessed her life. It was obvious to anyone after

an hour's exposure to her that Matthew Hatch could do no wrong in her eyes, commit no errors except those that she, through her intimacy, had the privilege to point out to him herself. But she was a hard worker, Peter had soon found out, available herself if needed in any emergency and able to do anything.

As Peter left her office, Matthew Hatch started in, almost bumping into Peter.

"Good morning, Doctor," Matthew Hatch said. "I see you're talking to my friend Mae West here."

"Don't you call me Mae West."

"All right, *Harriet*."

"Miss West to you today!"

"Well, *Miss West*, then." She finally reluctantly released a momentary sliver of a smile. "You must have had a busy weekend, Harriet."

"I was on the job, I can tell you."

Matthew Hatch stepped in to pat her on the shoulder and then turned back to Peter. "You're definitely a man of hidden talents. My wife says that you can play the piano and you're quite a dancer. I think you made a hit with her at the party." He winked at Peter. "I'll have to keep an eye on you two." He laughed. "And now I find you coming out of Miss West's office. Taking all my women away."

"It was a good party, Saturday," Peter said, smiling back and leaving before Matthew Hatch could see his beginning blush.

When he got to his office, he found Miss Lockwood, his own nurse, opening mail at his desk. "Oh, Dr. de Haan," she said, getting up, "I'm glad you're a little early. There's a lady here who's very upset and wants to see you right away."

"I am, as the saying goes, available," Peter said.

The patient was a young, good-looking woman named Micheline Long. She was dark-haired, small-featured, and her eyelids were swollen from tears or fatigue.

Peter looked at her chart as he walked into the treatment room and noticed she had been a regular patient of Matthew Hatch's for years, although there were no entries for office visits in the last three months.

"Mrs. Long, I'm Dr. de Haan." He shook her hand as he sat down. "You're not feeling well?"

"No, I'm not really. You *are* young, aren't you?"

"Well, I hadn't planned to retire for a while," Peter said, and smiled at her.

Staring directly at him she began crying silently. "Dr. de Haan, something terrible happened to me."

"Is that right?"

"I know you'll think I'm awful."

"I'm sure I won't."

"*I* think I'm awful. I don't know how I got into it. It doesn't seem possible."

"We all have that feeling at times."

"There's so much happened before. I know you don't know me. Or about my husband and me."

"The chart says he's a real-estate man. Is that right?"

"He was. Actually, you see, he's left me now and is working in San Francisco. Our problem has been, well, mainly that he is an alcoholic."

"I see." Peter sighed inwardly. Another one. He had had half a dozen alcoholics and their families in by now.

"It's just too embarrassing. I'm so upset and my stomach is killing me. You can see in there that Dr. Hatch has seen me before for my stomach. He found a little ulcer on an X-ray and he thought I should have it operated on, but I didn't want to have it done. Actually, I've gotten along pretty good the last six months with it."

"Do you take antacids and pills and also follow a diet?"

"No. Oh, I do take some pills. But Dr. Hatch said I could eat anything I wanted. It probably wouldn't make any difference. The pills seem to help. They're little green ones before meals."

"You have pain today?"

"Oh, yes. I'm burning like mad."

"Now, about what happened to you. . . ."

"God, it's embarrassing," she repeated. "As I said, we're separated and getting a divorce. My husband has had another woman friend off and on for years. But anyway, I hadn't gone out much since he left home about six months ago. Last night this friend of mine asked me to go to dinner with her, because it was her birthday. We went out to Danny's on the Berrenda Road. Well, of course, we had a couple of martinis before our steaks and an afterdinner drink in the bar. Lord, I can hardly believe it, even now. Anyway, we met some young men there. Seemed like nice young fellows, even if they were younger. We started dancing and this one kid, Tommy, seemed to take especially to me, while Phyllis, my girl friend, danced with the other kid. We had a swell time for a few hours. Then's when I made my mistake. I should have said to

Phyllis let's go home, but Tommy asked me if he could take me home and Phyllis right away said it was all right with her. She'd had more to drink than she should."

Mrs. Long was white-faced and dry-eyed now. "Anyway, Tommy and I went out the back way and when we got in the car he asked me if I wanted another drink someplace and I said no. I explained to him where I lived and then, as I was telling him, I realized we weren't on the regular road back to town. We had turned off and were on some ranch road."

"Had you started back over the regular highway at first?" Peter asked.

"Oh, yes, we were on it for a few minutes, I'm sure. Anyway, he stopped when I asked him what road we were on, turned off the motor and said, 'No, I just wanted to. . . .' Then he said something dirty. He meant he wanted to have intercourse with me. I said, 'No, Tommy. What do you mean? I wouldn't do that.' He kissed me and I realized he was terribly strong. Then he got mad when I wouldn't kiss him back. 'You'd better kiss me, Mickey,' he said then and he grabbed my neck with his left hand and squeezed. I was scared to death. I was afraid he might kill me. He did slap my face a couple of times, as if he was playing, but he really hurt. Then all of a sudden he put the front seat down, it was one of those kinds you can do that to, and he pushed me down on it. I was afraid I might get sick to my stomach, and hoping I would, too. Then he pulled my pants off and raped me."

Peter was shocked by her words, but tried to conceal it.

"After he finished he just laid there breathing hard. Then he turned back to me and said, 'If you tell anybody about this I'll kill you and don't forget it.' Then he took off my brassiere and put it in the glove compartment and started laughing. 'If you say anything, you know, it will be just your word against mine. And I'll have that for evidence.' It didn't make sense to me why, but he seemed to think he'd made a point. I began to think at least I wasn't going to get killed. Then he started getting excited again and made me do some awful things and finally raped me again. After that he got his clothes fixed up, combed his hair, and started driving back to town. He wouldn't take me home, but insisted on letting me off at the taxi office downtown. He did ask me if I had any money for a cab before he let me out. All the way back he talked about the evening as if nothing had happened, but before I got out he grabbed my hand and said, 'Don't forget what I said and I meant it too.' "

"You are going to the police, aren't you?" Peter tried to be matter-of-fact.

"No. God, I couldn't stand that, Doctor. I don't mean it's because I think he'd kill me. I just couldn't do it."

"I really think you should, Mrs. Long. They might be able to find this Tommy and prevent the same thing happening to some other woman. He could really hurt, or even kill, the next woman."

"Maybe he wouldn't do it again either. I don't know, but I *can't* tell anyone else. I'd be mixed up in an awful mess if I went to the police."

"Of course that's up to you. But I feel you should."

"What I'm really worried about, Doctor, is that I might get pregnant. Do you think I could get pregnant? Or get syphilis? I've been worrying about that."

"When was your last period?"

"I just got over it three or four days ago."

"Are you usually regular?"

"Pretty much. About every twenty-eight to thirty days."

"I don't think there's too much chance of your getting pregant, then. I should examine you today, though."

"I wish you would. That's one reason I wanted to come in. I thought I ought to be checked. And get something for my stomach."

"Did he hurt you at all?"

"Just a little. I was too scared to notice much pain, I guess. He was pretty big, I mean inside me."

"Why did you come to me about this?"

"I was just frantic to see somebody and you were the first doctor who had an appointment time."

"Is that the only reason?"

"I hope you won't write down anything about what I've told you, or let the nurses know about it. I'd just die if I felt anyone knew."

"No, I won't if you don't want me to."

"I suppose I ought to tell you why I didn't want to go to Dr. Hatch."

"How do you mean?"

"I've never told anybody before and this is a real secret, please."

"All right. I understand."

"It isn't just that I don't want him to know about what

happened now. It goes back to my trouble with Paul. Dr. Hatch was kind to me. Very kind. He came by the house a number of times to give me vitamin shots or sedatives when I was so upset about Paul and having so much stomach trouble. He'd talk to me and well, I just fell for him. I was in love with him and I told him so. He didn't seem to mind. He told me he liked me very much and he did kiss me once. There wasn't much else to it. Then, about a month ago, he said he had thought it over very carefully and he felt he shouldn't come to the house anymore. There were considerations, and he had decided not to. But I still have a feeling for him, to be honest with you, and you can see I'd be especially ashamed to have him find out about last night."

Peter was even more surprised by this disclosure than her initial one. Such coincidences in life. His episode with Rosalie Hatch on the weekend, and now this lady's connection with Dr. Hatch, and then her even more dramatic, really horrifying interlude in a car the previous night.

He went ahead with Mrs. Long's pelvic examination, which was negative.

"Did you douche, Mrs. Long?" Peter asked.

"Yes, as soon as I got home, with a strong vinegar solution."

"Well, I don't find evidence of any abnormality. Of course, I wouldn't expect to find much other than a bruise now."

"You mean you think I could still get a disease?"

"It's possible. Not probable but it's possible."

"I want to take something so I won't get any disease."

"We'll give you an antibiotic."

"Doctor, I feel terrible. I'm afraid I'm going to collapse. Do you think I could go to the hospital for a few days? I don't see how I could do my housework and take care of Vickie and Lee, feeling the way I do."

"You have a son and a daughter?"

"They're little girls. Lee is a girl."

"Do you have somebody to take care of them?"

"My mother lives in San Marcial and could do it."

"I'd be glad to put you in the hospital if you feel you need it, but of course Dr. Hatch makes rounds here all the time and would most likely see you."

"I didn't mean to go here. I thought you could get me a bed at Cima Valley Hospital."

"I don't know if I have privileges there yet. Just a minute, let me see." Peter went into his own office, called Frank Lewicki, told him the problem briefly.

"Put her in under my name and yours," Frank said. "I'll call the administrator and explain. Then when you are over there pick up a staff application blank."

In the late afternoon Peter walked into the Valley Hospital and stopped by its main office for his application, then went up to the third floor, to Room 313. Mrs. Long was in the bed by the window, poking at supper with an irresolute fork. Looking up at Peter as he came in she instantly flooded with tears.

"Is your stomach feeling any better, Mrs. Long?" Peter asked, wondering suddenly if she might not need an antidepressant, or even a psychiatrist to see her.

"I had a shot this afternoon when the pain got bad and it seems better now. I don't know why, I just can't stop crying. The poor girl in here with me has had to put up with a sad sack all day."

"Do you have a roommate?"

"She's in the bathroom."

Peter sat down in the bedside chair. "Well, your blood tests and urine look fine. There certainly was no anemia. We'll X-ray your stomach in the morning, so be sure not to eat or drink anything after midnight."

"All right."

"I'm going to give you some medicine for depression, too. That will pep you up a little."

"Good. I can use that, and something for my nerves."

She really was not bad-looking, even seeing her now at a poor time. Still it was surprising about Matthew Hatch. Rosalie was so much prettier. Peter wondered what Dr. Hatch's version of the affair might be. He could make it out as much less of a thing from his viewpoint, or Mrs. Long might actually have protected him. Peter considered it all as he listened to Mrs. Long's story about what a financial mess her husband had got them into.

The door to the bathroom opened and he was conscious of a dark-haired girl in a blue negligee coming out. She excused herself, passing in front of him with a toothbrush in her hand.

"This is Miss Alexio, Dr. de Haan. Anne Alexio. They tried to give me her tray tonight, fried steak and all. I didn't care one way or the other, but she did."

Peter bowed slightly. "Hello, Miss Alexio."

"Hello, Doctor," the young woman said and laughed. "I don't think I could have eaten those pureed baby foods. I'm glad I only have virus pneumonia."

"Mrs. Long, I'll be by in the morning," Peter said. "And I'm going to give you a shot tonight for pain and sleep."

"Thank you very much for being so kind with me today, Dr. de Haan. I do appreciate it."

As he left, Peter thought suddenly of the possibility that Mrs. Long might get interested in him, too. Some women were supposed to be that way, falling in love with every doctor they had. That was a chilling thought.

Driving downtown he tried to remember about Mrs. Long's roommate, Miss Alexio. It seemed he had seen her before, but he could not recall where. She was very attractive, with shining black hair, smooth fair skin, a high forehead above deep brown eyes and a delicate nose. An appearance one would not forget.

Suddenly he remembered that face in a car, and then he knew where. He had seen her in a white Plymouth convertible parked near his own apartment several times. He was sure it was she.

The next morning back at the Valley Hospital, Peter stopped by the X-ray department first. "I have a patient in Room Three-one-three, Mrs. Long. I wonder if her chest X-ray is ready yet, or any of the G.I. films from this morning," he said to the technician at the department window.

"Just a minute." The young man was back quickly. "Here's the chest X-ray from Three-one-three taken this morning."

Peter looked at the film. It showed the profile of a taller, slimmer woman than his patient, and there was a bare patch of streaky white infiltration in the right lung base. Turning it sideways he saw the name on top was Alexio. Room number 313.

"Here's the G.I. X-rays, Doc," the technician said. "The first ones. The patient's just getting her one-hour follow-up film now."

"Say, these chest plates are not my patient's. They're her roommate's in Three-one-three, Miss Alexio."

"Oh, I'm sorry. They were in the third-floor box, and I saw the Three-one-three and brought them. I guess they haven't taken the chest yet on your lady."

Peter looked at the films he had on Mrs. Long. No ulcer. Only stomach and duodenal imflammation and spasm. Good.

Mrs. Long was not back from X-ray when Peter got to the room, and he talked to Miss Alexio. "I thought I knew you," he said.

"Knew me?"

"I'm in the apartment house at Fourteen forty-eight Valleyview Drive, and you're at Eleven-forty? I took a look at your chart just now, that's how I know."

"Oh, I don't recognize you."

"I've seen you in a white convertible as I drove by. Is that your house?" Peter looked for an engagement ring, but saw none.

"My dad and I live there."

"And you teach out at San Marcial City College?"

"Yes."

"What do you teach?"

"Art primarily, and one English class."

"Really?"

"Don't I look like an art teacher?"

"No. You don't look like a teacher at all to me."

She laughed, showing white-white teeth.

"You know," he said, "I just saw your chest X-ray by mistake, looking for Mrs. Long's."

"How was it?"

"Well, not bad. I don't know what it looked like before, though."

"I saw it. Dr. Hard showed it to me, Dr. Herbert Hard, he's my doctor, and it was all white down there at the bottom, so that sounds better. Maybe he'll let me go home tomorrow then."

"I know Dr. Hard. He seems very nice."

"He is, but being here is awful. I had a three-week vacation set for after summer school, and I was going to go to Tahoe and Reno, so I wind up in the hospital. I've decided it's my brand of cigarettes. I think I'll change to those little thin cigars that you don't inhale."

"Oh, Anne, you'd look awful smoking cigars," Mrs. Long said, coming in the room just then with an escort from X-ray. Peter stood up.

"I was going to suggest chewing tobacco," he said. "It won't hurt lungs, and it has plenty of nicotine in it, but I have a hard time selling it."

Peter helped Mrs. Long into bed. She began to cry again. "I didn't sleep well after all, Doctor. Just too much on my mind."

"That's too bad. Your X-rays do look good, though, so far. I don't think there's any ulcer going to be found. Just a lot of irritation."

"I was afraid I might have to have that operation after all."

"No."

"Do you think I'll ever get over this terrible feeling?"

"Oh, I'm sure you will." Peter talked to her a while longer, and then told her he'd get another shot for her right away so she could doze with it through the morning.

As he left the room, Miss Alexio, who was reading a magazine, looked up. "I've decided you're right, and I ought to give up cigarettes. I'm going to start on Tiparillos or Copenhagen or something. Seriously, this is my second pneumonia in two years. I ought to do something."

"I agree."

"You know they tried to give my tray to Mrs. Long again this morning. I hope you don't decide to operate on her. I'm afraid I'm the one who would wind up in surgery."

"Not a chance for a mistake," Peter said, smiling at her as he left. "We could tell you by the cigar smoke."

9

THAT noon, going into the coffee room for lunch, Peter almost bumped into Joe Parmelee, the pathologist, coming out. "Excuse me, Dr. de Haan," Dr. Parmelee said. "I didn't hear you coming."

"Perfectly all right," Peter said, noticing the pathologist's dark blue suit, beautifully tailored, and complemented by a striking monogramed red-and-blue tie.

"You are fast on your feet, though, aren't you? I noticed that Saturday night at the medical party when you were dancing with Rosie Hatch."

Peter stared at Dr. Parmelee's too-brown features. Seen nearby, his sleek hair was suspiciously without gray compared to the many tiny wrinklings in his leathery skin. Peter decided he must be years older than he would care to admit. He looked like an aging theatrical type, the kind one saw around New York with spats and homburg and a klieg-light tan.

"She's a good dancer," Peter said.

"Close, too, isn't that right?"

"Are you trying to say something to me, Dr. Parmelee?"

"There may be a hundred thousand people in this city, now, Doctor, but it's still a small town. That's all I'm trying to say."

With an irritating slow grace, Joe Parmelee ambled out, as Peter poured some coffee and sipped it black for a minute, annoyed that he had let the pathologist get away without further comment.

Frank Lewicki and Harry Lawson came in together. Frank ordered a sandwich, while the stubby pediatrician sat down with a cup of hot water and a tea bag.

"Don't you drink coffee?" Peter, his anger just subsiding, asked Harry Lawson.

"I do for breakfast, but not after that. If I drink too much, it bothers my stomach."

"Frank, did you notice if Al Humphers' light was on as you came in?" Peter asked.

"I think he went home. Why?"

"I have a lady with a possible carcinoma of the vulva I wanted to talk to him about."

"Why do you send a patient like that to Al?" Harry asked. "He's not a board man in O.B.G.Y.N., you know."

"He isn't? I thought he was."

"No. He did general practice for years before he turned to O.B."

"Who would you send the woman to, Harry?"

"To Matt Hatch, of course."

"I'd suggest Silvana," Frank said.

"Now why do you say that, Frank?" Harry asked.

"I think Norman's better. Technically better and better judgment."

"Oh, I don't see that," Harry said.

"Matt operates on every damned thing he can lay his hands on. I've told you that before, Harry, and working with him every day you must realize it. Besides, I never knew any surgeon that had so much trouble post-op. Eviscerations, shock, infection, everything because he doesn't select people properly for surgery. And I've never seen anybody so rough with tissue, either. That's why he gets a lot of his complications, I'm sure."

"Oh, come on now. You know I've been scrubbing with him for five years on almost all his cases, and I can't stand to scrub with anybody else. He's not always good diagnostically, I'll admit, but when he gets a thing to do he does it quickly and well."

"Baloney. After surgery his patients act as if he had used a hacksaw and a garden rake in their abdomens. He thinks he can cure anything with a knife. I swear to God somebody ought to check him sometime to see if he has an erection while he's operating."

"Hell, Frank, I can't even talk to you about it," Harry said, red-faced and obviously getting angry.

"Well, Harry, would you honestly let him operate on you or your family?"

"Of course I would. You know I have."

"Well, you put your money where your mouth is, I admit. But I wouldn't let him take a mole off Gloria, literally."

"I don't get it, at all. What do you stay around here for if you feel this way about him? If you have so many of his post-op cases to look after, if it bothers you so much, what's the percentage in staying?"

Frank turned to Peter. "You know how it is here, de Haan. Everything's an emergency. You never saw so many emergencies. Did you ever hear of an emergency hemorrhoidectomy? We have them here. Emergency mastectomy, emergency herniorrhaphy, I mean for a hernia that's not incarcerated. Matt even did an emergency tonsillectomy one Saturday afternoon. Or he does it the reverse way. He tells some old lady to come in *next week* for her intestinal obstruction."

"What is it that's getting you down today, Frank? Is it that Emily Mosher case?" Harry asked.

"That didn't help things any. Listen to this, Peter. Here is a routine hysterectomy, seven A.M. this morning. She's already back in her room and in shock at nine thirty. He missed a bleeder. That's a trick he pulled on me before. But you practically have to club him to death to get him to admit it."

The telephone rang and Harry answered. "It's for you, Frank."

"Yes," Frank said, when he took the telephone. "All right, I'll be right up. And get three bottles of blood." He hung up. "Here we go with Mrs. Mosher."

Peter and Harry were silent for a few minutes after Frank left. Peter felt suddenly very worried. It appeared he had run straight into the center of a major clinic dissension concerned with the competency, or rather the possibility of incompetency, of the founder and owner. He was damned if he knew how to take the situation. He had to admit that here and there, from certain things, he had suspected there might be something wrong with Matthew Hatch professionally.

Harry said then, "Frank's an excitable fellow, Peter, and he takes everything so seriously and personally. He thinks nothing should be done any differently than it was at New York Medical Center. Matt's been out of medical school a long time and he's developed his own ways of doing things. This is something Frank doesn't stop to realize. And all he sees are the poor results, anyway, because he's called in to consult on them. The good results he never really knows about."

"Do you send your pediatric surgery to Dr. Hatch, Harry?"

"Actually, I send a lot of it to Norman. He spent extra time on pediatric surgery in his training. But I do send some of it to Matt. I'd have to say honestly that I think Norman gets results with the kids, though."

Peter leaned his head against the coffee room wall.

"I know what you're thinking, Peter," Harry said. "What the hell have you gotten into, or something like that. But let me reassure you. Frank's been here for over two years and I never heard him talk like that before." Harry seemed to be hesitating. "Matt is, I mean, well, let me tell you this. With Doris, my wife, Matt was the only one that realized she had something wrong. He was sure he could feel something in her right ovary area. Two gynecologists in San Francisco had already said there was nothing to explain her pain. Matt operated on her and found an early ovarian carcinoma. That's four years ago now and she's perfectly all right. Now, I mean, you can imagine how I feel about that. How *we* feel."

"I can understand, Harry."

"That Lewicki made me mad today. He doesn't talk much, but even so I know he is opinionated, too damned sure of himself. He really believes he knows the answers to everything."

"Do you think so?"

"Yes, I do. Well, gosh, it's one o'clock. I've got to go."

"Nothing to eat at all, Harry?"

"No, I'm trying to reduce. Tea for lunch."

Peter walked outside and across the lawn behind his building, thinking hard about Harry's and Frank's words. Maybe it was a complete mistake to stay. His contract had not seemed totally binding, especially if he didn't stay in the community, and he could give two weeks' notice and go back to Baltimore. It would be embarrassing and hard to explain, of course, but besides there was the money. He needed the income from this year to pay off his debts, get a little ahead to help him through residency.

Frank Lewicki was smart, sharp, though perhaps somewhat a man of causes. Was what he said accurate and objective, or distorted by the day's pique?

On the other hand, Harry did not seem especially sharp, but honest—God, painfully honest and earnest. Hard-working, slow-thinking, trusting, a man of loyalty and belief. Beholden to Matthew Hatch, in his own mind, for his wife's life. Was his point of view correct or was there much more to be said on each side and the truth in between?

Peter knew though that he would detest any man who did unnecessary surgery. "If you can do no good at least do no harm." But surgeons were different from internists, too, and they often fought each other mightily over whether an operation should be performed.

Dr. Hatch himself was obviously egocentric, absorbed in his own life and activities, appealing to the ordinary people who were his patients. Peter was impressed by his ability to work fantastically hard and fast with apparent ease, but he also realized that for an unclear reason he had not yet been able to decide if he liked Matthew Hatch or even if he trusted him. There was just something odd and skewed about him, something off-center, off-base.

When Peter was with Dr. Hatch, he found himself impressed, even absorbed in his comments, which often seemed acute. Then away from him, he was not sure of their solidity. Peter depreciated him in private, and then seemed to go through a reconstitution of belief and even liking for him each time they were together.

Peter recalled the previous Friday at lunch. Matthew Hatch had come in for his usual quick meal and started talking to them about setting up a colon cancer register in their hospital. "I had ten cases of carcinoma of the colon in June and July, Peter," he had said, "and most of them were inoperable at the time of surgery. And there must have been four or five in April and May. It would be very interesting to go over the records of the clinic to see if anything could be turned up as a clue to an earlier diagnosis. If my practice is any indication it seems to be definitely on the upswing in this locality. I wonder why."

Peter himself had seen one of the recent patients with colon malignancy who had come in to the emergency room. "Harry Adams, the man you operated on two weeks ago, Dr. Hatch, had had a lifetime of trouble moving his bowels. Do you suppose it's possible there could be a relation between long-standing spastic colitis, chronic constipation, and cancer of the colon, or maybe the use of specific types of laxatives or enemas and malignancy?"

"That's what I mean, Peter. If someone could pick up all these small points, such as how many people had had their appendix out, or had gallstones, who also went ahead to get a colon C.A., you might have something. I'd be happy to have the record room girls pull all the old charts on colon neoplasms and let you investigate the whole matter."

Peter was stimulated by the notion and by Matthew Hatch's immediate enthusiasm. In a moment he was floating into the steamy, exciting world of clinical research and medical discovery. And then the opalescent bubble so quickly created fractured abruptly when Harry said after Dr. Hatch left, "Funny, you know I scrubbed with Matt all during June and July and I can't remember ten C.A.'s of the colon. All I can think of is three or at the most four."

Peter recalled instructors in medical school, brilliant people, who were strangely unsatisfied with their own spectacular stores of knowledge and wished to be infallible, intellectually invincible, as the old Viennese medical men of the early century pretended they were. No one was expected now to be able to encompass all medical information, but these men were not able to admit to gaps in their knowledge.

Matthew Hatch seemed this way, untoppable. He could not put things on the line as they really were. He had to change everything, add a superlative to it, "the sickest woman I ever saw," or "the roughest gallbladder I ever did." Patients were impressed by these terms, but not physicians.

Peter worked abstractedly through the day. Making hospital rounds in the evening for Dr. Hatch, who was away at a meeting in Oakland for the day, he stopped to see an old patient of his, Mrs. Clara Gard, who had been in the hospital for several weeks. Her primary problem was recurrent cancer of the breast which had spread into her spine, and she was now in the last few months of her life.

"I'm tough," she said to Peter, smiling. He noticed how distorted her hands were with arthritis, but her face was smooth and white and her eyes perceptive, their clear blue magnified by her thick lenses.

"I believe you," he answered. He knew she had been through a series of operations, treatments, and illnesses that would have taken off a dozen lesser people.

"So you're Dr. Hatch's new young man. You really are just as good-looking as the nurses said."

"Don't tell me the nurses talk about silly things like that."

"Oh, you are quite the apple of their eye already, I can tell you. You know, Dr. Hatch has been taking care of me for sixteen years now, and of course I would never leave him, but when he's not here I rather think it would be nice to have you."

"Thank you. I hope we can get to know each other better." Peter was tired and the elderly soul seemed talkative, so he sank into the chair in her private room, her conversation in his ear but his thoughts off on the dilemma of Matthew Hatch.

"What do you think of Dr. Hatch yourself, by now?" she asked in a minute, piercing his abstraction with her question.

Surprised, Peter answered honestly, "I don't really feel I know him or understand him yet."

"Good for you. You tell the truth, too. I've known him since he first came to town and he is a wonderful man. He's done so much for me and my family, for so many families. He doesn't make friends easily, doesn't get close to people easily. But he and I are very close. Do you know since his mother died he thinks of me as his mother? He's told me so. He was very close to his mother. She worked like a demon to get him through school. When she died he was lost. I was in the hospital then and he came in my room every day and cried."

"Did you know his mother?"

"Oh, yes, very well. Her house was just a few blocks from mine. She was tough, like me, so we got along. These dizzy spells she had got worse, though, and he tried to make her go in to see Dr. Lewicki, but she didn't care for him—like me—and wouldn't go. Then all of a sudden, one day she had a big stroke and that was it. Of course Dr. Hatch blamed himself for not starting her on medicine to prevent it."

Peter nodded.

"He tells me everything. We had a fight a week ago about something he told me. Doctor's got his son's future all planned for him, you know. He has practically insisted that the boy go into pre-med. I told him to leave young Matthew alone. No child likes to be pushed too hard."

"I think it is wrong," Peter said, intrigued by the old lady's words. "A boy ought to have his own chance on a decision like that."

"That's right. That's what I told him."

"I have to go. They're ringing my call bell," Peter said.

"You're nice and easy to talk to, Dr. de Haan. I need a little conversation once in a while with someone young and interesting." She squeezed his hand with what strength she could manage from her trembling fingers.

10

DRIVING home Thursday afternoon, Peter saw Anne Alexio turning into her driveway in the white Plymouth. He stopped by the curb and waved. "Hello, there, how are you doing?"

The young woman, looking different, slimmer, her black hair up in a knot on top of her head, wearing a white suit with a turquoise scarf at the neck, stared for a moment and then waved back. "Hello, Dr. de Haan. Oh, I'm fine. I even went back to work today. Darn it."

"School hasn't started yet, has it?"

"Oh, I'm helping on the art program for next year in the elementary schools. It's something extra."

"Have you switched to Tiparillos?"

"No, I'm ashamed to say I'm still smoking cigarettes. I'm very weak. I couldn't stand the smell of cigar smoke, anyway. I'd rather be operated on."

Peter laughed. "I'm still holding out for the chewing tobacco."

"I am going to stop now, really."

"I'm sure you can do it."

"I'm glad that somebody believes me."

"I'm on your side. Good-bye."
"Good-bye, Dr. de Haan."
Driving on home, Peter turned the radio up loud and hummed with the Lucky Strike commercial. He looked at his mail, threw it on the sofa and picked up the telephone book. There was a number listed under Philip Alexio. He dialed it and a man answered.
"Mr. Alexio?"
"Yes, this is Alexio."
"I wanted to speak to your daughter, Anne, if I may."
"Anne? Certainly." He heard him calling her.
"Hello," she said, her voice smooth on the phone.
"Anne, this is Peter de Haan."
There was a pause. "Oh, yes."
"I called to ask if you could go out with me Saturday night. It's my evening off and I was thinking of dinner and maybe dancing."
"That sounds nice, but I'm sorry, I have a date."
"Oh. How about Friday night, tomorrow night?"
"I couldn't then either."
"Same person?"
"Yes, as a matter of fact."
"Any point in my asking about the next weekend?"
"I'd love to then. Jim won't even be in town. He's going on reserve duty."

By seven thirty on the last Saturday of August, Peter and Anne Alexio were slicing through east Oakland on the Nimitz Freeway. They came out along the water's edge and turned onto the Bay Bridge as the blue fluorescence of its mercury vapor lamps came on.
"You're not engaged to Jim whoever-he-is, are you?" Peter asked, as he gave the quarter to the attendant at the toll gate.
"No, nothing that serious, though I like him very much. We've been dating all summer. He's a law clerk for Andleman and Williams until he hears if he passed the state bar."
"Are you from San Marcial?"
"Oh, goodness no. Jim is, though."
"How long have you been here?"
"I was born in Mexico City."
"Really?"
"Yes. We lived there and around Southern California until I was about five, when Dad bought a business in Hawaii after

the war, a construction business, and we moved to the islands."

"Honolulu?"

"I grew up in Honolulu, and I love it there, really. I'd like to go back some day."

"You went to college here in California?"

"Yes, to Berkeley. Then a couple of years ago my father's company went broke, and he moved back to California, too. He finally got a good job with a big contractor here in San Marcial, but just about that time my mother got sick and they found she had cancer. After three or four months she died."

"That's really too bad, Anne."

"I felt so sorry for my dad. Everything he had was suddenly gone. After I finished school I found out there was an opening in art with the local j.c., the City College, and I moved here to be with him for a while."

"Is Alexio a Spanish name?"

"No, it's French."

They emerged from the Yerba Buena Island tunnel, and Peter stared at the lighted San Francisco skyline at dusk.

"San Francisco is marvelous," Anne said.

He looked at her. The lovely tilted nose, high forehead, strong chin, slender neck were profiled against the blue glow of the bridge lights.

"I suppose you're engaged?" she asked in her low voice, looking back.

"No," he answered.

"You're not *married*, are you?"

"No, not guilty."

She laughed. "I'm always going out with someone who turns out to be married. They never bother to tell you beforehand."

"I could never talk anyone into it."

"I'll bet."

The Côte d'Or was far out Leavenworth Street where it began its slope to the bay. They were twenty minutes early for their reservation, so the maître d' seated them in the bar to wait. It was small and dark and busy.

"I'll have a sidecar," Anne said to the waitress, and Peter told her a martini. After a second one each, they were taken back through a dark vestibule and came out in an elegant room, gold and white with large chandeliers.

"This is pretty, isn't it?" Anne whispered. A small orchestra was playing. They ordered dinner and then danced for a while on the tiny floor.

"I love this place," Anne said later over her lobster, "but it's expensive, isn't it? I didn't realize that."

"I'm enjoying it so much, I couldn't complain. Do you want to dance again?"

Anne nodded. On the floor she gave the impression of lightness, turning easily, staying close. Peter held her as tightly as he could and she did not seem to mind.

After dinner she took him to a small night club called Chiello's, and they listened to a young Spanish guitar player.

Sitting close to her on the banquette, he admired the style of her broad-collared yellow coat, nipped in sharply at the waist by its belt. The bar was so noisy it was hard to talk, and when a trio began playing, he said in her ear, "Isn't there someplace quieter where we can talk?"

"Don't you want to wait for the topless act?"

"Are you kidding? That's all I see all week."

Anne laughed charmingly—her voice was normally pitched, but when she laughed it came out low and throaty. "There's a psychedelic show around the corner that's really kooky," she said, still smiling.

"Come on now, I don't call that quiet."

"All right, I'll take you someplace else," she said.

In the car she directed him to Telegraph Hill. They got out to look at the view for a few minutes, a foggy breeze from the sea blowing in their faces, then went on down the Marina to old Fort Point at the end. The lights from streams of automobiles passed onto the Golden Gate Bridge directly overhead.

"I tried to tell you at Chiello's how nice you look tonight," Peter said as they watched the freezing black water of the Gate. He turned to her, next to him. "You have the best nose."

"Do you like it? I'm not sure that I do."

"I think it's perfect."

"I'd like it better straight."

"No, I wouldn't. I like that swoop."

"Isn't this a fantastic place?" she said, peering out at the bay and the towers of the bridge.

"Let's go to the end."

"It's too cold."

"No, come on."

The fog was thick, the foghorns loud, and the old fort

eerie ahead of them. He took her hand as they came to the end and leaned out over the giant shoring rocks of the seawall against which the waves slapped.

"This is sort of scary," Anne said, looking down at the foaming water.

"I like it."

"Don't get too far over," she told him, pulling up the giant collar of her coat.

He stepped back and put his arm around her. She looked up at him. "Please," he said. He drew her to him and kissed her. She came against him, soft and warm, putting her hands on the sides of his chest. Suddenly she pulled away.

"Don't do that," she said.

For some reason he had used his tongue without thinking to or planning to, without even realizing he was going to until it was done. "I'm sorry."

She stared at the fort for a moment. "Let's go back to the car," she said then.

Slamming her door of the Ford, Peter got in himself and began to apologize. "I didn't intend to do that. I can't explain why I did."

"I suddenly had a young-interne's-first-night-off feeling, and I didn't like it," she said.

"I've been cooped up in that damned hospital too long. I guess I've forgotten how to act in normal society. I'm just down to aboriginal man, all sex and no sensitivity."

She smiled. "You're crazy."

"Believe me, this is as much sense as I ever make."

"You are nice, and we do seem to have a good time together," she said, putting her hand on his arm.

They went back to North Beach and stopped at Enrico's for a nightcap. Anne ordered a café royale while Peter had hot chocolate with brandy. They watched the bereted and bearded people in the coffee house and talked. Peter found her pleasant, stimulating, filled with information and conviction.

At midnight they were on the Bay Bridge going back to San Marcial.

"What's Jim's last name?" Peter asked.

"Why?"

"I just wondered."

"Jim Hovey. James Hovey, junior."

"I don't like him."

"You don't know him."

"I just have a feeling about him."

"Well, don't."

At her door, Anne turned and said, "Thank you, Peter. I had a perfect time."

"I did, too."

"Will you kiss me?"

Peter did so lightly. She pulled him closer and kissed him more solidly, then drew away. "I like you very much," she said gently. "Please call me again."

He went home somewhat bewildered. He enjoyed kissing Anne Alexio. And he liked her. But she had sounded so suddenly serious at the end of the evening that it worried him. It would be fun to date her, and maybe to sleep with her, but he wasn't thinking of other things than that now.

Peter had never been busier in San Marcial than Monday and Tuesday of the next week. Sunday he had phoned Anne, but her father said she was out. Late Tuesday night, nearly ten, he called again, and told her how he had tried to reach her before.

"I didn't know that," Anne said. "I was hoping to hear from you."

"I wondered about tomorrow night. Can you do something with me?"

She told him of a play at the Straw Hat Theater in Concord, and they decided to go. The next evening, Peter, punctual as always, pushed Anne's bell at five minutes to seven.

"You're early. Come in for a minute," she said, taking him through a small dark entrance hall into a pleasantly furnished living room with prints and watercolors on its walls. Peter saw one of the latter, a portrait of a woman in white in a garden with vivid plants, was signed Anne Alexio.

Her father stood up as Anne introduced him. He was a tall, handsome man with graying dark hair, Anne's brown eyes, and a calm, friendly countenance. "Hello, Doctor." The hand he presented was broad and warm.

Peter was surprised at his appearance. He automatically pictured a rough man with a beer belly, smoker's cough, and weathered, venuled skin when someone mentioned a construction superintendent. Mr. Alexio could have been a customer's man for a brokerage firm as easily as someone in the building trades.

Driving to Concord, Anne asked, "Peter, if you go into

residency will you go back to the East Coast for it, or might you stay out here?"

"I don't know. I'd be interested in one of the big services, like the University of California or L.A. County, but if not, perhaps Boston or New York, or Baltimore."

Anne moved over next to him. "I think you ought to stay in California."

"You've talked me into it."

The stage settings were well done, but Peter found the play, Christopher Fry's *Venus Observed*, poorly performed and dull. Afterward they went backstage and Peter met and dutifully congratulated Anne's friend, Polly Andrus, who had designed the sets, and her husband Al, who was in the cast.

On the way home, Anne stayed close to him, listening to music on the car radio and talking.

"What time is it?" she asked as they drove in her driveway.

"Five after twelve."

"I guess Dad's in bed but left the lights on for me."

"Can you talk for a minute?"

"Yes."

"I enjoyed going to the play with you."

"So did I." She turned toward Peter and put her hand on his. "I do love you, you know."

Peter was too surprised to make any immediate reply. In a moment he reached over, put his hands behind her shoulder blades, and kissed her.

"You kiss so nicely," she said.

"Do you think so?"

"Yes, I know so. Do you love me?"

"Yes," Peter said.

"I'm not sure if I believe you. I don't know what happened to me. I can't get you out of my mind. I've thought about you continuously since Saturday night. Darling, I don't understand it myself. I've always said I could never be a doctor's wife, and look at me."

"Doctors aren't so bad."

"I thought it would be so boring waiting home all those nights. And all the kids I knew in pre-med in school were dull and grinds who were worrying about their grades all the time."

"What about Jim?"

"Jim is very nice, but I've never been in love with him."

"I thought you were."

"No, never." Anne kissed him again, and then put her head on his chest. "I can't believe it. Do you really love me?"

"Yes."

She sat up and looked at him. "You don't. All of a sudden I'm sure that you don't. Why did you say you did?"

"What do you mean?"

"You don't love me, do you? Why did you say you did?"

"I think I do, but I'm just not entirely sure."

"You don't. I feel so foolish. I thought surely you did, for some reason, or I wouldn't have said what I did."

"Maybe I will."

"Or won't. I better go in."

"Will you kiss me good night?"

"Do you really want me to?"

"Yes, I do."

"Come to the door with me and you can kiss me there."

Peter helped her out of the car and walked up the steps with his arm through hers.

She put the key in the lock and unlatched the door, then turned to him. "I still want to see you again," she said.

"You will."

She kissed Peter and said, "Please don't ever tell me again that you love me unless you really do. I can forgive you anything but that."

"Look," Peter said, wanting to explain.

"No, darling, don't say anything. Good night."

Peter drove home slowly and then sat in his living room for half an hour musing. Women were so different. Before they could take part in sex they had to think about love. Anne was so attractive, she walked, even moved, in the most graceful way. She was the essence of femininity, of sexuality. She was an artist and looked and dressed with the charm of one. And she was also a woman and needed to think like one. He must have attracted her physically, so before she could admit to this appeal she had to convince herself she was in love. For him the transition was too quick.

Still he did want to see her again. Maybe she could be persuaded to go out with him, dance with him, see plays, talk, kiss, sleep with him and not continue to insist on love from him. If she wanted to see him enough, she might settle on less than love from him, or less than marriage.

Or maybe he would change. She ought to have a little confidence in her own power at least, in this regard.

Thursday night he phoned her, and she was out at a

meeting, Mr. Alexio said. Friday night he phoned, late. Mr. Alexio said she had not felt well and had gone to bed early. Saturday afternoon he said she was visiting friends in San Francisco for the weekend, which Peter suddenly realized was for three days, including Labor Day on Monday. She had rebelled after all, hadn't she? She had decided to forget him, rub him out, before he took root, hadn't she? It was smart of her, but he didn't like it. As a matter of fact, Peter found it annoyed him. She was probably out with someone else, looking for someone new, tantalizing another young man to help erase Peter from her mind. How could that be fair? But perhaps it was best all around.

Peter sighed as he closed the front door to his apartment late Sunday night at the end of a difficult day on call: kids with coughs and rashes, cuts and swallowed pills; travelers on holiday with gastroenteritis and fainting spells; an accidental gunshot wound; a heart attack; a bee sting with an anaphylactic reaction. Everything had happened.

As he pulled off his coat and tie and poured himself a glass of milk, the phone rang and Peter, half asleep on his feet already, jumped to its startling sound. As he picked it up, he wondered if it could by any chance be Anne. But it was only the hospital operator saying that Dr. Hatch wanted to do a gastrectomy in an hour and needed an assistant. Harry Lawson was away for Labor Day. "Sure, I'll be over," Peter said. "Start at midnight? Okay."

11

PETER yawned as he walked into the brightly lit operating suite alive with the activities of nurses and orderlies. He could see the anesthesiologist adjusting an intravenous drip and getting ready to put down the intratracheal tube. The patient was asleep on the operating table; her lower abdomen was being sprayed with iodine.

Dr. Hatch's great head turned toward him as he opened the door to the dressing room. "Peter, how are you?" He waved an outsize arm as he pulled a green shirt over his massive chest.

"Fine, Dr. Hatch."

"Sorry to keep you up so late, but I thought this lady ought to be done tonight before she perforates. She's an old patient of mine with ulcer trouble. I've been trying to talk her into a stomach resection for a long time, and she's kept putting it off, but she can't get rid of her pain now. I've always found with these people that first you tell them they need surgery, don't force it, then just let them alone and pretty soon they come back and ask for it."

"Oh, by the way, what did you think of the woman I sent over Saturday with the big cyst in her breast?" Peter asked.

"What was her name?"

"Gardner."

"Oh, yes. I drained it with a needle, but I stuck her in the hospital. I'm going to take the whole thing out Tuesday morning. I think that's the best thing to do. It could be a malignant abscess or even a granuloma. Well, you're ready, aren't you? Let's wash up."

He put a friendly hand on Peter's shoulder as they went to the scrub room. Peter looked at the wide, cheerful, already sweating face grinning at him. "I like having you around, Peter. You have an inquiring mind, a wonderful manner with people, a real interest in them and feeling for them. Patients can tell when you care about them, one hundred percent. Mrs. Clara Gard thinks you're all right and she's a sharp apple, let me tell you. I wish, between you and me, I could drum a little of that warmth into your neighbor over there, Frank Lewicki."

After attaching the frictionproof covers to their shoes, they put on caps and masks and began scrubbing. Within two minutes Matthew Hatch turned off his water with the knee switch and left for the surgical pavilion, saying to Peter, "I already scrubbed tonight twice, and I think every germ on my hands has run for the hills before this."

Peter finished out his full five minutes. He went into the operating room with streaming hands which were quickly draped. Dr. Hatch had gown and gloves on and was standing with a scalpel in his hand. "Good, Peter, we're ready to go," he turned to look at the clock, "at just twenty-eight minutes after midnight. Let's see how long this job takes."

Peter hurried into the long gown offered him by the nurse, powdered his hands, and slipped on the gloves she held. He stepped quickly to the table as Dr. Hatch began the long slitting incision from high in the notch of the abdomen to well below the navel.

"Some people find it difficult to get used to my surgical tactics, Peter, because I'm inclined to be what you call a 'wet' surgeon. Some blood inside the abdomen doesn't bother me. But I do like to tie these bleeders in the skin carefully, because I've found they can give you difficulties later on. They lead to hematomas and I believe to stitch abscesses." After all visible bleeding points were clamped they tied them with silk. With sharp scalpel and blunt dissection Dr. Hatch went quickly down into the peritoneum, slicing it open with quick precision as Peter whistled to himself at his agility.

"This lady is tight, Gus," Matthew Hatch said to the anesthesiologist, pushing his hand on her abdomen. "Will you loosen her up a little?"

"Yes, sir. I'll give her more curare."

"We need good exposure, Peter, and we've got to have the abdomen well relaxed. I usually do a Bilroth Two on this kind. Lately I've been doing that almost entirely. I'd like to go over my gastrectomies in the last five years, collect the different procedures, and analyze them. See which ones have done the best." He went on working rapidly, moving his head up and down to peer into the opened abdominal cavity, taking out loops of gut to wrap in wet lap tapes, then exploring all quadrants vigorously, his long, green-sleeved arm getting bloodily moist to the elbow.

"Peter, Mrs. Long here has a lump on her left kidney, I think."

"Mrs. Long? Did you say Mrs. Long?"

"Yes, Micheline Long. Do you know her?"

Peter tried to cover his shock. "Micheline Long?"

"That's right."

"Yes, I believe I do."

"I think she told me she had seen you. You had her in the hospital, she said, but she went right on feeling bad and having stomach pain so she called me this evening. I examined her and thought she might be penetrating, so I told her she better have her surgery tonight, get her stomach out of there now. We have to do the appendix first, though. Say, I think that's only a cyst of the kidney I'm feeling. Her colon seems good and there are no nodes in the cul de sac. I always go all along the colon and small bowel, because I've picked up quite a few polyps and early cancers that way. Just a minute." He pulled out his right arm, changed hands and stuck his left arm in deeply. "Whoops, don't tell me the lady's pregnant."

Peter involuntarily sucked in his breath.

"Did you say something, Peter?"

"No."

"I thought you'd seen a bleeder. Nope, I don't think she's pregnant. Probably just about to have a period and I'm feeling the corpus luteum on that left ovary."

He soon had the stomach and duodenum exposed in the field and was carefully examining them. "Here's the ulcer in the duodenum. You can see that reaction on the posterior wall of the duodenum. I almost always find that when they are getting ready to perforate."

Peter felt the area. "You don't think that could be starting to heal, sir?"

"Not at all, Peter. After you've seen a few dozen more ulcers you'll get to know. Now let's see, how will I line this thing up? I think this piece of jejunum right here is what I should use for my anastomosis. I like to take a lot of the stomach, too. My best results are with a high resection, taking out a good three-fourths of the fundus of the stomach and leaving a small gastric pouch."

At two A.M. the operation was over, fast time, Peter knew. Matthew Hatch wrote quick orders in the chart, glanced at the anesthesiologist's sheet, and went to the dressing room. He dictated a note of his findings on the tape recorder there first, and then cheerfully talked while he took off his operating clothes and dressed. "That wasn't the simplest one technically, Peter, but I think she'll do all right."

"Then you feel she'll have an easy post-op course, Dr. Hatch?" Peter stood stiffly, even more erect than usual, feeling numb inside, but trying to talk naturally.

"Probably, but it's hard to say. I'd like very much to have you follow her with me, Peter. See her each day and write any orders you want. Please do that. Any time you want to with my patients I'm happy to have you check them and order anything you think I might have overlooked. I have that much confidence in you."

"Well, thank you."

"By the way, Harry Lawson, who's away for Labor Day, is also leaving the end of this week for the rest of the month. I'd like to have you scrub with me while he's on vacation. Is that all right with you?"

"Why, yes, sir. I guess that would be fine," Peter said after a pause.

"And you'll follow Mrs. Long with me on post-op, won't you? Give you a chance to see how I work."

12

MRS. LONG was doing satisfactorily the next morning. A catheter was threaded in her arm vein and fluid from a bottle hanging at her side dripped into it. "Some of the tough ones I get Frank Lewicki to see, Peter," Matthew Hatch had said on rounds. "This one won't be so bad, but maybe you could supervise the intravenous fluids. Talk to Frank about them, get his advice, and then you could help me on some of the other ones without having to bother him. I've found he gets a little upset when he's pushed too hard, anyway."

"I'll be glad to do that, Dr. Hatch." Peter was anxious to see Mrs. Long get well. He had slept restlessly because of his concern for her. He somehow felt responsible for her future now.

"Also, Peter, Harry Lawson told me he needs some time for catching up before he leaves Friday, and asked if you could start assisting me tomorrow, Tuesday morning. I was sure you wouldn't mind and told him yes. It's a full schedule and we'll begin at seven on the nose, so please come in at quarter to."

Going over Mrs. Long's chart afterward, Peter noticed at once that Matthew Hatch had ordered two units of blood although her blood loss on the operating table had been negligible in spite of Dr. Hatch's comment about being a "wet surgeon." Besides, two units of blood had been given during surgery for replacement. He made a note to ask Frank Lewicki about this also.

Mrs. Long looked up at him through her fog of sedation, but still with recognition. "Oh, Dr. de Haan, I don't want you to be mad at me for not coming back. I was feeling so awful, crying all the time, and Dr. Hatch said I just couldn't get well without this operation and that it had to be done immediately."

"Did your stomach pain get worse, Mrs. Long?"

"It was bothering me some, but it was definitely better with those medicines you gave me." Her answer was like a hammer cracking on his breastbone. Then she had been better with the antacid. Peter looked at her brown Gallic eyes, exaggeratedly big with her hair damped down from sweat. The gastric suction tube in her nose distorted the normally tiny mound of flesh in such a way as to give it a swollen, porcine look.

"Are you having much pain this morning?"

"It's been terrible, Doctor. I had a shot a while ago, but I need another one right now."

Peter percussed the bandaged wound. There was some unnatural tympany to the sound produced, indicating gaseous distension beneath. He listened with his stethoscope for bowel sounds, which were absent. "I'll be back to see you, Mrs. Long. I assisted on your surgery last night and Dr. Hatch asked me to follow along on your post-operative care."

"That's fine. It was nothing against you that I went back to Dr. Hatch. It's just that he's been taking care of me so long and I was so desperate."

"Did you tell him what you told me, Mrs. Long?" Peter asked.

"No, I didn't. Do you think I should have? Actually, I wanted to, but I'm not sure I could have brought myself to do it. He didn't give me time anyway. You know how he is. Quite a guy." A small smile appeared on her pale mouth.

"Yes," he said.

Peter came on Frank Lewicki in the coffee room later that morning. "You mean you're going to be assisting him all next month?" Frank asked when Peter began to explain the situation.

"Yes, I guess so."

"And he wants you to help with the post-operative care to save me? You poor bugger. I'm not surprised. Of course, he can't get George Carr to do it. He's too damned lazy and too unreliable after six P.M. And Matthew's patients have a nasty habit of turning up their toes at all hours. Also, I give him a little trouble about everything, which he damn well deserves. First of all, he knows nothing about fluid and electrolyte balance. If you just automatically crossed off everything he ordered in this regard and put down something different, I swear you would come out better. And blood, too. He orders too much blood all the time. With Mrs. Long, I'd hold the blood until you check her hemoglobin and hematocrit. If they are below ten and thirty you could give her a pint, otherwise I wouldn't."

"He worried me at surgery," Peter said, pouring a second cup of coffee for Frank Lewicki and himself, "not just because I wondered if the operation was really necessary, but other things. For instance, he went into the common bile duct and actually probed it, and I can't understand why. I'm afraid that will give her a hell of a lot tougher course. At least, that's what we were always told." Peter went on to tell Frank the whole story behind Mrs. Long's illness.

"I know what you mean," Frank said, buttering a piece of toast that had just popped up. "He's a bastard. I've thought about all this a lot, and my only justification for staying here, knowing what I do, is to tell myself I don't start or cause any of these things, and actually do my damnedest to keep them from happening. I fight Matthew tooth and nail all the time. Of course, many, many of his patients I never see." Frank sat down again and dunked the toast in his coffee. "He still tries sometimes to get me to approve his surgery, mainly by having me do a pre-op consultation, but I never mention anything about surgery in the write-up then. In essence you are supposed to say the patient is all right for surgery if needed. Matthew likes to twist even that into your saying the patient *needs* the surgical procedure he has scheduled, so be careful, protect yourself."

Driving home late on Labor Day afternoon, Peter saw a white convertible several cars ahead of him. In a block he had decided it was Anne's Plymouth. She must be coming back from San Francisco. They went up the hill of Valleyview Drive, and onto its higher flat stretches. Anne turned into her driveway and was out of the car as Peter came by. He slowed up along the curb, honked and waved cheerily, but kept going. Anne turned and waved, and watched him for a moment, Peter could see in the rear-view mirror, as he drove on. Then after he had passed her by, he wished he had stopped and talked to her.

Labor Day evening Micheline Long had bloody return from the stomach tube, which Mrs. Beauprey, now on the surgery floor, assured Peter was standard for first day post-op gastric resections. Mrs. Long's pain had been intense during the afternoon, and she was moist and cold feeling on the extremities when Peter saw her. Her blood tests had come back normal, so Peter had canceled the transfusions, hedging his order slightly by asking the nurse to get approval from Dr. Hatch for the change.

"You've had a lot of pain, haven't you?" Peter asked.

"It's been terrible, Dr. de Haan."

"You have to expect a few bad days after something like this, Mrs. Long."

"I know that, but I never thought they would be this bad."

Peter took her blood pressure and found it low at 80 over 60.

"I felt so nauseated tonight and I vomited some, too, Doctor."

"That shouldn't happen with the stomach tube in place. Did you bring up much?"

"Yes, quite a bit. The nurse can tell you."

Peter spent five minutes adjusting her Levine tube, and the return of fluid through it from her stomach was much better when he finished. "I'll try to see you get a comfortable night," he told her.

Talking to Mrs. Beauprey at the nurses' station, Peter told her how worried he was about Mrs. Long. "So much pain, Mrs. Beauprey, and she seems a little shocky, too. Cold and moist. We had better check her blood pressure at least every two hours tonight and give her Aramine I.M. if it goes down further."

"All right."

"If she has any trouble during the night be sure to have them phone me."

At one A.M. the nurse did call. Mrs. Long's pressure had dropped lower and they had given her Aramine with improvement, but her pain was intense, and Demerol was not relieving it. Peter ordered morphine and said Dr. Hatch probably should know if this did not work properly or if there was more trouble. The nurse told him she had called Dr. Hatch just after her shift started, and he told her to ask Dr. de Haan about any other problems, explaining that Peter was coming on the surgical service for a while and needed experience with post-operative difficulties.

Up at six o'clock and worried, Peter was in the hospital kitchen at quarter to seven for a quick cup of coffee before going upstairs to the operating suite. When he got up there, Dr. Hatch was already taking off his trousers in the dressing room.

"Good morning, sir."

"Peter," Matthew Hatch said jauntily, "how are you, my boy? Did you see Mrs. Long yet?"

"No, I didn't."

"She's doing fine."

"Oh, I'm glad to hear that. I've been really worrying about her. They called me during the night."

"That's what I heard. I was over about three A.M. doing an appendix on a young woman Dr. Susack sent down. Ruptured, with pus all over. She will be a sick young woman. I wish you'd look at her today and order anything you want."

"I'll be glad to."

Peter looked at Dr. Hatch. After a hard week followed by an even tougher weekend, with several hours of surgery during each of the last two nights, he started off a new day, a new week, looking and acting like a man fresh from a month in Bermuda. Whatever else, his birthright in vitality was irreproachable.

The first surgery of the morning was a bilateral herniorrhaphy, and though there was a huge scrotal sac, it went quickly. In forty-five minutes it was over, and the next patient was already being anesthetized in the second operating room. They regowned and began the thyroidectomy there. Again Dr. Hatch's technique was fast. The essential tissue landmarks were quickly identified and passed by. The large blue cyst in the right lobe of the thyroid was found and a specimen of it sent for frozen section.

Soon, Dr. Joe Parmelee put his head in the surgery door, impeccable in a starched knee-length white lab coat, his dark, four-in-hand tie knot kept neatly in place by a silver pin through the collar points, an untied mask held up to his face.

"Good morning there, Matt. It's a fine morning, isn't it?" His air of informal good nature, unlike Dr. Hatch's, seemed instantly false to Peter. He was almost feminine in his attention to detail in dress, annoying in the condescension he exuded like that of some important man's secretary. "I see you have a new partner there, Matt. Bright-eyed and bushy-tailed, I imagine. Good morning to you, Peter."

"What have you for me, Dr. Joe?" Matthew Hatch asked.

"That cyst looks benign, but you know how these thyroids are. The permanent sections can throw you a curve."

"It's clinically benign all right, too, so I'll just take out the nodule itself. Thanks, Joseph."

"You bet your life. Peter, keep your eyes on him. He's a whiz. You can learn what surgery's all about right here."

"A little bull mixed in, Peter, and sometimes I suspect more than a little," Dr. Hatch said after Dr. Parmelee had gone. "But he's a good, sound man."

Soon the thyroid patient had been sewn up and wheeled out. Peter saw it was not yet nine o'clock. Dr. Hatch bounced out of the room and came back in a moment. "We're scheduled in the other room next, but there'll be a half-hour wait, so I'm going to make rounds in the hospital. Why don't you come along?"

Dr. Hatch wheeled off in full operating dress, cap on his head, mask hanging at his neck, rubber gloves in place, baggy green pants showing under the blood-spattered gown, big rubber-soled cotton covers on his shoes. Peter discarded his own cap, mask, shoe covers, and long-sleeved outer gown before following, and caught up on B floor as Dr. Hatch walked into Room 46, the women's ward.

"Oh, Peter, there you are. This is the gal I was telling you about, with the appendix during the night. Doesn't she have bedroom eyes?" The girl herself smiled wanly and looked at Peter. "Mrs. Missy Grullas, isn't that right?" She nodded and Dr. Hatch scowled and then laughed. "What a name you have, dearie. This is Dr. de Haan, my assistant. I want him to check you over and help me keep track of you."

"Am I doing all right, Dr. Hatch? I still can't keep anything down."

"Fine, Missy, fine," he said. "You'll be all right."

As Dr. Hatch went on, Peter dropped behind to spend a moment with the large-eyed, plain-faced, toothy young woman. He felt her abdomen tentatively and found it soft through the bandaging. She looked dry, though, and her skin sprang back poorly when it was pinched, a sign of dehydration. She probably needed I.V. fluids.

"I'll see what Dr. Hatch has ordered for you, and then be around later to talk to you some more, Mrs. Grullas."

"Thank you. Will Dr. Hatch be back too?"

"I'm not sure."

"I just wondered how long I'd have to be here. I know my husband would want to know."

"Probably hard to say today, but I'd guess a week."

"Dr. Hatch is a wonderful surgeon, isn't he?"

Peter nodded and patted her shoulder. "I'll see you later on, Mrs. Grullas."

There was laughter from the corner of the ward where Matthew Hatch had been working over the dressings of an older woman in a bright blue bed jacket. The woman was saying, "You mean I have to go through that again tomorrow?"

"Nothing to it. We won't have to do it but twenty or thirty times more."

"If I thought you meant that I'd jump right out this window."

Dr. Hatch laughed again resonantly. "No, dear, I'm kidding you. I love you. You're my one and only girl friend." He gave the thin gray-haired woman a hug and reluctantly she began to smile.

"Good-bye, dear," Dr. Hatch said to her, still smiling as he started out the door. Peter mentioned to him what Mrs. Grullas had asked. He waved over to her as she looked their way and said, "Missy, if I have anything to say it won't be over three weeks and we'll have you home." He winked at her as she pinched her face up in a pout and then smiled back nicely as the door closed behind them.

"Hello, Andy," Dr. Hatch called to a man just stepping out of the elevator down the hall. "You're looking good after no sleep. We were just seeing your girl, Grullas."

Peter looked up to see a short, bonily thin man walking toward them. He was baggy-eyed and sallow in the face with thick curling gray hair and deeply tinted rimless glasses. His nose showed a red bulbousness while his eyes changed gaze continuously, nervously behind the dark pink lenses, and as he came up to them the odor of alcohol about him was unmistakable.

"Peter, this is Andy Susack from Bollerville in the north of the county. Andy, Peter de Haan." Dr. Susack grunted and offered a thin cold hand to Peter.

"You're Matt's new assistant?" he asked, but without waiting for an answer he turned at once from Peter to ask Matt, "How do you think Missy's doing?"

"Satisfactory, Andy."

"I'll probably be in to see her every day as long as I have that other man downstairs." Dr. Susack walked off into the ward without another word.

Peter looked at Matthew Hatch who shrugged and said, "Susack's always like that. A real oddball. It's a shame to watch a man ruin himself, Peter. Well, let's keep going."

The next room, a two-bed with the first bed empty, had a

cherubic elderly woman lying by the window in a full body cast. Dr. Hatch introduced Peter. "The loveliest member of the San Marcial Flower Club is Mrs. Liza McNaughton here who lifted one sack of Vigoro too many and darned if she didn't snap her back."

"It wasn't Vigoro, Doctor, but a chest of drawers."

"Anyway, she snapped lumbar vertebra number five, so that darned Les Leslie put this cast on her and that's no good."

"You look different this morning, Dr. Hatch. Did you get a haircut?" the lady asked.

"No, I just shaved, my dear." Dr. Hatch bent over and rubbed his cheek against the lady's as Peter watched in astonishment. "Did you ever feel anything that smooth, Liza? Like a baby's bottom." Mrs. McNaughton laughed, and Dr. Hatch caught her laugh, and reinforced it with his own. "Peter, let me ask you a question. Did you ever try to make love to a woman in a full body cast? It's tough, let me tell you, maybe impossible. That Les is sure not cooperative."

Twenty minutes later, still making rounds, Dr. Hatch looked at his watch and said, "I'm going downstairs for a minute, Peter, and I'll see you up in surgery. It's almost time to start. I'll have to finish rounds later."

"Yes, sir." Peter walked quickly to the end of the corridor and along the last jog in it to see Mrs. Long. Mrs. Beauprey was in the hallway and he called hello to her.

"Dr. de Haan, I tried to get you, but they said you were in surgery."

"Something the matter?"

"I'm so worried about Mrs. Long."

"Really? Dr. Hatch said she was doing fine."

"Well, we have to give her Aramine every half hour to keep her blood pressure above eighty. Her stomach is all blown up. She's not even passing any gas and at times there's just pure blood coming from her nasogastric tube."

"I wonder why Dr. Hatch thought she was doing all right."

"He was here before I came on shift. The girls said he just stuck his head in for a moment. Maybe she seemed better right then."

"What's her temperature?"

"It's a hundred and three this morning. They sponged her off during the night, too. I'm afraid to give her the castor oil."

"Castor oil?"

"Yes, Dr. Hatch ordered it this morning. Harris flushes to clean out the lower bowel, get some gas out, and an ounce and a half of castor oil through her nasogastric tube."

"I'll go see her."

"By the way, her husband, or ex-huband, I should say, is in there and would like to talk to one of you."

"Oh, Lord. I have to get back to surgery."

Mr. Long was at the bedside holding Micheline Long's hand and talking softly. When he saw Peter, he moved away toward the window on the far side of the bed. Peter nodded to him and picked up Mrs. Long's wrist. She opened her eyes and smiled. "I'm not feeling so good, Doctor." Her forehead was sweat-pocked and even with the fever her face was bloodless.

"I heard you weren't," Peter said. Her hands were cold too, her blood pressure only 85 over 70 as he took it. She winced and then cried out with pain as he felt her abdomen. Even through the bandages he found it tight-skinned and as hollow-sounding to percussion as kettledrums would be. Her heart raced as he listened to her chest with his stethoscope, and there were some rales of congestion in her lung bases.

"The pain is really bad today, Mrs. Long?"

"It's been just awful ever since yesterday afternoon, Dr. Hatch, I mean Dr. de Haan."

"I'll look over your chart and see what I can do to help you."

She smiled again, with her eyes closed.

"Doctor, may I see you for a minute?" Mr. Long asked then. He was medium-sized and dark with a ragged moustache on his upper lip. His brown suit was unpressed.

They walked into the corridor and Mr. Long said, "She seems plenty sick to me."

"I think she is. I don't know why she's so bad, really. I mean, her surgery came along all right."

"Did she really need to have this operation?"

Peter noticed that the man had a slight stammer. "What do you mean?"

"Just that I wonder if you also felt she had to have this done."

"She had had the ulcers for a long time."

"I know, I know. Well, maybe so, but of course I never have been much for surgery. I wouldn't let her have it done before when Hatch told her she needed it. And she got along all right without it. Now we're not together. I don't know if you—"

"She told me about the divorce."

"My drinking was the main problem, but I've stopped now, and I'm going to stay stopped. I do miss the kids and I had hopes we might even get back together. Seeing her now, though, I'm really scared. Is she going to make it, Doc? What's the score?"

"She definitely doesn't look good."

"Boy. Well, I've got to go to work. I'll be back later on in the afternoon."

"I'll talk to you then, Mr. Long."

At the nurses' station Mrs. Beauprey asked, "Do you think she should have a special nurse, Dr. de Haan?"

"I certainly do. I'll ask Dr. Hatch to see her again, too. I suppose some abscess in the incision or the abdominal wall is possible, though it seems awfully early for that."

"Is there anything else?"

"Yes, I want to get a blood culture, a C.B.C., and a portable film of her abdomen and chest."

"And the I.V.'s today?"

"Let's order her the same two thousand cc.'s as yesterday, and also have the lab do a blood sodium, potassium and CO_2."

Back in surgery, Peter found Dr. Hatch was not there yet, but the patient was already anesthetized and her abdomen was being draped.

"What are we doing on this patient?" Peter asked Marshall Wormser.

"She wanted her uterus out, so Matthew's obliging," Marshall answered sourly.

Peter looked at him. "What's her name?"

"Joslin."

"Just a hysterectomy?"

"He'll probably take out the gallbladder and maybe a kidney or two for kicks."

Peter was embarrassed to make a reply in front of the nurse, but Marshall pressed him. "Don't you agree with me, young Dr. de Haan? He's out for blood, this man."

"What do you mean, Marsh?"

"Never mind, kid. I just pop off sometimes."

Matthew Hatch came in as Peter was scrubbing. "Here we go, Peter. Are you scrubbing again?"

"Yes."

"You don't have to if you will leave your gloves and gown on like I do, you know." He pulled up his mask and stripped off his gloves and top gown. Then he regowned, put on fresh gloves and was quickly back at the surgical table. As he examined the square of iodine-tinted flesh he said, "Quite a week, this one, Peter. I was just looking at the schedule. By Friday we'll have done fifteen major surgeries, including four gallbladders. I don't know why so many gallbladders this week. It must be the season. We'll have to look at this young lady's gallbladder, too, by the way."

Peter could not keep from glancing at Marsh who looked back at him, saying, "Come on now, Matt, four gallbladders a week is the limit. That's all the Fish and Game Commission allows you."

Dr. Hatch laughed. "I think the anesthesia department is complaining, and they're off by noon every day. What a bunch of softies. Peter, I wanted to mention the old lady who's up for gallbladder operation Thursday morning, Mrs. Hollenhorst. She isn't in too good shape. Maybe you ought to check her before surgery."

Matthew started the lower midline incision and they were absorbed for a while in the surgery at hand. After they had the abdomen open Peter asked, "Was this woman we're operating on having menstrual troubles, Dr. Hatch?"

"She's got a mass in the region of her left ovary. It could be a cyst or a malignancy. Lots of pain with her periods, excessive bleeding. She's thirty-five and has four children, so she's just as well off without her uterus. Could be endometriosis, you know. Her uterus felt large to me, thick. I wasn't sure but what I could feel her gallbladder, too."

"You could feel her gallbladder?"

"Oh, sure, I can put my hands on them pretty well many times."

The benign, ordinary looking follicular cyst of her right ovary was removed and Matthew went on to removal of the uterus. "It's thick and I think it's endometriosis extending into the uterus wall. I wouldn't take it out always, in someone young who wanted more children I wouldn't, but she is toward the end of childbearing and has a good family and I think it's the best bet. Save her future troubles and surgeries."

Peter knew by now that one of the reasons for Matthew Hatch's speed was his ability to identify tissue, to know at all times what anatomical structure he had before him and what he wanted to do with it. He could see why Harry Lawson had said that after getting used to assisting Matthew it drove him nuts to work with anyone else. They all seemed slow as clods. But Peter was also beginning to notice that with the speed there was roughness in handling organs, neglect of the tender care of tissue he had seen his professors demonstrate. Tenderness was time-consuming. Dr. Hatch finished his swabbing of the now empty pelvis. "Well, time to get out of this hole. We won't strike oil here." The scrub nurse snorted at his comment.

Sewing up the abdomen, Peter said to Dr. Hatch, "I was awfully worried about Mrs. Long when I saw her this morning. Her pressure is hard to maintain even though she is getting Aramine right along. Her abdomen's distended and she's very uncomfortable."

"I'll be darned. She was having a good deal of pain during the night, I know, but when I saw her this morning I thought everything was better. I'll look in on her right after we finish here. I know she has some ileus, but I don't think too bad. I gave her castor oil this morning. I've found that's often a good way to get those bowels moving. Get some gas passed, the distension goes down, and everything starts working better."

Peter said nothing, but wondered how anyone treating an early paralytic ileus, where the normal peristaltic activity of the intestine is greatly reduced or absent, could want to use a highly irritating purgative. Laxatives couldn't make the paralyzed muscles in the intestinal walls start working and they could irritate the walls further and cause greater distension, greater danger. Still, Matthew Hatch had surely carried hundreds of people through these situations, so perhaps his judgment was better than Peter realized.

But was ileus Mrs. Long's main problem, anyway? It didn't seem so. Pain of the degree she had, fever, and shock did not fit in with the extent of her ileus alone.

Back in her room, Peter found Mrs. Long little changed. Dr. Hatch joked with her and gave no evidence of serious concern. In a few minutes they left her and went to the X-ray room to look at her films with Lew Condon. "Some ileus there, Matt," he said, in his deep, loud, and engaging voice. "Not a great deal. I don't think it's an obstruction. But there is dilatation of the first part of the jejunum and haziness in that same area. Could she have some localized fluid in there or infection?"

"I don't think so, Lew. She does have fever. I wouldn't be surprised if her main trouble wasn't above the diaphragm, out of the surgical field entirely. Damned anesthetists don't always keep the lungs expanded properly during surgery and we get small pockets of lung collapse, with a touch of pneumonia in them. I see that on a lot of my cases."

"Well, Matt, your young associate here," Lew Condon beamed a full, friendly smile toward Peter, "ordered a portable chest X-ray, too, but I don't see much on it. A few extra markings here and there, but nothing that looks significant enough to account for the trouble she seems to be having."

"I can't really believe there is anything wrong in her abdomen unless an incidental diverticulitis has popped up. Remember we had that one case like that last year."

Lew nodded.

Matthew Hatch sighed. "Well, keep an eye on her through the day, Peter, and let me know what develops. I expect by tomorrow we will see some improvement. And I'd increase her penicillin dosage."

"She couldn't be bleeding, Matt, could she?" Lew asked, still pondering. "Peter wrote on her slip that she was shocky and the floor nurse told me they were giving her Aramine."

"I'm sure not, Lew. Absolutely not. Everything inside her abdomen was tied and double-tied carefully."

Was this the "wet surgeon" talking now, Peter wondered, but he said only, "By the way, Dr. Hatch, Mr. Long was in the room this morning and wanted to talk to you sometime today."

"Sure, send him over to my office. He's a no-good louse, you know, but I'd be glad to see him if he wants to come over." Dr. Hatch pounded him on the shoulder and snorted, "Don't look so worried, Peter. It's not good for the patients." He laughed. "She's going to be all right. Cheer up, boy."

13

THROUGH the afternoon Peter was reassured by Dr. Hatch's remarks, which was strange in a way considering the distrust that was growing in him for the man's judgment. Still, he *did* feel better. He had a shorter than usual afternoon in the office and then visited Mrs. Long again before going downtown for dinner. She was having less pain, but was otherwise the same.

He ate at Charley Gin's, his favorite Chinese restaurant, and after dinner called Anne Alexio from Charley's phone. He told her he wanted to come by to see her, and in ten minutes she was sitting in the front seat of his car again, looking at him.

"I'm so surprised," he said.

"What do you mean?"

"At your hair."

"Do you like it? I had it cut short."

"I can see. It looks good. I think it's great." She seemed very beautiful to Peter. She was so young, so fresh-looking.

"I had to do something to pick up my spirits, so I cut my hair."

"You didn't enjoy your weekend then?"

"How could I? All I thought about was you."

"Really?" Peter couldn't understand her. He had been sure that she had done just the reverse—forgotten him, never thought of him at all.

"I shouldn't have said what I did Wednesday night. I'm sorry. I've been kicking myself ever since. At first, I thought I never wanted to see you again, and then I decided I did want to. Now at the moment I am happy to see you, but also scared."

"Why?"

"I don't know. I guess because I'm afraid you won't come back after tonight."

"You're the one that's sort of crazy. You know, I called you twice, no, three times, but you were in bed, or not there, and you didn't call back, and then you were gone for the weekend. I thought you had written me off."

"I didn't know you'd called. You might as well understand how bad my father is about messages. If he did give me one, he probably wouldn't have it straight."

Peter found his heart beating hard when he was looking at Anne and talking to her. She was exciting in a white blouse and blue skirt—college dress—with the scents of fresh lipstick and powder and perfume coming from her. "I do want to kiss you," he said, rather lamely.

"Do you? I want you to. But it's still light."

"I know."

"Why don't you come inside? My dad's going out to a meeting."

They walked up the drive and into the house, silently. Taking him into the living room, she asked, "Would you like some coffee?"

"No."

"Or tea."

"I had all the tea I could drink at Charley Gin's."

She sat down on the sofa and tucked her legs under her as a door slammed farther inside the house and there were footsteps up the hall toward them.

"Anne, I have to go now," her father said. "Oh, hello."

"Dad, this is Dr. de Haan, Peter de Haan, you met him the other night."

"Oh, yes, Doctor, nice to see you again. I'm late and have to run. Anne, I'll probably be home by eleven, but it could be twelve. Good night, Doctor." He shook hands with Peter and left.

"I like your father. He seems very nice."

"He is. I guess he's lonely, too, but certainly never complains about anything."

There was a pause in their conversation, then Anne said, "I didn't ask you if you wanted a drink. I just assumed you were on call or on duty or something. You sounded so serious."

"No, thanks, I don't want anything."

"You said you wanted to talk about something."

"I mainly wanted to tell you, I guess, that I've been thinking about you. No, there was something more logical and important-sounding than that, but now all I can seem to do is stare at you and think how beautiful you are."

She reached for his hand.

"May I kiss you now?" he asked.

"I wish you would."

Peter stood up and came to her, sat down by her, and she put her hand on his cheek.

"I am crazy about you," he said, kissing her.

She pulled away in a minute. "Are you really? I just can't stand to hear you say that if you don't mean it. It does awful things to me to think you don't mean it."

"I do mean it."

"Darling," she said. She kissed him, putting her arms

around him. After a while she stopped, and drew back. "I do love you."

"I love you, too," he said, holding her close. He touched her body, her buttocks, her waist, her shoulders, her breasts. He felt her nipples tighten under his fingers. "Darling, I want to be with you," he said.

Anne put her head on his chest and held tight to him for a while, breathing hard. Then she said, "Go down to my bedroom at the end of the hall, and I'll come there."

He went to the room and took off his clothes, placing them carefully on a bench at the foot of the bed. Soon Anne stepped in with only a dressing gown on, slipping it off as she closed the door. There was enough light in the room for him to see her clearly and she was dazzling. Her body was beautifully proportioned, firm and smooth-skinned as he felt it. Her breasts were larger than he had realized and high on her body. The nipples were dark and erect now with broad, soft, raised areolae surrounding them. His hands searched all of her, and she touched him before he laid her down on the bed.

Their climax was quick but full, and they lay back against each other afterward, warm and sweaty and relieved. In a while she left him, and Peter, dressing again, thought how wonderful she was, how completely sexual, too. She had enjoyed their being together fully, and there had been no tears or shame later, just the recollection of love and excitement.

Later they sat at the table in the kitchen sipping white wine Anne had found in the cupboard and chilled quickly in the freezer. "This is good," Peter said.

"Dad gets it from a winery here in the valley."

"It doesn't taste as good as you do, though."

"Peter, you embarrass me."

"You know I do love you. It's true. I've never said that to anybody before and meant it, but it's true now."

"Have you had lots of girls?"

"No, some."

"I don't want to hear about them."

"I don't want to know about you, either," Peter said.

"I was in love before with one boy two years ago, but then I fell out of love with him. Now I can't imagine why it ever began."

"Don't say another word. It sounds like my own epitaph."

"Never. I'll never change the way I feel about you. I know that."

"I love you. Honestly I do." Peter kissed her cheek, scarcely believing in what had happened. He had a feeling of absolute madness for this girl he hardly knew. The moment now in this kitchen he knew he would always remember, and yet while it went on even it seemed unreal.

Anne said, echoing his own state, "It's so hard for me to believe it. I'm fighting myself, saying not to believe it, because I don't want to get hurt and that's all I can think will happen. You're not just saying what you are because you wanted to go to bed with me and you did?"

"I am crazy about you."

"Do you want another glass of wine? I put it back in the refrigerator."

"No, I have to go, darling. I'm befuddled enough already. What an evening this has been. I have to go see Mrs. Micheline Long, for one thing, the lady who was in the hospital room with you."

"What's wrong with her?"

"She's very sick. Dr. Hatch operated on her Sunday night for stomach ulcers, and she isn't doing well at all."

"That's awful. I got to like her when she was in my room, and I felt so sorry for her."

"I must go. I should have seen her before now."

"Thank you for dropping by," Anne said, smiling.

" 'Dropping by,' indeed."

"I'm teasing you."

"Come out with me to the car. It's dark now, so I can kiss you there."

They walked up the hallway and out the front door. "It's lovely outside. So cool and clear," she said.

Peter took her arm and held it until they got to the sidewalk. "Good night, darling." They kissed and she held onto him, and they kissed again. "Good night."

"Good night, Peter. When will I see you?"

"I'll phone you tomorrow."

"I'm home from school by four fifteen, so call as early as you can."

"I'll make it four sixteen."

"Good-bye, darling."

14

THE next morning Mrs. Long's fever remained high, but her pressure seemed to be holding a little better without much Aramine. Her pain was still intense and Peter was struck by her look of shriveling up, of emaciation. Looking at her now he could not even recall the face of the attractive woman who had first sat in his office three weeks before. Her voice, too, was small from pain and fatigue and husky now from the throat irritated by the stomach tube. Occasionally she started to say something unrelated to their conversation to some person not in the room. She would catch herself and tell him she was sorry. "There I go again. I keep wandering off." And once she said, "Do they have the same band here at Danny's as they used to?" and she laughed.

Peter said, "This is the Hatch Hospital, dear, and the patients tell me there's a new bunch of noisemakers every night." She wobbled out another small laugh before an abortive cough made her grab her bandaged abdomen in pain.

Later on in the day—at lunchtime—she seemed brighter and perfectly clear in her thinking. She said to Peter, "I'm so sorry now I had this operation. I'm going to die. I know it. And I don't want to, Dr. de Haan. There's something terribly wrong, isn't there?"

"I think it's just your bowel slowing up, we call it ileus, from a mild inflammation inside. It could be around the operation site, or even in the pancreas, which sometimes gets inflamed." The pancreas. He had never thought of the pancreas. She could have a pancreatitis.

"Poor little Vickie and Lee. Who'll take care of them?" The tears began to roll down her cheeks.

"Oh, Mrs. Long, things will be better tomorrow and you'll forget how rough today is."

"You're very nice, Doctor."

He decided to get the lab to run a test on her at once for pancreas inflammation. Why hadn't he thought to do that before? Hadn't Matthew Hatch probed the common duct into the duodenum, even talked about whether he could feel a nodule in the pancreas and discussed the possibility of biopsying it?

Peter wrote an order on the chart for a serum amylase to be done *statim*. "Do you want me to call the lab man from lunch, Dr. de Haan?" the nurse asked.

"Yes, I certainly do. He can get it started."

Peter left the ward absorbed with the problem. He remembered cortisone drugs could pull people through pancreatitis sometimes, but they interfered with wound healing, too, and could be dangerous in a post-operative situation for that reason as well as for their tendency to interfere with the body's defenses to infection. Also, the cortisones made some people wild and unmanageable, which led to other difficulties.

Going over to C Ward, occupied with his own mental clouds, Peter made the turn at the top of the stairwell and almost ran into Norman Silvana.

"Peter, you about got me."

"Hello, Norman, I'm so glad to see you. I have a problem that maybe you can help me with." He quickly told Norman, who leaned against the banister as he listened, the whole story of Micheline Long, even including the rape and her worry over getting pregnant. "Anyway, at surgery, Dr. Hatch claimed she was perforating, though I couldn't see it. But besides that, he explored her common duct to be sure there was nothing there."

"Hell, I saw him take out half a normal colon one day because he couldn't think of anything else to do. He actually said, after I'd told him to close up, 'We've got to do something.' That's the first and last time I ever scrubbed with him."

"Is that right?"

"Mrs. Long probably wasn't perforating at all, Peter. Look, he tried to tell me the other day about the good results he got from gastric resection for duodenitis. For *duodenitis*. I gave it to him. I just said, 'You don't do resections for duodenitis, Matt, now what are you talking about?' Right in front of Miss West, too. Of course, she hates my guts, so there's nothing to lose there. And being in love with the great man, she thinks he gives off perfumed farts anyway." Norman smoothed down an errant slip of sleek black hair dropping onto his broad handsome forehead.

"Well," Peter said, "Mrs. Long's been in a mess since surgery, sick as hell. Her abdomen is tight, distended, nothing going through, and still Dr. Hatch gave her castor oil this morning."

"Yes, Dr. Hatchet likes castor oil in his post-op ileus patients. God, he really proves to you how much physiological abuse the human body can take. There's hardly anything I could think of that would be worse for a patient with ileus than giving her castor oil on her third post-op day. Besides, do you know exploring a common duct adds about three percent mortality—*three percent mortality!*—to a surgical procedure? Pancreatitis is much more possible just for one thing."

Peter rubbed his forehead. "Norman, I am really worried about her. She is sick as hell. She has fever, up to a hundred and two or a hundred and three through the day, and lots of pain."

"When did the pain start?" Norman asked.

"She had it the first day after surgery. I thought of pancreatitis this noon, and now that you mention it . . ."

"She probably broke her anastomosis and has a peritonitis. That's happened to him before."

"What I wanted to ask you was if you would see her for me and tell me what you think about her?"

"Oh, come on, Peter, don't ask me that. I don't like to get mixed up in any of his cases."

"You do all the time, don't you?"

"Very little. He gets Harry Lawson or Al Humphers to follow up on him when he goes away. I just won't do it. Of course, sometimes he leaves some real critical ones behind when he's on a trip and I have to take over with them and try to correct his mistakes."

"I would appreciate it if you could help with this one, Norman."

"You don't understand, Peter. I can't do it. The minute I put my head in that door as a consultant, I accept responsibility, I stick my neck out, I am involved in a case professionally and medico-legally that I don't want to have anything to do with. Besides, technically he's the one who should ask for consultation."

"Well, why do you and Frank stay here if you feel the way you do about him?" Peter was annoyed now.

"Look, he runs his practice and I run mine, the right way, and there's no connection at all between us there. And that's the way it's going to be or I will leave. Matt has a good understanding of how I feel, I'm sure, and is willing to keep me on, on that basis."

"Okay. Well, thanks."

"Right," said Norman, raising the gleaming pink flesh and perfectly trimmed nails of his right hand. "I'm sorry. And don't forget what I said about a tear in the anastomosis. It's probably pulled apart in there and is dumping stomach juices into the omentum and stirring up a hell of a peritonitis. That's my guess, Pete."

With a swing of his beautifully tailored shoulders, he went gracefully down the hallway, his dark, almost pretty Italian head casting a giant shadow on the opposite wall for a moment before he disappeared.

Peter stopped by to see Mrs. Grullas, who was improving, then looked in on the aging woman Matthew had asked him to see before gallbladder surgery Thursday morning. Her name was Lillian Hollenhorst and she was a sad-looking, sweet-talking old lady with pink cheeks and white hair on a balding head. Her once blue irises were now white with time. Because her thoughts wandered easily, she had to be put back frequently on the track of the conversation.

"Yes, I am tired tonight, Doctor. All these tests are hard on a person when they're past eighty-four, you know."

"Are you over eighty-four, really? You don't look over seventy."

Her mouth opened in a small round smile as if she were going to blow a smoke ring from one of her filtered cigarettes. "It's very nice of you to say that, Doctor."

"Tell me about your illness. When did you first get sick?"

"I've had these dizzy spells that make me sick to my stomach for years. Everything spins and I feel bad for a day or two. I can't remember just how often I have them. I think Dr. Hatch can tell you more about them. He talked to my daughter and Dr. McKay, too."

"When did you get sick most recently, Mrs. Hollenhorst?"

"I don't know. I guess last week. I was dizzy and vomited a lot last week."

"Has anything special been happening lately at home? I mean, any troubles to upset you?"

"Oh, it's been terrible. My daughter has been an awful worry. She's a nice person, but she gets so nervous and she and her husband don't get along anymore. She tries to run everything and of course her husband doesn't like it. No man does." She blinked her short, white eyelashes. "Then they both get to drinking and fight terrible. Oh, dear." Tears appeared in her eyes.

"That's too bad. I'm sorry to hear that."

Peter examined her briefly, talked to her a minute longer, and then said good-bye.

"Will you come back to see me?"

"Oh, yes."

"Dr. Hatch is going to operate on me tomorrow. Take out the gallbladder. He says it causing all the trouble. He's very nice, just like you."

Going through her chart at the desk, Peter found a report from the morning before of a gallbladder X-ray that was normal except for slight reduction in concentration of the testing dye. A G.I. series was negative, too. Although Matthew Hatch's short, written workup said for diagnosis merely "Gallbladder disease," the normal X-ray seemed to cancel out that impression and Peter could come up with no clear understanding of a reason for a cholecystectomy on Mrs. Hollenhorst. It seemed more like a simple case of vertigo in an old person from poor circulation to the labyrinth of the inner ear.

To take out her gallbladder when the X-ray of the organ was all right seemed to be madness. Peter shook his head as he sat thinking about it. Finally he wrote a short note which did not include any mention of gallbladder disease. The diagnosis Peter came to was cerebral arteriosclerosis with vertigo, and he said nothing about the proposed surgery in his note. After he finished, he went by the laboratory before starting afternoon office hours. The technician motioned to him from the water bath. "Just a minute, Doc. I'm almost done." Thirty seconds later he took some readings from the colorimeter, consulted a chart, and said, "Well, I guess it's up a little. The amylase is two hundred and twenty milligrams percent."

"What do you call your upper limit of normal here, Ted?"

"Oh, I think about a hundred and eighty. Her serum may be a little icteric, too."

"Thanks a lot. I don't know just what it means, whether there is pancreatitis or there isn't. I'd appreciate it, though, if the lab would run a urinary lipase tomorrow. If that were elevated too, it would give us a stronger lead."

"We'll do that."

"Thanks, Ted. You have a good lab here."

"Dr. Hatch sends us anyplace we need to go for new methods."

"That's helpful, isn't it?"

After office hours Peter took his suddenly weary frame up to Mrs. Long's room on B Ward again. She was much the same, shocky, in pain, drowsy from sedation and poor in color.

"Why don't you give her an oxygen mask through the night to see if she won't be more comfortable?" Peter said to the special nurse.

In his apartment, Peter turned on his radio to the FM station, sprawled on the couch, and dialed Anne's number. After a dozen rings, he hung up and dialed it again. Anne answered.

"Where have you been?" he asked. "This is Peter."

"Hello, darling. I thought you'd call before now. I had to go downtown for a minute and just walked in the door."

"I'm late, but I wanted to wait until I got home from the hospital to call you. I wasn't sure if you were there because I couldn't see your car as I came by."

"Have you eaten dinner?" she asked.

"No, I was just going to ask you. I thought we might go out."

"I did eat already, but I wouldn't mind sitting with you some place. Or I could cook you something here—bacon and eggs."

"Why don't you come down with me to Charley's?"

"All right. Are you tired? You sound tired."

"Not too bad."

"How is Mrs. Long? Is she better?" Anne asked.

"No, not really. I'll tell you."

Anne stared at him thoughtfully as she got in the car fifteen minutes later. "Hello, may I come over?"

"You must," Peter said, his spirits rising to see Anne, to look at her lovely neck, her turned-up nose and her large clear eyes. He put his arm around her for a moment and kissed her before he drove off downtown.

He had to park almost a block away from Charley's. "There must be something doing tonight," Peter said.

"It's just Dollar Days, I think," Anne replied.

"You don't mind walking?"

"Of course not."

"It's foggy tonight," Peter said. "It seems funny. I didn't expect it here this far inland."

"Oh, we have lots of fog every winter, and sometimes in the summer, too."

Though Charley was very busy, he gave them a booth in the back. Peter drew the curtain on it. "Don't you feel wicked now?" he asked Anne, who laughed.

"I feel more cozy than wicked," she said.

Anne had two bottles of beer while Peter ate his dinner and talked to her. "I'm worried about Dad, too," he told her. "There was a letter from Mother today and she said he was going back in the hospital this week for tests and treatment. His heart is what's bothering now, chest pains and shortness of breath."

"I'm sorry to hear that, Peter. And what about Mickey Long?"

"Oh, Anne, she's awful. I'm so disappointed because I'm not sure she should have been operated on in the first place."

"Why? Didn't Dr. Hatch do it?"

"Yes, he certainly did."

"I thought he was a very fine surgeon."

"I don't know. I'm beginning to wonder about him."

"Well, that's terrible if she had surgery she didn't need."

"Maybe I'm wrong. Anyway, she's bad. But I do have one good thing to think about, do you know?"

"What's that?"

"You. I love to sit here and listen to you and talk to you."

"It is fun."

"You know the fog made your hair curly."

"It always does."

"I enjoyed walking along the street with you, looking in the shop windows."

Anne tilted her head to one side. "I wish you could kiss me right now," she said.

"The curtain's closed."

"There's a table between us."

"I don't care." He leaned over and kissed her nose before they stood up to leave.

Outside the sidewalks were a little wet now, and the street signs were blurred in the mist. When he got in the car, Peter snapped on the windshield wipers.

Turning through the smoky stop-and-go signal at Valleyview Drive, Peter felt weak-kneed and shaky for a moment, and realized he was getting excited. Anne was so close and so lovely.

"Darling," he asked, "is your father home?"

"He had to go to Los Angeles."

"Then you're home alone, and I am too. That seems a shame."

"Are you suggesting something?"

"Why don't you stay with me?"

"Should I do that?" She turned to look at him.

"I think so."

"Do you really love me, Peter?"

"I do, terribly." He stopped in front of her house, turned off the lights and the motor, and kissed her hard. "I do love you," Peter said, and it was a new feeling to him, the intensity of which was almost frightening. He had never truly loved any girl before, he realized. "Won't you stay with me?"

"All right, I will," Anne said. "I don't quite understand why you can make me do anything you want to. I seem to like it, though."

"Will you come now?"

"No. Let me off here. I want to get some things. No, first show me where your apartment is and then I'll come up to you. I hope you have back stairs."

"I do."

"Do you think I ought to start taking pills, or anything?"

"I'd rather you didn't. They're all right, and I know safe enough, but still there's occasional trouble with them. Right now I'd feel better not to. I'll give you something to use, or use something myself. Is that all right?"

"Of course. You're my doctor. My lovely doctor."

When she rang the back bell, Peter had lowered the lights in the apartment, and switched on the FM station in the front room.

"Darling," she said, "I think someone downstairs saw me."

"I don't care. Do you?"

"No."

Peter kissed her, feeling her body against him. She was trembling slightly, and suddenly quiet as she left him and went in the bedroom. In a few minutes she opened the door in her nightgown.

"You're so beautiful," he said, taking her hands in his.

"Kiss me," she said, and he did, standing up at first, and then after he placed her on the bed. They caressed each other, and when he entered her in a moment, she let out a quick cry.

"Am I hurting you?" he asked.

"God, no."

Peter made love slowly then, and Anne seemed to understand why he wanted to. When he could not put off the final moment further, the end came for both of them, longer and sharper than the first time. They had learned more of each other in the one night before than seemed possible, Peter thought.

As they relaxed silently afterward, Peter smiled into the dark because her hand was only an inch away and he could touch it whenever he wanted to. He fell asleep still smiling.

The phone rang at three A.M. and Peter had to reach over Anne, who was moving uncertainly in her sleep at its sound, to answer it. "Yes, this is Dr. de Haan."

It was B Ward about Mrs. Long. Her fever had gone up to 104.6 rectally. She was incoherent and noisy and they wondered about sedation and something else for the fever. Peter ordered another sedative and then, after thinking, gave her a starting injection of 50 milligrams of prednisolone, a cortisone derivative.

"What in the world is that?" Anne asked, sitting up.

"Nothing, darling. Just the hospital."

"The hospital? Oh. I'll have to get used to that, won't I? I couldn't imagine where I was."

"Shh. Don't worry. You're wonderful. Go back to sleep."

But Peter lay there for an hour watching Anne in the eerie half-light of the room and thinking about Mickey Long, before he finally slept again.

15

THEY had coffee and cinnamon buns together at six in the morning in his kitchenette, and then crept down the back stairs hand in hand before kissing on the last step. They went to their separate cars, and drove out like strangers.

Before surgery Peter went to see Mrs. Long. She was drowsing, but lifted her eyelids as he came in and smiled a little. "I'm still here," she said.

The nurse handed him her temperature chart. Her fever was down to 101 rectally. Perhaps the cortisone had helped. "How's the pain?" Peter asked.

"A little better right now." She spoke slowly and with effort. Her breathing was less labored, but she was still cold to the touch and moist. "I was going to say today though I don't even know what day it is."

"It's Thursday."

"Already? Wasn't I operated on Saturday night?"

"No, Sunday night."

"Oh, I can't keep anything straight."

She cried a little as Peter felt her abdomen, which was still rigid but slightly less tender. Listening for a minute he heard no bowel sounds. He said, "I'll be back later on in the morning. Meanwhile, I'm going to get your abdomen X-rayed again."

Leaving her room, Peter found Mr. Long waiting directly outside in the hallway. "Doctor, how's she doing? I waited for hours yesterday for Dr. Hatch and finally had to leave."

Peter motioned him down the corridor away from her room. "I'm not pleased at all with the way things are going, Mr. Long. Though she may be a little better this morning, she certainly is very ill."

"I knew she shouldn't have had that operation. That god-dam Dr. Hatch. Excuse me, but I've never had any use for him."

"I still think you ought to talk to Dr. Hatch yourself, Mr. Long. He's operating this morning for only an hour or so. I believe you could catch him about eight thirty."

"I will. I'd like to give him a piece of my mind. What's causing her trouble now anyway? Is it infection?"

"It acts like infection, what we call a 'collection' of pus inside the abdomen at the operative site. Or it could be the pancreas. Sometimes after surgery it can get inflamed, not really an infection, but a severe inflammation with fever and pain."

"Do you think she might die, Dr. de Haan?"

"She might. I certainly hope not."

"She better not." Peter noticed the man's eyes were blood-shot and he could smell on him the sour ethanolic breath of the morning-after.

"I'm watching her very closely, Mr. Long, and doing everything I can for her."

"I know, Doc, and don't think I don't appreciate it. I'm not mad at *you*."

In the surgery dressing room Matthew Hatch greeted him

with a smile and an upraised hand, a telephone to his left ear and only one leg of his scrub suit on.

"All right, then," Dr. Hatch said over the phone, "I'll talk to you about it this afternoon. Meet me at my house at five sharp. Okay?"

He nodded silently a few times, said good-bye and hung up. "Boy, those stockbrókers get up early to snag you. They're like cattle buyers, they try to do business with you when you're half asleep."

"I've thought about buying a mutual fund," Peter said. "Maybe putting fifty or a hundred dollars a month into one."

"I'd say no, Peter. A good broker can do better for you. You have to save up more at a time to work with them, but ultimately they pay off. Well, I'll be out scrubbing. Take your time, I can start without you."

"I'll be right there."

Making the incision in Mrs. Hollenhorst's abdomen, Dr. Hatch asked Peter, "What did you think of this old gal? Quite a character, isn't she?"

"Yes, she looks like one of the leads in *Arsenic and Old Lace*."

"You're right there. You know, she used to be quite a drinker."

"I wondered."

"What do you think we'll find on her?"

Peter looked at Matthew Hatch and momentarily lost a bleeder he was holding. "I don't know."

"There is something wrong with this old lady. I can just feel it and I think it's in her abdomen. I think it's her gallbladder. I wouldn't be surprised if we found a malignancy there."

"Really?"

"Yes. I've never seen her look so bad. She has had spells like this before, I know, but apparently this is the worst one. I definitely thought I could feel her gallbladder on examination. The X-rays didn't show this clearly, but I saw some haziness at the tip of the gallbladder that could be tiny stones or sediment. Lew didn't report it out, but I asked him about it and he said it was possible. I look at all my own X-rays and make my own interpretations of them and rely on that a lot. Not that Lew Condon isn't a fine radiologist. But he hasn't been looking at X-rays for twenty-three years on patient after patient whom he's also seen in practice and followed very closely. Lew often puzzles over my diagnoses of intestinal obstruction after looking at X-rays before surgery. This is the reason I can do it, I think."

Peter wondered if Dr. Matthew Hatch might occasionally have moments of self-doubt or clairvoyant flashes of self-realization. Or was his head permanently in the sand with any unpleasant thought immediately extinguished? Did he never face up to the fact that surgery was a *very* lucrative business and if one did not care where the chips flew or what planer was used to slice them off with, a fortune could be made out of operating and operating and operating? People liked to have surgery done on them. When it was offered, in what they could only conceive to be good faith and good judgment, they were sitting ducks. A doctor could capitalize on this. Did Matthew Hatch? It appeared he must. If so, was it done consciously? That scarcely seemed possible. Certainly he had rationalized the wish inside him for money and power into what he considered an acceptable, perhaps even a superior form of medical conduct. Still there was no getting away from what the man was doing.

Peter was beginning to feel with Matthew Hatch what he had felt when he talked to men on the death row in a Maryland prison once. Or the way he had on his first trip into a psychotic ward at a state hospital. Everyone seemed so normal to him in these places he couldn't believe he was with murderers or insane people. Now, unable to understand Dr. Hatch's thought processes, he could scarcely believe in the reality of his actions.

Perhaps his own judgments were getting too harsh now, almost paranoid, his own mental pressures giving him strange thoughts. Maybe Mrs. Hollenhorst would turn out to have a gallbladder full of stones and the good Dr. Hatch would be justified. But would that justify him? No, not really. Unless he had some magical sixth sense in his fingertips, who would have subjected this old woman to a problematic, almost certainly an unnecessary cholecystectomy? So many things were matters of medical opinion, and medical opinion varied so, but here he could not imagine there would be much variation. Surely, no good surgeon would have operated on her. Peter was suddenly appalled at the thought of how many Matthew Hatches there might be in the small cities and big cities, the hamlets and skyscraper medical buildings of the United States.

"Hold that retractor harder, please, Peter."

"Yes, sir."

"There certainly are some adhesions around the ovaries and into the colon. I think she had an old appendicitis here. Okay, let's go ahead and look inside by the gallbladder. You can get some sutures ready on needles."

"Two-O, Doctor?"

"Two-O's fine."

The gallbladder was exposed in a few minutes and although there were a few adhesive tags to the liver at its edges it looked large and reasonably healthy.

Matthew felt it and squeezed its end. "I think I feel a little gravel in there. It's definitely thick, I'd say, to feel. The wall is thickened."

"Are you going to take it out?" Peter asked.

"Certainly," Matthew said absentmindedly. "This is the type of case where you have to explore the common duct, too, the same as with Mrs. Long." Removing the gallbladder took the next fifteen minutes. When it was opened on the metal tray by the table, only yellow bile gushed out into the pan holding it. "I don't see any stones. The bile doesn't look normal, though, and the wall is thickened," Matthew Hatch said. "Okay, let's get into the common duct with the probes. The stones may have gotten out." He carefully selected two pliable metal probes from the sterile stand. The first did not pass easily, so he took the second and tried passing it. It seemed to be held up in the pancreas substance on several more attempts, until finally Matthew forced it on through the ampulla of Vater and into the small intestine lumen of the duodenum. "There we are. Any stones in there—and I have an idea that's what was holding up the probe—they'll be out into the gut now. Good enough. Let's close up."

Putting on his clothes in the dressing room afterward, Dr. Hatch hummed and whistled, stopping to say something to Peter occasionally about the morning's surgery. "I think you'll find a lot of improvement in this lady now if you follow her through the next few months. That was a pathological gallbladder, I'm sure."

"She wasn't too difficult a one."

"No, pretty easy. Say, I just thought, there's a good medical and surgical seminar over in San Francisco next month at Norton Memorial Hospital. I go for the two days almost every year. Excellent teaching. A good bunch of fellows who are *practical*. They talk about things you can use. Why don't you come along with me?"

"Maybe I could." Peter hesitated a moment and then went

on. "You know, I thought of pancreatitis with Mrs. Long yesterday and had the lab run a serum amylase on her. It was only slightly elevated. But her fever went so high during the night that I took a chance and gave her some cortisone. Her temperature is way down this morning and she looks better and talks better, too."

"I'd say that's good thinking. I certainly approve. We have had some pancreatitis cases here after surgery and they are dillies."

"Her husband's waiting over in the room, too. I know he would like to talk to you very much."

"Fine. Let's go. This is her fourth post-operative day, isn't it? I've always found that the fourth day, in the ones having a rough time, is the big one. What's going to happen and whether they are going to make it or not becomes clear. Most of the times when I have to go in and open them up again for abscess accumulations and what have you, it's on the fifth day, after that key fourth. We'll have to make a decision today or tomorrow about opening her up again."

"I didn't realize you were thinking of that."

"Yes, we have to."

"I didn't know you were worried about her," Peter added lamely.

Mr. Long was sitting morosely in a chair in the room, the shiny oil of stress on his face. He stood up as he saw Matthew Hatch, who waved to him and shook hands momentarily, then went to the patient. He held her wrist for a few seconds before quickly undoing her abdominal binder to palpate her belly. Mrs. Long mumbled something.

"What did you say, Micheline?"

"I feel worse again. I thought I was better for a little bit this morning, Matthew."

"Oh, you'll be ready for a dance lesson this afternoon, Mickey. You're doing okay." He laughed.

"I'm not going to make it through this."

Dr. Hatch snorted contemptuously. "Not going to make it? What are you talking about. You're the healthiest person I've seen all week."

"Please don't fool me."

"You only need one little thing fixed. So we're going to take you back to surgery and fix it."

"I can't stand that. Are you kidding?" She lifted her head up to look at him, her face triangular now from its thinness.

"No, I'm not kidding. You need one more operation to get well." His tone became abruptly serious.

"I can't stand any more operations."

"It needs to be done, dear, and I'm going to do it for you this afternoon."

"I don't think I can stand it. Do you have to do it?"

"Yes. I'll tell Nick here about it and he can explain it to you. We'll schedule it for about five thirty."

Peter had seen Nick Long's eyes widen and his tired face stiffen as Matthew Hatch mentioned the new operation. Then resistance had dropped from his face and body almost tangibly. He looked lighter in the hallway, like a sweated-out and beaten fighter who would drop with a tap. "You have to operate this afternoon, Dr. Hatch?"

"Absolutely, no question about it." He turned away for a minute to Peter. "Did you get another amylase for today?"

"Yes, it's back on the chart already and it's still about two hundred."

"Good. Will you order three pints of blood for her and have at least one in her before we go to surgery? Thanks a lot."

"What's wrong with her, Doctor? What are you going to operate on?" Mr. Long asked.

Dr. Hatch answered flatly, not graciously. "She has infection or at least some inflammatory process in the abdomen. It may be a pancreas inflammation. Or it could be an abscess collection, just plain infection. It's certainly a serious situation and we'll have to operate today. We just can't wait any longer."

"I would like to have a surgical consultation, then, Doctor," Mr. Long said, a vestige of manly resistance abruptly returned.

"You really have no legal relation to her now, you know, Nick."

"I'm still her husband. We don't have a final decree."

"Your consent is not needed for surgery. You are not responsible for her bills or care, except as agreed through court, and I understand you haven't even been paying the alimony and child support. There's no need for me to satisfy you as to what you want to do with Mickey. You haven't earned that right."

"I know, Doctor. Heaven help me, I know." He was meek again as sweat came out on his pallid skin. "I'm only thinking of Micheline, Doctor."

"For her life to be saved she needs this operation. She has to have it. It will only be extra expense and delay to have a consultation. Possibly I can save her life with this operation, but I don't think so. I'm afraid she is going to die, regardless of what we do now. As you know, I've been trying to get her to have this surgery done for a long time and I think she just put it off too long, was too far down, with her processes of defense and repair too poor to carry her through. She didn't even bleed normally at surgery. You noticed that, didn't you, Peter?" Peter looked at him, but made no answer before Matthew Hatch went quickly on, "And she didn't take the anesthesia well, either."

Nick Long sighed heavily and threw his hands up in the air mutely.

"That's the story then, Nick. She'll be scheduled at five thirty."

Dr. Hatch explained to Peter as they walked down the corridor, "Actually, I put it on strong there for Nick because I've always found that's the best thing to do, as I told you in the case of the Lopez boy." Peter was surprised again at the accuracy of the Hatch memory when it suited the surgeon.

"She may not die at all," Dr. Hatch went on. "Really, you know, I blame the anesthesiologists a lot for the difficulty here and in a number of other cases recently. They don't seem to know when they are getting in trouble with a patient, so they can respond in the right way to help us out. I can tell you things used to go smoother with Bud Knowles when he was doing our anesthesia. He was crackerjack. Thirty minutes after the procedure, they were awake and almost singing. No shock. No post-operative troubles. But with Marsh Wormser it's always a bad day and he usually has his back up about something, too, spouting off. If he just wouldn't talk so much it would sure please me."

They went downstairs in the elevator and into the coffee room. Sitting down at one of the tables, Dr. Hatch continued, "To explain what I mean, I think that with too heavy anesthesia something goes wrong with the patients biochemically. I told you I was a wet surgeon. I was joking a little really, to see how you'd take it. I don't mind some oozing as I go along, but everything that keeps oozing through the surgery I tie, if you notice. I don't leave bleeders behind and the larger vessels I tie very carefully. Since Marshall's been here I've had too many hemorrhaging patients, too many wound disruptions. I told Marsh exactly what I thought. Too damned much anesthesia was throwing these people off metabolically and they bled, or they didn't heal. Too much premedication before anesthesia, especially. He got mad as hell at me, I know. He didn't say an awful lot, but ever since he has been more careful."

"He's a pleasant guy with me most of the time," Peter said, not wishing Marshall Wormser to go completely undefended.

"He's good with the patients all right, too. A regular bullshit artist. One more thing—I don't take any sugar, thanks—maybe we ought to check Mickey Long before surgery for gamma globulin deficiency. Frank Lewicki turned it up in some of our patients that had infection after surgery. Then some that bled had fibrinogen deficiency. You can stop the bleeding right away with fibrinogen I.V. Expensive as hell, but saves a life. Get the lab to run the screening tests for those, will you, before surgery?"

"All right, Dr. Hatch."

"Swell. I'll see you about five fifteen then. It's nice to have you helping me. I knew you were just what the place needed." His smile was engaging as he said good-bye and walked briskly out the side door.

Peter was back to see Mrs. Long at two thirty. She was asleep when he came in, but roused to talk a bit and sip at water and ice chips, her lips swollen and cracked from dryness while her tongue and the inside of her mouth were covered with sheets of pink and gray detritus. Her fever was up again to 102 even with continued cortisone.

Marshall Wormser came in then, shaking his head and swearing, but he said nothing directly to Peter, who was sitting in the corner writing in the chart. Marshall grunted at Peter as he left to get his attention, and then raised his hands and his eyes to the ceiling.

In surgery a small amount of cyclopropane anesthetic was given to Mrs. Long and she was draped, then Dr. Hatch and Peter came at once to the operating table. Quickly, almost roughly, Matthew Hatch cut and removed her sutures and the old incision gaped open between his thick oversize hands. The odor was immediately nauseating. "Boy, there's a lot of pus here, Peter."

Marshall slipped the suction machine on as Dr. Hatch went rapidly deeper into the necrotic fluid with the suction tip. "Did you want to take a culture now?" Peter asked in reminder.

"Oh, yes, let's do it right away before we go any further. We may want to get another one later on, too."

Sterile swabs were dipped into the purulent material and put back into sterile test tubes. Then Dr. Hatch proceeded into the abdomen, tearing the fresh scar tissue with blunt dissection and his hands. There were thick adhesions around the upper end of the small intestine, too, near the surgically created connection between it and the stomach. Finally the debris, the fresh scars, and infected matter had been cleaned away enough to allow the site of the new junction between the side of the small intestine loop and the stomach to be seen.

"See, Peter. Look." Dr. Hatch pointed to a wide breach in the linkage he had fashioned four days before between the stomach pouch and the small intestine. Half of the connection was ripped away with a florid dumping of stomach and intestinal contents into the abdominal cavity. "This is what I mean. What I was talking about. This is just the kind of thing that happens." Dr. Hatch pushed the stomach away to look at the pancreas and again shook his head. "Peter, this pancreas is inflamed all over too. It's sick. Look, some of the pancreas here is almost like anchovy paste." With the handle of his scalpel he scooped out material from the surface of the organ.

"Well, I've got work to do. We'll have to revise the resection further. Trim more of it away." He began at once, cutting, juxtaposing, fitting, and resuturing for the next hour.

When it was done, Matthew Hatch said, "That was a job. Peter, would you please write her orders? I'll dictate the surgical procedure first thing in the morning. I'm due at a wedding. Overdue, as a matter of fact, and ought to run. Please call me tonight if you have any problems about her I can help you with. And get the lab hot on that culture." More softly he added, "And check the position of the nasogastric tube. I think our anesthesiologist had it down too far last time, which is why she blew out her stump."

Mrs. Long's shock was more profound after the surgery. Peter supervised the starting of a stronger medicine for her blood pressure and ordered a continuance of the cortisone. Going downstairs he talked to the lab man to be sure that their specimen had been plated for culture and then talked to Anne on the phone for a while before a thoughtful, slow dinner at Charley's.

16

FRIDAY morning the surgery schedule was lighter. Mrs. Long was holding her own, really more comfortable. Late in the day she told Peter, "I never expected to be around after another operation, and here I am even feeling better." Her face was gaunt, and with the fever down, much paler.

Peter had dinner that night with Anne and her father. Mr. Alexio told long, laughable stories about problems he had had with the Mexican workers when he was trying to build bridges between Guadalajara and Guanajuato. Anne's Hawaiian teriyaki, tossed salad, and lemon pie were excellent.

After dinner Mr. Alexio stepped back into his study for a few hours' work while Peter and Anne went in the living room. Sitting down on the sofa, close to Anne, Peter said, "My mother would be interesed in your beef teriyaki."

"It's simple to fix. I could show her so easily. Tell me, Peter," she asked, "what's she like?"

"Hmm, it's hard to describe someone. I think the simplest thing is to say she's like me, or I should say, I'm like her. She doesn't look like me, I don't mean. I look like a de Haan. She's small, gray-haired, thin like her family, the Dauphneys. She's fun, truly good sense of humor, and also peculiar about a few things. She's a terrible smoker, which I'm not, but otherwise we're really alike. Always have to be on time, and when we do something, it has to be just so—everything has its place and it has to be kept in place—and if we start something we always finish it."

"You don't ever seem to get angry or upset. Is she that way?"

"We really are the same there. We have the same sort of temper. We don't get mad easily at all, but when we do, we stay mad for a long time, or even forever."

"I don't know if I believe that. Are you that way?" Anne asked as the phone rang. It was for Peter, and after answering it, he came back in the living room slowly.

Anne watched him. "Was it about Mrs. Long, Peter?"

"No, it's something else. You know I've been helping Dr. Hatch, assisting him lately. We operated on this old woman yesterday, took out her gallbladder. They just called to say that she collapsed and died suddenly. They don't know from what. The nurse seems to think that she might have vomited and aspirated the vomitus. It's just a means of strangulation, and happens every so often."

"How awful. What was her name?"

"Lillian Hollenhorst."

"There's a big Hollenhorst ranch in the north county."

"It may be some connection. She lived on a ranch with her daughter. Damn that Dr. Hatch. I can't understand why he operated on her."

"You've said things like that before, darling. Don't medical societies and state boards take doctors' licenses away for operating unnecessarily?"

"I'm afraid it doesn't work out that clearly or easily."

"How old was Mrs. Hollenhorst?"

"Eighty-four or five."

"Oh, that old. Couldn't anything happen to someone eighty-four? Was she sick for a long time?"

"She hasn't been well for years and I'm sure if you make it up to eighty-four that's far beyond average and good enough. But we don't push people over cliffs when they get to a certain age."

"You feel this patient wasn't in condition to have surgery?"

"No, though that's not the whole point. I don't understand what the operation was done for at all. Of course, I wouldn't want you to mention it to anyone."

"I understand."

"But we took out Mrs. Hollenhorst's gallbladder yesterday and I don't know why."

"Why do you take out gallbladders? Isn't it for stones?"

"Yes, you might. She didn't have any, though. Dr. Hatch just *felt* she had something wrong with her gallbladder although the X-rays of it were normal, and so was the gallbladder itself when he took it out, as far as I could tell. But he put a probe into the common duct and said he found resistance, he suggested it was from a stone that had already passed out of the gallbladder. Then he implied that this opening up of the duct would be a great deal of help."

Anne put down the portfolio and stood up. "It might be

that there was a stone in this duct, then? You can't really say there wasn't?"

"No, that's the trouble with this kind of thing. It has to do with opinions and judgments. It's on the borderline of actuality. Enough so you can't put the finger on someone easily if they are used to the situation and clever about it."

Anne, standing in front of him, took hold of Peter's hands. "Do you mean you think that Dr. Hatch is a psychopath doing this sort of surgery deliberately?"

"I don't know what he is. I can't understand him. Some doctors do come to believe that they can cure anything with their knives. This could have happened to Dr. Hatch. He may think he's a sort of god and the scalpel is his wand of divine grace. There's one thing he must be aware of, which is that his surgery brings in a lot of money every year. I suppose he may have been affected by the money involved and long ago rationalized away his actions."

"Does he seem like that kind of person?" Anne asked, her hands cold in his.

"That's what I haven't decided. I know he tells people he has devoted his life to medicine. I think he believes his operations are fully justified. Patients are funny, too. They don't mind being abused or treated roughly if they are just noticed. I hear people say, 'Every time I go to Dr. Hatch he wants to cut me up or stick me with a needle,' then they laugh and add how wonderful he is and how much he's done for them."

Anne moved closer to Peter and put her head on his shoulder. "I suppose you have to go right away."

"The lady's dead, so I guess there isn't too much hurry. I'll have to sign some papers and talk to the family."

"What you say upsets me," Anne said. "We're all so selfish. You know what I think of right away is that you'll decide you want to leave here because you hate Dr. Hatch so much."

"I wouldn't leave here without you. You know that."

"You better not try."

They kissed and she said, "I hate to think of next weekend. I have to go to Fresno to that darned Art Institute. I don't want to go away, even for three days. Isn't that foolish?"

"No, it's nice."

17

MICHELINE Long did well until Monday afternoon. That morning their first case in surgery was a radical neck dissection, and the second a forty-five-year-old postal worker sent down by Dr. Susack's office. Peter was called over at six A.M. to examine the postman, found an acute diverticulitis, and decided antibiotics were in order to start treatment. Matthew Hatch had come up the hall after Peter's examination and at once recognized the man lying on the emergency stretcher. "You're Joe Chandler, aren't you?" he called. "The assistant postmaster up at Bollerville?"

"Yes. How do you know me, Doc?"

"Don't you remember when we talked about leasing space for a branch of the clinic in the post office building?"

"Oh, sure. That was over five years ago."

"And Dr. de Haan just told me you're here with a pain in your belly. You're probably pregnant. With a mailman this is what we call a special delivery here. Yes, sir, special delivery," he mused, beginning to feel the man's abdomen cautiously.

"Oh, Doc, hey, that really hurts."

Matthew examined him rectally, and then became serious for the first time. "Joe, this isn't a good thing. I can feel your lower colon on the left side and it's thickened, perhaps ruptured. I'm sure there's a small abscess there." Peter could not believe it. No one could get that much information out of feeling the intact abdominal wall and putting a finger in the rectum. "I've always found the best thing is to go right in and open the abdomen. We can take out the bad section that's infected and sew the two ends together. But you need this done right away, now, this morning, no waiting."

"Don't you want any X-rays or blood tests or anything, Doc?"

"We'll get some, but they wouldn't change my opinion."

"You think it's cancer, Doc?"

"No. Just a bad infection that needs fixing."

"Well, if you say it has to be. I don't want it unless it has to be."

"I've been through this too many times, Joe. I know."

"Well, tell my wife, will you? Talk it over with her, Doc, and if she says okay, well, okay then."

"Fine, Joe, and we'll plan to take you up to surgery, oh, about nine. Right after my first case."

Peter had disagreed completely. Absolutely. He would never have thought the man should have such rapid surgery. He could perhaps have gotten by without any. Here it was starting all over again.

In the afternoon Mrs. Long's pain came back again intensely. She had a sudden shaking chill and spiked a high fever. The center of the abdomen mounded up like a large melon, a taut drumhead pierced by its awful drainage tubes. It almost seemed as if looking at it would cause pain, and even the gentlest pressure brought a shriek from her.

She asked, after Peter changed her dressings late in the day, "Have you seen Nick, Dr. de Haan?"

"No, not today. I did see him last night for a minute."

"There are some good things about him, you know. We were so happy when we were first married and the last few days I feel that he's close to me again. He says he will stop drinking and that would make the girls so happy. You don't know my girls, do you?" Peter shook his head. "Miss West arranged for them to come in once to see me, but everything was strange and they looked so scared."

"Maybe we can get them back in tonight. I could fix it up."

"Oh, would you? I'll try to remember to tell Nick."

Beads of sweat came out on her small nose and she could not talk anymore. She went to sleep and Peter did not bring the children in because she would not have known it.

Nick Long was quiet and there was no liquor on his breath when Peter adjusted Micheline's abdominal binder and took her blood pressure the next day on his late evening rounds. When he finished, Nick Long stepped up with tears in his eyes.

"I appreciate what you've done for Mickey, Doctor. Tremendously. The whole thing's my fault, too. If I hadn't been such a bastard she wouldn't have gotten the ulcers in the first place."

"It's hard to say, Mr. Long."

"I have the girls out in the car. You said they could see their mother again."

"Do you think it would bother them?" Peter asked.

"I don't," Mr. Long said. "It might help them. They've been playing hospital, and talking about her all the time anyway, Mickey's mother says."

"Well, why don't you get them?"

In a few minutes he was back with two little girls, one blond with a pony tail, big glasses, and her mother's pert nose. She looked healthily plump but tired, with purple smudges beneath her eyes. Her younger sister was only half her size, about seven years old with dark hair and dark eyes that stared at everything. She was chewing gum and asked a question for every step she took up the hallway. She started by asking, "Are you my mother's doctor?"

"Yes," Peter answered smiling.

"Is she going to get well?"

"I don't know for sure. She's very sick. What's your name?"

"I'm Vickie. Do you have to give her shots?"

"Sometimes."

"They're terrible. I have to take them, too. They always make me cry."

Her father stuck his head back from inside the room. "Come on in, Vickie."

"Will you take me in, Doctor?" Vickie asked, grabbing Peter's arm with sudden fear on her face.

"Of course, Vickie."

Peter left the room with each girl holding one of Micheline Long's slender white hands, the nails still flecked with red polish, and Mr. Long surveying the group sadly.

The next morning Mickey Long's fever stayed far up and she was totally disoriented. "The sun is hurting my eyes," she said to Peter. "Can't you get Mary to close the shade?" It was an overcast morning.

The room was filled with an unpleasant odor that was the pervasive smell of bowel fistulas, the infected holes that burrowed through the abdominal wall from the intestines allowing the leak of fecal material into her bandages. Changing her dressings, Peter's stomach began to writhe and grind. Finally he got her abdomen covered over with heaps of absorbent ABD pads, and put his attention back on the dying woman's heart and lungs in an attempt to figure out some way he could stimulate and nourish them. Oxygen was begun again, antibiotics changed and medicine for shock restarted because her blood pressure was drifting rapidly downward.

When he came back late that same afternoon her face was redder and she seemed even more gaunt. The nurse awakened her and she asked, "Is it time for another shot? They won't give me enough to keep me comfortable and they make me wait so long after I ask for one."

"It's just that we don't want to make you too dopey," Peter said. "As it is you're sleeping most of the time."

Looking over Peter's shoulder she said, "Well, here's Dr. Hatch." Peter did not know if this was another hallucination, but looking back he saw his employer and clinic chief at the door. Dr. Hatch came in smiling, wearing a long white coat and the thick-rimmed glasses he occasionally used.

"How are you going, dearie?" he asked gaily.

She only groaned in reply.

"Now, Mickey, you are doing better. At least you're awake this afternoon."

"Dr. Hatch, have them get me another pain shot. I have so much pain."

"I will, Mickey. I just wanted to tell you that I think you need another handsome young doctor to see you, so I'm asking Dr. Silvana to feel your tummy. Do you know him?"

"I don't think so. Are you going away?"

"No, I just want him to see you, so we can talk about you behind your back."

"My breathing is funny. Why is my breath so short?"

"We'll fix that up. I'll see you later, doll. Good-bye." He motioned Peter and left the room.

Outside he said, "I wanted Norman to see her for a couple of reasons. First, he has awfully good judgment a lot of times on these tough cases and then, too, I might have to operate on her again. I'd like to have him assist to see what his judgment would be about things as we went along."

"You really think more surgery might help?"

"Norman's going to see her early this evening and we'll wait for what he says. He'll call me. The other thing is that that slinky little bastard of a husband of hers might cause us some trouble. He's trying to get their interlocutory decree set aside, I heard, and he got her to sign some paper the other day. He's probably just hoping to get a crack at a suit and I think it would be smart therefore to have Norman's examination and opinion on the chart." He paused, but when Peter said nothing went on, "That Long has never liked me. Mickey had a crush on me a while back, for over a year as a matter of fact. One of those silly things that patients get to feeling sometimes, and her husband always resented it and me."

"That can happen."

"Everybody else doing all right?"

"The old man with the colon C.A., Mr. Styron, was coughing a lot this morning, so I put him on the Bennett valve."

"Good. You're a real help to me. Say, why do you think Mrs. Long is so short of breath? Is it coming from pneumonia? Heart failure?"

"Maybe the abdominal distension pushing up on the diaphragm." What the hell did he expect? The patient was dying from abdominal suppuration and he wondered why she was short of breath?

"Well, don't look so worried, boy. You can't take things so hard. I know how you feel, but in this business you have to roll with the punches. You do the best you can and then you can't worry about what else happens. If you do you just destroy your effectiveness to your patients."

Norman Silvana came to see Micheline Long while Peter was still making late afternoon chart rounds at the nurses' desk. "I thought you were coming back this evening, Norman," Peter said when he saw him coming out of her room.

"We're going out tonight, so I wanted to do it now. It's almost six, isn't it?"

"Five after."

"Hell."

"This is the patient I talked to you about, Norman, and asked you to see last week."

"Oh, is it?" Norman looked at Peter. "I can tell you this. She's another one of those messes Matt gets into and wants somebody to help pull him out of. Hell, there's nothing you can do for her. She's a goner. She may not even live through the night. Matthew asks me to see her with about one-tenth of the details. He says, 'Mrs. Long's having some trouble with a fecal fistula after a gastrectomy,' like someone else might tell you a patient had pimples on her face. She's probably got a *half a dozen* fecal fistulas. She's moribund."

"He told me he thought he might have to open her up again and was thinking you should help if he did, so he could get the benefit of your advice."

"It would just be a form of murder. She couldn't possibly

live through it, but even if she did there's nothing can be done surgically to help her."

"Are you going to call him?"

"Yes. What's his home phone?"

"It's right here, Evergreen 7-8998."

Norman dialed the number and waited. "Hello, Rosalie, this is Norman Silvana. May I talk to Matthew?" Another wait. "Matt, this is Norman. Yes. I just saw Mrs. Long. I don't think anything can be done for her. I went over her abdomen and looked at her chart and I've just been talking to Peter about her. The only thing I could think of to give her would possibly be blood plasma or I.V. protein. I don't really think they'd help much, though." He listened for several moments. "She *is* very dyspneic, but she has a fever of a hundred and three or a hundred and four and is entitled to some heavy breathing. Besides, she's getting three or four antibiotics now." There was another pause and then he said, "She *could* have pneumonia or heart failure, but I don't think that's her primary problem. I think this is the picture of intra-abdominal sepsis. Peritonitis. I can't see how the anesthesia would cause any of her trouble." He listened again. "I absolutely don't think she should be opened up. It would kill her." Pause. "Well, if you think her husband could have anything in his mind like that it would be even more reason for you not to go in again." Pause. "She would never live through it, Matt, in the condition she's in. She'd die on the table." Pause. "All right, I'll look at her again in the morning and I'm putting a note on the chart."

Norman snapped the receiver in its cradle with a loud click. "Let that bird get an idea in his head and you have to talk to him like a Dutch uncle to get it out. You know he really was going to open that girl up tonight. All he wants me to do is not say no to what *he* wants to do, but I'll be goddamned if I will."

"I was astounded when he mentioned another surgery this evening. I'm awfully glad you talked him out of it."

"At least for the night I did and I think he has a full schedule in the morning. But she'll be so bad tomorrow that even he won't suggest it."

Peter awakened the next morning at five and could not go back to sleep; finally he got up and dressed. He was in Mrs. Long's room just after six. Her fever was up to 105 and she moaned continuously when she wasn't talking incoherently. The nurse said, "I haven't been able to understand what she has been saying, Doctor. It seems to be French words she's using some of the time."

"French. I didn't know she spoke French."

"Her husband told me she was raised in Canada and used to speak some French as a child, so I guess that's where it comes from."

She loosed then a torrent of gibberish, thrashing in bed and pulling at her restraints. "That's unearthly, isn't it?" Peter said.

"She pulled her 'INTRACATH' out during the night too, Doctor, so she hasn't had any fluids since four o'clock."

"Does she have any blood pressure?"

"I can't be sure about it, at least not for the last hour. I've been giving her Aramine by hypo."

"Hell, we'll have to start on that right away. I thought she was sweating a lot. I wish you had let me know."

"I hated to bother you."

Peter de Haan looked at Mickey Long again before he started working on her, thinking once more how completely unrecognizable she had become. Her face was red and puffy now, the black hair a tangled mess and her nostrils exploded and bulbous, their scarlet rims scabbed from pressing catheters. Her abdomen was pathologically tumid, her wasted arms and legs patterned in black-and-blue from needles. She was an example in ersatz living, oxygenated, infused, suctioned, and stimulated. Her heartbeat was fast and steady, but obviously weaker in sound. Only when she opened her lids and he could see her black unfocused eyes could he really recognize her. He forced himself to think about the dying woman's failing physiology, to try to decide what to do next. He wrote orders rapidly and during morning surgery he dashed out between each operation to see her. After surgery was over at eleven thirty Peter sprinted for her room.

"She just stopped breathing, Doctor. I was putting in a call for you. She stiffened up too and her color turned blue," the nurse told him.

Peter listened to her heart at once. The beats were slow now and irregular. Her pupils were dilating. She took in an occasional gasp of air and there was no clear pulse at the wrists.

"Her temperature was a hundred and six about thirty minutes ago, Doctor."

"Rectal?"

"Yes."

"I'm going to run down and get some Coramine. Set the oxygen higher for now, will you?" He got the drug and on the way back saw Mr. Long stepping out of the elevator with the two little girls that Peter recognized as Micheline's daughters. "I didn't know you were bringing the girls today, Mr. Long."

"I wanted them to see their mother again, Doctor. As long as she's here I want them to see her every possible chance." He was unsteady today, exuding almost visible alcoholic vapors.

"She's awfully sick, Mr. Long. They can't come in now."

"I want them to. I don't care."

"No, it's impossible. Not now."

"Is she that bad?"

"She's very sick." Peter left them standing in the hall, the girls with their hands in their father's. In the room he saw Micheline stiffen again and take a giant gasp. The nurse said, "That's the first time she's inhaled since you left."

After putting the Coramine into the I.V. tubing, Peter tried artificial respiration by chest compression, but nothing happened except for a few minor respiratory gulps. Then there were no heart sounds and the pupils became widely dilated.

Peter walked out of the room and said, "She's gone, Mr. Long. She just passed away." The older girl began crying, but Mr. Long and Vickie only stared.

"I can't believe it, Doctor," Mr. Long said. "I want to see her."

"If you want to go in alone, you may."

"Oh, I don't want to without the girls. Thank you for what you tried to do."

"Did Mama really die away?" the smaller girl broke her silence to ask.

Her father nodded as he turned the girls away. Just before he got to the elevator he looked back and said again, voicelessly now, "Thank you, Doctor."

18

THURSDAY night Peter went home and collapsed on his couch, bone-tired, almost nauseated in his tiredness. He slept for an hour and awakened to the phone ringing. It was Anne telling him she did not want to go away the next day for the weekend, but with the good news she would be back Sunday morning because part of her meeting had been cancelled. They arranged to play tennis at the country club in the morning and go into Oakland for dinner.

Friday and Saturday passed in a plaster of paris world. Early Saturday night Peter sat under the vaulted ceiling of the bar at the San Marcial Inn, tapping his foot on the rung of his stool, musing unhappily. After a third Rob Roy, he decided to call Frank Lewicki.

"Could you stand a wandering Hatch Clinic employee in your home tonight, Frank, or are you barricading your doors as I ask?"

"Peter, come on over. Marsh Wormser is here. His family's out of town, so he had dinner with us."

"I'll get a bite and be out."

As he paid his check and stood up to leave, Peter was surprised to see Rosalie Hatch walk through the entrance, glance around and then sit down across from him. He gathered up his change and walked around the bar in time to hear her order a stinger.

"Why, Peter, I didn't see you in here."

"I was just about to leave after getting quietly high on the other side of this dark den."

"Well, sit down. How are you?"

"I'm fine. Well, not as good as I might be. But not bad. Is Dr. Hatch with you?"

"No, I was at a little party upstairs for the lady who just finished as president of the Women's League this year. They're having a business meeting now—the nominating committee for next year. I decided to have a nightcap while I'm waiting for a ride home."

"Will you get nominated for something, do you think?"

"I was president two years ago, so I don't think so."

"Good."

"It is good. It's so much work."

"I'll have another Rob Roy, too," he said to the waiting bartender, "with a twist of lemon."

"Oh, Rob Roys," she said. "They're awfully strong, aren't they?"

"I guess."

"I don't think I'd like them. I don't care for Scotch." But a moment later when he was served she asked, "May I taste the Rob Roy?"

"Certainly."

She sipped it. "No, I don't like that at all." Making a face she picked up her own drink. "You know I haven't seen you for a while."

He nodded. Not since the night of the summer party, he knew they both were thinking.

"I heard from Matt that you have a girl friend."

"I didn't realize he knew but I do."

"I'm glad to hear that. You *should* have." She looked at him and frowned. Peter recognized that knitting of her forehead. It was the same expression she'd made at the country club when she was tight. "Matt knows a lot about people and things at the clinic that he doesn't let on."

"I suppose he does."

"Which brings us to Matthew. You know, I worry about him. There's something I've wanted to ask about him for a long time, but I've never had the courage to do it. Perhaps I could talk to you sometime about it."

"Surely."

"Could I talk to you tonight?"

"Yes."

"Not here. I wouldn't want to here."

They agreed to go out to his car to talk, and then he would take her home on his way to the Lewickis'.

"Tell me," Rosalie said, swinging her stool toward him as they started to leave, "are the Lewickis good friends of yours?"

"I guess as good as anyone."

"I like Frank. I really do."

"I do too."

"I know he's abrupt and Matthew doesn't think he always handles patients too well, but he respects his ability. Gloria and I have never gotten along, though."

"You haven't?"

"I guess it all started because I phoned her one afternoon about two o'clock and got my head torn off. 'I was taking my afternoon nap. Would you please call back?' Of course I said to heck with her, and have never tried to call her since."

She finished her stinger and they walked out to Peter's car in the parking lot. It was dark there, and Peter could smell her same perfume as they sat talking.

"I guess I'm trying to put off what I wanted to tell you." She fought for control briefly, swallowing and blinking her eyes. "In the last year Matt has gone through periods lasting a couple of months when he just wasn't interested in me. I thought there must be some other woman or women, and I even accused him of this, or at least asked him about it. Of course there wasn't anybody. It's been awfully hard on me. I'd get to wanting to make love and yet we'd go a month or more without. I guess I'm terrible to talk about this."

"Not at all."

"I know that's one of the reasons I acted the way I did with you at the summer party. Right after that, things changed and were all right for a while, but now they seem to be going bad again."

"And you don't know why?"

"Of course, Matt has a great deal of responsibility, and works very hard, much too hard. I know that early this year they did suspect for a while that he had some heart trouble. Some electrocardiograms were off for an insurance exam, but apparently the changes turned out to be the result of medication he was taking for hay fever. When he stopped the pills, the tracings went right back to normal."

"Do you think he's been especially nervous or tense in these last years?"

"He has a lot more going on inside him than people realize. I'm the only one he confides in really. He gets depressed sometimes, and other times he's a hundred miles up in the air, just the opposite of depressed. He'll go and go then, and never wear out. But he's not really a nervous person, or a worrier in any ordinary sense. If he's worried about something it's for a good reason."

"He's only forty-eight, isn't he?"

"He'll be forty-nine next month. Of course, he goes to bed early, gets up early, works all day. All in all, I don't get to see much of him, and I've thought maybe just not enough for him to stay interested in me."

"When you do have relations is it all right?"

"Sometimes and sometimes not. It's variable."

"You know, men do on occasion lose their ability for sex in the forties, even the early forties. With diabetes and other diseases, even before then. I've seen a number of people lose the ability, though, who didn't seem to have much else wrong with them, and it's just a temporary thing. As a matter of fact, this is usually the case. It's a temporary affair that goes back to normal soon."

"I guess what I've really worried about is that there is something wrong with him, and that he needs some kind of care. You know how wives are, they get to worrying about everything, even cancer. What you say certainly reassures me. I haven't been able to talk to anybody about this, and even Matt won't discuss it, so now I feel better. Of course you wouldn't mention it to anyone."

"I won't. I never would."

"I know you must be wanting to go, so why don't you take me home."

"Sure." Peter backed out of the lot and started east. Rosalie Hatch moved toward him on the seat.

"Do you have a handkerchief, Peter?" she asked.

"Yes." He gave her his, and saw her put it up to her eyes. She handed it back to him, and then kept her hand on his thigh. Suddenly he remembered her large nipples, and felt excited, then thinking of Anne, was at once ashamed and uninterested.

"You're a very nice person," she said. Peter didn't reply.

Shortly they were at Santa Rita and Sharpe. "We're at your corner already," Peter said.

"Why don't you go around the circle and let me off by the back door? It's only nine, I know, but Matthew's in bed, I'm sure. He was out fishing all day."

The big house was white and gleaming in the glow of its outside lights. Its close-planted cypresses looked black against the night sky, flanking the gardens around the house like rows of giant stiff guards. Peter remembered how impressed he had been with it all a short few months before and sighed. What price anything?

"I wonder if I'll ever be sorry I didn't go to your apartment?" Rosalie said as Peter stopped.

"Do you think you will be?"

"I don't know. I better not have another chance," she said, putting her hand on his shoulder.

"You don't think so?"

"No," Rosalie said as she rubbed her hand across the top of his shoulder. She leaned over and pulled his head toward her with her hand, and kissed him squarely on the mouth. "Definitely not. Thank you, Peter, and good night."

He went with her to the back door where she smiled at him, turned her key in the lock, and disappeared. Peter drove off muttering to himself, "I'll be damned, I *will* be damned." On the way to Lewickis' he pondered Rosalié Hatch and her problem further. There was Matthew sexually uninterested, semi-impotent some of the time. Could his relationship with Micheline Long have anything to do with it? Peter had noticed, too, the new young surgical nurse in the O.R. obviously had a crush on him, and he seemed to be aware of it. He spent extra time kidding her, teasing her so she blushed or got momentarily angry, talking to her after surgery. Maybe this *was* the answer, Dr. Hatch played around some. Or could deep concerns in him with sexual adequacy have any connection to the way he performed in the operating room? And then here was Rosalie Hatch out alone Saturday night acting tight. Was it possible she had a secret problem with alcohol?

At the Lewickis' Gloria greeted him at the door warmly, and took him into the family room at once. She was in a tight sheath and heels, and looked neatly attractive. Peter wondered if her life was really so patterned that she couldn't stand any interruption of it. Of course, it was her prerogative to have it that way.

He waved to Frank and Marsh and said, "I'm sorry I took so long. I ran into Rosalie Hatch just after I called and had a drink with her."

"Did you have something to eat?" Frank asked.

"No, I never got around to it."

"Gloria, fix him a roast beef sandwich."

"Oh, no, please don't bother," Peter said.

"It's no bother and we have lots left over." Gloria went to the kitchen and soon brought Peter back the sandwich and a glass of cold Dutch beer.

As he began eating, Frank said to him, "You saw Rosalie Hatch, did you?"

"Yes. I sort of like her but I'm in rather an anti-Hatch mood right now," Peter said between swallows.

"We were just talking about your baptism under fire this

last ten days," Frank said. "You must have earned the fig leaf cluster by now, Peter."

"That Micheline Long case really got to me. God! To see that girl die by inches when she didn't even need any surgery in the first place."

"It's amazing how he can take a perfectly well person and after four or five operations for ulcer and intestinal obstruction get them to where they're sick as hell. Or usually not just sick, but dead," Marshall said. "It takes quite a talent."

"Don't you want your beer?" Frank asked Peter.

"I think I'd prefer Scotch. I'm not sure how beer goes with Rob Roys." Frank waved his hand in understanding and left for the kitchen.

"Marsh, do you think Dr. Hatch's surgical judgment is ever really any good?" Peter asked.

"No, it's lousy, or rather nonexistent. Do you know he's killed more people than the plague?" Marshall's prominent eyes protruded more and the pale pastiness of his complexion increased as he talked. "Why do you think I'm over here guzzling Frank's liquor like there's no tomorrow? Cases like that Long woman kill me, too. I'm getting to where I can't live with myself. Thank God I go back on the outside hospital circuit the first of November and partner Gus takes over the Hatch for a while." He chewed on the butt of a smoldering cigar held between his bloodless lips. "You wonder why I don't leave Hatch, probably, and I wonder why you don't leave and Frank wonders why we both don't leave and so on. You get the picture?"

"Rather."

"But maybe you really are planning to quit?"

"It could happen."

"Ah, but you probably find yourself in a position of nonaffluence, like me, or a relative lack of means, the relative quality being at all times in the mind of the one figuring. Let me tell you about me. First, I didn't like the last surgeon I worked for down at the Valley, so I quit him and came up here. Matt's not employing me. I could maybe even live without him now, if he didn't get me kicked off the county hospital staff for leaving him, which he probably could. And that's where I begin to worry. I've got a kid starting college this month and three more coming up in the next few years, a fifth later on. I'm afraid to give it all up and start over again. My wife would probably shoot me. The trouble is we're too fat. We doctors are just too fat. If we only made nine or ten thousand a year it would be different. We could act on our principles. Thanks, Frank." Frank was back with more drinks for everyone but Gloria, who had motioned no.

"I never heard you talk like that, Marsh," she said.

"You're just like my wife, Gloria, you never listen to what I say. I talk like this all the time."

"Well, excuse me," Gloria said blandly.

"Peter, as I was saying, it's hard to speak right out and say what you think, or quit when you would be throwing away an income of forty or fifty thousand a year."

"Hard. It's impossible in my case," Frank laughed. "I don't make that much a year."

"Well, so you make thirty thousand, the idea is the same."

"We were talking about Matthew Hatch, Frank. I have been thoroughly disgusted with him this week," Peter said.

"I gathered that."

"Listen, Frank, I want to tell you something. Marsh, you know this, I'm sure, but listen to what my figures show." Peter pulled some small file cards from his pocket. "I looked over each chart on every patient that we operated on this past week and a half. Now in that time, besides Mrs. Long's gastrectomy and an operation for perforation of a gastric stump, he did two other stomach resections, four inguinal hernia repairs, three hysterectomies, one radical neck dissection, one thyroid nodule removal, three hemorrhoidectomies, one adhesionectomy for supposed small bowel obstruction, two breast biopsies, an emergency appendectomy, four gallbladder removals, and two varicose vein strippings. And then there were assorted small ops like removal of a leg cyst, some D and C's and such."

"He's really been cutting lately, hasn't he?" Frank said.

"You know how I feel about Mrs. Long," Peter said. "I don't think she should ever have been operated on. She never had an adequate trial of medical management and she had no active ulcer at surgery. I saw the area and it was definitely healing, I'd say. She was more a psychiatric case than a surgical one." Peter took a deep breath. He felt nervous, even shaky, but happy to be opening up. "Now out of all those cases there were only three or four that I think required immediate surgery. Some could have been watched and some were on older patients who should have been left alone. Two cholecystectomies did have gallstones when opened, but then there was that old woman with normal gallbladder X-rays who had a normal gallbladder at surgery.

She came in with dizziness and she still would have been dizzy when she went home, I imagine, if she hadn't died. That was Mrs. Hollenhorst."

"Poor old Mrs. Hollenhorst never knew what hit her. Of course it's always the anesthesia that's wrong," Marshall said, "or sometimes the nurses didn't watch the patient properly, so the patient vomited and made the incision come loose. All these people get operated on and then the trouble begins, but somehow it never has anything to do with the surgery."

"I'm beginning to see that that's the way it goes," Peter said. "But let me tell you about one of those stomach resections. It was a young fellow twenty-three years old who had just come in the clinic for the first time two days before. His X-rays showed a severe inflammation of the duodenum with possible superficial ulceration, but he had no antacid before surgery, not one drop. The poor guy deserved a few weeks of medical therapy, something to calm him down and relieve his pain. At least a trial of medicine before he had his stomach out."

"Yes, and I can tell you that in about one out of three of his resections he gets a dumping syndrome with vomiting, diarrhea, sweating, the works," Frank said, "from poor selection and because he takes out so much of the stomach, I guess."

"The thing that gets me," Marshall said, "is that everything has to be done right away. Everything is an emergency. Here we even have one or two emergency hemorrhoidectomies a month," Marshall said. "He's just doing more work lately, too, I don't know why. I think he must be taking Dexedrine again like last year. When he gets on those things he eats them like popcorn."

"He has cycles. There's no question about it. And I have the idea they occur most often just before he goes away on a trip," Frank said. "He's traveling east for three weeks in November to go to meetings and then Rosalie is going to meet him in Florida for a tour of the Caribbean. I can't believe it's conscious money-madness, though. Can it be unconscious money-madness?"

"Why in hell couldn't it be conscious?" Marshall asked. "I think when a patient walks in the door he sees dollar signs instead of pupils in their eyes."

"I can't believe he actually thinks that way," Frank said. "You know he really feels he does what's best for people all the time. He's very moralistic about it and he gets mad as hell, not openly to the patient, but underneath, if he feels they think otherwise."

"I'm going to get another drink," Marshall said.

"Give me your glass, too," Frank said to Peter as he stood up.

Marshall and Frank went off to the kitchen as Peter turned to Gloria. "By my calculations," he said, "at least forty percent of his surgery is not clearly necessary. As far a I'm concerned *one* unnecessary surgery in a lifetime is a crime, so to see eight or ten in the past week and a half is too much, way too much to take. I'm ready to quit, contract or no contract."

"That's too bad."

Marshall came back with the characteristic looping simian swing to his arms as he walked.

"How can a man smile and smile and be such a damned villain?" he asked. "Oh, I don't mean you, Peter."

"Of course his office practice is miserable, too," Frank said, sitting down by Gloria and putting his hand on hers. "One thing I found out, maybe you've caught it, Peter, is that he really can't take blood pressure. After about a year of trying to figure out how he got some of the readings he did, I decided that he just can't or doesn't bother to do it properly. He can get one-twenty over eighty on someone I see the same day and find two hundred over one-ten."

"I've noticed that, too," Peter said.

"Some of his work is done adequately, I'm sure," Frank went on. "He's not stupid. He's noncritical, but not stupid. He often knows the latest thinking or the newest drugs, but he gets on these wild times, like now apparently, cutting everybody up and there is no living with him."

"Do you remember when Matthew had the disk operation himself?" Marshall asked Frank. "He had Dr. Nussbaum come over from Oakland to do it, would *not* go to the hospital in Oakland. Then the pain he had was so great, he claimed it was so great, that's the point really, that he demanded enough morphine to practically give him a respiratory arrest."

"Oh, he is not a normal man, I'm sure of that," Frank said. "Hell, when Bill Arrow had that blowup and decided to quit, after telling him off, Matt was practically psychotic for a while. He accused Bill of stealing patients and made Miss West search every box of his stuff he carried out."

"At the same time he laughed and joked with the patients

as if he had never been happier. It was odd as hell," Marshall added.

"What I'd like to know is what can be done about Dr. Hatch?" Peter said. "Harry Lawson seems to think he's Jesus incarnate and I guess Al Humphers has him tagged as perfectly all right. I gather Dr. Koepff doesn't have opinions on much of anything, and I don't have any idea how Les Leslie feels about him."

"Just ask Les sometime. You'll get the picture real quick," Marshall said, slumped in his chair now, his eyebrows raised in their "so what else is new?" look.

"How about Lew Condon?"

"He's wise to him too, but then he's got such a sweet deal, and besides feels removed enough from direct patient care to believe his skirts are staying clean," Marshall answered.

"How about you? You've got a sweet deal, too, haven't you? Why do you get upset about it?" Peter asked.

"I feel like Lady Macbeth at times, going around my house trying to wash the blood off at night. Lew Condon doesn't get the scent like I do. He's so goddamn patrician, anyway, he wouldn't believe any of the common folk could suffer."

"I don't feel that way about Lew," Frank put in.

"What I'm getting at is everybody's reaction to Dr. Hatch," Peter said. "If the group in general feels that he's incompetent, what can be done about him?"

"If you take away Big Daddy, don't forget, you take away the group. Without him, everyone would have to start over," Marshall said.

"Perhaps someone could talk to him about it in some way," Peter said, "so he would realize how we all felt. I suppose it could wind up doing no good, but it might be worth trying."

Frank was leaning back in his chair, his tie loosened, but now he sat forward and said, "Actually, Peter, I convinced Al Humphers once that Matt had made some errors on two surgical patients sent to Matt by him, and then Al, in his typical self-righteous manner, took Matt over the coals for them. Result: Nothing. Matt denied all accusations, and ultimately just about got Al to thinking I was entirely wrong on everything I'd said."

"You can't talk to that man, Peter. He just does not hear anything he does not want to hear," Marshall said.

"So what can we all do about controlling someone like Matthew Hatch?" Peter asked. "I still want to know.

Shouldn't somebody put in a formal complaint about him to the County Society or the State. I mean it. It's not right that he shouldn't be stopped some way, is it?"

"Let me give you the word on this business, kiddo," said Marshall, lighting a cigarette off the butt of the previous one, and taking another gulp from his glass before his explanation. "Take Dr. Susack from Bollerville, a real shit of a doctor. Pardon me, Gloria, but a real prince of a doctor, spelled p-r-i-c-k. He's strictly out for every cent he can make. He's the shot doctor to end all shot doctors. Sometimes he'll give those poor Filipinos and Mexicans from the field labor group *two or three shots a day* for the flu. Awhile back, after a couple of his patients got hepatitis, they found out he was even giving some shots *right through their clothes,* when he was too busy. No kidding, the patients would come in, bend over, and he'd inject the B-Twelve or whatever without them even dropping their pants down."

Marshall coughed harshly before he went on. "This guy Susack appears as a real menace, then. He doesn't know, I'll try not to be vulgar now, a heart attack from a strangulated hernia, but he knows how to charge and make money. The Professional Relations Committee of the County Society, you know, the 'grievance committee,' even heard a complaint about him where the patient said he gave him three blood transfusions in the office at fifty dollars each. The patient said it didn't look like blood to him and afterward he found out it wasn't blood at all, just red-tinted fluid, because no blood had ever been checked out of the blood bank for him. Of course Susack said the guy had it all wrong and never would give any money back, though the committee 'suggested' he do so."

"You're out of booze, Marsh. I'll get Peter and you another one," Frank said. "Go on with your story, I can hear in the kitchen."

"Okay, Frank. Well, that's just the beginning, Pete. Also, everyone in this county knows he's an alcoholic and a drug addict. The narcotics inspectors used to be always fussing around the county trying to get something on him, but never could. Why, I don't know. You could tell he was on the stuff by just glancing at him. His pupils would look like a Siamese cat's on the Sahara Desert at high noon and he'd be slurring words, dreamy and way off. Besides all the dope stuff, he's sent several cases to our hospital that were treated badly and ultimately died. Two tonsillectomies he did in his office died, a little boy and a little girl. Koepff worked on one of them and won't even speak to him now." He paused for breath and a sip on the fresh drink Frank handed him before continuing.

"He did spend time in the state hospital for alcoholism three years ago after trying to run over a girl friend on the sidewalk with his car. That brought enough public notice of his situation that he was officially put on probation by the State Board of Medical Examiners. But after all this—with him drunk or coked one day a week, so his office nurse has to run things for him, with him clearly incompetent medically, regardless of his other problems—do you think our own Professional Relations Committee has done anything about him, do you think our medical society members have gone to meetings stamping their feet and demanding something be done or toss him out? They have not. Nobody's done anything. It's a goddam disgrace and it's wrong. The doctors aren't doing right by themselves. I don't think they deserve to control themselves anymore. But if you realize a guy like Susack can't even be controlled, what chance do you think you have going through the chain of command to get something done about a guy like Hatch, with a big practice, many influential friends, an active prosperous clinic employing a number of competent doctors? His position is perfect. He has a hundred miles of cover-up. If we try to do anything we cut our own throats. I never heard of *anyone* being disciplined in San Marcial County anyway. I asked one of the other members recently and he didn't seem to think it had ever happened."

Frank listened carefully to what Marshall was saying, nodding his head in agreement every now and then. He leaned back against the couch and said, "But, Marshall, we know that some doctors are going to be imperfect, as barbers and dentists and auto mechanics and lawyers are imperfect."

"Yes, but even lawyers, for example, control their own better than we do. Probably everyone controls their own better than we do. And while the rest of them are only involved with money and property, or teeth or hair or something, we're playing around with human life and human health. Like Peter, I think performing *one* unnecessary major operation is at least as bad as armed robbery and should be treated accordingly. But it isn't. What's going to happen is that the state and the government are going to crack down on us. That's what's going to happen. I'm convinced of it. They've already started, really, with Medicare."

"For God's sake, Marsh, get down to a little more rational level," Frank said angrily. "There are some rotters in medicine, as in everything, but medicine is also a unique occupation. We've come a long way in the last fifty years making it an improved, efficient affair, and it's getting better all the time. It needs to stay free, out of government control. The patient's confidence in his doctor is essential. It helps all of us every day to get people well. If we admitted we needed the government to police us, which I don't believe for a moment we do, that confidence would be destroyed."

"Listen," Marshall said, "this Medicare thing is just the start. In ten years the government will be controlling medicine all the way and we won't have to decide anything. That's because they just can't trust us to insure that only good physicians are available to the public."

"But, Marshall," Peter asked, "don't you think we can develop something? I do. With hospital accreditation boards and tissue and record committees, and the hospital utilization review committees of Medicare, we should be able to clamp down on the crummy doctors and show we mean business."

"Take accreditation," Marshall said. "Matthew's applied for it now, because he needs it to hold his Medicare and the other insurance patients, and the Conjoint Commission is coming around in a few months. I'll bet you anything the place passes. Then with these hospital committees, it's still doctors judging doctors, and is there anything in the past to make you think they're going to do anything but gently tap wrists? Of course all we're even *talking* about controlling here is hospital practice. Nothing is mentioned about office practice, which is a hell of a lot of the practice of medicine."

"Lookit, Marsh," Frank said, standing up to stare at him, "I admit we ought to do better on this discipline business, but I think we are making progress and I think we will make more, and I hate bastards who go around moaning the blues, and saying we ought to turn everything over to the government, or at least are so defeatist they're willing to let what we have go by default."

"I'm just saying again what I said. The doctors better show signs of being able to insure quality medicine or they're going to fall flat on their faces and be run over by the Department of Health, Education and Welfare—Democratic party steamroller."

"I'm the junior assistant here, I know," Peter said, "so before you two get into a fight, I'm going to agree with both of you. I think private doctors can give better and more individualized care to patients, and I don't think the American people really want medicine fully controlled by the government. But I think, too, with Marsh, that the doctors obviously have never done the job they should with medical discipline, and they're just simply going to have to find a way to do it, or go under. So now we all agree with each other. Don't you think so, Gloria?" Peter asked as he looked at her blinking her eyes on the couch.

"I thought I'd been forgotten. You three are certainly having a time tonight, I must admit. What I say is that I hope George Carr will run out, nightgown stuffed in his pants, if somebody needs a doctor in a hurry."

"He ought to be able to take call one night a year," Frank said. "The damned turd."

Peter put down his glass suddenly and looked at his watch. Twenty minutes after twelve. "God, I've got to get home," he announced, "while I can still make it, and let you poor Lewickis go to bed, too. I hate to think of making rounds in the morning. Hey, Marshall, let's allow the kindly Lewickis the surcease of our absence and the friendliness of their bed."

19

HALF an hour later, though, Peter was sitting with Marshall in a downtown bar having "one last drink." Marshall was saying, "Dammit, Pete, I don't know why Frank won't face up to these things."

"Did you think Gloria would be the kind to take afternoon naps?"

"What?"

"Oh, nothing. Do you know I really didn't like you when I first met you?"

"Yeh."

"But you're a pretty good guy. You're very smart. I think you're smart."

"I been around, believe me. I was in practice for a while myself before I went into anesthesia. You're not dry behind the ears yet. Give yourself a few years and you'll understand this whole mess better, the way Frank should. He gives me a pain in the ass sometimes, he's so goddam cautious and conservative. Some of you guys should sit down and really talk tough to Hatch, get rough with him. I think you might get someplace that way."

"Do you? I'm not sure. Say, do you know he's always making nasty cracks about you?"

"The shit. Actually, I'm not surprised."

"You know, he is easy to work with."

"He is *now*. I understand he didn't use to be, but he's quieted down a lot."

"He never seems to bother anybody around the clinic. He hardly ever fires anybody, still he wants complete loyalty from the employees and is hurt by anything short of that."

"He's about as soft-hearted as a water buffalo, I'd say. And something else, maybe you don't know this, but he makes a hell of a lot of money out of you guys. Why shouldn't he pay you guys well. He's got a sweet package going for him there. I figure he makes between two hundred and fifty and three hundred thousand dollars a year. Of that, close to one hundred thousand from the lab and X-ray alone."

"I wouldn't doubt it. But you know, I've been trying to understand him a little better, what makes him tick—"

"Give up, Doc. You can't analyze a guy like that."

"Don't you feel confused about him?"

"Not at all, buddy. I judge only what I know and see directly and don't listen to character references and grateful patients. And I think he stinks as a doctor and a surgeon and a person. He's a damn megalomaniac. He confuses himself with God. I think hanging is too good for him."

Peter was silent for a minute as Marshall talked to the waitress. After she left he said, "I've been trying to figure out what made Dr. Hatch such a success, and I decided on a few things. First, he gives a patient anything he thinks the patient might want, tranquilizers, vitamins, excuses from work, whatever. Then, he never admits a mistake. And he never accepts their complaints as being neurotic. He would rather take a sixteen-year-old girl and operate on her abdomen than give her any help with the emotional problem that's causing her abdominal pain."

"If he can't X-ray it or cut it out, either it doesn't exist or he gives it shots."

"That's right. I realize there are other M.D.'s who are bad, but he's about the worst I can imagine."

"You hit into a poor setup, Peter, let's face it. You ought to get over to one of the other groups in town. They don't make as much money, but they're good, competent men."

"I'll probably leave at the end of a year here, Marsh. I'm sort of caught in a trap right now, what with a low bank balance and even my family needing some help. You know what I mean?"

"Of course I do. You're honest in your approach, at least. What gets me is that most docs won't be honest in their thinking. For instance, about how the patient-physician relationship must be preserved. The patients must be *free* to choose their own doctors. They must be saved from socialistic shackles that might not allow the *free* American to *freely* choose his own doctor. This is really hypocritical. Most doctors don't give a damn about the freedom of their patients compared with how they worry about preserving *their own* freedom and *their own* income. And for thinking and talking this way for decades they wind up with Medicare shoved down their throats. I call it justice."

"It seems impossible to change anything, though, people or anything."

"Yeh. That's so."

"Marsh, you know, I'm awfully tight. I'd probably pass right out in this cockeyed booth, except that I'm dizzy and this keeps me upright, because I know I'd feel so much worse lying down."

"I better get you home."

"My car's right outside."

"Well, you leave your car here. I'll take you home and then get your car to you, Pete."

"How can you do that if you're driving your own?"

"Just figure that's my problem."

"Okay. Are you all right?"

"Hell, yes. I'm fine. I never get drunk. Let's go, kid."

The next morning Peter felt far better than he had anticipated. After a dish of peaches, a glass of milk, and two aspirins, he went to the hospital. It was after eleven, but Frank Lewicki was just making rounds, too, looking swollen-eyed and tired. "Boy, you guys really got me clonged," he said.

"Eyes straight ahead, standing erect, I look to the future, and pretend I have no past—like last night."

"You sound awfully chipper," Frank said crossly.

"I really don't feel bad. I expected to spend a week in bed. You know, Marsh and I had three or four more at the White Cat or the White Bird or whatever the name of that place is, after we left your house."

Frank rolled his eyes in agony. "You did? My God. It must be youth."

Peter picked Anne up at her house at noon. She was in tennis clothes, with a broad white band in her hair.

Peter beat her as usual, but not badly. The previous evening caught up with his legs before the first set was over, and he only scraped by for the second set win.

After they finished they went to the club terrace for a sandwich.

"Are you going to have a drink before lunch?" Anne asked him.

"Don't mention liquor to me."

"What's the matter?"

"Oh, I was disgusted with everything at the clinic last night and I got blotto over at Frank's house."

"And I thought you were purposely letting me do better when we played."

During lunch they talked about hangovers and tennis courts and old tennis tournaments. Over dessert of cheese-cake, Anne looked up and asked, "How's Micheline Long doing, by the way? You haven't even mentioned her."

"She died Thursday."

"Oh, Peter, she didn't."

"She sure did. That's one reason I got drunk last night, because I was so depressed about it."

"I'm so sorry to hear that. She had two children, didn't she?"

Peter suddenly had to clear his throat.

"Didn't she have two children?"

"Yes. Let's talk about something else, all right?"

Anne looked at his face and was silent.

After lunch they took a back road to town, stopping at a hill overlooking San Marcial to sit and watch for a while. Anne moved close to him, and then kissed him. "Darling, I worry about you."

"You shouldn't."

"I can't help it, baby." She had never used this word before. Was she suddenly maternal because of his tears, Peter wondered.

"Peter, hold me." He did.

"Will you stay with me tonight?" he asked. "You must."

"I can't. What will I say? My father's home."

"Say something, anything."

"I could come for a few hours."

"Please. You know I want to marry you."

"You do?"

"Yes, of course." He could not believe what he was saying for a moment, but he meant it, didn't he? "Yes, of course, we're going to be married. Next June. Before I leave here. We have to be. If you want to be. Do you want to be?"

"Oh, darling, you know I do. I didn't know if you felt the same way, but you must know I do want to mary you."

They rode peacefully into San Marcial after that, both happily quiet, warm together in the afternoon sun, absorbing their new world.

The next morning Peter was in surgery past eleven and then busy in the office until near six. Mrs. Beauprey had told him in the morning Mrs. Clara Gard was going home that day, so before he left for dinner, he stopped by her room to say good-bye. As he came to the short hallway leading to her door, Matthew Hatch stepped out of it. "There's a fine lady in there, Peter," he said with a full smile. "I've never found her equal."

Mrs. Gard was equally enthusiastic about Dr. Hatch, Peter found. "He's a real man, Dr. de Haan. You wouldn't believe he was so sensitive, that he had so much real feeling. And do you know, every Monday I'm in the hospital he sends me a bouquet of red roses, and he has never forgotten to send me a postcard any time he takes a trip."

Just *try* to understand this Hatch, Peter thought to himself. It was impossible. He was a man of split images, multiple ways, prismatic, kaleidoscopic. Perceptive at times, and yet childishly self-deceiving; on occasion tender, gentle, and "sensitive," and still megalomaniacal, calculating and a "money surgeon." The strength of his personality was obvious. He was buoyant, colorful, humorous, ingratiating, pleasant, even warm and likable. But from his joints blood-red sawdust leaked all over the floors.

Dr. Hatch apparently disapproved of the use of alcohol and cigarettes, and yet at lunch this Monday, Dean Mason, the pharmacist, had confirmed Marsh's assertion about how he misused Dexedrine capsules at times. "He must take six or eight of the big ones in a day," Mason said. "And then

Seconal at night to sleep." But this was just when he was supposedly trying to reduce, Mason implied.

Peter left Mrs. Gard's room perplexed, ready to give up on Matthew Hatch and his own efforts to pierce the mechanism there.

That Monday evening Peter was called back to the emergency room to see a patient sent in from Berrenda with abdominal pain. The elderly Dr. Hogarth of Berrenda had probably been to a medical meeting recently, Peter thought, because he sent this young dairy worker to the hospital with a diagnosis of possible porphyria.

Peter dialed Frank Lewicki's number for a question. "Frank, old Doc Hogarth sent a guy into the E.R. with cramping pain in his abdomen that acts to me like a simple gastroenteritis. His wife even had it a few days ago. But what's the easy test you can do for porphyria? He brings up this possibility, so I suppose I should rule it out."

"What you mean, Peter, is the Watson-Schwartz test for porphobilinogen."

"That's right. I'll ask the lab if they can do it."

"Sure they can."

"That's what I wanted to know. Thanks."

"Say, it was too bad about Mr. Long, wasn't it?"

"How do you mean?"

"That Micheline Long's husband. The patient of yours who died Thursday."

"What happened?"

"It was in the papers tonight. Didn't you see it?"

"What was? I haven't read any papers today."

"He jumped off the Bay Bridge."

"You're kidding."

"Absolutely not. Kidding? What the hell."

Peter saw the light in the hallway was flickering from a large moth caught inside the frosted globe.

"Are you still there, Peter?"

"Yes."

"According to the papers he went directly from some bar in San Francisco when it closed to the bridge, stopped near the first tower and jumped off. They recovered his body before noon and he was identified then."

"The poor kids, Frank, the poor damned kids."

That night in bed, shaking sadness descended on Peter again. How could he, even in his thoughts, have called Dr. Hatch colorful, humorous, pleasant, likable, *warm* and likable. Hatch the butcherer. Hatch the hatchet man. Hatch the obsequious oily murderer. Those were the better names. Marshall was right. Hanging was too good for him, and something had to be done about him.

PART TWO

20

OFF the surgical service, no longer Dr. Hatch's assistant, Peter was at once much happier. He avoided Dr. Hatch, letting the post-operative care drift back to Harry Lawson and Frank Lewicki. The Hatches were away on vacation in early October, too, and afterward things seemed slower on his service. The events of September came to seem a dream to Peter, a nightmare time, a storm lived through and passed, whose reality now was questionable.

The hospital and his practice were still important to him, but he spent whatever time he could with Anne, asking for more afternoons and weekends off to be with her. They went boating, even water-skiing, explored roads and mountains and beaches, played tennis and ate dinner out on Saturdays or Sundays. As the fair weather of September passed, there were concerts to hear, plays, singers, and bands to take in, and Anne even led him through the galleries and museums of the area.

Peter found her the most cheerful person to be with, and surprisingly tireless. She was happy to fill every day with as many activities as possible. To him, naturally reserved in manner, she seemed very gregarious. She loved people, loved to talk to strangers, to everyone, to get their opinions, to learn to know them and understand them, "comprehend them," as she put it. At the boat docks, in the coffee houses and the art galleries, they came on people she had met and remembered.

He also learned she could be jealous. At the end of October the San Marcial Medical Society Auxiliary had their annual benefit. This year it was a revue of light opera and musical comedy put together by a group of San Francisco players. They met Matthew and Rosalie Hatch at the door to the auditorium. Dr. Hatch was resplendent in a blue silk suit with bright red tie, and was charming in manner to Anne, gay and teasing. They all sat together during the show, and talked with each other at intermission. Rosalie looked tired, but was dressed beautifully in white chiffon. She seemed to make a point of being attentive and friendly with Anne, Peter thought.

Sitting at a table in the San Marcial Inn bar afterward for a drink, Peter found Anne disturbed. "Is there something I don't know?" she said.

"Why, what do you mean?"

"That Mrs. Hatch. I thought she acted very strangely."

"What do you mean?"

"She looked at you as if she owned you or as if she was in love with you or had slept with you or something." Anne spoke in an unnatural way for her, through tight lips with her words clipped. "There is something, isn't there?"

"Not really."

"Now tell me what you mean by that? Don't put me off."

Peter told her what had happened briefly, of course not emphasizing the events, but being truthful, and he hoped fair all the way around.

"Do you mean that you were out with her the night I was in Fresno?"

"I wasn't *out* with her. I met her here and took her home and went on to Lewickis'."

"I could tell there was something between you and that woman. I knew it, and I was furious about it. I could see her putting her hand on your arm, too."

"I've told you the whole thing. That's it, that's all there is to it, and it has no meaning to me, and shouldn't to you."

"You know, I just realized I'm really jealous. I've never been like this before. I could *smack* her for doing what she did. And I can't really believe it. Don't misunderstand me, I can see she's very attractive, but for *Mrs. Hatch*, who's married to the head of the clinic and who has grown children and all, I find it surprising."

"Can't we forget it, just drop it?"

"I don't blame any woman for getting her hands on you, either, you know. Don't think I can't understand that. But what was it she wanted to tell you about Dr. Hatch?"

"I consider it confidential, a professional confidence, and don't think I should tell anybody."

"I see."

"Did you like Dr. Hatch?"

"I can't stand him."

"Really? Don't you think he's good-looking?"

"Not at all. I think he's sort of odd-looking, strange. And he seemed so phony to me. All that teasing and fake gallantry. He's obviously got a monstrous ego. I can't stand him. I don't know how you do."

"Well, of course I don't very well."

On the way home, she stayed very close to him, holding his arm and kissing his neck. Her good-night kisses were very warm, impassioned. "I do love you and want you to be all mine," she said. "I guess I'm very possessive. I don't like any other woman thinking she has any part of you." Peter laughed and kissed her again before he left.

Anne had the last part of Thanksgiving week off from classes and Peter took his first vacation from the clinic then. They decided to go to Rio Hondo, a small beach town south of Santa Cruz, where Anne had a friend from Hawaii who was also a teacher. "I can stay with Lynn," she said. "I know she wouldn't mind and there are all kinds of little places, inns and motels, where you could get a room. We could have a couple of wonderful days. I really should get back Saturday night, because I promised Dad I would cook a turkey for him Sunday. And you must come too. Dad finally has a friend, I mean a woman he's interested in, so I asked him to ask her."

He picked Anne up at the junior college late Wednesday afternoon. She was poised on the steps waiting for him in a short-skirted burgundy suit. A matching broad ribbon held back her black hair, which was longer again, and she had a polo coat thrown over her arm. In the weakened slant of the late day's sun rays her face was in soft shadows, her hair blowing in the breeze as she came across the broad, leaf-strewn walk to the car. Peter gave her a soft hug around the shoulders before he opened the car door.

"I can't believe it," he said, driving away. "We're off on our weekend."

Anne laughed in her throaty way. "Isn't it delicious?"

They decided to stop in Palo Alto for dinner. At a quarter to seven they were sitting near the fire at L'Omelette having a martini, the special L'Ommy's one, as Anne pointed out, with an olive, a twist of lemon, *and* an onion in it.

"This is good," Peter said. "I didn't know you liked martinis, though."

"I didn't either, but I'm growing a taste for them. I think I'll give up sidecars for a while."

After a third excellent martini served at their table, they devoured their coquilles St. Jacques appetizers, and chicken breasts with cream and mushroom sauce.

"You know what I've wanted to ask you to do," Peter said over coffee after dinner.

"What?"

"Call Lynn."

"Why?"

"To tell her you can't stay with her after all, but that you'll see her tomorrow for a visit. You said there were all kinds of places there, and I don't see why I should stay alone if I don't have to."

"Of course, it would be wonderful, but I don't think I should."

"I really want you to want to, even if you won't," Peter said, a little tight still, which increased his feeling of enchantment by her.

She looked at him fiercely, and then gave him a little kiss through the air. "All right, darling, I'll stay with you. I want to and I will. But let me phone Lynn from here, so I won't have that on my mind."

After her call, they walked to the car and Anne got in quickly. He slammed the door with a tinny crash of its metal timbers, and slid in the other side. "Please kiss me, Peter," she said, and he pulled her to him. She extended the kiss, holding onto his face as he started to move away. "I do love you," she said. "So much."

Her head was in Peter's lap as he drove absorbedly over the winding road beyond Los Gatos, finally passing over the coastal range to drop down into the flat outskirts of Santa Cruz where he turned southward. The salty smell of the sea air struck them as they went through Santa Cruz and Capitola to reach Rio Hondo, where they turned directly to the beach.

"When I visited Lynn last year I saw a nice place down this way, down here. No, keep going, darling." And then she said, "There it is."

They drove into a large two-story motel, white with green shutters, a shake roof, and a large central lawn indented by the kidney-shape of a steaming swimming pool. "What are you going to say?" Anne asked softly. Peter only shrugged, and smiled at her.

The night air was a moist brine on his face as he waited for the manager to answer the night bell. "My wife and I wanted one of your good rooms," he said to the moustached night manager when he finally came.

"The best one we have left is on the second floor at the end. The cocktail lounge is underneath, but it closes at eleven here."

"I think that would be all right."

"Sign here."

"We'll probably stay two nights."

"If you'd just pay for tonight in advance."

Anne opened the door with the key as Peter carried up their suitcases. "Oh, this is nice," she said. "It's a big room. And the ocean's right there. What's that music?"

"That's from the bar downstairs. The manager said it closes at eleven."

He put her suitcases on the luggage rack. "Are you tired?" he asked.

"No, why?" She looked at Peter.

"You look sort of funny," he said. "Is something the matter?"

"I just wonder if I made a mistake."

"You mean to come here?"

"Yes. Did I?"

"No, of course not."

"I don't want you to take me for granted."

"I don't and I won't." He took off her coat carefully and then pulled her to him and kissed her.

Catching her breath in a moment, Anne took the band out of her hair and hugged him, sinking her chin in his chest.

They undressed and she touched him as they stood, and then knelt down to kiss him. In a bit he said, "You'd better stop."

"Really?"

"Definitely."

"I shouldn't do that . . ."

"I don't mind."

". . . but it's exciting to me, too."

They lay back on the bed then and he kissed her nipples into hard red buds before he got inside her. Their climax came soon, and they stayed on the bed afterward resting from it, talking and kissing.

Later they changed into casual clothes, sweater and slacks for him and sweater and skirt for Anne, and went down to the bar. There was a man playing the piano, and three or four other couples. They all sat at the tables near the piano and sang the songs that were played and laughed when they didn't know the words.

"I'm surprised," Peter said as they went up their stairs. "You knew the words to almost everything."

"Yes, I always remember words."

"I like that. I think that's just what I do like."

"You're funny when you're tight. I like you too this way, with the clinic and everything out of your head, and just me and us on your mind."

"We're lucky to get a double bed," he said. "Usually these motels always have twins."

"How do you know?"

"I don't mean I've ever been in one with a girl, but just with other fellows on trips."

"I'll bet. Really, have you ever been in a motel with another girl before?"

"Of course not. And to prove to you I didn't plan to bring you here, I don't even have any pajamas. You'll have to put up with me in shorts."

"I know I'll love you in shorts. And wait until you see my entrancing outfit." She picked up her small case and went in the bathroom. Peter turned on the television.

A few minutes later she came out in a two-piece beige pajama suit. "You couldn't call this too glamorous, could you? You see, I didn't plan right for this trip, either. Is that an old movie?"

"I think it's *Casablanca* with Bogart."

"Are you going to watch?"

"Maybe for a while. Do you want to?"

"No, not really. But leave it on."

"No, I'll turn it off."

"I thought you'd want to make love."

"Of course I do. I didn't know about you," Peter said.

"You didn't."

He turned off the flickering light of the set. Later, before she went to sleep, Peter said, "It was good for you, tonight, wasn't it?"

"If it were any better I couldn't stand it."

"Do you love me?"

"Oh, yes, you are my love."

"Really?"
"Yes."
He kissed her gently on the mouth. "Are you tired?"
"Yes."
"Good night, darling. Remember if you wake up, you can move over close by me if you want to."
"That's wonderful. Don't think I'll forget, because I won't. I only wish we could be together every night, and never had to be away from each other."
Peter watched her for a while as she went to sleep, so silent and childlike now. Lying back, he could hear the quiet breaking of shore waves. Suddenly he thought of the Hatch Clinic, and Dr. Hatch, and shivered. For the first time in his medical life he had the feeling of a wish to escape. He realized he would rather not go back in four days, would rather never go back. Somehow, he thought, he should correct that Hatch situation. If only he knew how.
Thinking ahead, dreaming ahead, he saw himself a major figure in medicine, getting up at a national meeting and proposing a program to sweep the world of Hatches that carried by acclamation.
But to hell with medical incompetents, doctors like Matthew Hatch. There was Anne at his side to consider. Think of what children they would have together, big tall kids, some with black hair, some towheads, gangly and, he hoped, good-looking. The babies in their tasseled caps, and the older ones astonishing their teachers with their brightness and spirit. He had never really considered what his own children might look like or be like before and it was fun. He'd have to remember to tell Anne about it in the morning. She stirred a little as he thought of her, and turned on her back.
"Hello, darling," he said.
"What time is it? Are you still awake?" she asked when he kissed her.
"Only about twelve thirty," he answered. "Go back to sleep."
She murmured and turned over as Peter sank back again, cheerfully welcoming the cap of sleep drawing tight over his skull.
In the morning he got coffee and doughnuts and orange juice for them from the motel coffee shop. They ate happily, and then went swimming in the surf. Afterward they walked along the beach for half an hour in the remarkable bright sun and warmth of a late fall Indian summer day in California.

"I didn't tell you, but when I talked to Lynn, I said we'd be over there by two in the afternoon, so she's expecting us for turkey dinner. This is Thanksgiving Day, you know."

"A disconcerting development," Peter said. "I told the motel we'd be here two nights."

"I should stay with Lynn tonight. If she doesn't have a cot for you, then you'll have to look out for yourself."

"Oh, all right," Peter said sighing. "I'll behave. I won't even spill cranberry sauce on her tablecloth."

"You better not," Anne said, hitting him on the arm and then running away from him down the beach. He caught up with her and tackled her on the soft warm sand. They laughed and kissed then, and walked up to their room.

On the road back through Los Gatos and Los Altos Saturday they ran into clouds, and by the time they reached Redwood City it was raining lightly. They rolled along the slick black surface of the Bayshore Highway and by the airport, locked into place in a myriad of slow-moving cars.

"God, I wish I didn't have to go back to that Hatch Clinic Monday," Peter said. "Still I can stand anything for seven months more."

The Sunday dinner at Anne's was a success even though the rolls got burned a little in her excitement. Peter liked Mr. Alexio's new friend, Elizabeth Young, a willowy blond widow with grown children whose husband, a dentist, had died, and who now worked for her husband's former partner. Mr. Alexio had met her in the office when he went to get his teeth checked, and they joked about this now.

The two of them had an air of immediate intimacy, of belonging together as if they had been with one another for years, that Peter found remarkable and was also happy for. He went home that night glad, too, that he was on such good terms with and liked so much the father of the girl he was going to marry.

21

THE time between the holidays passed quickly. Peter was absorbed again in his work, learning all the things that weren't taught in medical school or training programs. Much of what had to be understood was how to handle people; when to tell them their problems were psychosomatic and when not to tell them; who could be told they were going to die, and who could not be trusted with the information; how to talk long enough to people to satisfy them, without talking too long. Occasional patients could scarcely be kept in the office sufficient time to be questioned and examined properly. Far more others, though, had practically to be driven out of the examining rooms. To dispose of them without taking too long over them, and still keep them as patients, was sometimes an impossibility and always an art.

To explain illnesses, tests, and treatments to patients clearly and concisely was a continuous challenge. Some individuals were impervious to medical information. After the most careful explanation, these patients would ask in a few weeks, with irritation, "What exactly is wrong with me, Doctor? My family have asked me and I just have had to tell them that you won't say. Why are you doctors so secretive?"

The telephone callers could be a difficulty. A day could not be gotten through for some patients if they had not checked in with their doctor once or twice. People called in the black deadness of the witching hours to wonder if they should take enemas, to complain that they had not gone to sleep with their Seconal. The near-addicts were on the phone night and day pushing for medicine, pain pills, narcotic injections, stronger sleeping potions. People called at midnight, hoping they had not awakened him, and at five thirty A.M. to catch him before he left for the office. When they thought he slept, Peter could not say.

With luck he saw Dr. Hatch only once or twice a week now. The clinic head was unchanged in his attitude toward him, as far as Peter could tell, joking often, cordial but always rushed.

Peter, on the other hand, walked on rounds with Frank Lewicki whenever he could to pick up all possible of his frequent pearls. He also scrubbed with Les Leslie at surgery occasionally, enjoying orthopedics more under Les' capable instruction, and in the delivery room he learned better forcep techniques from Al Humphers.

In the first week of December, Peter and Anne's lives seemed to snowball into a desperate rush of work before Christmas which kept them apart most evenings. Anne told her father that they planned to become officially engaged the first part of the new year, and Peter thought Mr. Alexio was genuinely pleased.

Christmas afternoon as Peter was getting ready to go to Anne's house for dinner his mother called him at his apartment.

"How are you? Is anything wrong?" he asked.

"Peter, something has happened to your father." She sounded calm.

"What do you mean something has happened? Did he have another heart attack?"

"Yes, he did. It was very sudden and nothing could be done. He passed away about an hour ago."

"Oh, no. Oh, Mother, I'm sorry. Are you all right?"

"Yes, I think so."

"What happened?"

"We were sitting in the front room watching television after Christmas dinner and Dad said he didn't feel well. He thought maybe the dressing from the turkey hadn't agreed with him, and kidded me about it. All of a sudden he took a big gasp and fell forward off the sofa. I called Dr. Mohler who came at once, but your father was gone. He said it must have been instantaneous."

"You're sure you're all right, Mother?"

"I'll be fine. Harriet Crafts from next door is here and wants to stay all night with me, but I don't think I'll need her. I have my sleeping pill I can take. Of course, I've expected this for a long time. Still when it happens, well, you know what I mean."

"Are you going to take him to White-Haydn's?"

"Yes, the men from there, I think the older one is Mr. Haydn, are here now." All at once he could hear his mother crying softly. Peter waited through a short silence then, and Mrs. Crafts' voice came on. "Give us a minute, Peter. I think everything caught up with your mother suddenly." A pause, and Mrs. Crafts said, "Here she is back again."

"I'm sorry, Peter," she said, "but I just couldn't stand to see them take him out the door."

"Mother, I'll come home. I can get a plane out tonight, and be home in the morning."

"I know it's expensive."

"Never mind, dear, that's all right. You take care of yourself, and let Mrs. Crafts stay with you tonight. I'd feel better about it. And if the weather's not a problem, I'll see you probably at nine or ten o'clock in the morning."

22

TWENTY minutes after landing at Friendship Airport, Peter was in the old familiar world of North Charles Street, passing the pleasant greens and the Georgian brick buildings of Johns Hopkins University, and the houses and apartments of Homewood. Crossing Cold Spring Lane, they drove on into the Towson suburb of Baltimore, and shortly turned off Charles Street. In three blocks they were at the de Haan home, which looked surprisingly older and gloomier to Peter.

His mother, tired and thin-looking, was waiting on the porch for him, one hand to her mouth silencing a cough, the other holding a cigarette, as she tried to mobilize a smile. She hugged him and then cried very briefly on his shoulder, before saying, "Come inside, Peter. I've got bacon and eggs on the stove for you."

The house seemed mustier and dingier, and already there was a feeling of physical loss as he stepped into the living room. He could picture his father sitting here in his leather chair, white-haired and slender, but still preserving the straight spine of all the de Haans as he sipped tea and watched the ten o'clock news. His essential vigor, even dimmed by his infirmities, had always permeated the household, and his absence now was as perceivable as a missing wall.

Peter put his suitcase down at the foot of the stairs and went through the dining room, where his grandfather's scratched old portrait still hung over the battered buffet there, into the kitchen on his mother's arm. His older sister Dora was there, down from New Hampshire with her husband, Francis.

Dora gave him a small hug and a kiss that brushed his cheek.

"I didn't know you were here," he said. Peter was almost startled at her stoutness. She must have gained twenty-five pounds since he had seen her last. She was only thirty-two, but she now seemed catapulted into middle age with graying hair, legs showing veins, and small facial lines like her mother's.

"We started down right away last night, and got here about one this morning."

"How are young Francis and Cathy?" Peter asked.

"Fine. Home with the baby-sitter."

Francis Arnot had been drinking coffee at the breakfast table, and got up to shake hands. "I'm sorry about your father, Peter." Francis had a wide, coarse-featured face, tanned and placid. Peter had always been happy his sister had married such an imperturbable fellow, who apparently enjoyed being the stabilizer for their ship.

"Peter, before you eat, come here a minute, please." Dora dragged him out onto the back porch and shut the kitchen door. "Do you know Mother says that Dad wanted to be cremated, and she's determined to do it. Now don't you think that's awful?"

"No, not at all."

"You *don't?*"

"Why not, if he wanted it that way?"

Mrs. de Haan put her head out the back door, her blue eyes glinting with life for the moment. "Peter," she said, "I'm sure Dora is telling you how shocked she is about cremating Dad, but that's exactly what he wanted. He left written instructions for everything, which included a plain pine box and cremation, and I think we should do what he asked."

"Okay, Mom. Let us talk a little and we'll be in."

Peter went with Dora and his mother to the funeral parlor in the late morning. The undertaker did seem disturbed by their requests, Peter could tell: plain wooden coffin, closed casket, private services, cremation, deposit of the ashes in an urn already purchased in a small country cemetery. It appeared to bother his sense of the proprieties for doctors' funerals, but he at last, always polite, went along with their wishes. It was now one o'clock, Sunday afternoon. White-Haydn's had four funerals planned for Monday, so Tuesday morning was set for Dr. de Haan's services.

Peter spent the afternoon with his mother and sister. There were a number of visitors, Dr. Lee and Dr. Harry Kiefer, Miss Oma Smith, his father's office nurse for years, and others Peter did not know.

They had a cold supper together late, and Peter slept in his old room at night. It seemed bare, unreal to him now. Though he missed Anne, and would have liked to see her, or talk to her, somehow she did not fit into the room. Here was his past, and she was of the future.

In the morning he got up early and drove the family Chevrolet through town to the Biddle Medical Center. The old car seemed doubly balky and decrepit now. Without power steering, it handled like a truck. He had no current parking sticker, but the guard at the gate saw the old one, recognized him, and let him into the staff lot. Peter found himself excited as he went through the side door to the main entrance and crossed its giant marble floor.

He paused at the massive doors of the medical school, then stepped through them to the row of elevators by the main desk inside. The first one was open, and he rode it rapidly up to the sixth floor, where he asked at the surgery department for Dan Sankoff.

"You're Doctor . . . ?" the middle-aged, red-haired receptionist's voice trailed off uncertainly.

"De Haan, Peter de Haan."

"Oh, yes. I thought I recognized you. Everyone looks so different when they don't have on their whites."

Gone six months, Peter thought, and my absence not even noticed. Well, that was sort of good in a way. He felt as if he were still part of the hospital.

"I'm sorry, Dr. de Haan. Dr. Sankoff is scrubbed and operating at the moment. They said it would be an hour before he's through."

"I know this is the first day after Christmas weekend, but is Dr. Cunningham here, by any chance?"

"You might be able to catch him. He has no appointments for today, but he was in a little while ago doing some extra work. I'll ring him."

There was a brief, unintelligible conversation over the intercom, before she said, "Go right down to his office."

As Peter walked in the doorway, the tall physician stood

up at once, swinging his wide shoulders vigorously as he shook hands. His smile was broad and genuine. "Peter, how the hell are you? What are you doing in Baltimore?"

Peter explained, and Dr. Cunningham, sinking back in his chair, listened, his brown eyes sympathetic as Peter talked.

"You know your father was a fine man."

Peter was surprised at the comment. "I remember you told me once you had known him, but it was only slightly."

"I'll have to explain. When I was a medical student I worked at the old Provident Hospital as a sort of orderly, an *extern*, at nights. Your father at that time took quite a few patients to Provident, and I got to know him. He actually paid some attention to me, which none of the other staff doctors did. He'd tell me about his patient's problems in the old laboratory on the second floor, and he was the first one to show me how to run a urinalysis. He'd bring in X-rays occasionally, too, and so gave me my first taste of clinical medicine. I didn't see him for years at a time, and he wouldn't have recalled all this, I'm sure, but I certainly thought a lot of him."

"That's interesting," Peter said, his voice suddenly thick. He cut his sentence short.

"How are you finding California?" Dr. Cunningham asked.

"Good enough. Some things I don't like about the group I'm in."

"What are they?"

"Well, it's a long story. The man in charge just doesn't seem competent."

Dr. Cunningham gave Peter a long look from his trout eyes, and pulled his shirt collar down over his Adam's apple. "You'll be going back in residency in a year or two, then?"

"I might very well do that. I plan to, in fact. Perhaps in San Francisco."

"Listen, Peter, I'm awfully anxious to have you see some of the letters we got on that paper we presented last spring at the National Surgical College. Take twenty minutes and read them through."

Peter sat down on the old lounge in the corner of his consultation room, as Dr. Cunningham worked at his desk. In a half hour the doctor signed the last paper and stood up to shake hands again before leaving.

"Now, Peter," he said, "don't forget to keep in touch with me. I mean it. And when I come out to the Federation meetings in San Francisco this spring, we'll have to spend a day together."

"That would be wonderful. Thank you again for everything, Dr. Cunningham."

"Good luck, my boy."

Peter talked to Dan Sankoff after he had finished his surgery for the morning, and then to several other old friends and former fellow interns. Driving home, the feeling that he had never left Biddle came back, that he was going home now to stay in his old room, to take up his old ways. It was good to feel a part of things again, but it made him uneasy, too. It was disturbing, he decided, because all this was not in Anne's world: she had no place here and he did not want her left out of anything that was his.

He thought of Dan's news of the marriage and pregnancy of Doris Lund, a girl he had dated a few times, and then at once pictured Anne the same way, in maternity clothes, appearing as a Kodachrome of young matronly charm at bridge luncheons; then she would feel the baby kick and they would both be solemnly anxious to see what it looked like. For a moment, it was there. In his mind's eye he could see a tiny dark-haired organism, held easily in two hands, with minuscule fingernails, and a crying, flushed, sucking, Chinese-eyed face. He smiled in delight at the vision.

The funeral the next day was anticlimactic. There were only a few people there besides the family. His mother's best friend, Vera Miller, came; also the Crafts from next door, and Doctor Mohler, who had especially asked to be present. His father's only sister, Bertha Milne, whom Peter had not seen for a decade, came down from Hagerstown with her husband, a retired lawyer plagued with arthritis and diabetes.

Peter had been thankful that the minister's eulogy and benediction had been brief, the funeral itself as low-keyed as possible. This was his father's wish and it was sensible. He was pleased afterward, too, when Aunt Bertha asked if he thought he could get his mother to come up to Hagerstown for the night. Dora and Francis were starting back for New Hampshire at once and his aunt thought it might be good for Mrs. de Haan to get away from home this first night. He accepted the invitation without asking her and she did not complain when he announced his decision to her later.

The afternoon was cold and sunny and the conversation was Aunt Bertha's idea of a light one: the identity of those bushes by the road (she had majored in botany at college), the dead dog on the highway shoulder, the way everything was building up, the gloomy future of Maryland, racists and the troubles they caused. She had not liked the idea of a private family funeral, Peter knew, but she at least commented on what she called the simple beauty of the services.

As they talked to each other, Peter watched the landscape go by and thought about his father. What had happened to all those patients of Dr. Henry de Haan who had called him morning and night, deluged him with Christmas cards, told Peter's mother when she met them at the store or post office how much they loved him? Gone, certainly gone. Not heard from nowadays. Yet his father *had* left behind a heritage of care, had he not, in a great group of people who had been influenced by him, helped by him, and in turn liked him, even loved him, always recalled him, tied him to some pivotal action in their lives. These people might not be in view now, his son might never know them, but they were there. As evidence, Dr. Howard Cunningham. And to the whistling of the windwings of the car Peter decided this was a substantial legacy.

The Milnes' house was a large two-story one which was stuffed full of dreary old furniture. An elderly woman servant prepared a simple, cold dinner, and in the evening Peter sipped brandy and chatted with his aunt and mother while Mr. Milne, heavy and flushed, largely silent through the day, drowsed in his armchair.

Peter slept uneasily that night, awakening once with a start of fear, unsure where he was, fighting a nightmare. After a quiet morning of talk and a substantial lunch, his aunt drove them down to the bus station.

The return trip to Baltimore was enjoyable for him. He appreciated his mother more than ever on the ride. She was in command of herself, refusing of self-pity, pleasant, warm, joking a few times. She told Peter how Henry de Haan had been anxious that she remarry so she wouldn't "screw herself up the way most damned women do after their husbands die." She imitated his father's speech perfectly with these last words, and they both laughed.

"He was such a fine person, Peter, and smart, you know, humorous, good company, even after his stroke. I couldn't have been luckier. Of course, his life was all medicine always, and when he had his stroke, in a sense it did stop. But he still had you. It was such a wonderful thing for him that you went into medicine. My greatest sadness about his dying is that he didn't get the chance to see you farther along in it."

As the taxi let them out at the house in Towson, Peter saw the mailbox was stuffed with cards and letters, and his mother stopped to empty it as he went on up the steps. Walking slowly across the porch, he wondered if perhaps he should not suggest right now to his mother that she sell this place. The land itself was worth $25,000 or more anyway and she could buy a duplex somewhere, live in one part and rent the other. She was going to be so alone in this big place.

"Peter, there's a telegram here for you," she called.

"Who could that be from?" he said, coming down the stairs.

He ripped the envelope open and read, "Anne ill in hospital. Need you here. Call at once. Frank Lewicki."

"My God, Mother," Peter said, "it's from Frank and he says Anne's sick in the hospital."

"Oh, my dear."

Sitting at the telephone table in the hallway, Peter listened with great impatience to the usual beeps and clicks and woodwind sounds before Frank came on and told he had been trying to reach him for hours.

"What's wrong with Anne?"

"She's had vaginal bleeding. Cramping and bleeding. Quite severely."

"No, Frank!"

"Yes, damnit. It seems she's either aborting or has a tubal pregnancy; she's in surgery here."

"Surgery. Who's taking care of her? Norman Silvana or Humphers?"

"They're both out of town. Her father, I suppose scared to death, brought her in to Matthew, and he's operating right now."

"Matthew Hatch, for Christ's sake. MATTHEW HATCH! You must be kidding. How could she let *him* operate?"

"I don't know, Peter. I stumbled on the whole thing. I was seeing a patient who went sour and I just happened to notice Anne's name on the ward roster."

"Well, what's happening in the surgery? When did they start?"

"It must be half an hour ago. I haven't been in there. I've been trying like hell to get you on the phone. I finally got your aunt's name through the funeral parlor and I called her.

She told me when you'd left her place and I had the telegram sent to the house."

"You don't know what's going on with the operation then?"

"I know she was shocky on admission and Matthew slugged her with Demerol and Sparine right away, then got some blood started on her pronto, which she apparently needed."

"I have to know what's going on, Frank. Can't you find out and call me back?"

"I will. Wait a second, Marsh has his head out the surgery door." There were footsteps and hurried voices and more footsteps, then Frank was back on the phone. "Well, Marsh says things are going as well as they can with 'Doctor God.' He says there's been no more bleeding on the table, and Matthew's exploring the pelvis and abdomen now. He doesn't know what's the cause of it all, but I guess they figure the bleeding's from a miscarriage. He says her pressure is fine and her pulse."

"Listen, I'll get back there as fast as I can. Mom's all right, and she'll understand. And get hold of Al Humphers or Norman Silvana if you can, will you please—Al might be more likely, Norman never wants to stick his neck out—and have one of them supervise matters, see things are done right. Please do that, will you, Frank, and make any excuse you need to Matt until I get there. I'll appreciate it like nothing else ever, before or after."

"Okay, Peter. I'll do everything possible."

23

THE trip east had been one of sadness. The flight back west was more one of desperation. Peter had time enough to talk to Frank for just a moment before catching the first takeoff to the Coast. The word from Frank was that Anne was out of surgery and in good condition. He did not have other details of the surgery yet, because he had been too busy with his own patient.

The superjet airliner had a ghastly sex-comedy for its

movie, which Peter could not stand to watch, except that he could not bring himself to read either, or bear to think about Anne, so he kept looking back at the screen, watching Hollywood's current Aeneas and Dido for a few moments before the bald, unbelievable shock of Anne's trouble came slamming back into his consciousness, blotting out all other images.

At least she was alive and in good shape, he thought to himself. Of course, with Matthew Hatch doing the surgery, ripping tissue and mishandling bowel, God only knew what troubles she might have post-operatively. But at least she would live, wouldn't she? Of course that was the important thing, and she would. That goddam Hatch.

Peter had made a mistake himself, a bad one, the most serious one he could have made. He should have left the Hatch Clinic before now. He should not have continued to take money, a salary, from someone he despised, from a pig of a greedy surgeon. If he had broken with the place probably Mr. Alexio would have taken her somewhere else, to the Valley Hospital or the Cabrillo.

God, though, nothing could happen to Anne. He could only accept her illness for moments at a time and then, with any distraction from it, he had to go through the agony of understanding it all over again. It was only when they were past the middle of the flight, and after dozens of repeated shivers of disbelief, that the reality of what had happened began to stand up for him.

He had never loved her more than now when she was injured, not dying, she certainly couldn't die, but balanced on a ledge of danger without him there to pull her up and hold her.

When I get back to San Marcial, he thought, and Anne is all right, I must do something about myself professionally. I'll start applying for residencies. Maybe Anne and I could even come back to Baltimore and live with Mom. That would help her. But Anne might not want to leave the West Coast, and I'm not sure I do. I could go out for myself in practice. Start an office of my own in San Marcial, perhaps.

Why am I thinking all these disconnected, branching thoughts, Peter wondered. I must try to concentrate on Anne now. Is it possible that thinking positively for her can actually help her? It always seems that we can help someone by thinking about them strongly enough. But if it *can* help her, I will think for her, send up prayers and thoughts and hope, and positively affirm in my mind the best for her. I must prepare for trouble, but think optimistically for her, be calm with her when I see her, gentle, reassuring, never let on with her if she is in trouble, not let her realize how disturbed I am that that bloody Hatch cut into her.

Peter discovered in the middle of an imaginary kiss on Anne's cheek, and caress of her hand, that the movie screen was blank. A moment later the pilot announced that they were twenty minutes away from landing.

A light rain was falling at the airport, and the wheels of the airplane were noisily slick on the glistening runway surface. It seemed an hour and a half, but it was ten minutes later that Peter was on a pay phone to the Hatch Hospital. It was Thursday morning, although only a quarter after six Pacific Standard Time, so Peter did not try to bother Frank Lewicki, who would be asleep, but talked directly to the floor nurse on D Ward.

"She seems fine," a Mrs. Shirley said.

"Wonderful. That's good. Is she awake?"

"Just now woke up. Of course, she's still somewhat groggy. She asked about you, Dr. de Haan, and I told her you were coming, I understood, so I guess I'm right."

"I'm at the airport in San Francisco. I'll be there in about an hour, I expect."

"I'll tell her."

"Thanks, Mrs. Shirley."

Then his car wouldn't start. His battery was fading when suddenly the engine coughed, caught hold, and he was off. He drove rapidly, almost recklessly, and afterward could recall nothing of the trip over the Bay Bridge and through the East Bay.

San Marcial looked somehow older and smaller, more countrified, with an increase in open spaces and less green than seemed natural. The Hatch Hospital was gloomy in the early morning dewiness, tiny after the Biddle Center. Peter parked in back. Inside the building everything was reassuringly familiar again, and Baltimore was at once very far away, nonexistent.

The elevator stood on the ground floor with its door open as if waiting for him. On D Ward the day nurse, a Mrs. Richter, was at the desk.

"Hello, Dr. de Haan," she said. "Did you just get back?"

"Yes. How is Miss Anne Alexio doing?"

"I haven't seen her yet since I came on, but I understand she's all right. Just finished breakfast."

"Where is she?"

"Two-o-four. They haven't gone in to bathe her, so you can see her right now." Mrs. Richter unconsciously made it clear that Anne was not his patient. With your own patients you went in to see them even if they were being bathed. The nurses simply pulled a towel over them and got out.

Peter knocked on the closed door. An unfamiliar aide opened it a crack. "I'm Dr. de Haan. I wanted to see Miss Alexio." Peter's chest was tight from worry, and his hands felt cold and clumsy. After a long thirty-second wait, the aide opened the door again and he walked in.

Anne was lying there, pale without makeup, smiling for him. "Darling, I'm so happy to see you."

Peter leaned over and kissed her. "It's so good to be able to do that," he said.

"Have you been very worried?"

"Yes, but now I'm not. Do you hurt much?"

"I do this morning."

Peter took her hand, which was moist, and colder than his. Her hair was bedraggled, as if she'd just come out of swimming. "God, I missed you, Peter, and needed you. I knew you wouldn't want Dr. Hatch for me," she said, lowering her voice, "but I was so damnably sick, I couldn't care. I just had to have somebody and of course Daddy couldn't find anybody else. I told him not to get Dr. Hatch, when I could still talk. I remember he was very surprised, but he said he couldn't locate any other doctor. After that it's all vague. I recall seeing Dr. Hatch when I got here, though. He gave me a shot right away, and that's all I know until I woke up from the surgery."

"I didn't even look at your chart as I came in. I wanted to see you right away. So I don't know what the surgical findings were. They must have opened up your abdomen; I mean, that's what Frank said, but I don't understand it all. If you were bleeding from a miscarriage, of course they wouldn't go into your abdomen. They'd just do a D and C."

"I can't tell you, darling," she said. "But Frank Lewicki knows. Why don't you talk to him?"

"Well, let me go look at your chart and I'll call Frank Lewicki, too, while they're bathing you, and then come back."

"Darling, I have to tell you something first. I couldn't do it at Christmas. I was going to, but then after your father died, I couldn't."

"Yes."

"I was sure I was pregnant before you left. I was more than two weeks over my regular period, and I just felt different, sick and funny."

"I didn't think we'd have any trouble. Certainly we were careful."

"It must have been down at Rio Hondo at Thanksgiving, and you know what happened there."

"You should have told me before I left."

"I guess so." She sighed. "Well, go find Frank and talk to him, and come back soon." She squeezed his hand. "I love you."

Peter found Frank in the downstairs corridor, his face serious.

"Let's sit in the emergency room, Peter. There's nobody in there, and I don't think we'll be bothered."

"Sure, but why so gloomy, Frank?" What the hell was wrong?

"Sit down, Peter."

"All right, but for God's sake, what's the big production?"

"As you know, when I was on the phone to you yesterday, I didn't know what surgery had been done. Afterward, of course, I found out."

"Don't tell me now he cut a ureter?"

"No, not that, but he did remove her uterus."

"Her uterus? What the hell for?"

"Matthew apparently opened her abdomen up to start with because he thought she might have a tubal pregnancy."

"Of course that occurred to me. But they don't usually have much vaginal bleeding."

"I guess he felt her shock was out of proportion, or, I don't know. You should talk to him. Anyway, she was bleeding, her uterus was enlarged, he didn't know what from, there was no tubal pregnancy, he was afraid he couldn't control the bleeding otherwise, he says. He was afraid she might have tried to induce an abortion and that infection or perforation could be a problem, and besides he says she definitely had endometriosis, there were some of the chocolate cysts of endometriosis broken, and so he couldn't tell if perforation had occurred, or if the bleeding was simply from endometriosis implants. I got all this from Marsh, who came in late himself, but has most of the story. He says that

Matthew figured she probably couldn't get pregnant with this endometriosis anyway, and that the safest thing all around would be to take out her uterus, to do the hysterectomy."

"Jesus, Frank, I can't believe it."

"I suppose the path. report will show a pregnant uterus with early miscarriage. I presume she hadn't tried to do anything about it herself, had she?"

"No, of course not. God, it just sounds like a typical D-and-C situation. Of course you can't ever tell about that goddam Hatch. I hope for his sake she really had endometriosis, that the slides really show it, because I'd want to kill him if they don't."

"I don't even know whether he tried to biopsy any of the chocolate cysts. Anyway, it's all a damned shame. Maybe she needed her uterus out, but with Matthew you never know, you always wonder." Frank Lewicki lit a cigarette and breathed it deeply, then exhaled and sighed.

"Does Anne know anything about this?" Peter asked.

Frank looked over at Peter. "As a matter of fact, she does. I saw her this morning and she insisted I tell her what I knew, so I did. She cried like hell for about five minutes, and then said she didn't want to be the one to tell you. She said she couldn't stand to see your face when you found out. She asked me to do it."

"Poor girl. You know how we've been about having kids. No, of course you don't. We've both been nuts over the idea."

"Do you want me to go back up with you to Anne's room?"

"No, I'll go alone. Thanks for your help, Frank."

Peter read the license in the elevator while the cab rose slowly; Overhead traction vehicle, 10,000 pounds gross weight. . . .

The D Ward corridor seemed hazy and the forty feet down the hallway to Anne's room were unbelievably long and hard to traverse. His mind repeated to itself as he walked in the door: Overhead traction vehicle, 10,000 pounds gross weight . . . , and then he suddenly felt stupid to know that he was going to cry. He sat down at the side of Anne's bed, sorry for her that he must do it then, not wanting to hurt her in doing it. She rubbed his neck with her cool hands.

"Frank told you," she said, and after a while he lifted up his head and held her hand.

"Yes."

"God, it's awful," she said. She looked white as she squeezed his fingers. "I do love you."

"I love you, too," he said. "And I need you."

"Do you still? I don't know how you can. You can't want me."

"Of course, I do."

"He did have to do it, didn't he, Peter? I mean, could somebody else have found another way out?"

"No," Peter told her, speaking slowly and carefully. "Apparently from what Frank said anyone would have had to do the same."

"I didn't know that pregnancies could wind up so badly."

"I guess Dr. Hatch thought you might have a *tubal* pregnancy, rather than a pregnancy in the uterus where it should occur, and so decided to open you up. Instead he found endometriosis inside you at surgery. This is where there are a lot of so-called chocolate cysts around your tubes and ovaries and uterus. They're tumors of a sort and will grow and cause all kinds of trouble without being really malignant or cancerous. He doubted you could ever get pregnant again because of them, and he thought he ought to take out your uterus to save your ovaries. When you take out the uterus, the other cysts that are in the ovaries and tubes will usually go down, and also the other way around, taking out the ovaries will do the same thing for the uterine cysts, but at your age he thought it was better to take out your uterus than your ovaries, which is completely right."

"It was necessary then, but it's still terrible. I really don't want to talk about it anymore. I can't stand to."

"I know. You should rest for a while now, anyway. I'll come back later on."

At the nurses' station, Peter called Marshall Wormser's house. His sleepy voice answered the phone.

"I wanted to ask you, Marsh, about the surgery yesterday on Anne. I've talked to Frank Lewicki, but I'm still a little confused, and there are no notes on the chart to help me."

"Not much to tell, buddy. Matthew, with his usual diagnostic acumen, thought she had an ectopic pregnancy, but of course she didn't. He seemed afraid to do a D and C first, from what I could gather, but wanted to open her up right away. At surgery there was nothing but some endometriosis with implants various places, including on the uterus. I thought Matthew might trim the cysts off the ovaries, then perhaps close her up and do a D and C, but he said with the bleeding and the endometriosis, he'd better take out the uterus. I began fussing with him right then. I was shocked, I mean. It could have been the right thing to do, but I didn't think so. It seemed an awful bad choice to me. Her ovaries didn't look too much involved, and I said so. He got really mad. I mean, I don't think I ever saw him really mad before. He was in control of his voice, but it sure sounded different. He asked me to leave the 'amphitheater,' but I got stubborn and wouldn't go. He went ahead and finished, took out the uterus, and when he opened it up afterward in the utility room there was a definite early pregnancy inside."

"I'm so sick I wasn't here to get somebody else for her, Marsh."

"I didn't tell you everything. After we'd been shouting some comments back and forth, he finally said, 'Marsh, this is my decision, and you have nothing to do with it. One more word from you, though, and you're going to be through here, do you understand?' Well, of course I'd have been willing to make a federal case out of it, but there really wasn't anything I could do at that point, short of knocking him out, tearing the scalpel out of his hand, and finishing it myself, which I seriously considered for a moment. Of course, he might have been right about what he was doing. I just always expect him to be wrong, but I didn't really know, and I didn't know how to find out, so I shut up. Mad as hell, of course, and I imagine turning from red to white to blue, but I shut up. Afterward, the slimy bastard tried to jolly me up, after he'd dressed and was on his way out. 'You can go straight to hell,' I said, and walked off. So I might not have a job there after my vacation this week, but what the hell."

"I appreciate what you did, Marsh. I suppose she had an inevitable miscarriage going, so you can imagine how that makes me feel. I have to consider myself responsible for the whole thing. God, if only Silvana or Humphers could have been around."

"My friend," Marshall said, "what can I do for you? I'd like to help in some way. Do you want me to come down to the hospital? Or would you rather come out to the house and have a drink with me here?"

"No, I want to talk to Dr. Hatch first before I do anything else."

"Now take it easy. Don't do something you'll be sorry for. Maybe I better be with you when you talk to him."

"I don't know what you're so worried about. I don't intend

to shoot him. I'm not going to kill him. I'm just going to *talk* to the bastard."

"All right, already. I'll be around home all day, so come on out after a while. Come out for lunch."

"Maybe. Thanks a lot, Marsh. I really mean it."

Peter hung up the phone and went slowly through the mists still rolling in the hall, then down the staircase to the coffee room. He sat there sipping from his cup and looking out the high windows. For a moment then he could feel, deep within, sands shifting, accommodations being made, acceptances and understandings starting. He loved Anne, there was no question there. He still did. And after all they could adopt children, couldn't they?

Then all at once he felt as bad as at the first moment, like crying again, like hitting his fist through the table in front of him. They had both wanted children so much, how could they feel the same about, do the same for, be the same with, someone else's?

The gravel-spitting crunch of a car sounded outside, and through the coffee room window, in the spaces between buildings and bushes, Peter could see Dr. Hatch's long black Cadillac glide by like a canoe on a pond.

Impulsively he put down his cup and headed for the back door. He pushed through the double screen door there, but Dr. Hatch wasn't on the walk yet. Peter went on out to the parking lot. The trunk of the Cadillac was open and Dr. Hatch was inside the car, lifting camera cases off the rear seat. Peter stepped out across the gravel as Dr. Hatch settled three cases in the trunk and looked up.

"Well, hello, Peter, you're back already, are you?"

Peter found his hands shaking, and he knew he was pale. He said, "May I speak to you, Dr. Hatch?"

"Of course. I was just getting some guns and camera equipment arranged here. We're going out to Whale Lake this afternoon."

"I'm very upset."

"I know you must be." He stepped to Peter and slapped his shoulder. "It seems like everything's hitting you all at once."

"It certainly does."

Dr. Hatch exhaled his breath, looking at Peter curiously, and then slammed shut the trunk of his car. "Let's go inside and sit down in the coffee room, get a cup of java, and be comfortable."

"All right."

Peter's coffee was still sitting on the table, and he picked it up as Dr. Hatch got out his bowl and filled it, then closed the connecting kitchen door behind him, and stood by the urn, drinking noisily for a moment.

"Too damned bad, Peter," he said. "It was too bad, your fine girl friend there." He looked directly at Peter than. "She was pregnant, you know."

"I was told that, and it's medically possible, because we did have intercourse though we took precautions. I still don't understand, though, how someone who is twenty-two years old and miscarries turns up with a hysterectomy."

"Now, Peter, you know me, and you know I've always been conservative and careful about the female organs, ovaries *and* uterus. We just found a mess inside your young lady that could only be corrected by hysterectomy, in my best judgment, and believe me I took a long, hard think about everything while I was trying to make up my mind. She had serious uterine bleeding, she had uterine, tubal, and ovarian endometriosis when we looked inside. I thought we were going to find a tubal pregnancy, frankly. But instead both ovaries were clearly and deeply involved with the chocolate cysts. Take out her ovaries or her uterus, that was my dilemma. Either way she was sterilized. I think we did the right thing."

"I can't agree. I can't see any reason why she couldn't have had conservàtive surgical care. Why couldn't you just have done a D and C? At least it would have given us a chance to have a baby. Besides, you're saying she had endometriosis, and you didn't even have a frozen section to back up your impression."

"Now, listen, Peter, I know endometriosis when I see it."

"I still don't see how you could justify sterilizing a woman Anne's age with a nonfatal diagnosis. You could at least have left the uterus and one ovary in, and she could have had testosterone therapy for a while, so maybe we could have had a child or two. Why couldn't you have gotten some *competent* gynecologic advice before you went ahead?"

"Now you're being insulting. There's no other word for it." Dr. Hatch set his bowl down on the drainboard. "I think you're very disturbed now, and just not talking sense. It takes a lot of guts to practice medicine. It takes guts to make decisions like I had to on your Anne Alexio yesterday, but I do my best and my conscience is clear. I sleep well at night.

You just go on home now. When you want to come and apologize to me, and thank me for what I've done and tried to do, then I'll talk to you again. I don't want you around here working, though, until you get your mental balance. That's an order."

Dr. Hatch's voice had been soft through the conversation, but at the end it got louder and momentarily shaky. He stared at Peter, breathing heavily, then threw his paper napkin on the floor and walked out of the room, his right hand under his left coat flap, his leather heels clicking sharply down the hallway until they disappeared in the corridor to A and B Wards.

Oh, God, how I hate that man, Peter thought. Christ, if he could just *once* admit he made a mistake. If he could have admitted he made a mistake in opening Anne's abdomen and so closed her up and done a D and C, there'd be no trouble now. He can't close up a belly without taking something out, though. He's incapable of such a simple, honest act.

In some way, subtly or grossly, Peter reflected, staring at the bubbling, steaming coffee urn, I must do something about him. As his mind raced on, Peter felt excited. It was not immature, he said to himself, it was not simply anger or revenge that made him feel this way, and although excited he was thinking clearly when he decided it was necessary for someone to act against this man, and in turntable fashion, make *him* suffer.

As he went outside and walked down the sidewalk of Archer Street, reconsidering, wondering if this was some momentary insane flare inside him, more and more his notion turned dispassionate, but persevered and became determined. As he walked and thought and quieted down, the sense grew in him and seemed final and irrevocable, that he would have to take on this new responsibility.

PART THREE

24

FIVE days later, Monday, January 3rd, Peter was in the chair in Matthew Hatch's anteroom waiting to see him. Anne was better after a painful Friday and Saturday and already up and around. She was peaked but lovely, the dark swallow wings of her eyelashes outlining deep brown eyes made more vivid by the thinness and pallor of her face. She seemed happy with him, and Peter wondered if the significance of what had happened had completely unfolded to her yet. Perhaps it would later on, and there would be hell to pay then. Either that or she was just tougher than he had ever understood.

At any rate, he had made his decision about the clinic, and now he was waiting to talk to Dr. Hatch about it. Even as he sat in the anteroom with his mind made up, he felt tired, and he knew he looked tired. Besides, he was worried about the interview with Dr. Hatch. It needed to go right. He had gone over what he planned to say a dozen times to be sure it would come out as he wanted. Now as he listened to the ticking of the ornate gold clock on the corner table, his stomach felt tight. As the clock struck eleven, he heard the heel clicks start down the linoleum-decked hallway, and then Dr. Hatch was there.

"Hello, Peter," he said, motioning him into his office. "Come on in. I understood you wanted to talk to me."

"Yes, I did."

Dr. Hatch spoke to his secretary, "Would you leave us alone, please, Josie?"

She smiled at them and walked out. Dr. Hatch settled in

the chair behind his great crescentic ebony desk. "Sit down over there, Peter. Now, what's on your mind?"

"Dr. Hatch, I came here because I wanted to apologize to you. You must realize that with my father's dying, and then this trouble with Anne, I was thrown completely off base. I'm seeing things clearer now, and I feel quite bad about how I spoke to you."

"Well, Peter, I see. I'm happy you came to talk to me, and I'm not surprised. No, I'm pleased."

"I really appreciate what you did for Anne, and she's getting along fine now." He was doing it right—it was easy after all—and Matthew Hatch was going along with it, wasn't he? Peter sighed as he felt his stomach relax. It would not be hard to do what he wanted, after all, would it?

"I expected she'd do swell, Peter. And I am sorry for losing my temper with you the other day. It's not characteristic of me at all, believe me. I might say I've had some upsetting things in my own life recently, that perhaps have thrown me off balance, too."

"I wanted to tell you I would like to get back to work as soon as possible," Peter said. "I only hope you will accept my apology for the other day."

"Peter, of course. I appreciate your coming to me now. I'm sure it wasn't easy to do. I think we have a great, great future here together, and I'm pleased to have you on the job again. I had it tabbed before, just what your reaction was."

Peter stood up as the older doctor rose. "Thank you, Dr. Hatch," he said, thinking, so it was done, the strategy was working, the tactical engagement had begun.

"I think I follow your actions possibly better than you do yourself. You see, my own mother got sick and died two years ago, and I've never been so upset." He walked around his desk now, and took hold of Peter's elbow, his hand hot through Peter's coat sleeve. "I was taking care of her myself. I think if someone else had been doing it, I probably would have blown up at them just the way you did at me. Of course, it was a blood vessel thing my mother had, and not at all amenable to treatment, but I blamed myself for her death, and was off work two weeks. I couldn't see anyone without getting tears in my eyes. So I understand you, better than you realize."

Peter remembered hearing from Frank and Norman about the elder Mrs. Hatch's death. Apparently, Dr. Hatch would not admit she had died, but kept pumping blood and medicines into her body long after the life-substance had irretrievably gone out of her. Norm had said Miss West and he had had to shut off the I.V.'s, take the syringes out of his hands, and lead him out of the room finally.

"Dr. Hatch," Peter said, "I've thought a lot about my future, too, and I've about decided to go into surgery. I can stay on for a while here with you, then take off three years in San Francisco or Oakland for a surgical residency, and after that come back to the clinic."

"That would be real fine," Dr. Hatch said, smiling now. "And you know, Peter, we'd be glad to help in any plans like that. Perhaps we can have you assisting in surgery again here when Harry's away or too busy."

Peter went back to work that morning, plans in his head, and anger in his gut. I must continue to find ways to get into his confidence, to soften, to macerate his resistance, he thought, to find his vulnerable point and dig in there.

He wondered if he could carry out his scheme with his emotions so intense. Perhaps I'll get an ulcer, he thought. All that acid and bile filling my sick, disgusted stomach might erode it, or give me regional ileitis, or ulcerative colitis; or I could just wind up in the psychiatrist's hands. Maybe, too, I'll find out just how tough I am. I might as well know.

The hardest part of it all is that I can't tell Anne what I'm doing. She may guess from the way I act, how I talk to her, that there is something beyond her understanding, but she mustn't know what. She must never know why she can't have babies, that some other doctor might have been able to give us one or two or three babies, but Dr. Hatch allowed us none.

At noon he went up to Anne's room, and found her sitting up staunchly in a chair. "You look tired. Are you?" she asked at once.

"Oh, a little. I'm back at work today."

"Darling, will you close the door to the room for a minute?"

"Of course. Why, what's the matter?"

"I want to talk to you. Peter, you've been so different the last two days, and I think I understand why. I just have to get this clear." Her brown eyes darkened from the widening of her pupils as she talked.

"What do you mean I'm different?" Peter asked.

"I can see where it would be a tremendous shock to any man if he found out he couldn't have children."

"What are you getting at?"

"I know every man wants children, and might lose interest in a woman if he found out she couldn't have babies." She was talking fast now, and her voice was a little trembly. "I know you're kind, and I know how difficult it would be for you ever to tell me something that would hurt me. But please, dear Peter, I must know if you're not going to be able to love me any more because I can't have babies. Actually, it really makes sense to me. If I were in your position, I can see how I might feel that way. So please tell me, if you don't think you can marry me now, and . . ." Anne stopped, short of tears, staring at Peter.

"Oh, darling," he said, "you are foolish. I can't just stop loving you, and I won't. You mean so much to me, I couldn't ever give you up, and I don't want to. Of course, I want children. Until now, I guess I never knew how very much I did want them. But I want you more than anything, and if we have to adopt children to be satisfied, we'll do that. We'll find some fine children, and enjoy ourselves with them. I find that all I truly care about is that we can stay together. Is that clear?"

"Peter, I love you so fantastically. Give me a kiss, no, not a little one, a really big kiss. Now get out of here and let me cry."

25

PETER'S next month was agonizing: it was so hard for him to work. He tried to get back to seeing his patients, old and new, with the same old zestful donation of himself, but he knew his absent-mindedness was obvious at times. His daily encounter with Dr. Hatch in the hallway or coffee room, the flash of his car in the parking space or passing it in traffic, a glimpse of the front gate of his house when out on a call, each made his insides roll. He was acutely aware of the man's presence, his comings and goings. He did everything possible to be engaging and pleasing each time he saw him, and attempted to make every encounter in some way meaningful. Then afterward, he replayed them like phonograph records.

He wanted to seem normal, happy, adjusted to and delighted with the Hatch Clinic, but his eyes betrayed him. He could not help noticing when shaving in the mornings, or brushing his teeth in the evenings, that they looked like a zealot's, dark-shadowed, red-rimmed, and hollowed out as he lost weight.

In the middle of January a disturbing thing happened. A month or more earlier, an investigating team from the Conjoint Committee for Accrediting Hospitals, representing the National Society of Hospitals, and the National Colleges of Medicine and of Surgery, had spent several days at the Hatch Hospital. Peter had thought there was little chance of getting the approval of this official, countrywide group for the Hatch Hospital. The physical plant had some real defects and was not being maintained as it should be, but besides, the Conjoint Committee was supposedly careful about accrediting small, privately owned, so-called proprietary hospitals.

His prediction was wrong. At a special meeting the chief inspector had even told the staff of the deficiencies, histories and physicals on the charts not as good as they should be, the need for more formal hospital meetings, plus better minutes for the various hospital committees, improvements in central supply's sterilizing techniques, and so forth, but still the word came through on January 17th from Washington headquarters of the Conjoint Committee that the hospital had been accredited.

"That's depressing. It really depresses me," he told Anne, at her house that night. "God, I can't get over why they would accredit that place. I thought that was one way Hatch could be slowed up."

Anne was dressing every day and doing things around the house, but it was supposed to be two weeks more before she went back to work. She was graver now than she had been, Peter noticed, not so vivacious. "Peter, all you seem to have on your mind is Dr. Hatch," she said. "Do you realize that's all you talk about, or seem to think about?"

"Now, Anne, that's not true."

"Is there something that I should know that you haven't told me?"

"No, of course not."

"I keep thinking I have cancer or leprosy and nobody's telling me."

"Oh, darling."

"You do love me?"

"Yes, of course. You know I do."

"You haven't said so for a week. Oh, I'm sorry. Don't mind me. I just feel there's something different about you and I don't know what or why. I wonder, for instance, if Dr. Hatch really did do something wrong with me and I don't know it."

"Absolutely no, I've told you that."

"Well, I've decided on what I'm going to do, and I wanted to tell you before anyone else. As you know, they have a substitute for me at the college—they've had to get one. He's doing a good job, I hear, so I think I'll not return there next semester. I've decided instead I'll go up to Berkeley and get an apartment and start school again. I can probably just about finish the work for my master's in one semester and a summer session, and I need to do it sometime anyway."

"You don't need anything if we're going to get married."

"You'll be back in training for a few years, and not making too much. And even after you get in practice, I'm certainly not going to be home raising children."

"It is not very nice to say that."

"I'm sorry. But it's true. Peter, you must know how I love you. I couldn't imagine ever loving anyone else in the way I do you, but I'm not sure but what it's best for us if I go away. You're working hard, you have your mind on things at the hospital and clinic, you're bothered and unhappy with the Hatch setup, you're trying to decide where to go for your training, your father died, I had my trouble, and everything. You've just had too much for one person to take. I think you need more time for yourself, now; to think, I mean, and to rest, too. You're getting so thin, and you look tired all the time. I won't be too far away, and I'll come home some of the weekends."

Peter looked at her lovely face, such smooth skin there, and at her shoulders, small and delicate, and her breasts, stretching tightly against the white wool sweater she was wearing. "I'll let you go on one condition," he said.

"What's that?" she asked, watching him looking at her.

"That you'll take this with you." Peter took a box out of his pocket and opened it to show a diamond ring.

"Oh, Peter, you did get it."

"I wasn't going to give it to you until tomorrow, because

it's my mother's birthday, but all of a sudden today seems like the right day."

She put the ring on and said, "Isn't it beautiful?" and bent over to kiss him softly.

"Do you like it?"

"It's wonderful. You hadn't mentioned it, and I wasn't sure I was still going to get it."

Peter ached again then to think of what Dr. Hatch had done to them, and for a moment he wasn't sure that his love for Anne would not turn into mere pity and a wish to be kind. Perhaps it was better that she be in Berkeley for a while. Certainly an increasing amount of his time was going to be taken up by his plans anyway.

Anne moved to Berkeley as January ended, still cold, but with the rains beginning to push out the greens of the hillsides and country pasturelands. Peter was on a schedule of long hours. After Dr. Hatch indicated he was interested in help, he would often start at seven working up new patients scheduled for surgery. In the evenings he stayed more closely on call, following the post-surgical patients, studying the old charts of the hospital in the record room to which he had been allowed a key by Dr. Hatch.

Every few weekends Anne came home, and they always had dinner together and often went dancing. She had an aversion to making love at his apartment now, so on the occasional Saturdays or Sundays he could get to Berkeley, he would sometimes spend an evening or a night there with her. Once she was morose when he came, not sure she loved him anymore, she said, and thinking they should break up. Peter went back to San Marcial that night, but scarcely slept. Then she had called early, crying wretchedly, telling him she had not meant what she said, blaming her words on the martinis and wine, saying she had decided it was not fair to him to continue with her, and she had determined she should make the break, but now did not have the guts to stick with it. Then after that when she saw him she was quieter, happy-seeming when they were together, more loving and tender than ever, and more mature in her manner, like a little girl grown up overnight after her parents died. Through her torments she became more beautiful. Peter noticed how men's heads snapped around when they went in a restaurant together, and he himself just sat staring at her some nights, tongue-tied at her loveliness.

When he was not with her, Peter felt glum and witless, but

his obsession with Dr. Hatch was still with him constantly; it consumed him. Peter remembered Frank Lewicki had said one night at his house that every little good fight, each significant, if minor, social or legislative change, usually turned out to be another cleansing of the Augean stables. It had taken twenty-five years in the state of California, Frank had pointed out, to get one fair housing bill on the books and within a year the voters had knocked it out through a referendum. "Just try to change the size of one form in this hospital," Frank had said, "and listen to the moans and screams from doctors, nurses, billing girls, printers, who have you. So when you talk about trying to change some fundamental fact of medical conduct, trying to get doctors to police themselves better, to separate and straighten out the Hatches, it is like pulling teeth from a thousand rabid polar bears. Then there may be a reason for things being as they are," he had gone on. "If some doctors were given *too much* disciplining power over others there would be obvious chances for abuse. One doctor might get too popular in a community, cut into other doctors' practices, and he could be ganged up on, accused of improper methods, and closed down."

"Oh, hell," Peter had said, adamant in his idealism, "I can't believe there aren't enough good men in every medical community to help on this kind of thing if they're given a hard enough push. And the doctors have to do it themselves. They're the only ones who can spot the scurfy ones. Then they should rout them out. Look, what if you multiply Dr. Hatch by the nation. Say there are five percent bums—that's what it figures out in this county, and I expect that it's close to the national average—then it's five percent of two hundred and forty thousand doctors in this country which is twelve thousand. Twelve thousand acquisitive doctors, killing and maiming people with their bad care, that's quite a burden for the old folks at home, practically a national catastrophe, an unrecognized goddam plague. I know that perfecting the world is impossible. Improvement is always possible, though. My God, if just half those abusing doctors could be brought to terms, it would be something bigger than penicillin."

"Peter, you simply don't understand how hard it is to change anything," Frank had said, "no matter how important it might seem to you to do so. I can think of fifty things I'd like to have changed tomorrow. If I were a dictator, I would change them. But short of that, I believe devoting my life to any one of them, the simplest one of them, would accomplish nothing."

"Frank, you are a defeatist."

But since Anne's illness they had talked little. Peter talked to no one but his patients. At times he felt like a confidential agent, entrusted with great secrets, living a double life. But more often his rancor merely addled his brains and fatigued his body.

Then at the end of February, his campaign began suddenly and beautifully to pay off. First, Harry Lawson got ill. So Peter was asked to assist again, to be back where he wanted to be, across the surgical table from Dr. Hatch. After Harry was off a week with influenza, and then another few days with epididymitis, he and Peter and Matthew Hatch had a conference. It was decided, to Peter's surprise, that he would take over as Dr. Hatch's regular assistant, with Harry available for fill-in as needed.

After Anne's operation, Peter had noticed, and some of the other doctors had even mentioned, how much slower the hospital seemed, how many fewer patients Dr. Hatch had in. His surgical schedule was running half of usual. Lew Condon, the radiologist, said to Peter one day as they were looking at films on one of Dr. Hatch's patients, "I'm surprised at Matthew. This fellow with a big ulcer in the duodenum is one of those I thought Matt would certainly have operated on. Matt said absolutely not, though, he didn't think surgery was in order."

After Peter started as assistant, however, the volume of work at once burgeoned. He wondered why? What went on in that circuitous mind? He was supposed to be taking a hunting trip in August and September. Was that the reason for the pickup? Were there financial problems in the clinic? Or was he on Dexedrine pills?

Peter thought he noticed a growing excitement in Dr. Hatch as the tempo of the days increased. There was surgery after bloody surgery, so many unnecessary, with a half-dozen, then a dozen, then twenty post-operative patients in the hospital all the time. Emergency surgeries at five thirty after office hours occurred several times a week, with other surgeries, supposedly more pressing, *during* office hours. There were swarms of people in his waiting room staying hours just to see Dr. Hatch for a minute. He was the great healer at work, kidding everyone, apparently serious with no one, though the patients took in his every gesture, and slept with his every word. "Laugh your way through surgery," Peter de Haan would sing to himself. "Laughing makes your troubles incidental—you think."

The hospital became a disaster area to Peter again, a world of its own. The bleeding and hurting and dying patients he had to see and succor daily engulfed him, shut off the reality of any other life. One holocaustic day after another kept him so busy he did not have time or energy left to consider how he should advance his plans. He began to worry that now inside the gates he still might not find the way to the destruction he looked for, or that if the opening appeared, he would overlook it from fatigue or confusion.

He had never thought he could become a fanatic, but except for visits with Anne occasionally, his world became circumscribed to the examining tables, the surgeries, the patients' rooms of the Hatch Hospital and Clinic. As weeks passed and he could not find the answer to his problem, he was increasingly troubled with anxieties over his ability, only a month ago never questioned, to cut this Gordian knot. His days became feverish blurs of activity, his nights hours of work and then tossing sleep punctuated by frequent, piercing nightmares that shook him awake.

Dr. Hatch began a daily litany, repulsive to Peter but apparently exciting to the older doctor, about what a wonderful team they made together, how he had never had a better assistant, how together they could build their group into a medical organization that would rank with the great centers of the world. He began to talk of building a huge new hospital and clinic on property he owned west of town, and even spoke of the possibility of starting a medical school associated with it. "We need another medical university in this state, badly," he said, "but one that would use doctors who really practice, who know medicine from experience, to teach students the last two years. We could do it here."

Dr. Hatch was losing weight, too, apparently dieting strenuously already for his hunting trip in the fall. With his face thinner, pupils wide from the Dexedrine Peter now saw him taking daily, and also growing a heavy beard for his trip, Dr. Hatch himself looked steadily more messianic as one wild day followed another. On some long, meat-market mornings, Peter found himself so caught up in the man's own life from their constant communion that he would laugh at Dr. Hatch's joke about the poor devil whose supposed hernia he was lopping off right then, before the guilty rebound of stomach pain would stab into him a moment later.

Peter wondered if he himself were courting psychosis, but felt his awareness of this chance made it less likely, though in any event he could not find room in his busy thoughts for concern over the possibility.

Long, worried letters came from his mother asking for more information about him, wondering why he wrote so little, but most of these he did not answer, sparing himself no time for activities external to his central one. Instead he gave her several minutes of reassurance by phone every few weeks. Anne, too, continued to complain about his vagueness and vacancy of manner still, his less frequent trips to Berkeley, his haggardness and irritability with her. When he visited her, she cooked his favorite dishes, and dressed with special care in the clothes and even negligees he particularly liked, in efforts to shake his apathy. But he could not share his present world with her, and could not loosen his concentration on it for her. He often left her seeming petulant or gloomy or even angry, and this added to his concerns. He loved her, but his usual feelings were blocked off now, his love along with the others.

He plunged ever more devotedly into the hospital work. The post-operative care Dr. Hatch left almost entirely to Peter now, really seeming to enjoy the role of the great white surgeon who only had to take out an occasional suture, or open the odd stitch abscess, but in general did not soil his hands or dilute down his talents for such lesser duties, saving himself instead for the great masterful exercises in the surgical amphitheater for which he was so supremely able. Peter made early rounds, and then afterward, later on in the mornings, they made rounds together, Dr. Hatch like a general at the head of an inspection party with Miss West and two floor nurses usually trailing. He kidded and wisecracked mercilessly with the patients, but gave clear indication of the preciousness of his time by the speed with which he traveled. His prestige with patients was such that every word he spoke to them was at once solidified and retained, as if it had been handed out in metal type. His few flippant words would be passed back and forth by the patient to his nurses, visitors, to other patients, other doctors. They would gradually be stretched by the patient to compose a complete up-to-the-minute analysis of his case and its progress so far. Granted a certain aptness and pithiness to Dr. Hatch's comments, it was still annoying to Peter when patients retained nothing of his careful explanations, but kept the Hatch utterances engrained on their brains.

Peter did not mind his subordinate role, though. At least with him watching everything, the patients got no more castor oil when they had abdominal ileus with vomiting, no pint after pint of unnecessary blood transfusions, no diet orders for general trays three days after a gastrectomy, no wild orders for intravenous fluids, like saline solutions for cardiacs, and heavy potassium dosages for Addisonians. The routine ordering of penicillin, streptomycin and Chloromycetin on all patients after surgery was stopped his first day as assistant. Peter could see that the patients prospered under his care, and this was at least one consolation in the midst of his general torment. For Dr. Hatch's abuses continued and were terribly wearing.

There were so many times when Peter could not slow his vengeful hand, and unnecessary herniorrhaphies in eighty-year-olds resulted, healthy uteruses were scooped out, hemorrhoids removed because one drop of blood had been passed, and every last little knob of cystic mastitis was taken from breasts scarcely mature. Cancer was cut from abdomens like ambergris being chopped out of dead sperm whales, and the patients returned to their rooms at times literally dripping blood on the floor with Dr. Hatch's steamroller approach to the surgical treatment of malignancies, the madman slashing of livers and intestines; the poor people would sometimes die three, four, six hours after surgery, sapping Peter's strength and time to even get them to last that long. Dr. Hatch would tell the family in the corridor, "Maybe this is the best way. Perhaps God was showing his mercy. There was no hope. The cancer was spread everywhere." Peter knew these patients, with chemotherapy and X-ray treatment and luck and good care and no surgery, might have at least had a decent year or two with their families.

With many of these cases, Peter, even scheming to outmaneuver or outtalk Matthew Hatch, simply could do nothing. There was a blank wall put into place suddenly if he went too far, as one night when he had not wanted a seven-year-old boy opened up for acute appendicitis because he thought he was merely homesick and constipated. Dr. Hatch had turned away from Peter in the middle of a sentence, picked up and carried the boy in his own arms directly to surgery, waiting solemnly there for the operation to start, for the boy to be saved by his hand. The next morning over the operating table there had been no mention of the incident. Dr. Hatch instead had gone into his usual glowing report to the operating room nurses of how helpful Peter was being to him.

So Peter worked and worried, watched and waited, eyes burning, stomach aflame, until finally his patience gained its end.

26

PETER came out of the Hatch Hospital back door late one night in April tired, excited, thrilled in a cold and deadly way from the discovery of that evening. An hour before, he had rushed away from the autopsy table to go through all the records on the patient he had just seen dissected by Dr. Joe Parmelee. He had asked the night girl in the office to photostat the man's complete chart for him before morning. "A case I might report," he told the girl. "I'll be in at six A.M. to pick up the copies."

As he settled in his car cushions, he said to himself, "This is it, isn't it? This *is* it." In his strange and unnatural mental state—exhausted but alert, apprehensive but resigned—he heard the chimes in the belfry of the Methodist church gong out twelve muted, shimmering sounds as he went down the gravel drive past the records building and out onto Liberty Street. Did the stroke of midnight coming now have some special meaning, he wondered. Was it an omen? Or was it just twelve o'clock Pacific Standard Time and he was going nuts?

He had heard of the success syndrome, where the striving executive finally got the vice-presidency he had been trying for the past fifteen years and promptly shot himself. There was always a measure of discouragement in reaching one's goal. Why should he think he had gotten anywhere yet, though, and feel let down? Simply because he thought he had found the patient, the case, he could hang Dr. Hatch on, didn't mean that tomorrow morning, next week, in a month, it would not all blow up in his face. The first lawyer he went to might laugh in his face, explain how stupid he was being, show him the obvious holes in the matter that any half-assed legal mind could use to attack and destroy it all.

Peter sped abstractedly home. He undressed slowly in his apartment, thinking back over the case which had suddenly become the focus of his soul. Four days before Mr. Louis Corti, a thirty-two-year-old building contractor and father of three, had been admitted directly to the hospital from the office by Matthew Hatch. He had been in quite severe abdominal pain, and the clinical impression was acute cholecystitis, which meant acute infection of the gallbladder. Immediate surgery was scheduled by Dr. Hatch, and at the end of his office hours on this Monday, April 4th, he came over, scrubbed, and with Peter as his assistant began the operation at five thirty.

Peter had had no chance to see this man beforehand, but as usual was at once wondering what pathology if any would really be uncovered instead of Dr. Hatch's prediction. Exploration did show unquestionable inflammation of the gallbladder, though, with many gray, slimy, multifaceted stones in the organ. Dr. Hatch was quick in his dissection and removal of the scarred-down gallbladder. Peter by this time more secure in his relationship with Dr. Hatch, and with a profound continuing distrust of the man's every move medically, had often been able to slow down his excessive speed, or gotten him to decide against too radical resection of a stomach or against taking out a perfectly harmless, adhesed or scarred segment of colon.

Again this early evening of April, Peter urged Dr. Hatch to go more slowly, saying, "Give me time to catch these bleeders, please, Doctor." But a meeting was in the offing; Dr. Hatch was talking to a women's club that night about his travels, so Peter could not get him to reduce his frantic pace. His usual gallbladder took close to an hour. This one was finished in an unbelievable thirty-three minutes, and was harder than most. Putting the last stitches in the abdomen, Dr. Hatch asked Peter to dress the wound, saying, "I'm almost late now. Have to pick up my slides downtown at Jermin's, too. They're waiting for me. So you write the orders for me, please, Peter. I'm sure he'll be all right. He's a tough, healthy young guy, a building contractor. Tells me he's building six houses at once right now and two stores. Might even get him to work on a new suite for us in a year or two. See you later." He was away from the table then and off on the run, slapping the ancient surgery nurse's behind as he left the suite.

Louis Corti did well overnight. Peter liked the handsome young Italian at once, when he could talk after surgery, because even sick and in pain, he managed a big smile with impressive, pearly teeth, brushing back his black hair with the thick rough hand of a carpenter to say, "I'm here to get well, so whatever you say goes, Doc, except please no enemas, huh? I mean if I have to okay, but otherwise please no enemas, all right? Aside from that, I'm your pigeon."

Peter laughed "Did my eyes shine as if they had the thought of enemas flashing behind them, Mr. Corti? By the way, my name is de Haan, Dr. de Haan, in case you don't remember."

"I know you, Doc. But call me Lou. When you say Mr. Corti, I think you mean my father. No, listen, I've heard about you already. You took care of my wife's aunt, Mrs. Allende. She says you saved her life, and brought her through after she had her operation. As a matter of fact she brought me here when I got sick. My wife Peggy—she used to be Peggy Bassi, maybe you know the Bassis—was shook anyway, and she didn't have anybody to leave the kids with."

"How many children do you have?"

He smiled again, once more showing the alabaster teeth. "Three, Doc, but with good Catholics like us, I guess there'll be four before long."

"Well, I hope so."

"My father-in-law says I'm going to have to sleep over the garage if there's any more. He's such a character, though, he might be kidding."

"I won't make any comment, because the doctor who cracks jokes on the first post-op day takes a chance of breaking his patient's stitches, which doesn't go over good with anybody."

Lou Corti tried to laugh, and moaned instead. "I get what you mean," he said, as he leaned back and settled down while Peter gently palpated and percussed his bandaged belly, and checked the bile draining into the plastic bag from his abdominal T-tube.

As he listened to his lungs, Lou Corti asked him, "How many stones did I have?"

"Shh, just a minute. There. Oh, seven or eight. Do you want them?"

"What do you mean, do I want them?"

"Some people like to take them home in a bottle. Or put them on a watch chain, or something."

"Not me. I want to forget them. Say, who's the night nurse on this floor?"

"Mrs. Harris was on last night, I think."

"Say, she's a doll. She's wonderful. Good doctors and good nurses, how can I go wrong? Don't smile, Doc, I mean it."

That evening Lou Corti was doing perfectly well, but the next morning he felt nauseated and had a fever of 100. "Just don't feel good today, Doc. I guess the operation's catching up with me."

"I think so. You had a much better first day yesterday than usual, so I'm not surprised. Is your pain bothering you much?"

"Not too bad. All I can say is that I feel crummy, period."

"I'll come back this evening and check on you, but meanwhile I'd concentrate on fluids and just skip any solids, I mean even the custard and Jell-O."

"I will. If we were mixing concrete, I might put in my two cents, but you're the boss here."

Peter was late getting to Lou Corti's room that night, and when he did he found his temperature up over 101.5, and the patient feeling even worse, though still unable to give any localizing symptoms.

"Lou, how's the abdominal pain?"

"Well, of course there is some, Doc, in the right side where I got cut, but whether it's more than you'd expect, I don't know."

"Let's see what time it is. After eight. I guess I better break the lab man out, Lou, and get some blood work and a urine done on you just to be sure. We'll give you some antibiotics, too, in case you might be getting any infection in the gallbladder bed, or in the small biliary radicles. These are tiny bile ducts that thread up into the liver from the big common bile duct that connects with the gallbladder. When you get those smaller ducts infected, it's called a cholangitis."

"Colingitis, or schmolingitis, whatever it is, Doc, fix it up, please, and I'll be happy, because I feel lousy."

"Lou, just to check again, your chart indicates no allergies to drugs. Can you take all the antibiotics for infection, penicillin, the mycins, the sulfa drugs, all the rest?"

"I think so. I got penicillin in the Army for pneumonia, and Dr. Hatch always orders it for me when I get a cold. Only thing I'm allergic to is work—and enemas, right, Doc?"

Checking with the lab man in an hour, Peter found him rushing around anxious to finish his evening's work.

"What's the hurry, Steve?" he asked.

"I like to watch the Gordon Griffin show, and it's on at nine thirty tonight."

Peter realized that he had not seen a television show since he was home at Christmas. He lived in a world apart from television, too.

"Here's the blood count on Corti, Dr. de Haan," Steve said. "The white count is up a little, that's all. I have the urine cultures going, but there wasn't much in the microscopic of the urine. I think the serum looks a little icteric, though. Is he jaundiced?"

"I haven't noticed it. Was there bile in the urine?"

"I didn't check for that, and I threw the specimen out already."

"Well, we'll do it tomorrow."

"I could get another spec and do it tonight, Doc, but I did want to catch Gordon Griffin."

"Okay, already, Gordon Griffin," he said and Steve laughed.

Peter walked back up to Lou Corti's room to look at his eyeballs. "You asleep, Lou?" he asked.

"No, Doc, hell, no. What's the matter?"

"Nothing. I just want to look in your eyes. Don't turn on your light. I'll just use my pocket flash." Peter shone his beam at Lou Corti's eyes. There was no yellow.

"What's going on, Doc? Something wrong?"

"No, just checking something. See you in the morning."

It was a sleepless night for Peter, one in a succession of them. A few hours of rest, then awake for an hour, then a few more hours of rest. He dragged himself out of bed at six, still worried about Lou Corti and his others. After a cup of quickly brewed coffee, he hesitated, then finally, for the second time in a week, took a Dexedrine tablet. He did not want to get into the Matthew Hatch category of six or eight of these tablets a day, but it did not seem unreasonable to take just one of the pills occasionally to get his feet tracking in a straight line.

At the hospital before seven, he saw a pre-op patient quickly, then stopped by Lou Corti's bed. He was awake and smiled, but Peter saw he was chilling. "You're shaking, Lou," he said. "Do you feel bad?"

"I think the problem is they're spiking my water here in

the hospital, Doc. I feel like I've got a first-class hangover, and the flu at the same time. Could that be my trouble?"

Peter smiled at the nervy young builder. "It would be unusual. Let's see what your temperature is." He put a thermometer in his mouth and checked his pulse. It felt weaker, surprisingly weaker. Peter then took Lou Corti's blood pressure. He frowned at that and pulled the thermometer out. It registered 103.5.

"Your fever's higher this morning, Lou. We'll have to use some different antibiotics."

"Nothing by mouth, Doc. I couldn't keep it down."

"We'll give them as shots."

After the morning surgeries Peter begged off making rounds with Dr. Hatch and went straight to the laboratory. Steve saw him come in and stood up. "Dr. de Haan," he said, "your man Corti's got a crazy white count this morning. The total's only seventy-seven hundred but there are thirty-nine percent segs., thirty-four percent stabs, two percent juveniles and two percent myelocytes, plus twenty-three percent lymphs. He couldn't be getting a leukemia, could he?"

"It must be some acute infection. I don't know from what, though. I don't know where it is."

"His bilirubin's elevated a little at two point four. I didn't get any bile in his urine, but there is some albumin. His amylase was normal at eighty."

"Normal amylase, huh. Well, that rules out his pancreas. Okay, Steve, thanks." Peter picked up the telephone and put in a call for Norman Silvana. His nurse answered.

"Hello, Mrs. Prock, this is Dr. de Haan. Is Dr. Silvana there? Well, will you ask him to see a patient for me in consultation? Louis Corti, on D Ward, the surgery ward, Room Two twenty-two, the first bed. Wait a minute, you better say that Dr. Hatch *and* I want him to see the patient. That's right. And ask him if he'd see him as soon as possible."

Exactly at noontime, Norman Silvana called Peter. "I was just seeing your patient, Corti, Peter. Can you come over?"

On the ward, Peter found Norman Silvana, black and handsome as ever, scowling over Lou Corti's chart. "This guy's really sick, Peter. You've got to get going on him right away. I can scarcely catch a pressure on him over fifty. His fever's about one hundred four. And he just mumbles and rambles, nothing coherent at all."

"Why the hell didn't the nurses tell me? I asked them to

take his pressure every half hour and let me know if there was any change."

"It's been below eighty on the last two checks on the chart."

"It's that dumb Dora that's relieving today, Bickerson. She doesn't know her ass."

"Anyway, you sure need blood cultures, and urine cultures, and every antibiotic you can think of, I.M. and I.V. This could be the cold shock of a gram-negative bacteria. I'm not sure."

"I think he might be having infection in his bile ducts."

"Cholangitis, sure, that's one of the possibilities. But when I examined him, I felt there was a mass in his right upper quadrant. More than just the ordinary post-operative mass. I don't know if it's liver, or just what. I'm sure it's not feces."

"He did seem to be tender there."

"I think you have to consider a peritonitis due to bile, too—they're wicked—and also an abscess collection on the right side there above the liver and below the diaphragm. But also there may be something causing serious liver damage with acute necrosis and death of the liver." He moved closer to Peter and said sotto voce, "You know this crazy Hatch. You can't ever tell what could have happened to his patients."

"I'll get going right away, Norman. I had better tell his wife how damned sick he is, too."

"Incidentally, Pete, I think he's going to need his abdomen opened again. So tell the hound of the Baskervilles and watch him pounce." Norman laughed softly at his own joke as he left.

Peter inserted an intravenous catheter into Lou Corti. The man who even that morning had seemed lively in spirit although ill now roused only intermittently to the ministrations. The drip of antibiotics for infection and Levophed for blood pressure elevation began into the bloodstream of the patient through the slender tube in his right arm vein. The crystalline glucose solution in the hanging bottle was yellowed by Terramycin, while white penicillin and amber Chloromycetin were pumped into his buttocks. When his blood pressure failed to rise, oxygen by nasal cannula was begun, and hydrocortisone was injected directly into the tubing leading in the vein for fast effect.

In half an hour, Lou Corti's vital signs were improved, and Peter left to call Mrs. Corti. She was obviously stunned by

Peter's message. As he was explaining her husband's fresh difficulties, Peter watched a bounding Matthew Hatch go past him and into the patient's room. "Fine, Mrs. Corti," Peter said finally, "I'm glad you're able to come right over. You definitely should."

Peter walked back to the bedside, anger at Matthew Hatch flooding him again. Somehow the bastard had caused this, hadn't he, but how? What had happened? The surgery went all right, but it was too fast. He couldn't slow Dr. Hatch down that afternoon. Or was this case just an example of the bad fortune everyone on occasion had in medicine, something gone wrong that no one could have foreseen or prevented. Peter shook his head, uncertain, pushing down for the moment his instinctive, hopping hatred of the slimy substance that he conceived to be Matthew Hatch's soul to which nothing seemed to matter but its own gratification.

Peter had concluded recently that Dr. Hatch had more understanding of the nature of his own actions than he had previously suspected. This view followed the visit to the clinic of Dr. Hatch's sister, a tall attractive matron from Illinois. Dr. Hatch had worked her up for arthritis, then had Frank Lewicki see her too, and Peter had overheard their conversation about her in the hallway one day.

Dr. Hatch had asked, "You think she's definitely got arthritis, then, in her elbows and hands?"

"I think so. Arthritis is a loose term, of course. I'd say it's mostly hypertrophic osteoarthritis, but there could be some rheumatoid, too. They'll definitely occur together, and she may have both. But no serious rheumatoid disease."

"Tell me, what do you think of intravenous hydrocortisone, you know, with Pyramidon or the salicylates added to it, say three times a week for a few weeks or months? I mean, this is my sister I want to treat and I like to be sure. I've heard there were side effects to this kind of therapy."

Frank's face had flushed and he had muttered, "Oh, I think something like aspirin or even Butazolidin by mouth would give better long-term results." Then when Matthew had gone, Frank had blown up to Peter. "Why, that son of a bitch. He's given everyone and his dog cortisone in the vein with salicylates and that screwy Pyramidon added to it for years, and we all screamed at him about the side effects. He happens to charge eleven dollars and ninety cents a shot for it, see? Now all of a sudden, though, he wonders if it's the right thing to use, which it isn't, when it's his own *sister* involved. The hypocritical bastard."

Peter had decided then that Matthew Hatch must have considerable awareness of that dark, bloody, really nonschizoid heart of his, and had hated him triply for every speck of insight he might possess. There was such a thing as double-think, but it wasn't all double-think with Dr. Hatch.

Walking into Lou Corti's room, Peter found his fists tightening defensively. Without looking up, Dr. Hatch said, "Peter, this looks bad here. There's some toxic manifestation in this young man, possibly from the anesthetic combination used, or maybe infection. I don't believe there's any surgical problem at all, though, and in any event he's much too ill to be opened up again."

Peter's fingernails pressed into his palms. "I don't agree. I think there's enough chance of a subdiaphragmatic abscess, or inflammatory process in the gallbladder bed, or even in the pancreas, that exploratory surgery is in order right now."

Matthew Hatch straightened up now and looked over at Peter in surprise, his face tightening in irritation and calculation. Peter watched his discus-thrower's hand duck under the cover of his coat and begin a torturous rubbing and probing process there over the apex of his heart. He spoke softly and calmly. "I don't think you've seen quite as many of these cases as I have, Peter, and I'm saying that this man should not have a surgical investigation now. I've always found in a situation like this where infection's a problem you need antibiotics and more antibiotics until you find the one that works."

Bullshit, thought Peter. "I disagree strongly as I've indicated. I asked Norm Silvana to look at him, too, and he agrees with what I've said, or perhaps I should say, I agree with him."

"Is that right?" Matthew Hatch said. "You didn't even consult me. Why wasn't I told about this situation earlier, Peter? I think I should have been, don't you?" His speech sank to near inaudibility, and he laughed a little, but Peter caught the anger behind the soft words and the smiling face.

Peter coughed thoughtfully but said nothing. Matthew Hatch resumed talking, louder now, apparently interpreting Peter's silence as evidence of intimidation. "Let's get Norman over here and thrash this out." He turned to the nurse in the room. "Call Dr. Silvana and ask him to come right over. And I want a full-time top-notch special on with this boy all the time. Please tell Miss West to see that this is done." Dr. Hatch pushed the partially detached bandage back from the wound and felt Lou Corti's abdomen again, then covered him up.

Norman met them a few minutes later in the hallway. Peter was standing silently. Dr. Hatch had the chart in his hand and was reading it, scribbling notes on it here and there. Norman started off the conversation without any pleasantries in typical Silvana style. "This boy has to be operated on, Matt," he said.

"It'll kill him to do that," Dr. Hatch said firmly and rather loudly.

"Oh, come on now, Matthew, he's certainly going to die if you don't find something at surgery you can fix."

Dr. Hatch spoke even louder, warming up to the fight. "I admit that his trouble here might be toxicity from the anesthetic mixture—don't smile, Norman, I definitely do see this—with widespread oozing in places from capillaries damaged by the anesthetic. Of course, I do admit that this could be simply a case of hepatorenal syndrome, acute, severe, and I've never known anyone to do anything for them. They get better or they don't. But to operate on someone with a hepatorenal syndrome is like turning a wind machine on a fire."

Dr. Hatch looked pleased with his metaphor, but Norman was staring him straight in the face impassively. "You don't seem to get the picture, Matt. Why kid ourselves? You don't know and I don't know what's wrong with this fellow. I think something is wrong with his liver, frankly, acute liver damage, acute yellow atrophy, but if there is an abscess in there, then surgery could conceivably offer him something."

Matthew Hatch's face lost its brief glow of enjoyment and hardened back into annoyance as Norman talked. "Let me tell you, just blow one whiff of nitrous oxide in the left ear of this man," Dr. Hatch said then, "and he'll go out like a light. Surgery on him now would be homicide, and I won't permit it. You needn't say anything more to me." His voice was angry, and then it relaxed as he checked himself. "I've always found, Norman, that I follow my consultants' opinions just so far, and then I'm strictly on my own. You must remember I've been in this business a long time, and I've seen a lot of cases, for many more years than you—"

Norman stepped a little closer at this moment and put his face directly in front of Dr. Hatch's. "Listen, Matt, this guy might have an abscess in his abdomen that could have ruptured. If it could be cleaned out, his life might be saved. Supposing his liver is being damaged. Why? It might be from some adhesion, some inflammation or injury interfering with the circulation to the liver. If this could be relieved, it might help the situation tremendously."

"I think some blood might help him," Matthew suggested. "His shock might be from hemorrhage, from blood or fluid loss."

"Blood probably wouldn't hurt him, but he needs more than that," Norman insisted. "This isn't the shock of hemorrhage. With hemorrhagic shock you get *wet* skin, but his is dry, and the hematocrit and hemoglobin would at least go down a little, if not a lot, but his are actually going *up*. This is the cold shock of toxicity, possibly of gram-negative infection."

"I've always found there are a few practical things you have to think of, too, Norm. For instance, sometimes you don't do things because of the medico-legal situation. If you operated on this boy, he'd die right on the table and that sort of thing scares me. You might find yourself right in the middle of a suit."

"I've given you my opinion. If you don't want to pay any attention to it, that's your problem." Norman's face was flushed and his speech was slurring with his own anger.

Matthew Hatch smiled, then laughed, and put his hand on Norman Silvana's shoulder. "Norm, I respect your opinion. I just override it this time, but I probably won't the next. But you don't feel blood can hurt, and I say blood is a good thing, so we're going to give him some more blood, plenty of antibiotics, and I think you may find this boy will surprise us."

Norman Silvana sighed and shrugged his shoulders. "Just do it your way, then, Matt, and leave me out of it." He turned on his heel and walked off.

Matthew smiled again, inhaled deeply and looked around at some footsteps behind him which were those of an aide from the floor.

"Dr. Hatch?" she said.

"Yes, Millie, what is it?" he asked pleasantly, with no trace of upset in his voice any longer.

"Mrs. Corti is here." She was waiting down the corridor, dark and pretty, pale, frightened-looking, with swollen lids above high, smooth cheekbones. She wore a brown fur coat and a blue scarf over her head. Holding her self-possession with an obvious effort, she nodded and smiled fleetingly at each doctor.

"Dr. Hatch," she said, "what is wrong? Is he going to be all right?"

"He's awful sick, Peggy. I don't know if we can pull him through this."

"Is it really that bad?" she asked tonelessly.

"I frankly don't think he'll make the grade."

"I can't believe it, I can't believe you're saying that. It's impossible, it seems so unreal, I mean. He's going to die?"

"I think he will."

"I want to see him. May I see him?"

"You can, though he's not really conscious."

"I want to go in."

"I have an emergency in the office, Peggy, but Dr. de Haan can take you."

As she moved, Mrs. Corti swayed a little, and Peter steadied her with a hand under her elbow.

"Has the priest been called?" she asked.

"No, but I'll see to it right away."

"Please, Father McLaughlin of St. John's Church if you can get him."

"I'll try," Peter said as he guided her down the hall to her husband's room.

"Wait a minute," he asked, going in the room before her. Lou Corti was lying quietly, his black curling hair vivid against his pillow. His hands and arms were as cold as if they had been iced. Frigid sweat spotted his face and chest, and gathered in the trough at the V of his neck like rainwater in a ditch.

"How's his pressure?" Peter asked the special nurse.

"Very poor, Doctor. I can hardly get it."

"His wife's outside in the hall. I'm going to bring her in."

"I've just noticed, Doctor, that he has begun to breathe irregularly, as if he's Cheyne-Stoking."

"An aminophylline suppository might help him."

"I'm really afraid to leave him, Doctor."

"I'll bring his wife in and then get one for you."

"Is the blood going fast enough?"

"Oh, that's started already? He doesn't need it, anyway, but that's why his pressure's lower. He still has to have the Levophed, you see, and there's none in the blood. There's an ampul of Levophed on the dresser. Just add that directly to the blood. Take the needle out of the stopper and stick it in through the same hole."

Peter leaned out the door and called to Mrs. Corti. She came in slowly and fearfully, but went straight toward the bedside and grasped her husband's hand. "Lou, can you hear me?" she asked softly. She put her head down by his, and then turned to kiss his cheek. "Lou, it's Peggy," she said louder, and he moaned a little. "Open your eyes and look at me. You're going to be all right." She wobbled his head gently, and his eyes opened with a momentary focus as he said, "Oh, Peggy." The lids rolled shut again, and he moaned, but made no other response to her pleadings and kisses.

Peter stepped down the hallway for the suppository, and was quickly back in the room. Mrs. Corti was sitting in a chair pulled up to the bedside now, her eyes closed too, holding her husband's hand.

"Let her have a few minutes with him," Peter whispered to the nurse. "And then you can insert this. I think she should stay in the hospital, so tell her that, will you?"

Two hours later, at the end of his office hours, Peter came back to find Peggy Corti in the same chair, her coat still on, her husband's hand still in hers. The P.M. nurse, a Mrs. Thollander, was on duty now, and she spoke at once. "I was just going to call you, Doctor. The patient started a chill a few minutes ago." She pulled out a rectal thermometer, wiped it, looked at it, and handed it to Peter. It read 106 degrees. Peter glanced down at Peggy Corti as she stared up at him with wondering eyes.

"Will you come outside with me for a minute, Mrs. Corti?"

In the corridor Peter said to her, "Your husband's doing very poorly, and I'm concerned as to whether he'll make it through the night. I wanted to be sure everyone in the family realized just how bad he was in case they would like to see him, or just so they would know."

"That's what Father McLaughlin said, too, so my sister was going to call everyone. His mother died, of course, but his father should know, and his sister."

"He's getting worse, weaker. His fever's very high. The last reading is a hundred and six degrees." Peter felt angry at the situation, sorry for this woman, defeated and impotent in trying to find a way to save this man from dying.

"Oh, God, I don't know what I'll do if something happens to him," Mrs. Corti moaned, her eyes dripping huge tears.

Peter walked off to get her a Kleenex from the utility cupboard. When he got back she was quiet, calmer.

"You should have somebody here with you," Peter said, looking at the black streaks of mascara on her cheeks.

"I'll call my sister. She can come over, Doctor. Thank you for being so kind. I know that you're doing everything you can."

Peter ate mechanically through the small supper he had the kitchen serve him in the coffee room, and then spent the evening going in and out of the Corti room. At seven thirty the patient became restless and began calling out incoherently. For a while he needed three or four aides to restrain him. Then he had a sharp, shaking chill again, and lapsed into coma and unresponsiveness at ten. It was a chiaroscuro night for Peter after that, remembered in all shades of black and white and gray as he was sleeping and waking, up and down, exposed to brief visions of the Corti room with whispering nurses while he adjusted tubes, took blood pressures, started and restarted I.V.'s, then slept and awakened and repeated the same things. Peggy Corti stayed through the night, with four or five of the family centered in the day room at the end of the corridor taking turns with her at sitting in the room.

At eight in the morning Lou Corti had a major convulsive seizure. Peter got Peggy Corti and the family into the hallway, intubated the patient, and kept him breathing through the tube until the sudden cessation of heartbeats a half hour later. Peter stood for a moment in the center of the room thinking about the family outside. It was so hard to measure the intensity of grief. Lou Corti's sister had cried, moaned, screamed in the room. Except at the very first, Peggy Corti had been quiet, perceiving, mostly dry-eyed, greeting everyone politely. His father had been impassive. How should he tell them now? Who would be best to tell first? They were all waiting in the hallway, though, and Peter told them together. The Corti sister dropped forward in a swoon with a sharp crack that made him afraid she had broken her kneecaps. Two of the younger men carried her down to the day room. Peggy Corti went in by the bed, and kissed her husband's forehead a last time before leaving. Matthew Hatch arrived while she was still in the room and she squeezed his hand and thanked him. Peter listened, nauseated, while Dr. Hatch gave his usual speech. "We did everything we could for him, Peggy, and you did, too, but nothing could have helped this time. It was quick for him, though, and there wasn't much suffering." Peter fought the hostile hot burning in his stomach pit. "Even at surgery I could tell there was something terribly wrong with his tissues, and frankly I'm convinced that we were dealing with an early cancer. Call it an old doctor's intuition. Of course, we talked yesterday about opening him up again, but he just seemed too sick. I don't think he could have gotten through even the mildest anesthetic."

"Do you think another examination now would help you to understand what happened to him better, Dr. Hatch?" Peggy Corti asked. "Would it help you for medical science or for your other patients?"

"I don't think so, Peggy. We understood things very well as it was. We knew that there was severe overwhelming infection after a badly infected gallbladder. And then liver and kidney failure following this. And as I say, malignancy, early, might be behind it all."

How smart he was, Peter thought. Take the ignorant people and kill off their relatives, and just breathe the word cancer, the word stroke, the words heart attack or kidney failure, and everything was explained. They could tell the friends, the other relatives, the lodge fellows and the vestry members and their neighbors, it was a heart attack after stomach surgery, it was a hemorrhage, it was cancer all over, possibly leukemia, and so it became understandable, and errors in judgment, mistakes in management were neatly covered up. Peter had seen it so many times with the families of Dr. Hatch's patients. It worked so smoothly. No one wanted to believe, few people could stand to believe, the monstrous horror that a husband, wife, father, daughter, son could have died from medical carelessness or incompetence.

As George Bernard Shaw had said, Death was a way to raise the prestige of a doctor. If important people died under his care, he came in for a great deal of attention and comment, and invariably his practice increased. If he's good enough for Mr. Moneybags, or Mr. Politician, who died last month, he should be good enough for me, would be the way the thinking would go. People were crazy, crazy-thinkers, unpredictable, hard to understand.

Matthew finally left with a shake of his large head, his hair long in back now like the mane of a lion. Peggy Corti started to leave herself, and then fell against Peter's breast, her hands on his shoulders, sobbing, "I can't hold back any longer."

"Don't try to," Peter said. "It'll be good for you to cry."

"I just can't go home and face the kids."

"Maybe I can get you something to help."

She drew back and blew her nose. "I don't want any medicine to put me to sleep."

"Well, come downstairs and sit with me in the lobby for a minute. I want to ask you something anyway."

"What is it? Why can't you ask me now?"

"Let's go down first."

She looked back once more at the now covered body of her husband, and then cried again in the elevator as it descended. In the lobby, she sat down, leaning forward on the lounge with her head in her hands, sobbing noiselessly.

"Mrs. Corti?"

"Yes?" she said in a minute.

"I would like to get permission from you for an autopsy on your husband to try to determine the cause of death more accurately. It would be a great help to us, I believe."

She looked at him. "But I asked Dr. Hatch, and he didn't think it would be necessary."

"I heard what he said, but . . ." Peter hesitated, "I think he was just thinking of your feelings. I'm sure he really wanted the examination, but hated to put you through any more suffering."

"He is the finest man, isn't he? You could just tell how bad he felt. I've never seen him look so sad. I'm sure he had tears in his eyes when he talked to me. It must be hard on him to do such great work and then have these kinds of things happen. At any rate, I know we couldn't have had a better doctor for Lou. Maybe what you say is true, though. I can understand how he might want the examination but wouldn't want to hurt me or upset me to get it."

"That's the situation."

"No," she said, quite alert, "I have no objection. I know Lou wouldn't have minded either. In the past he even said if something happened to him and medical science could use his eyes, or his heart, or his body, for anything, he'd want them to do it."

"You'll have to sign a paper to approve this."

"I'd want to know exactly what you find, no matter what it is."

"Of course. You understand it takes a few weeks for slides to be made and all, before there's a final report, but preliminary diagnosis and report is made right away."

"Just so I know everything when you find it out."

"Fine. I'll go get the paper for you to sign, and I'm going to have the nurse bring you a very mild sedative." On his way to the emergency room to get an autopsy permission slip, Peter saw the hearse coming in the back alley, and hurried to get his paper signed before they left with the body. He got to Lou Corti's room with it just as the two morticians were lifting him on their stretcher. "I'm Dr. de Haan," Peter said to the older man, very stout and red-faced. "I just had the wife, Mrs. Corti, sign this slip for a postmortem and wanted to give it to you."

"Is that right?" said the man, puffing heavily with his exertion. "I'm Doug Reddleman, Doctor, of Reddleman Brothers Funeral Home." He put out a beefy hand with a red liver palm, smelling of whiskey as he exhaled. "I don't think I've met you before, Doc. We like to cooperate on all these cases. When will you do the autopsy?"

"I'll call Dr. Parmelee and probably he'll do it late this afternoon or tonight."

"I was sure surprised about young Lou here. Him and his dad used to go hunting with me when he was a kid. Best bird shot I ever saw for a boy his age. Of course, we take care of all the Corti family and the Bassi family, too, when any of them passes away. But, boy, I was surprised about young Louie. I was talking to him not more than three weeks ago. He told me he had almost a half a million dollars of contracts under way. It's too damned bad."

"It sure is," Peter said.

27

THAT evening Peter was sidestepping caskets and cadavers to get to the hideaway room in Reddleman's Funeral Home's basement where autopsies were done. There was a door of wickerwork and opaque glass to go through, and then a brightly lighted, low-ceilinged interior whose gray walls were swept by the arcing blast of a noisy old black fan overhead.

Dr. Joe Parmelee, bow tie and all, was there already,

donning the prosector's rubber apron as Peter walked in. The small black suitcase of the autopsy surgeon lay open on the wooden sink exposing its large dissecting knives, big enough to carve turkeys, and specimen bottles filled with Formalin, gloves, large and small scissors, as well as a small rotary handsaw for opening the brain case.

Joe pointed out the other man in the room, a taller, also aproned, and healthier-looking version of Doug Reddleman. "Peter, this is Henry Reddleman. Henry, Dr. de Haan."

Joe Parmelee stepped toward the starkly nude body as the door snapped open. Peter looked up to see Norman Silvana walk in, a hat in his hand and wearing a black raincoat. Peter had called Dr. Parmelee late in the day to lessen the chance he might get in touch with Dr. Hatch before the autopsy, but for a moment he had been certain that it must be Matthew Hatch coming in the room.

"Hello, Norman," Joe called as he began the crunching, bilateral incisions through Lou Corti's costal cartilages with his largest knife. Norman nodded pleasantly at him without saying anything.

"Norm," Peter said, "I'm surprised to see you here. I should have called you, but I forgot to do it."

"I've got my own spies," Norman said cheerfully.

"You didn't let Matthew know either," Joe Parmelee said, pulling up the sternal bone to expose the glistening, colorful organs wedged into the chest. "I told him I'd phone him afterward and give him the results, though," Dr. Parmelee said, cutting quickly through the abdominal wall to lay that cavity bare, too, and slicing through the tail of the right upper quadrant suture line as he did so.

At least Matthew Hatch had not stopped it, Peter thought, as Joe Parmelee intoned in his best prosector's manner, "A small amount of peritoneal fluid, serous, nonpurulent, here. Since you gentlemen are mostly interested in the abdominal cavity, I presume, I'll go through the thoracic organs quickly." He deftly and speedily removed the lungs, heart, and mediastinal structures en bloc in the Saphir style. The lungs were detached and sectioned, the aorta slit longitudinally and inspected, the heart vessels palpated and serially nicked open in quick order. "A little congestion in the lungs, a few petechial hemorrhages in the heart muscle, all compatible with a death in shock, possibly toxemic shock. Coronaries are certainly good. No arteriosclerotic hardening of his arteries at all. I'll look at his heart valves later on."

Then the pathologist removed all of the intestines, stomach to rectum, and took the shining, slippery coils to the sink in a pan. With large surgical scissors he opened the gut retrograde, rectum to colon to small intestine. As he got to the duodenum, he shrugged and screwed up his face. "I think our boy had an ulcer here at one time, though it's healed now, but aside from this I see nothing more than a few subserosal and submucosal hemorrhages in the whole gastrointestinal tract."

Then he plunged again into the gaping abdominal cavity, deserted now, shelled-out and fluid-filled. Soon the retroperitoneal kidneys were out, capsules peeled off, sectioned, and then Dr. Parmelee was looking carefully into the remaining organ cluster at the surgical site in the right upper quadrant.

"This liver looks sick," he said, poking at it and into it. "It's soft and mushy, necrotic." There were mattress sutures to be seen in the gallbladder bed. He pulled the liver up to cut the peritoneal attachments still left and so remove it.

Norman Silvana was leaning over the table, peering intently. "Joe, what's this?" he asked, pointing to a small, wine-red mass in the hollow of the liver just below the mattress sutures.

"That's some blood clot right there between the common bile duct and the hepatic artery."

"Well, take it off, will you? I want to see what's there."

"Sure. I was going to take everything out first, but I'll do it now." He carefully removed clot and early adhesions from the biliary tree area, and Norman pointed again with his tapering index finger, its beautifully manicured nail sparkling from the sharp overhead light as he said, "Look, there. Do you see? It's what I expected. The cystic artery to the gallbladder should have the ligature around it. But that's not the cystic artery to the gallbladder with the knot around it. *That's the hepatic artery to the liver that's been tied off.*" His voice was not loud or strident, rather soft and strained, intense. He was white-faced as he kept looking closely at the liver bed, his finger still outstretched.

After a definite, palpable gap before realization, Peter felt his neck muscles jerk stiffly as if a noose had tightened on them, and his heart began pounding against his chest cage. Matthew Hatch had really made a slip, an overt slip, a bad error.

In contrast to Dr. Silvana's pallor, Joe Parmelee flushed, angrily it seemed, and saying, "Norman!" he nodded toward the Reddleman brother, who saw the move and busied himself adjusting the water faucet at the foot of the table as Joe glared back at Norman with a meaning obvious by now. The pathologist then removed the liver silently, cutting it into wedges on the wooden board of his table like a butcher slicing steaks off a sirloin. Norman Silvana stared impassively at the procedure.

Peter could not give his attention to the rest of the post-mortem. Sealing himself off from the realities of the room, he was absorbed in contemplation of the horror of the findings, their monstrous aspect, and still thinking what he might do about them. It was clear-cut malpractice, wasn't it?

Beneath the grate that held the cadaver, water circled rapidly, carrying away the dwindling drops of blood and body juice from Mr. Louis Corti. Peter stared at the eddies, trying vainly now to gather his focus, to understand if he was accurately appraising the meaning of that 3-0 gut ligature pulled tightly around the artery to the liver. The sheer shock of the event, at the end of a trying week, when he was grossly tired, along with the growing excitement in him at the finding, seemed to make it impossible for him to analyze it all appropriately.

"Are you leaving?" Joe Parmelee asked, bringing Peter back to earthly awareness. He pulled his eyes up from the clearing whorls of water to discover that the question was addressed to Norman Silvana, who merely grunted out, "Yes," as he caught up his hat and burst out the door.

Finally, the dank room had been left to its Reddleman brothers. Joe Parmelee had returned the jumbled organs to the body spaces, and the larger Reddleman had arrived to help with sewing up the corpse, and the other, subsequent cosmetic arrangements.

Peter went out with Dr. Parmelee, who was muttering small complaints about Norman Silvana. "What's the matter with that guy, Peter? He's going to get into trouble some day. He needs to be more careful about what he says."

Peter had rushed to the hospital then to review more carefully Lou Corti's entire record, and after that had aranged for full photostating of the chart before he left for home.

In bed finally, he got up several times to write down recollections of various events of the evening, and then thinking fiercely, fell stonily asleep with the lights in his room still on at their brightest.

PART FOUR

28

PETER stumbled through the next few days, trying to work and trying to think out his plan for future action, and then at times wondering simply if he should go ahead with any plan, but knowing he would and waiting to see how the gross autopsy turned out.

The report came as an infuriating surprise. His copy was sent over by the record room the Tuesday after Louis Corti's death. Walking into his office, Peter saw the three-page photostat, stapled and marked with his name on the routing slip, sitting in his "IN" box. Waving away his nurse, who arrived at the same moment with a cluster of messages in her hand, he sat down to read through the sheets. He glanced at the bottom of the final page first and stared in amazement at what he read. Joe Parmelee's official conclusions were:

> GROSS DIAGNOSIS: 1. Immediate and principal cause of death: Acute hepatic necrosis
> 2. Status post-cholecystectomy
>
> NOTE: Microscopic examination and final diagnoses will follow.

Peter went back quickly to the section called "Synopsis of Principal Anatomical Findings" and skirted through it to the significant paragraph:

> The liver is enlarged, extremely soft, necrotic and friable. Mattress sutures are present at the gallbladder bed. There is a large hematomatous blood clot occupying the liver adjacent to the hepatic artery. [There was no amplification of this

statement, Peter noted. *None* at all.] There is considerable induration and hemorrhage in the connective tissue surrounding the common duct, but the T-tube is in place and securely sutured. Multiple sections through the liver show the vascular channels are filled with well-formed thrombi and there is a large pseudocyst measuring 7 cms. in diameter filled with necrotic debris and occupying the upper and middle portion of the right lobe of the liver. The left lobe is approximately twice normal size and it also shows uniform infarction with resulting softening and friability in all areas.

Not one damned word mentioned about the tie around the hepatic artery.

Peter picked up his phone. "Get Dr. Parmelee for me on the line as soon as you can," he told the operator. "Well, get him out of surgery if you have to. I don't care."

Peter found himself shaking with anger. "Dr. Parmelee, this is Peter de Haan. I was just reading over your gross autopsy findings on Louis Corti and I don't understand them. I mean, what's the cause of the dead liver supposed to be?"

"That report is written clearly and exactly the way I want it, and you should have no difficulty making it out."

"Come on now, Joe, what in the world is an autopsy done for if you don't put the facts down about it afterwards?"

"I told you once to be careful about what you did and said, and that applies right now. There are just a whole hell of a lot of things you don't understand, young man."

Peter slammed down the phone, and he hoped the noise of the crash of the receiver got partly over the line to Joe Parmelee's ear.

The next few days were hard for Peter to get through. He wanted to talk to Mrs. Corti, he had definitely decided he would do that, and he was waiting for the right time.

The Saturday morning after the funeral he called her. She seemed surprised that he wanted to come to the house, but said she could see him that afternoon. At two he drove out to her home. It was new, with the yard only partially landscaped in front, the lawn delicate shoots of a bright, virginal green, the fence around it unpainted. Inside the house still smelled of plaster and paint, and was not fully furnished.

"Please excuse everything." Peggy Corti was pale and thinner. "We just moved in a month ago. Louis built this bigger place so we'd have more room." Tears came into her eyes.

"It's very nice," Peter said.

"I'm sorry for crying. Seeing you just makes it all come back so strongly."

"I wanted to tell you about the autopsy, and I wanted to tell you in person, because something unexpected turned up which I think you should know about."

"From the way you sounded, I thought that you must have something special to say. Was it cancer? Is that what you found?"

"No, not at all. It wasn't that." Peter halted, wondering how to start.

"It wasn't? I thought . . ." she said, before being interrupted by a curly haired girl who ran in screaming, and collapsed in her mother's lap. "What is it, Nancy?" The girl blurted out something about her brother. Her mother patted the seat of her playsuit.

"You tell your Aunt Teresa that I said Steven must give it back to you." Mrs. Corti sighed as the girl walked off, rubbing her eyes. "My sister, Teresa, has been helping with the children some. I asked her over this afternoon, so I could talk to you without being interrupted, but it didn't work, did it? Please go ahead."

"At the postmortem we found that he died from liver failure."

"Liver failure? Was that from the gallbladder infection?"

How easy it all could be, Peter thought. All he need say was, yes, the gallbladder infection had spread into the liver. It would satisfy Mrs. Corti, even in a sense, please her to hear it. It was *too* easy. There were too many premature grave markers in the cemeteries put there through gross neglect and mishandling of patients by doctors who were never brought to judgment. For every case of malpractice in the courts, there were fifty or a hundred unknown ones. The medical guild was strong, tight-lipped. No one told. The relatives never knew. The creed of the guild was, all for one and one for all, and no leaks. A good doctor deserved a few breaks. For a rare, honest error or shortcoming he probably earned the support and shelter of the guild. But Peter realized he was sitting in this living room talking to this sad young mother—and about to give her very bad, upsetting, if very truthful news—because the medical guild apparently protected *all* doctors, indiscriminately, without regard to competence. In essence, the guild decreed that the doctor comes first, let the patients look out for themselves. A drinking toast: our profession, may it always be right, but our profession, right or wrong.

And now Peter wanted to take a step himself toward cracking this obvious wrong. He wanted to do something here and now about it. He felt dizzy from the responsibility as Peggy Corti asked him again, "Did you mean the liver infection came from the gallbladder, Doctor?"

"No, it didn't," Peter said slowly.

"It didn't? Where did it come from?"

"The liver was not really infected. It was damaged."

"I don't understand."

Peter breathed deeply, selecting his words carefully as he went on with his explanation. "We found a suture tied around the main artery to the liver damaging it. The liver went on to die from the lack of blood supply, and this caused the fever which we thought might be from infection."

"Are you saying there was a knot tied around this blood vein—"

"It was not a vein but an artery. A vein takes blood from something. An artery carries the fresh, oxygenated blood to an area or organ."

"It was your fault, you mean, that you tied a string, or what do you call it, a suture, around my husband's artery?"

"I was there at the surgery, but I didn't see this happen. I didn't know it until I saw the autopsy examination. I wasn't the surgeon, you know, I was just the assistant."

"Are you trying to say that Dr. Hatch was the one that did this? Do you mean that Lou shouldn't have died, but did because something was done wrong at the surgery?"

"Yes."

"I can't believe that. Dr. Hatch is a wonderful man and a wonderful surgeon. If he did anything wrong, I know he would tell me. He wouldn't let somebody else tell me." She stood up, tears rolling off her cheekbones. "Why are you saying this to me? That's a terrible thing to say." Peggy Corti's sister came running in from the other room. She was larger, stouter than Peggy, and older, perhaps forty with gray showing in her short brown hair.

"What's the matter, Peg, for heaven's sakes?" she asked. "What are you crying about?"

"Dr. de Haan here is saying some things I just can't believe or understand."

Peter sighed. "I think perhaps I'd better go now and come back some other time. You see, I had told Mrs. Corti I wanted an autopsy on her husband, and I would report to her honestly and faithfully on the findings. I was doing that, but the findings, unfortunately, are very disturbing."

"What do you mean, Doctor?" the sister asked.

Peggy Corti wiped her eyes and nose now with a handkerchief, and said, "Teresa, he's been trying to tell me that Dr. Hatch tied off some artery to the liver by mistake, and because of that Lou died."

"That doesn't sound possible," her sister said. "Is that really what you told Peg, Doctor?"

"It was," Peter said.

"I think it's very wrong of you to come here and talk like this. After all, don't you know Dr. Hatch has been our family doctor for years, for all the Bassis and the Cortis, and we have complete confidence in him."

"I believe you should realize how hard it is for me to bring this news," Peter said. "I feel very bad about the whole thing." Peggy Corti was sitting on the arm of an upholstered chair now, staring at Peter, a handkerchief over her mouth and nose.

"Does Dr. Hatch know you're here?" Teresa asked. "Did he want you to come?"

"No, he doesn't know anything about it."

"I bet he doesn't. Does he think that Louis died from what you say? Have you talked to him about that?"

"No."

Peggy Corti took her handkerchief down and asked now, "Do you mean you didn't talk to Dr. Hatch about this, and yet you're here talking to me? That doesn't even make sense."

The sister was shaking her head. "All right, Peg, I think that I'm going to ask this young doctor to leave, right now. We don't want to talk to you, Doctor, do you understand?"

Peter stood up. "Of course I understand and my sympathies are all with you. I mean it. I could tell you why I didn't talk to Dr. Hatch, but I don't think you would see my point. I'm very, very sorry to be the one to give you this word. I would like to come back some time when you both feel I could, especially when Mrs. Corti feels I could, to talk to her. We shouldn't leave it all like this. It will be too hard on everyone."

Peter picked up his topcoat from the davenport, and walked erectly to the front door, opened it, and closed it carefully behind him without turning around. Driving back to the hospital, his hands squeezed the steering wheel tightly. One die was rolled. Would he have a chance to roll another? The question was an anxious one, and its answer came soon.

Late in the afternoon Peter was told a Mr. Corti was waiting for him in the small visitors' lobby off A Ward. He went there at once.

Mr. Corti was a large man, taller, with bigger shoulders than his son Louis, and handsome with his thick gray hair and gray-white moustache, as well as sprightly, quick-moving, full of gestures.

He said hello and shook Peter's hand. "Where do we speak?"

"I guess right here is as good as any place." Peter walked to the wall and switched on the overhead fluorescent lights. "Sit down, Mr. Corti."

"Doctor, let me tell you first," Mr. Corti said in his surprisingly high-pitched, husky voice. "My son, Louis, is my only son. Three daughters and one son. I love him very much. You know this. Now I think many things. I even wish as a young man that I never leave Livorno and come to America. Maybe this would not have happened to me then. I work hard all my life, up early in the morning, three or four o'clock, going till eight at night in the fields at first, then as a carpenter, and after that in my own store. Louis, I help a little bit, sure, he's my son, I'm his father, but he's in building, a contractor, and he does well. A good boy. Hard-working like me, and starting to make money pretty good. Maybe sooner or later he make more than I do, but what does that mean, nothing. Everything I do, everything he do, it means nothing now. Nothing means anything. Still, this is no reason to upset his wife or me with foolish talk."

"Mr. Corti, you must understand that we did an examination on your son after he died, with your daughter-in-law, Margaret Corti's, permission. She asked only that we tell her completely what we found wrong, which is her right. So that is what I did." Peter stopped, suddenly sorry for the older man.

Mr. Corti, looking steadily at Peter, flashed a momentary white-toothed smile and said, "Tell me please what you saw on my son?"

Peter explained all the findings, carefully and fully this time. Amadeo Corti listened, his head averted, but nodding. When Peter finished and was silent, Mr. Corti looked at him to see that there was no more, and then he said, "It didn't seem right to me that he should die. He was so young, so strong and healthy. Why couldn't he go through an operation? I didn't see why not. So did something go wrong with the operation, I wondered? And now you tell me it did. Is that right, young doctor? Is this what you tell me?"

"This is what I believe."

"So will it bring my boy back? No."

"I understand that."

"You work for Dr. Hatch, right?"

"Yes."

"He pays you?"

"Yes."

"But he doesn't know you're talking to my daughter and me?"

"No, he doesn't."

"Maybe you lose your job."

"I don't care. I am doing something which I believe is right, and that is first, while other things are second."

"I like to hear you say that. Sometimes people get busy, too busy, too big shot. They don't build their buildings good, they don't clean the fish like they should, they don't fix their vegetables nice in the grocery store. They get sloppy and that's bad business. Always a person must look out to do things careful, not too fast, and watch for everything. So I say to myself when Louis gets so sick, did the doctor do something wrong? Dr. Hatch I know a long time, but I think he's too busy now. Last time I go to him, I wait for hours, and then I see him for two minutes. He give me a pill that makes me sick, and I can't take it. So you see, I think I understand."

"I believe you do," Peter said, suddenly thinking of Baltimore in the annual bright freshness of spring and early summer, of times past and a time ahead without worries and dreadful responsibilities, without dead people and doubtful dreams of dreams.

"You have something else on your mind, young man; and I know that. You are very angry at Dr. Hatch for doing this, no? What is on your mind? You tell me, please."

"You're right. I feel very bad about this, and other things I've seen Dr. Hatch do. I think you should know that."

"If this is something very wrong that Dr. Hatch has done, then somebody could make him be sued, couldn't they?"

"It's possible."

"You understand, I wouldn't think that was right, we

wouldn't. No. What would money be, what could money do?"

Peter sat up straight, the juices in his body come to life and working again. "So who's going to send your grandchildren to college, and give the girl a wedding, and put the boys in business? Who's going to pay for the house, and the new cars, and the clothes and food? You may be well off, but not that well off. Now listen, Mr. Corti, I want to tell you something. I begged Dr. Hatch to slow down when he was operating on Louis. No, he was too busy, too much the big shot, as you say. He had to get to a meeting to talk to people about his trip to South America. He couldn't slow up enough to do a good, careful job on your son. I've seen him do the same thing other times. I don't like it. I think your great Dr. Hatch, the wonderful family doctor of the Cortis and the Bassis, is no good. I want to see him hang. He deserves it. If you go to court, I will testify on the witness stand in behalf of your family and your daughter-in-law, if you will give me that privilege. I believe I can win this case for you and hurt this man who needs to be hurt for what he did to your son and to other people. Also we could get some money for your daughter-in-law, and for your three grandchildren. Sit here and think it over for a while before you leave. Good night, Mr. Corti."

29

ON the highway out of Cima Valley that evening, Peter said to Anne, "You know, your dad's really a great guy. He's never mentioned anything to me about your being in the hospital, never treated me any differently, though I'm sure he was terribly worried at the time and wouldn't have minded killing me."

"I don't know. I don't think so. He always liked you."

"I'm glad." Peter reached out and squeezed her hand.

"You seem better tonight, Peter."

He shrugged, smiling.

"You don't even look as tired."

"That's what your father said."

"What's the reason?"

"It's just nice to be with you for a weekend, and I love you, and therefore I'm happy."

"Is that all?"

"I guess it's partly because I've got Dr. Hatch in a spot finally."

"What do you mean?"

"I've run onto a case that he goofed up too much. Maybe we can put the thumbscrews on yet."

"Are you going to take it to the medical society?"

"I don't know. I'd like to do something about it."

"I don't see why you should be pleased about things that are so messy and awful."

Traffic got heavier as they turned on the new Orange Freeway into Oakland, and they said little until they got to the restaurant. The Taj Mahal consisted of three large, modernistic rooms decorated with Indian bric-a-brac and turbaned waiters, and was situated on the top floor of an old hotel overlooking Lake Merritt. It was still early when they arrived, and they were able to get a table in an alcove by a window.

"It's beautiful here," Anne said, smiling in delight. "The view is so perfect. And we're off by ourselves."

"Yes, I like it too. I'll get us a drink before we order."

After two-martinis, they started on dinner.

"This is good curry," Anne said, "and I've decided I like your abalone with shrimp sauce, too. I had some last weekend."

"You did? Where?"

"Oh, I've been going to tell you. Now don't get angry. Stanley Evans is a boy I've known for a long time at Berkeley. He came over to my place and had a drink with me last Friday night and asked me to go out to dinner with him. He's an old friend, and I was tired and depressed and didn't feel like cooking, so I decided to go. Don't look that way, it wasn't anything. We only went down to Busbie's by the railroad tracks, you know, the big fish place. Anyway, I saw the abalone with shrimp sauce on their menu and tried it and liked it. That's all there is to tell you."

"What the hell kind of a fake story is that?"

"What are you talking like that for?"

"I'm not supposed to make any comment even when you tell me you're out having dates, is that the idea?"

"I didn't have a date. I only had dinner with an old friend

who's about as sexy as Marshall Wormser. We just like to talk to each other. There's nothing more than that to it."

"Neither one of us should be so naive as to believe that."

"Peter, what is the matter with you? You're so different."

"Are you trying to say you don't love me anymore?"

"Of course not. I *am* getting sick and tired of hearing about that damned Dr. Hatch, though. That's all you have on your mind and it seems unnatural."

"I think it's the most important thing I could have on my mind, and I don't agree with you at all."

"I want you to tell me something. You won't ever talk about it, but I think I should know. He did do something wrong with me, didn't he? That's the reason that you're so gone on getting even with him, isn't it? But what did he do?"

"If you know that he did something wrong, why do you bother to ask me?"

"He did then. You finally admit it, don't you?"

"Yes, he did. But I felt the same way about him before he ever touched you."

"What did he do wrong? I want to know what it was? He should never have done a hysterectomy, is that it?"

"Yes."

"Oh, God. I worried about that, but then I thought it couldn't be. I guess I didn't want to believe it could have happened."

"It doesn't do you any good to know. I shouldn't have told you."

"You should have told me right away, that's what you should have done. I can't ever forgive you for not telling me. Oh, God, that makes me sick."

"Anne, I don't know what I said it for. I may be wrong. I just *think* that it wasn't necessary, but I'm not sure."

"Now, please, don't do that now. Don't start off telling me it was so, and then say it wasn't, and expect me to believe that."

"Finish your dinner, darling, and we can talk about it after a while."

"I'm not going to finish my dinner. I'm going to get out of here right now."

"What are you talking about?"

She stood up, grabbing her coat. "Peter, I want you to listen to me. I'm leaving here and going to Berkeley, and I'm going alone. I don't want to make a scene, I just want to do this. I'll get a taxi, and I don't want you to follow me. If you do, I won't talk to you. I can't believe there's any feeling for me left on your side, and I don't know how I feel myself. So, *please, don't* follow me, and don't try to call me or to see me. I think we should stay away from each other for a while until we can decide a few fundamental things. If you sit and think about it for a minute I know you'll agree with me. Good-bye, Peter."

She walked out carefully, with poise, beautiful to Peter as she retreated, her slim shoulders straight across the top, the bracelet on her wrist flashing reflections of light from the restaurant's chandeliers, her head never turning.

Peter watched her leave, believing until she disappeared that she would come back. He paid the bill then and took the grindingly slow elevator down to the first floor, plunging out the lobby doors of the old hotel to the sidewalk, but Anne was not there. A parking attendant lounged by the entrance and Peter asked him if he had seen a girl in a red dress in the last few minutes. Yes, he had. She had got in a Yellow Cab and gone.

At home in his apartment an hour later, Peter dialed Anne's number. "Darling, this is Peter. For God's sake, why did you do that? You know I love you and want to marry you. What more can I say to convince you?"

"I don't see how you can convince me, because I don't believe you know what you think yourself right now. You're too confused, with everything on your mind, to think straight."

"You're wrong about this."

"I'm sure I'm right, Peter, and I believe what I said that we shouldn't see each other at all for a few months. Let's find out what happens when we don't."

"Would we still be engaged, or not, or what?"

"I don't know whether to say yes, or no. I just can't say."

But the next Tuesday the ring came to Peter at the clinic by registered mail, with a little note inside its package that said, "I think it's best that I not keep this now. Anne."

30

THERE was no word from the Corti family, and none from Anne. A dozen times Peter thought to call her, or Mr. Corti, and decided against doing so. He was too numbed to be despondent, too tired to take a drink for fear he would lose control when he might need control, and always jumpy, waiting for the ceiling to crumble finally, watching for the plummeting Damaclean sword that had to be dodged.

Then Saturday, the 23rd of April, several things happened at once as the consequences of his actions. Peter was in the hallway of the surgical floor, stretched over the nurses' desk writing progress notes, when Dr. Hatch came striding up and slammed down a chart.

"Say, de Haan," Matthew Hatch said, clomping him painfully on the shoulder in what Peter took to be only a more robust greeting than usual, "this morning Joe Parmelee talked to me, and said you were riding him about the autopsy on Lou Corti. You know that boy died of hepatorenal syndrome and toxemic shock, plus a bad anesthetic, you have to admit that. And then right now I just came from my office. Old man Corti and his daughter-in-law were there and it sounded to me talking like they might want to sue me, or some such nonsense. I asked them if they had seen you and they wouldn't answer me, which made me think I'd better talk to you. What's going on, Pete?"

"Did Joe Parmelee tell you the autopsy findings?"

"*Tell* me about them? He showed them to me. He brought all the organs up to me and we went over them that same night. I know what Norm Silvana said, too, but that's all crazy. I showed Joe that the tie was right around the cystic artery. There was a little tie around one of the other small arteries in the gallbladder bed, too, but that was of no significance. I recall very well identifying the hepatic artery at surgery and putting it aside. I told Joe where it was and how he, or in this case, Norman Silvana, might have gotten confused. The cystic artery was a little anterior to where it usually is, that's all. The ligature was right where it should have been, though, around the cystic artery, and this boy died from hepatorenal and toxemic shock. That was a really bad, very infected and acute gallbladder, and the infection spread into his liver and into his bloodstream. So what's the fuss? And what gives with the Corti family? Did you talk to them?"

"I did. She consented to an autopsy—"

"That was your first mistake. This was not the kind of case nor the family to ask for an autopsy." Dr. Hatch's breathing was noticeably heavy and his face was flushing. Peter on the contrary felt calm, even soothed by the thought that the showdown had come. "I don't follow you there at all, Matt." He had never before called Dr. Hatch by his first name.

"Now let's be careful, boy. What do you mean, you don't follow me? What I said is perfectly simple."

"I know. You never make a mistake. Really, how can you even *talk* about this? You didn't see the autopsy. Taking the organs out and carrying them to you, I'm sure all the relationships would be lost. I was *there*, you know, and I saw where that tie was placed. And Norman knows where it was, too. He doesn't need you to tell him."

"Hell, that boy doesn't do enough surgery in a year to tell me where the belly button is."

"What do you mean, anyway," Peter went on, "this isn't the kind of case you do an autopsy on? I can only gather you're talking about self-protection. Anyway, yes, I talked to the Cortis, and I told them the truth about the post. I had promised Mrs. Corti to do that. Frankly, I think she has a perfect right to sue, and a good case. Whether she will or not, I haven't any idea."

"After what I've done for you, you mean to stand there and talk to me this way, suggest somebody should sue me? You're not a doctor, you're no physician, you're a goddam Communist." Dr. Hatch's neck veins were swollen ropes.

"That's the kind of stupid, illogical comment I would expect from you."

"No one talks to me that way," Matthew Hatch roared. "You get out of my hospital. And until a formal apology is made to me, and a full explanation of your activities given, *and accepted by me,* you are barred from any and all buildings of the hospital and clinic."

"You have no right to do that."

"I own this place."

"This is a publicly used hospital assertedly run by its staff and operating under by-laws. You know that, and you know that the rules say I have to be dismissed by the executive board after hearing."

"You got your prick into that girl, I didn't, and that started all this thing, didn't it? It's your fault she got pregnant, so don't try to make me the guilty one around here. I want you *out* now, and if you don't believe I mean what I say, you come back this afternoon again and you'll meet a deputy sheriff with a restraining order."

"Before I leave here, I'm going to make rounds on all the patients I've been seeing and tell them I've been summarily relieved from duty here by you against my will, and that you or your appointee will be taking over, and I will write this on each chart. If you attempt to interfere with me on this, I *will* fight you." Peter turned on his heel and started down the hallway, then looked back to say, "See you in court." Dr. Hatch glared at the back of his head as Peter continued along the corridor, while several heads of nurses and aides appeared out of doorways to see what the commotion was. The phone rang just then and one of the nurses answered it, and then called after Peter in a shaky voice, "Dr. de Haan, telephone." Peter stopped in the hall. "A Mr. Corti calling you."

"I'll take it," Peter called back.

"Don't you dare talk on the phone here," Dr. Hatch said, stepping up to take the receiver from the nurse and hang it up. Peter shrugged and walked off.

That evening he spent at Peggy Corti's house, talking to her and to her father-in-law, Mr. Corti.

"I want to help you do what's right," he told them, feeling that there was no point spending time on Dr. Hatch's other wrongs, or the grievous shortcomings of the County Medical Society in allowing doctors like Hatch and Susack and Delaney to practice, or the similar failings of the state and national medical societies. The Corti's problem was not to reorganize the ethical structure of medicine, but a much simpler one: Should they sue Dr. Hatch because of a seeming act of malpractice performed against their Louis?

Even so, Peter thought, every invasion had its initial beachhead, every legal reform its Gideon case, and each social change required suffering protagonists. Perhaps in the small beginning which Peter was now committing them to, these grieving people could turn Lou Corti's death into one of greater, more general help than they could conceive.

Still this was not their concern. They had an honest case, and they were thinking on it honestly, undecided what to do.

At first Peter had taken the wrong turn with them. They did not care about the money. The losing of a life needlessly, and retaliation to someone who had caused that, were the principal considerations. In the old man's Tuscan heart the publicity for the family in acting against Dr. Hatch would be vindicated only if it appeared suitable vengeance was obtained.

"I think we should do something on it," Mr. Corti said finally. "I don't think we should go with it if Dr. Hatch didn't do something really wrong. But you feel, Dr. de Haan, that man did do something really wrong, and you get up in court when the time comes and swear that way, don't you?"

"Yes, I will."

"Are you going to lose your job for sure then?"

"I already did. I was fired this morning."

"No, you really mean that?" the old man said, surprise showing through the deeply grooved skin of his features.

"Dr. de Haan, did you?" Peggy Corti asked.

"Of course," Peter laughed, throwing his hands up. "It's true."

Mrs. Corti at once broke into soundless sobs and streaming tears. Peter turned away so as not to watch her cry. In a few moments she recovered to say, "Grandpa, this is all I need to know. If this doctor feels so strong that Dr. Hatch did something wrong with Louis, we should take his word for it. We have to go ahead and do something, I think."

"That's right," Mr. Corti said. "I think so, too." He leaned forward and clapped his rough old hand on Peter's. "My boy, and I don't mean to show no respect, my young man, *my doctor*, I think we go along with you and do something. I can see you have some reason to get into this, to do this strong thing, and your reason is a good reason from God. So we go do this together." He smiled.

"What will you do for a job, I mean, how . . . ?" Peggy Corti asked.

"I'll have to find other work, and it may not be easy," Peter answered. "I can stay here for three or four months for hearings and depositions, and come back after that if necessary for a trial, but I need to have *some* income during that time."

Corti's face went abruptly serious again. "You mean," he said sadly, "you want money from us?"

"I guess it's only right that he should get something for all the help," Peggy Corti said.

"Oh, no, I don't want anything. Well, I want *something*, but not money. I want very much to see Dr. Hatch get properly repaid for what he did. But it would be completely wrong for me to get any money, and I don't want that. I imagine Mrs. Corti has enough financial problems on her hands without me being one of them."

"You're so right, Doctor," she said. "I've been amazed. I mean, we were doing so well, and with my husband's death everything has fallen apart. All the people who had contracts are canceling them, and everybody we owe to is worried and wants their bills paid at once with no money coming in."

Mr. Corti put in, "Even the 'countant shakes his head. 'Some mess,' he says."

"I'm going to have to go to work eventually, no question about that," Peggy Corti added. "Sell the business and go to work. But it will take six months to get everything settled before I can do that." She looked at Peter and smiled. "Well, I've got coffee and cake in the kitchen, so we can have something to eat while we talk."

Peter enjoyed the rest of the evening. The Cortis' definite decision to go ahead with the suit buoyed him through their discussions.

What attorney to use was their biggest problem. They knew many good lawyers in San Marcial, but whether these men were able to handle a malpractice case, or would want to, was something else again.

"I talk to my friend, Bill Johnson, tomorrow," Mr. Corti said to Peter. "He's a fine lawyer."

"I certainly wouldn't go to any lawyer locally unless you're sure he has no connection with any member of the Hatch Clinic."

"Come to think, young doctor, I see Dr. Hatch himself in the office there one day. I think he say about a will."

"You see, you could run into the situation where he'd have to refuse to handle the case, and then you'd worry that he'd go ahead and prematurely hand on the information that you were suing."

"Bill Johnson would do nothing like that, I know, but I understand what you say. So Peggy and I we think about it and talk and take time."

"Well, don't take too much time," Peter said, smiling. "And I pray we can get a good lawyer. I say 'we' because I want to help, too, all I can." Peter stood up. "I must go, Mr. Corti, and Mrs. Corti. Thank you very much."

"Thank *us*, young doctor? Thank *you*." The rugged old man grabbed Peter's hand suddenly and squeezed, throwing him off balance. Peter recovered, laughing.

"We are partners now," Mr. Corti said. "So good luck to us."

31

THE next morning Peter, feeling odd, like a soldier just returned from a battlefront and unable to comprehend there would be no more bloody calls to combat, roused himself and fixed a large breakfast of eggs, toast, cereal, and coffee. Anne was on his mind, of course, but still through the day he found himself moving freer, the band around his head and chest loosening, his soul greatly relieved that he did not have to go through the grinding agony of caring for the Hatch victims.

Monday he applied for and Tuesday got a job as temporary emergency physician at the San Marcial County Hospital, being assigned to the night shift, six P.M. to six A.M. Within a week the medical director let him go. Supposedly the board of supervisors would not approve any more county physicians. This was the reason given for his being fired. Peter knew that Dr. Hatch's influence had been at work, but he had one cause célèbre already, and did not care to try for two.

The week he worked at the county hospital he realized that the medical grapevine was operating well. Many of his acquaintances, even Lew Condon, no longer spoke to him. Frank Lewicki was different, too, strained in his manner, more defensive than cordial. Peter was deeply discouraged at this. He had thought more highly of this taciturn, dry, and sharp-witted physician than any other in his months in San Marcial. Still he gritted his teeth, wondering at how scared most doctors ran, how easily they could be threatened.

At least Marshall Wormser stuck with him, feeding him, encouraging him, giving him news of the repercussions he had caused. Marshall told him how Norman Silvana had been angry at Peter's actions, and had called him a "stupid young cock" in the coffee room, how George Carr had gone into a long tirade on the way Communism was breaking into the medical profession, and even Frank Lewicki had shaken his head sadly over the affair. Marshall told of his own repartees, gems of black nastiness, with Joe Parmelee, and Matthew Hatch, too.

Disturbing as some of these reports were, the details of which Marshall in no way spared him, Peter still felt enduringly grateful for this corpulent Jewish anesthesiologist's helping arm, listening ear, and friendly support.

He thought of Anne often, and got her on the phone twice. She was busy both times and couldn't talk long she said; at first because she had an examination coming up, and then a term paper was confronting her. The last time she said, "Peter, I don't think you should call me anymore. It's just because I still feel so unsure about us, and I suspect you do too, whether you'll admit it or not. We need more time apart to find out if what's between us is really love, if it's strong enough to last."

He agreed finally with her logic, and was reassured by her earnestness.

In the three weeks after he left the Hatch Clinic, he gained back ten pounds. Lying in the sun by his apartment pool he lost his gaunt, insurrectionist look. Preferring assignments that left his days free for conferences and appearances as needed in the future, he found another job as night physician for the old Fabiola Hospital in East Oakland. The Corti family was going ahead with their plans for suit, and Peter talked to them or saw them every few days. They had located a famous trial lawyer, a plaintiff's expert with malpractice experience, in San Francisco, and had an appointment arranged with him on his return from hearings in the East. Peggy Corti's sister, Teresa Tolley, was no longer hostile to Peter, but rather quite friendly. She told Peter, "I thought you were the most miserable mean fraud and stinker at first, unbelievably cruel in what you were doing to Peggy and Dad Corti, but now I see it just the reverse. You've saved their lives, I think, by giving them something to keep busy with. They think about the case and talk about it, write notes and call each other up several times a day, and it seems to be more a blessing than anything else."

Apparently none of the doctors at Fabiola Hospital knew what had happened with Peter in San Marcial so they were cordial to him. The hospital was old and rather small, situated out in East Oakland where the Negro population was rising so there were even a few colored physicians on the mainly general practitioner staff.

Peter got to know one of the young doctors at Fabiola who had just gone into practice. In the staff lounge one night, waiting to scrub on an appendectomy, Peter told him something about why he was there, about the Lou Corti case. The doctor was interested and asked questions. Peter went ahead to tell him more of the horrors of working at the Hatch Hospital, and about this one particular terrible Corti affair.

"They *should* sue him," the young doctor said.

"That's what I've advised them," Peter said. "That's why I got fired, as a matter of fact."

"Say, there's a tremendous lawyer here in Oakland, the father of a friend of mine, named Cousman. He's a wonderful person, not one of these attorneys who only think about money. He'll take a case he believes in even if the people have nothing. He does some malpractice and personal injury cases right along, at times representing doctors, at times plaintiffs, so he knows both ends. If you could possibly get those people to him, I know you'd be doing them a favor."

Peter thought about the doctor's advice, then a few days later called the lawyer's office and so started a three-day chase. Mr. Cousman had just left, or was in court, or in San Jose for the day, or unable to talk. He would probably answer a message if left, his aides stated, but he never did.

Late one afternoon, Peter went to Mr. Cousman's office in Oakland. It was sparsely furnished though large and neat, with three willowy young women at desks typing documents with impressive speed, while an elderly receptionist worked incoming and outgoing calls on a Multiplex telephone system, chanting at intervals, "Cousman, Draper, and Feldman."

In a hiatus, she looked up at Peter inquiringly.

"I'm Doctor de Haan," Peter said. "I've been trying to get hold of Mr. Cousman for several days. I wanted to talk to him today for a few minutes if possible, or make a definite appointment to see him some other day."

The receptionist looked at him uncertainly. "Dr. de Haan? Have you been a client here before?"

"No, I haven't."

"One moment please. Cousman, Draper, and Feldman. Mr. Feldman? I'll connect you, Mr. Mortenson." She turned back to Peter. "Mr. Cousman takes on very few new clients. Would you be willing to see Mr. Draper or Mr. Feldman?"

"No, I'm afraid not."

"May I ask the general nature of your problem?"

"Malpractice."

She kept looking at him and Peter felt she wanted to ask more about the problem, to define it better, but then she dipped into her Auto-Call panel. "Mr. Cousman, there's a Dr. de Haan here who wants to talk to you today, or make an appointment to see you in the near future, about a malpractice case. He's not a previous client of the office." Peter was aware of some indistinct but loud words over the receiver, and the receptionist looked up again and asked, "*You* are being sued, sir, isn't that correct?"

"No, I want to sue someone."

A slight emotion furled her forehead skin and she spoke again into her headphone, then turned back to Peter.

"If you'll wait twenty minutes, Mr. Cousman will see you today." She smiled more pleasantly at Peter now that he was a client. "He fooled me. Please sit down."

In half an hour a far door of the office opened, a short man stepped out and called, "Dr. de Haan."

Peter stood up hurriedly, heading toward the open paneled door with gilt "A. O. Cousman" emblazoned on it. The caller retreated into the office itself, and he was staring out his window with his back to the door as Peter came in. The lawyer spoke without turning. "If those pigeons stay around here I'm going to bring my own twelve-gauge Parker down and blast their chubby heads off, Doctor."

Peter closed the door behind him and looked around. After the drab outer offices, this room was surprisingly luxurious. It was deeply carpeted in rich green velvet pile, paneled with dark gray oak, with one entire wall taken up by bookshelves, while two other walls were laden with diplomas, engraved plaques, and large inscribed photographs. Behind a gigantic, highly polished walnut desk, the final wall was made up primarily of faceted windows. The lawyer turned against the concave interior arc of the desk, pushing its high-backed chair to one side while he pounded a closed fist into his palm as if he were pulverizing avian skulls before Peter's eyes. Then he stepped around his desk and shook hands with Peter, a large hand for his size, warm and dry. "You are on the young side, Dr. de Haan. I'm A. O. Cousman."

"Hello, sir," Peter said, looking in fascination at the small man as he came charging at him noiselessly on the cushioned floor, slightly bent forward in attack, his skimpy gray hair combed straight forward onto his high forehead like a senator's from ancient Rome. His unconventional clothes were at once noticeable. His dark blue suit was of rich material, cut obviously to measure and overgenerously. It was set off by a red-and-blue figured tie which was abnormally broad and knotted very loosely at the neck between the points of a collar far larger than usual. A diamond stickpin adorned the tie, and his vest had a Phi Beta Kappa key hanging from the gold watch chain which traversed it. The lawyer's nose was prominent and beaky while the eyes were blue and alert.

"Now, did I understand that you want to bring suit, Doctor?" Mr. Cousman asked, indicating a chair for Peter as he took up a post in front of his desk.

"I'm representing a patient who wants to bring suit."

"Really," Mr. Cousman said, his facial manner brightening as he nodded his head to one side in interest. "Tell me exactly what you mean."

Peter went briefly over the details of the case and his reasons for involvement in it. He had summarized beforehand what he would say, thinking it might be important to present his facts quickly but convincingly enough to intrigue the lawyer into accepting the case.

Mr. Cousman listened silently, without facial or bodily movement, eyes averted as Peter spoke.

"A nice recapitulation," he said when Peter stopped. "I've heard of Dr. Matthew Hatch, because I sued him once before. Yes, about seven or eight years ago. It was only for a few thousand dollars, possibly ten, and it was settled out of court. He'd left a cast on a boy's leg too long which resulted in a pressure necrosis. Open-and-shut problem, if such exists. Sometimes I think not. But I spoke to the man then and didn't like him. Nope. Sort of an odd-looking duck, too, I thought, with those buggy eyes and the head that's too big. Well, anyway, we would have to prove to a jury that this man committed malpractice, and I'm not sure it can be done, even with your help, from what you tell me. You say the

Cortis, too, have already got an appointment with another lawyer."

"Yes, but he won't be back for at least another week. Then I heard of you, how good you are, and besides it would be so much more convenient to work with someone closer to San Marcial. I think the Cortis would follow along on my recommendation if you thought you would be able to take on the case."

"I want you to tell me more about your own feelings toward Dr. Hatch. What has brought you to this point?"

Peter told the attorney of the problems he had found practicing with Dr. Hatch, the fantastic, unbelievable trail of mismanagement and manslaughter in which he had tried to work. Then he told Mr. Cousman about Anne and her surgery, which had made it clear to him that he must, regardless of the sacrifice involved, make an effort to do something about Dr. Hatch.

"Your personal position is no help to any lawyer, you understand," Mr. Cousman said. "You'd undoubtedly be cross-examined on it, and I think it would make the case weaker. These malpractice cases are very difficult, Doctor. I can understand your position, why you think so strongly you want to do something. You must also realize it is highly unusual, and quite possibly unique, to have a physician in a lawyer's office urging him to take on a malpractice action with the doctor himself asking to be allowed to act as an expert witness. It makes me have to consider things carefully." He smiled a roguish smile, sitting behind his desk with his thumbs in the watch pockets of his vest. "I admit that the case rather interests me. Mind you, I don't say I'll definitely take it yet. I'll have to talk to the family and make some serious investigation of the facts here first."

He flipped a switch under his desk, and an overhead light came on, softly illuminating the room against the fading day outside. "You know, Dr. de Haan, even the friendliness or hostility of the judge can make or break a suit. He can cut off some of these actions at the knees."

"I realize that there are many problems involved," Peter said. "But I did convince the Cortis, who were unsure at first, that they have a right to sue. They would never have known about the botch if it hadn't been for me, and that is one of the things that's so maddening. If you can believe it, Dr. Hatch is the most successful doctor in San Marcial, both in popularity and in bank deposits, and yet he personally does away with six or eight people a year, I'd guess, not even counting how many he puts through strung-out illnesses at tremendous expense. I'm sure that copies of him are scattered about in the towns and cities of the country. In San Marcial, the doctors cannot bring themselves to do anything about him collectively or individually, and I imagine that the same thing happens with physicians in the other cities."

"Frankly, I recoil at the picture you bring out and rebel, I admit, at your accusations. It's hard to believe that almost every community doesn't have good medical men in such a majority that the bad actors aren't kept under better control than you imply."

"There are practically no disciplinary actions against doctors in the state of California—I've looked this up—or even in the United States, Mr. Cousman, for anything but the grossest of abuses, insanity, narcotics use or illegal sale, conviction for abortion or other felonies, repeated molesting of women patients, things like that. Medical societies simply *don't* do any disciplining. They have now five new regional advisory boards to the State Board to help with discipline, but there is no intention of having these boards really dig into problems that don't fall into the categories I just mentioned."

Mr. Cousman sat quietly listening, and then rolled his jolly blue eyes when he spoke. "Okay, now let me ask you a question, Doctor. Wouldn't it be just as well, and serve your purposes better if you want to be a reformer of some kind, to present this story to your county medical society? To try for once to get some real backing from your colleagues before one of your own tribunals? None of these friends of yours are going to testify willingly or helpfully in court, you know, but they might be on your side in a disciplinary hearing before the executive committee of your own society."

"What I've just been saying shows that this wouldn't work. There are quite a few doctors in the society who have a very good understanding of how Dr. Hatch operates and who hate him, but they have never done anything about him in any formal way, and I know they never will. There's nothing that indicates to me any sudden change of interest by them in disciplining other doctors. Dr. Hatch has committed an offense against an individual which I think is basis for a suit. This man's family is entitled to a chance in a court before a judge and jury, and I think they should get it, if possible."

"All right. I follow your points. Now incidentally, what kind of operation did your fiancée have?"

"Hysterectomy," Peter said, watching the reflex toneless whistle of the lawyer's lips after his answer, and cogitating on the man as he did so. He seemed to be sharp, not really nutty but eccentric and perhaps just the extroverted, tough, cock-sure kind of individual who might be able to win a malpractice case.

"So, let me explain," Mr. Cousman said. "In court the plaintiff's case is presented first, the plaintiff being the person who is bringing the suit. Now the plaintiff has to make a strong enough case first, which is called a *prima facie* case, one which on the face of it appears to have enough real merit that the judge feels a defense of its assertions is warranted. He can chop the suit off right here, call it a non-suit, and that's what could happen in the case you bring to me, especially if the defense's objections to you as an expert witness, which would undoubtedly be made, were upheld by the court. You know if you've been doing any reading in law books that an ordinary witness can testify only as to facts, but an expert witness can and must judge facts which the jurors could not understand or interpret properly, and then the expert witness must give an opinion. In a malpractice case his opinion, more or less to the effect that a proper standard of care has not been adhered to, is ordinarily a necessity for the plaintiff's case. The jury will often get conflicting expert testimony, and then it is up to them to deliberate and ultimately decide which expert is the most believable. If we can't use you as an expert witness, but just an ordinary one, since you are so new in practice and not specializing in any field—these would be the points they would get you on—then we must get other expert witnesses. We'd have a devil of a time getting some good enough to oppose the array that the defense for a man like Dr. Hatch could no doubt present, but we would have to have enough hope for good expert testimony on our side to believe we could get past non-suit, or there would be no sense in starting the whole thing."

The lawyer lit up a cigar, and began blowing fragrant clouds of black smoke into the room. "You've got some strong points to the case you present, though, and if we get past non-suit we'd have a chance to get at Dr. Hatch on the stand under cross-examination. I would probably have to take him apart some way to win the judgment." Mr.

Cousman scratched his head briskly and noisily, mussing up his Roman locks, then closed his eyelids tight and wrinkled his face in thought.

"All right, let me tell you how I see our steps. You bring the family in here to me so I can interview them. We'll have to talk money, for one thing. I'll want a retainer of two thousand dollars to start off an investigation to see if we really have a case. You know, transcripts of official records of the hospital, research on my part or my staff's on the law involved in this situation, the expenses of depositions to be taken from the principals, as well as from nurses, aides, record-room clerks, and so forth. Then we'll have to reconsider and see how good our case is, see if we really do have a case."

"I'm sure the Cortis would be happy to come to you and cancel with the San Francisco attorney."

"I can do better for them than the big city guys," Mr. Cousman said, smiling.

"I believe you can," Peter replied, looking at the old lawyer with warmth and confidence.

"You really want to see this guy in the electric chair, don't you, young Dr. de Haan? You're a good salesman. I'm already beginning to build up that fire in my gizzard I need to get going on a case and win it. I like to find people who should be hated. I like to find lousy husbands, nasty, cheating, blood-sucking wives, filthy and fraudulent businessmen, or money-hungry, holier-than-thou doctors. I like to sue them, make them enemies of mine, set them up in court as my adversaries." He pounded his fist on the table. "Then I like to put an arrow in the heart of this enemy and watch him fall to the ground, *hard*. I just think I might enjoy seeing this Hatch fellow bite the dust."

"Fine."

"Dr. de Haan, I want you to go home and put down in writing everything that has happened in this entire case, anything you know, all details that come to your mind, and in chronological order."

"I'll do it."

Peter watched Mr. Cousman's face as he stood up and looked out the window at the street below. "You realize," he said, facing Peter, "this is a most curious case. For instance you, Dr. de Haan, as one of the doctors involved in the case would normally be named as one of the co-defendants, yet here you are at the same time the agent provocateur. I guess we'll have to ask for a non-suit for you at the end of the plaintiff's case."

"I wondered about that," Peter said as a delicious, warm feeling flooded him. After all this time it was pleasant to realize suddenly that he had a helper and an ally.

32

A WEEK later, Peggy Corti, demure in a gray suit with large blue hat, sat with her father-in-law, Amadeo Corti, and Peter in Mr. Cousman's office. "You know," Mr. Cousman said, "I'm going to ask for a very large award."

Peter waited for the Cortis to speak, but they only stared silently, so he asked, "How much do you mean?"

"I think close to a million dollars."

Peggy and Mr. Corti pushed back in their seats in surprise. Peter felt his own eyebrows involuntarily rise. What if they could get such an award? That would surely put a crimp into Hatch. His coverage for a single case was for a top of $300,000 Peter knew. If a judgment for even $350,000 could be obtained, some of it would have to come out of Matthew's own pocket. Of course, even a judgment for $25,000 would do some good. It would help the Cortis and hurt Dr. Hatch. Insurance companies did not like clients who were sued and lost cases.

Mr. Corti said to the lawyer, "It could be a mistake asking for too much?"

"I understand what you mean, Mr. Corti. Besides, you have the kind of a great loss for which money is no real compensation. But you do have a right to some retributive act, and money is the only one available."

"Sir, I am born in Livorno and I live here as a working man all my life without education, so please use smaller words."

Mr. Cousman smiled. "I will, sir. You seem a very fine man, Mr. Corti. I would like to have known your son. I want to try to recreate him for the jury, let them see what he was like so they will understand the heaviness his absence brings to the family. As you can tell from what I say, I believe we have a case. With the permission of everyone here, I am going to file preliminary, that is, first papers, tomorrow."

"I don't understand why you think of asking for so much, Mr. Cousman," Peggy Corti said, her brow creased in worry.

"You must realize, Mrs. Corti, that what we ask for, or as we lawyers put it, what we pray for, we don't ordinarily get. That's the first thing. Ask for a million, you get fifty thousand. But more than that, your husband was a young man, just starting to make an important income at thirty-two. I have already heard from your accountant, and he says Louis would probably have made thirty to thirty-five thousand dollars this year before taxes, and did make twenty-nine thousand dollars last year. Simple arithmetic shows that thirty thousand times thirty-three years, the time that Louis might have been expected to work before retirement, comes out to nine hundred and ninety thousand dollars. And he probably would have done better than that. He was deprived of that earning opportunity by what I believe and will contend to have been an act of gross negligence on the part of Dr. Hatch. There is your lawsuit. The amount can be changed, up or down, but it must be something big."

"My daughter here don't want to make the jury think she ask for too much," Mr. Corti said.

"Of course, besides the loss of earnings, there is the cost of the illness which though it lasted less than a week, comes to over two thousand dollars. But maybe we can cut things down some. If we just figured twenty-five thousand a year, that would be eight hundred and twenty-five thousand. As I say, if we do get the verdict, the jury or the judge, either one, can cut it down. And of course to avoid retrial, reversal on error, years waiting for appeals to go through, we might accept a settlement during or after the trial for much less."

Mr. Corti shrugged his shoulders, and his eyes went up into his head. "Okay, whatever you say. She's the wife, and I'm the grocerman, and you're the lawyer. That's that."

They all smiled at each other now, and Peter felt that forces had been joined, the battle begun. It was an exciting moment for him.

The following week depositions were started. The first ones were in Mr. Cousman's office, with a court reporter present, and two of Dr. Hatch's attorneys, Mr. Shannon Sheaffer, the insurance company's lawyer from San Francisco, and Mr. Martin Tupper, Dr. Hatch's San Marcial legal aide. With Peter listening in, Mr. Cousman started questioning two nurses from the Hatch Hospital the first day, one from the floor and one from the surgery. They both stuck rigidly to the theme that the patient's care had been good in the operating room and on the ward. Mr. Cousman spent considerably more time with the spindly, white-haired, tough and briny Miss Masters from the surgery, whose belief in the godlike qualities of Dr. Hatch he found hard to dent.

"Miss Masters," he asked, after explaining to her what a deposition was and putting her through the customary questions about her length of employment and her duties as operating room supervisor, "Have you worked many times with Dr. Hatch in the operating room?"

"Oh, yes, of course. I work with him almost entirely."

"Do you recall the surgery on Mr. Louis Corti, beginning approximately at five thirty P.M. on Monday, April fourth of this year?"

"I do, very clearly."

"Can you tell me who all was in the room at the time that this surgery was begun, as near as you can recollect?"

"The patient, Mr. Corti, the surgeon, Dr. Matthew Hatch, the assistant, Dr. de Haan, the anesthetist, Dr. Marshall Wormser, and Mrs. Alice McCann, the utility nurse."

"And what does the other nurse do, what did Mrs. McCann do?"

"I was the scrub nurse. I was sterile, in gown and gloves, helping the doctor. Mrs. McCann was unsterile, able to walk around the room, and get us things we might need, move the lights, call the pathologist, for instance, if needed. We always have a scrub nurse and a utility nurse for every major operation."

"There were six of you then in the room, including the patient?"

"Yes, sir."

"Could you describe the appearance of the operating room?"

It was funny. Peter knew her so well, the rigid-spined, self-assured tyrant of the O.R., who was pale now as she sweated out the meaning of these simple questions. Her lawyers, their boredom obvious, listened as Mr. Cousman finally carried her through a description of the operating room and on to the events of the surgery on Louis Corti as she had seen them, including her interpretation of the condition of the patient during that time.

"Now, Miss Masters, did you hear any comments between

Dr. Hatch and Dr. de Haan about the speed of the surgery? Strike that. Were you impressed with the speed with which Dr. Hatch completed this surgery?"

Miss Masters, pinker again and starting to assert herself, snapped out in her midwestern twang, "Now, do you mean that you—" but Dr. Hatch's San Francisco attorney was on his feet interrupting.

"Just a minute, please, Mr. Cousman," Mr. Sheaffer said. "I am assuming that we are reserving all objections except as to form until the time of the trial."

"Yes, that is the standard stipulation. I'm also glad to see that you're still with us, Mr. Sheaffer. I thought we might have lost you." Mr. Cousman smiled fleetingly.

"Not for a moment, Mr. Cousman. Well, we did not stipulate to it before, but I am glad to do so now. I understand that under the rules we do not need to do it any longer, that it is instead reserved as a matter of statute, but so that it will be doubly clear for the record for both of us, I will so stipulate."

"Thank you, Mr. Sheaffer," Mr. Cousman said pleasantly.

"Miss Masters," Mr. Sheaffer told her, "you may answer that last question."

The reporter read it back to her, "MR. COUSMAN: Were you impressed with the speed with which Dr. Hatch completed this surgery?"

She looked confused again before finally saying, "No."

"Have you been a scrub nurse for a great many gallbladder operations?"

"After twenty-five years as a surgical nurse, of course I have."

"Would you be able to say how long a cholecystectomy takes on the average?"

Miss Masters pressed her lips together before replying. "I'd say approximately an hour or an hour and a half."

"Do you recall how long it took for the cholecystectomy on Mr. Corti?" Mr. Cousman asked rapidly, depositing his notes on his desk and looking directly at Miss Masters.

"No, I don't, but you must realize that Dr. Hatch is much faster than the other doctors."

"Please answer only the question I ask. I am not interested in additional comments." His tone was somber. "If I were to say that the surgery took exactly thirty-three minutes according to the official record from the time the incision in the skin was made to the time the final suture was tied, would you think that that was a rapid time for a cholecystectomy?"

"Not for Dr. Hatch."

"That is not an answer to the question I asked you."

"I don't know how to answer that question without that explanation."

"Nevertheless, I would like to have you answer it with a yes or no."

"I will say yes then."

"How much time do you allow for the other doctors who operate at the Hatch Hospital to do a cholecystectomy?"

"Usually thirty minutes longer than Dr. Hatch."

"Does he always work faster than the other doctors who operate at your hospital?"

"Oh, of course. That's what I've been trying to tell you."

"Were you conscious that Dr. Hatch was in a hurry doing the surgery on Mr. Corti?"

"I was not."

"Did he indicate in his actions or in his speech anything that would lead you to believe that he was rushing this piece of surgery?"

"He did not. I just said that."

"Who is your employer?"

"Dr. Hatch."

"Then when you receive your paychecks they are signed by him, by Dr. Hatch?"

"Yes."

"Now, was Mr. Corti's condition good to the best of your knowledge at the time he left the operating room?"

"Yes."

"Was there any reason for you to think that a surgical mistake had been made during the course of the surgery on this man?"

"There was none."

"Did you have any further contact with the patient after he left surgery?"

"I did not." Miss Masters was red-faced now, sweating enough for curling gray tendrils to form at her temples.

"Thank you. I have no further questions. Mr. Sheaffer."

"No questions by me," Mr. Sheaffer said.

"I have no questions," Mr. Tupper said.

Mrs. Eyraud, the daytime charge nurse on D Ward, was interrogated next by Mr. Cousman, mainly on such matters as how many injections Mr. Corti had needed for pain, and how many for infection, what degree of fever he had run, how much mental confusion he had shown, how much agitation, fear, and suffering had been observed in him. She was a soft-spoken witness, but tried to minimize all of Louis Corti's difficulties.

When the depositions were concluded, the attorneys nodded gravely at each other, neither side in as good humor apparently as when they had started, and made arrangements for Peter to give a deposition the following week in San Marcial at Mr. Tupper's office. Arrangements were discussed for depositions to be taken from Dr. Hatch, and also Dr. Parmelee and Dr. Silvana, without any definite time being set. Mr. Cousman asked for the opportunity to take depositions from at least two of the defendant's expert witnesses, but a decision on this request was not immediately reached.

Peter stayed behind in the office to talk to Cousman. After going through every book on a medico-legal topic he could find in the last month, and steeping himself in the words and phrases, Peter was starting to feel legalistic himself. "What did you think of the depositions?" he asked.

Mr. Cousman smiled as he chewed on a cigar. "Peter, I think that they're getting an idea of our tactics. I haven't dealt with this Amsterdam Insurance Company much, and they don't know me well either. They're mostly in Southern California rather than in the Bay Area. I presume they thought they were getting into a hick crowd here, but maybe they'll think differently after today."

"I know the first nurse, Miss Masters, very well. She'll be on Dr. Hatch's side one hundred percent all the way through."

"We instruct witnesses at times by our questioning of them. For instance, we gave Miss Masters a little information today she didn't have before. You'd be surprised how some people, if they're open-minded at all, will change their attitudes during the course of several appearances, and as they learn there is another side, one with some merit, even change their testimony."

"That's interesting. Say, do you want me to come to Dr. Hatch's deposition, or any of the others, Silvana or Parmelee?"

"No, I don't think so. You'd destroy the casual nature of the affair which is important to maintain. People don't realize, sitting casually around a lawyer's office, how binding every word they say still is. Later on, you can hang them on their carelessness or cockiness. Of course, I'll want you to read their depositions, and comment on them."

"You still don't know when you're going to take Matthew Hatch's deposition?"

"I've already called his office five times. He's busy, he's going to a meeting in San Francisco for the weekend, he's in surgery. We'll pin him down, though, even if we have to get a court order. By the way, I need a good deal more briefing myself on all the technical details of a cholecystectomy. Can you sit down with me and some of your surgical textbooks and go over it all soon?"

"Sure, anytime. I'm free all afternoon every day until seven in the evening."

"Tomorrow's Thursday, I don't have anything in court, and no special appointments. How about two or three hours of your time then? Try to find a good illustration of the gallbladder area at surgery that we can blow up, too." Mr. Cousman stood up, suddenly cheery, and bounced around his desk to say good-bye to Peter.

33

A WEEK later Peter went through the giving of his deposition. Before it, he and Mr. Cousman had several conferences which were hours long and wearing, but Peter enjoyed them, enjoyed getting to know the lawyer better. At a light lunch in Oakland just prior to driving to San Marcial for the deposition, Mr. Cousman stopped discussing the Corti case and spent their hour together telling Peter fascinating stories of some of his previous encounters in the law. One involved property lines in an oil belt where the argument over boundaries concerned land worth a hundred million dollars. After a year of testimony in court his client had won. Then there were stories of sexual deviates, rich women who had shot their husbands, Arabian princes, and one about a modern Svengali who had entranced a wealthy dowager and fleeced her out of half a million dollars.

Just before lunch was over, Mrs. Cousman joined them for coffee and a small brandy. Peter was surprised by her. She was small, very dark, much younger than her husband, attractive and rather shy.

Driving to San Marcial, Peter asked, "Mrs. Cousman isn't the mother of your young Todd, is she?"

"Oh, no. She and Todd are about the same age. The first Mrs. Cousman and I separated many years ago and she has since died. Mrs. de Vega, I call the second Mrs. Cousman that for clarity, was kind enough and temporarily unhinged enough to honor me by accepting my proposal of marriage only nine years ago. She helped raise Todd, though, who's back East with a law firm now, but may come here someday with me."

"Your Mrs. de Vega reminds me of my Anne. I wish you could meet her someday. Of course, I'm not even seeing her now myself, but that should change."

"Sometime I'll take us all out to dinner at the finest place in the Bay Area. It's a private restaurant on Russian Hill, and belongs to a Frenchman, who I happen to know is also part Malaysian."

Lawyer Tupper's office was in the aging Johnston Building. Mr. Tupper's own consultation room was comfortably if simply furnished. Walking in, Peter was interested to see Dr. Joseph Parmelee there talking to the San Francisco man, Shannon Sheaffer. Joe looked up and smiled his blank, meaningless smile.

In a quiet but obviously deliberate way, without notes of any sort, Mr. Sheaffer went at Peter hip and thigh, hammer and tongs. He was working to confuse, trying to find contradictions or misstatements in his testimony, with his calm, repetitive, often circuitous questions.

He also asked him about Anne, how well he knew her, what their relationship was, what surgery she had had, and where she was now.

Then abruptly, after two and a half hours, it was over, and all in all had been less complete, covered less ground than Peter had been prepared for.

"Do you suppose they haven't gotten a satisfactory statement from Dr. Hatch or the others yet, so they don't know what to ask?" Peter said.

"Maybe so," Mr. Cousman answered, seeming preoccupied.

"What's the matter?" Peter asked. "Did I do something wrong? I suppose it might seem I'm stupid or dishonest in not recognizing the error Dr. Hatch made during surgery, but when a person's working deep in the belly you really can't see that well and I'm not a good enough surgeon to recognize every mistake that might be made."

"No, that's not what's on my mind, Peter. You did perfectly all right. I'm just surprised, as you are, at what they didn't ask you. I mean, Sheaffer didn't even go into the postoperative care, which is damned important. Of course, they may be intent on settling before the trial, or have star witnesses, or shiny tricks, up their sleeves. You get noses in your fingertips and ears in your rear end in this business, and I find it just a little fishy today, which worries me. But I work best when I'm worried, so I always try to worry."

The next Monday Mr. Cousman finally got to take Dr. Hatch's deposition.

"I'm making him take the entire day off," he told Peter on the phone at noon, "so I can question him the whole time. I have a thousand things to ask him, literally, and I can't get them all in. But the good news is this, he's cocky, cocky as hell, and his lawyers aren't getting through to him to take it easy, be careful. At first he said, 'I don't have to answer your silly questions, you know. I'm here as a favor to you.' And then later he said, 'I'm not here to help anybody but myself.' Those kinds of statements can create a bad impression on a jury."

"I understand," Peter said, shaking his head to get himself more awake.

"I called to ask you," Mr. Cousman said, "when you open the peritoneum, how long before you'd actually see the gallbladder?"

"Well, it would take a few minutes usually to clear away intestines and omentum."

"All right, I just wanted to be sure about that for the attack this afternoon. I'm going to skim over that surgical anatomy book again, and then read through the section in Collins, before I go steaming back in there."

Two days later they got together to review Matthew Hatch's deposition which the reporter had just finished typing. Mr. Cousman was obviously excited. "You see what he said here," he told Peter, "he said he always knew where everything was in the gallbladder bed within *thirty seconds* after the gallbladder was exposed. And again he says, now let's see where that is, yes, here he says, 'I can do a gallbladder operation, and do it well, in thirty-five or forty minutes and I *have* done that. Thirty-three minutes is not too fast for me. You see I've done over nine hundred gallbladder operations.' "

"Anytime he tells you anything that involves a figure, you can cut what he says to one-half or even a third and you'll come closer to the truth," Peter said.

"I realize that. Now is there any way we could check his assertions about the nine hundred operations?"

"I don't know. It would be hard unless you had the cooperation of his record room, and I'm sure we wouldn't."

"He admitted he took out the appendix too in the thirty-three minutes."

"I noticed that."

Mr. Cousman shook his head and went on. "I'm trying to find some of the people at the club meeting he presented his slides to that night after surgery, to see if he rushed in, or what. He says it was something that made no difference to him, that he didn't even have to show up, and that there was no necessity to hurry to it."

"It could be worthwhile to follow that up."

"Now another thing he said, I think rashly, was that he operates immediately on all acute gallbladders."

"Which he does," Peter put in.

"I know, but now we have him saying it during his deposition, it's down in black and white as his testimony. As you pointed out to me, and all the texts I pick up seem to say, there are times when you go right in, and other times you might do everything possible medically to tide the patient over the acute, shocky phase of the illness, and then in a week or two when he's in better shape, with the infection subsided, go ahead and operate. This is what a reasonable doctor would understand and explain, but that isn't his tactic. He isn't being cautious or prudent in his answers. He says, 'Look here, with my infallible judgment I go right in and take out all those acute gallbladders right now, *Stat.*, regardless of what anyone else says to do.' "

"Tell me, did you get around to the operation?"

"Well, first let me say that I think a *res ipsa loquitur* plea is going to be out. We'll mention it, and try to give it a go, but I think the only place it would have a chance would be on an appeal, because this Hatch is going to make it tough for us. If he conceded he'd tied the artery off, but that it was not negligence, rather was needed for some reason, or inescapable because of cancer being present, we'll say, then we might have a *res ipsa*, you see. But he's not going to concede a thing, much less that he did anything wrong, or that anything went wrong. As far as he's concerned, he did a beautiful job. The patient died. As you say, if he doesn't want to see something or believe something, it doesn't exist."

"That's true, but not completely. Some light filters through." Peter told him about Frank Lewicki's conversation with Matthew Hatch on the use of intravenous cortisone and Pyramidon, a dangerous mixture which he indiscriminately injected by the gallon into his patients, but then suddenly wondered if it was right when he was treating his sister. "And he uses Chloromycetin as if it were water, for colds or anything, which even by act of the state legislature is to be considered only in life-threatening illnesses, but still he asked me if I thought he should give it to his wife when she had a bad sore throat."

"That's very interesting to me. I'm really trying to understand this man. Personally, I think he's a psychopath. We get them in the law too, of course, and they are bastards to handle. But this Hatch is a real crook to me, a criminal. That's the way I think of him. You know, I'm hating him more all the time."

"I want to see him hurt and beaten, but I can't really hate him. I should hate him, but I don't. I'm still trying to understand him."

"Just a minute, listen to this exchange:

"COUSMAN: Now, Dr. Hatch, Dr. de Haan has already given his deposition and in it he states that he observed the autopsy on Mr. Louis Corti and noted the hepatic artery to have a ligature around it rather than the cystic artery, the artery which was supposed to be tied off. Would you comment on this statement of Dr. de Haan's?

"HATCH: I am absolutely certain that he was in error. I always identify the hepatic artery, and the cystic artery branching off it, as I did in this case, and of course tie off the cystic branch. I recall distinctly doing that in this case. Dr. de Haan is a young and very inexperienced doctor and I believe incapable of accurately identifying these structures inside the abdomen.

"COUSMAN: Since you were not at the autopsy how can you be sure that this artery was not found to be tied off?

"HATCH: I rely of course partly on my pathologist, Dr. Parmelee, who did not report the hepatic artery to be tied off. I examined the organ specimens later that night, though, after Dr. Parmelee called me, and found no suture around the hepatic artery, but rather around the cystic artery.

"COUSMAN: You admit that examining any specimens 'later that night' would hardly be the same as viewing them in place, nor as legally admissible evidence, when the organs had been cut up and detached from their normal relationships?

"HATCH: Well, I know what I saw. The whole thing is a pile of nonsense and stupidity by an unhappy young man with a grudge.

"COUSMAN: I wonder if you would mind confining your statements to simple answers to my questions, please, Doctor. I'm trying to get at some understanding of this business of the hepatic artery.

"HATCH: I'm not here to help you do anything, Mr. Cousman. You might as well get that straight.

"COUSMAN: However that may be, isn't it true that when the hepatic artery is mistakenly ligated at surgery the patient dies of high fever and toxemia with signs of liver failure?

"HATCH: I don't know anything about the condition. I've had no experience with it.

"COUSMAN: You mean to say that you are a general surgeon who has done hundreds of cholecystectomies during your professional life, and you have no knowledge of the papers or literature on the subject of this possible calamity of improper gallbladder surgery?

"HATCH: Of course I am familiar with the printed matter, and I've talked to others who knew of this condition. I just mean I know nothing of it from my own personal experience."

"Do you see what I mean, Peter? He's a difficult, obstructing witness who's going to make you pull any information out of him with a claw hammer. But you know, I think I can get him in court."

"He's a complicated person."

"It's like going on a tiger hunt, you know, for me, and I'm already eager to taste blood."

"What do you plan to do?"

"I'm not going to let out all my little secrets and surprises. Really, they have to stew and simmer inside for a while to come out right. To give you a little better answer, though, I think I can get to Hatch, for one thing, through the autopsy report. Even though its conclusion is simply, 'Acute hepatic necrosis,' and there is no mention of a ligature around the wrong artery in it, the entire record there, the descriptions and the pathologic terms, leads one to that inescapable conclusion. I think I can trap Parmelee and Hatch on it whether they admit anything about the ligature or not. I have a top-notch pathologist looking it over now, and this feeling of mine is a result of our conversations. Incidentally, I'm subpoenaing the slides for him to look over too. He won't testify for us, but he helps me with thoughts and suggestions."

"That's great. You take on Silvana next, and Hatch's expert witnesses, possibly, and then are you going to try to get a date set in court?"

"Yes. I'm worried about that Silvana one. Oh, of course there'll be a deposition, too, on Parmelee. I'm not going to work him over too much now, though. I think with him I'll save my big guns for the jury." He stood up and handed Peter the Hatch transcript. "I want you to read this whole thing, and make notes on every thought that comes to you about it, please."

In a few days when Peter saw Mr. Cousman again he found the attorney's fears about Norman Silvana's deposition had been confirmed. "He's definitely a hostile witness. He was evasive with me, but I believe he won't lie. He may try to distort the truth, but not lie. Today he wouldn't say if the ligature was around the artery or not. He kept saying it had appeared to him that it was around the artery, but it might not have been. He knows very well that he is virtually positive it was around the hepatic artery, but he's taking what seems to him the only possible way out without lying or perjuring himself. He's a hard-head, isn't he?"

"He is. He's tough, and has a mind of his own, but he's not stupid and he's a good doctor. I respect him. He doesn't like Matthew Hatch at all, but on the other hand he thinks that a malpractice suit is ordinarily a combination effort of Lucifer and the Marquis de Sade."

"I wish he'd change, because to have him on our side would be a real cushion for us."

"Do you think it would do any good for me to talk to him?"

"No, I don't really believe so. I'm not sure that you should talk with him when he is a hostile witness. It could be misinterpreted."

"But you need someone to back up my testimony that the artery was really tied off."

"Yes, but there is a funny thing, you can get too good a case, too. Juries have an innate respect for a doctor, particularly one like Hatch who will probably give a strong, self-assured appearance, and make the jury react emotionally against the plaintiff's side. They don't like to do something that would punish a doctor forever, when it seems he was caught in a momentary lapse, perhaps because of overwhelming professional pressures. At times, juries have even thought that a doctor's mishandling of a case seemed so bad, so atrocious, that they decided if they found him guilty he might be sent to prison for criminal malpractice, and have therefore brought in a verdict for the defendant rather than destroy the man's whole life, which they may have felt was essentially a deserving one. So you have to present a case where the preponderance of evidence points toward your side, but you have to leave the doctor-defendant the chance for his self-respect in the eyes of the jury, even if you know him to be a miserable crook like Hatch. It's a fine, but often important point in these cases."

"That's a depressing analysis."

"Do you know that in over fifty-five percent of malpractice cases tried in courts the ultimate finding is for the defendant, which doesn't even consider the thousands of ones that are thrown out, dismissed, or withdrawn before trial?"

"Why are you telling me all this? You're supposed to be our fountain of confidence, bucking up all the plaintiff's people. You'll be scaring us off instead."

"What it would take to scare you off is four howitzers pointed at your head by grinning, insane Eurasian sadists eagerly reaching for their firing buttons."

34

THOUGH he had talked to Anne several times on the telephone, after two months of not seeing her, Peter drove to Berkeley and waited outside her apartment late one afternoon until she came home.

"Hello," she said, as he came up the steps while she unlocked her front door, "how long have you been here?"

"An hour."

"I'm surprised. Come on in."

Her studio room had sketches and partly finished oils on the walls, and a view of a leafy garden out the back window. Peter noticed that one of the drawings looked like a side view of him.

"Darling," he said. "I miss you so much. That's what I came over here today to say."

"I miss you, too. It's hard not to call you or see you, but I still think it's the right thing."

"It's terribly lonely."

"You ought to go out some. I told you I've been dating."

"I don't want to. I guess you just feel that we're all through, and won't say so. Is that what it amounts to?"

"No, you know that's not so. I've always told you the exact truth."

They talked for an hour longer, but she remained distant, no longer his Anne, and though she kissed him lightly on the lips as he left, he was unhappy after his visit. While he was with her, she had a telephone call, and he was sure it was her friend, Stanley. They talked easily, familiarly, and she laughed several times at what he said. Peter refused to ask her whom she was talking to and she did not say. Driving to Oakland, he decided that Stanley was controlling her now more than he was and he felt almost glad to run into a heavy workload at the Fabiola Hospital that night to dilute his despondency. He should do what Anne was doing, find a friend. There were several attractive, unmarried nurses around Fabiola, but they did not interest him. The sad fact was that Anne had spoiled everyone else for him.

That evening there was a phone call from Rosalie Hatch. "I wanted to find out why you're doing all this," she said. "I've been so shocked and so upset. You know how close I felt to you. I can't believe you'd do a thing like this to Matthew, and I can't get it out of my head that you're really doing it to me." Peter could tell suddenly that she had been drinking. Her voice was too careful—still there were slight imprecisions in it. "I know I flirted with you, but you couldn't have expected me to go ahead with an affair with you, not with my family and husband and everything. God knows I'd gladly sleep with you now, or would have then, if it meant you'd stop this business. It's going to drive Matthew crazy."

Peter did not believe anyone could be such a point-misser,

but on the other hand, knowing Matthew Hatch, he could imagine what warped impressions, what misinformation he might give her. "Rosalie, you had nothing to do with this affair. It just is completely unrelated to you. I'm sorry for how upsetting it must be to you, but you should know I feel I'm right in what I'm doing."

"I don't see how you can say that." She sounded angry now. "And I don't suppose you'd *admit* what happened between us had anything to do with the suit anyway. But for God's sake won't you call this whole thing off?"

"I can't do that, Rosalie. If I wanted to, I couldn't, and I don't want to."

"I can make a lot of trouble for you. If I tell what happened between us, it would look pretty bad for you, you know."

"Oh, Rosalie, don't be ridiculous. There's really nothing to tell, and if there were, it wouldn't have anything to do with the case." Peter sighed in annoyance. "Besides which, I think it would be personally foolish for you to do such a thing. It would create more of a problem for you than for me."

"I'm not going to talk to you anymore. There's just no sense in it. Good night." She hung up sharply then, and Peter did not hear from her again.

The pre-trial activities took place the last week in June, surprisingly soon, Mr. Cousman told Peter. The judge cut Dr. Hatch's expert witnesses down from six to three. Little else was accomplished except that all doctor and hospital expenses for Louis Corti were attested to as legitimate and proper by both sides so as to avoid any dispute during the trial itself. At the end of the pre-trial, the judge astonished Mr. Cousman by saying that several cases on his calendar had had their venue changed, so there would be an opportunity to try this case starting Wednesday, July 20th, if the attorneys felt this was adequate time for preparation. Both sides agreed at once, Mr. Cousman quite happily. He said to Peter, "The jury finds it more interesting to get right into something when it's fresh. Incidentally, I believe you ought to be present during the selection of the jury. It would be a good psychological point for our side."

Peter sat fascinated through the whole first day in court that was required to *voir dire* and empanel the jury. There was a surprise right at the start of the day. Shannon Sheaffer and Martin Tupper stepped forward to announce that Houston Tolliver of San Francisco would also be associated with them in the case, along with a Robert Mongan, who had already been associated. An official filing of this move was handed to the court and accepted by the judge, a small, red-faced, great-nosed Mr. Fielding.

Mr. Tolliver stepped up to take over the questioning as Alfred O. Cousman leaned back, smiling at Peter. "I guess we've really got them more scared than we ever realized. They've got the biggest name in the field for Hatch, old Hugh Tolliver. Now we'll see some real fireworks, believe me."

From the vantage of his seat at the bench inside the court's railing, and just behind Mr. Cousman's table, Peter watched the new attorney with interest. He was tall, with long, wavy gray hair and a small gray moustache. He was a little stouter than he should have been, but vigorous in manner. His dress, in contrast to Mr. Cousman's, was somber and inconspicuous, a dark blue suit with an almost invisible pinstripe, a small-knotted solid blue tie. The only extravagant touch was a fluffed-up white handkerchief in his breast pocket.

Peter was afraid Mr. Alfred Cousman, his good friend now as well as lawyer for his side, would seem eccentric, certainly physically inconspicuous, almost bumbling beside his imposing cross-Bay rival.

He watched as Mr. Cousman got up to interview the jurors. "I want to emphasize," Mr. Cousman said, "that we are selecting jurors for a case involving claimed negligent treatment of a patient by a doctor. This is a trial to recover damages for alleged injury, but the complaint does not state or imply, and judgment for the plaintiff, the party I represent, will not imply criminal or unethical conduct by the defendant. Also, I want you to understand that there is great difficulty in getting doctor witnesses to testify against their colleagues, in getting them to give expert medical evidence for the plaintiff, and that this fact makes the plaintiff's case more difficult to collect and present. Additionally, I think it should be made clear at the outset that for us to be granted a verdict only requires that we present proof to a preponderance. This is not a criminal case, and if the judge so instructs you, and he will, it will be to the effect that it is not necessary for us to prove our case beyond a reasonable doubt or to a moral certainty. The evidence we present must be stronger than the defendant's, but if it is just a little bit stronger, if there is only a slightly greater ring of truth to it, we are still entitled to the verdict."

Peter realized now that his fears about their lawyer were unnecessary. He noted that Mr. Cousman's speech was precise, and that his manner and spirit had at once taken the attention of everyone in the courtroom.

"Now, Mr. Christy," Mr. Cousman said, "you are first here, and I would like to ask you if you are a great admirer of the medical profession and of their accomplishments in our times?"

"I am, sir, in my way."

"Your occupation, Mr. Christy?"

"I'm a retired fireman, sir."

"I see. Did you at any time assist in any fire rescue squad work?"

"I did a great deal of that up until the last few years of my time in the fire department."

"Did your work often involve your rendering artificial respiration and pressure breathing to people who had become acutely ill before they were transferred to the hospitals for care?"

"Yes, sir, it did."

"Did you enjoy that type of work?"

"Very much."

Mr. Cousman asked a number of other questions, and then turned the man over to the defendant's attorney.

"Thank you," Mr. Tolliver said. "Mr. Christy, have you ever served as a juror in a case such as this?"

"No, sir, I haven't. I was a juror once for a robbery case a long time ago."

"Do you realize that a doctor does not guarantee a cure when you come to him for treatment?"

"Yes, I think I understand that."

"Do you feel that doctors in general overcharge?"

"No, I don't."

By lunchtime the two lawyers had seen three juror candidates excused for cause, while Mr. Tolliver had issued three peremptory challenges, and Mr. Cousman had turned out four.

"What was wrong with that fireman?" Peter asked him at lunch, intrigued by the processes of the legal mind.

"He bothered me. He was involved in all those rescue missions in the past, and I'm sure he has built up a feeling of camaraderie with the medical profession. Firemen, policemen, people like that, work a great deal on what I would call preconceived ideas—they know who's good, what's good, they believe in things instinctively, and it's harder to affect them logically. They make up their minds quickly and then are difficult to change. Besides, this Christy seemed *too* anxious to be on the jury. He was trying to answer the questions to satisfy me."

"What do you think of Mr. Tolliver, and of the judge?"

"Hugh, of course, I've worked with before, as you know. He has a splendid courtroom presence, and impresses the hell out of everybody right away. I just let him do it, let him take over the bit of making everybody realize just how tremendous he is, and then after a while they all get used to it and aren't impressed anymore, which is when I put on my elevator shoes, stretch out my chest, and start flapping my wings."

"Do you really have elevator shoes?" Peter laughed.

"Sure I do. Wait and see. Oh, about the judge, I know him too. I never had a case before him, but one of my partners did. He was in practice for a long time himself; I imagine had a lot of professional men as his clients. He's a squirrely little guy with his big nose and big head and those great big blue coyote eyes of his. I imagine he'll be prejudiced in favor of Dr. Hatch, but still I hope fair."

By the end of the day the jury panel had been selected. There were four women and eight men, and another man as alternate. Cousman had wanted to get married people on the jury, and ten of these people were married. There were two Italians on the panel, one man and one woman, but there was also a former patient of Dr. Hatch's whom Mr. Tolliver had gotten through when Mr. Cousman ran out of peremptory challenges. Mr. Cousman had wanted more women, too, he told Peter, because of the young-bereaved-mother situation, but he had had to settle for four, because so many of the women were too young, or unmarried, or both. They wound up in their eight men with an automobile salesman, a cattle ranch foreman, a jeweler from south county Reading, a young junior high school teacher of mathematics and science, a retired printer, a middle-aged assistant bank cashier, a well-dressed dandy who was in charge of the county's credit union, and finally Mr. Louis Guyton, a prominent farmer in the county, paunchy with weathered skin, and though near sixty still with coal-black hair. Mr. Guyton was promptly named foreman. For the female contingent of the jury there was a spinster county librarian, a housewife and mother of four, a childless woman in her sixties whose husband had a local florist shop, and lastly, a divorced and childless woman of forty who was secretary of the local Housing Authority office. The alternate was a postal clerk, middle-aged, spectacled, humpbacked.

"How long do you think the trial will last?" Peter asked.

"Oh, I'd say twelve court days," Mr. Cousman answered. He was in error by only one day.

35

THE jurors were taking the box, talking to each other, and the gallery was noisily settling into seats, but all hushed as the Corti family came in the next morning. Mrs. Corti had not acceded to Mr. Cousman's request for black, but arrived in a discreet blue suit with white blouse instead, and a small blue hat, gloves, high heels. Her eyes flashed moistly, her cheeks were flushed, as she brought four-year-old Nancy in a fancy pink dress and six-year-old Steven in slacks and sweater with snap-on bow tie onto the bench next to Peter. Mr. Cousman came over promptly, extending his hand in courtly greeting, smiling at her, speaking to her and then to the children in turn.

"Good morning. Good morning. The baby isn't coming, Mrs. Corti?" he asked.

"She had a little temp this morning, Mr. Cousman. I left her home with Teresa."

"That's all right. That's fine. And your father-in-law?"

"He's talking to someone in the hall. He'll be right in."

"Good. Have him sit by you folks when he gets here."

The clerk rose then to intone, "Now hear this, this court is in session, Superior Court, Division Three, of San Marcial County, state of California, the Honorable Russell Fielding presiding." The judge, his white hair flying, strode in looking stern. As everyone rose, Peter glanced around to see Dr. Hatch walk in the double doors, face rosy, eyes darting everywhere, and at a distance looking relaxed and handsome. He smiled and waved at friends before passing through the swinging gate to sit down with his four lawyers at the slick-surfaced, highlighted defendant's table.

The gallery was surprisingly full. Peter estimated there

were forty or fifty onlookers there. The day before, the trial had leaped to the top of the second page in the newspaper, which undoubtedly accounted for many of the spectators. "$825,000 Suit Against Local Doctor for Death After Surgery," the headline had said. Inspecting some of the faces in the gallery he saw six or eight doctors and several nurses from San Marcial, besides a lab technician he knew, and Miss West from the Hatch with a friend. Peter sat down wondering wearily if even the gallery would be unfriendly now.

All the combatants were there in good bib and tucker, clean-shaven or made-up, solemn-faced for the moment, awash with aftershave and antiperspirants, bloodstreams suffused with adrenaline and hydrocortisone, waiting expectantly for the start. Even the jurors bent forward to hear the first words. Peter swallowed on his abruptly dry throat as the ruddy countenance of the judge surveyed the doings, like a seasoned actor looking over the house, before he said to Mr. Cousman, "Counselor for the plaintiff, are you ready to proceed with your opening statement to the jury?"

"I am, your Honor."

Peter saw that Mr. Cousman's hands trembled as he lifted papers from his table and put them down, but when he walked out to face the jury, and began speaking to them, his voice was steady and measured. He quickly summarized the issues of their suit, and began his introductory statements on the evidence they were going to present. Soon he came to the operation itself.

"An acutely infected gallbladder, one that was near rupture according to Dr. Hatch's own words in a statement taken before this trial, was then removed. The evidence will show that this major and delicate procedure, with a thinned, fragile gallbladder, took only *thirty-three* minutes, 'skin-to-skin,' as the medical saying goes." Mr. Cousman paused, looking thoughtfully toward Mrs. Corti for a moment. Then he began to describe Peter's role in the tragic tangle.

"Dr. de Haan, though not being able during the surgery to see the specific act of negligence we are charging, will testify as to the fact of Dr. Hatch's speed, and to the fact that he specifically requested the defendant to note his haste and to slow down. We will further establish that the defendant was the guest speaker at a dinner held by the Daughters of Hibernia in the San Marcial South County Auditorium, some twenty minutes distant by automobile, starting at six fifteen.

There is a presumption that he was hurrying to get to this meeting, and therefore was reckless in his approach to surgery on this fine, trusting young man, failing to visualize clearly the anatomical structures as is proper and necessary in this kind of operation. As a result of this negligent failure, we contend the defendant in error placed a suture around and tied off the main trunk of the hepatic artery which supplies the entire liver with blood, instead of tying off the cystic artery to the gallbladder as he should have. The cystic artery is a branch off this main hepatic artery, and without careful and at times tedious dissection of all the structures in the area of the gallbladder, important surgical errors can be made here with tragic results, such as we contend occurred in the case at issue here." Mr. Cousman took several deep sighing breaths himself as his words died off, then stepped to the middle of the jury panel, where he stationed himself, facing them all directly.

"We will further establish that the defendant was multiply negligent in the post-operative care of the patient, and was also negligent in not performing further exploratory surgery at the urging of a surgical consultant, Dr. Norman Silvana. In fact, Dr. Silvana and Dr. de Haan both urged a further operation, suspecting the problem that existed, but the defendant steadfastly denied them. After the death of the patient, Dr. Hatch, the defendant, told the family when they requested it, that no post-mortem examination was necessary. This examination was obtained then only through the efforts of Dr. de Haan, who will describe for you the findings thereof, including the cut and tied hepatic artery to the liver."

Mr. Cousman moved to the plaintiff's table now and pointed to a collection of papers and exhibits. "Some of our evidence is here. Hospital records, depositions by principal witnesses, charts we have prepared for you on the anatomy of the gallbladder bed, checks and bills showing the expenses of Louis Corti's illness, and financial statements showing the past and present earnings of Mr. Corti, a young man on the rise. We hope to take you then into the future of Louis Corti, to show you what he could reasonably have been expected to accomplish in the three decades of active business life he should have had left to him, and this will allow us to justify to you the very large damages of eight hundred and twenty-seven thousand, two hundred and ten dollars we are asking. You must understand that the law recognizes nothing can compensate a family for the loss of a father, nothing can replace his care, love, comfort and protection, thus certain limits are set on the monetary damages allowed so that sentiment is not allowed to run away with a jury. But the law does provide for recovery of income lost by death, and so we shall prove our claim this way, for young Louis Corti was on his way to an excellent income."

Mr. Cousman slapped down the papers and returned to the jury box. Now he spoke harshly, angrily, clenching his fists as he talked. "We expect to show that all these damages are proper, are appropriate, and that the call for them does arise from the reckless character of the surgery Dr. Matthew Hatch did perform on this man, ceasing for improper reasons to exercise his proper professional skill in the care of this outstanding young husband and father. Athletes strive to break the four-minute mile record and the fifteen-foot high jump, but there are no records kept, no necessary barriers to be broken in the performance of surgical procedures. Results, not speed, are the criteria here. 'Haste makes waste, but speed is often fraught with disaster,' to quote a voice from the past, Elbert Hubbard. The law only requires that a doctor perform his medical duties with average skill and learning consistent with that possessed by doctors in his own or similar localities. The law does require, though, in every event and in all events the utmost good faith of the doctor, and does not tolerate any degree of fraud or deceit. It is the position of the plaintiff that the defendant did fail to exercise the required degree of care and skill in this case, negligently tying off the vitally important artery to the liver in Mr. Corti, and in so doing causing his death. Additionally, the plaintiff also hopes to establish that there was evident lack of good faith on the part of Dr. Hatch in his relationship with this patient both at the time of surgery and subsequently in the management of this case. After death the wife was only told that infection and poor anesthesia had caused her husband's demise. You will note as partial refutation to that statement that we are not including the anesthesiologist in this complaint."

Mr. Cousman's body relaxed now, his shoulders slouched mildly, as his quietest words of the day followed. "We are not here to punish this doctor or take away his license. We are not asking you to condemn him to notoriety or to loss of the right to practice medicine. We are not exposing him to criminal negligence charges. We are merely asking you to hear the evidence, to decide on the facts of the case, and then hopefully to determine that this bereaved family deserves some reasonable recompense for what they have lost. In summary, then, it is our claim that Dr. Hatch acted negligently, and that this family deserves a judgment through the law."

Mr. Cousman walked slowly, almost sadly back to his table. Peter leaned forward and whispered to him. "That was great. Marvelous, but I thought you weren't going to wear your elevator shoes yet, and here I see you have them on."

"What? Oh, yes. That's surprise, the supreme element necessary to survive in courtrooms. I even fool myself sometimes."

The judge looked over the courtroom still filling with spectators, many of whom had taken the brief gap in activity to whisper and shuffle around. He pounded down his gavel twice, and said to the defendant's table, "Are you ready to proceed with your opening statement to the jury, Mr. Tolliver?"

"Yes, of course I am, your Honor." The mellifluous voice sounded through the corners and recesses of the room, and those souls not quieted by the gavel subsided into interested silence at Mr. Tolliver's resonance. He stood up, a small unopened notebook in his hand, and walked to the jury box. "That was an eloquent statement by Mr. Cousman, ladies and gentlemen of the jury," he said, standing directly before them for all to see his tall, straight form, his handsome, moustached face, his sturdiness, his assurance, "but statements are one thing, and proof is another. In a suit of this sort it is necessary for the plaintiff to convince three-fourths of the members of a jury such as you that the preponderance of evidence bears out his or her contentions. The plaintiff's case is presented first. After it, the judge may decide that there is not sufficient evidence to support the plaintiff's claims and dismiss the complaint, or deliver a directed verdict for the defendant. Only after this point is passed does the defense come into play. And still the defense need not disprove anything, nor rebut anything. Rather, it is always up to the plaintiff to bring evidence to bear to preponderantly prove his claim. I introduce my remarks with these words of explanation to help you through your journey here these next days or weeks. Don't look for us, the defendants, to disprove the charges, rather, look for the plaintiff to prove them, to make them stick, to make you believe in them against our efforts to undermine your belief. And we'll do just that, we will undermine your impressions for the plaintiff, because we have good, strong, believable, honest, negating facts to present." Mr. Tolliver now moved along to the back of the jury box talking as he walked, firm in his manner, careful with his words.

"You must all realize, too, that the plaintiffs must not only prove that the negligence which they accuse the defendant of took place, but they must show this act was the direct, effective, what we in law call the 'proximate' cause of the patient's injury for which they are seeking recovery of damages."

Mr. Tolliver was going to be a difficult adversary, Peter realized. He had expected verbal fireworks from him, declamations, hand-wringing, loud, slick, moving phrases. Next to Mr. Cousman's skillful opening statement, these circusy sounds and affectations would probably have been grainy and ineffective. Instead, Tolliver had taken off on an entirely new tack, straight erudition and instructionism. How wise it was. The jury, if not yet warming in just the way they had for Mr. Cousman, was listening carefully.

"Now, other important matters to keep in your minds are first, that the plaintiff's proof of cause must go beyond merely indicating the possibility that Mr. Corti's death resulted from the negligence of the defendant, for the jury cannot speculate on causation of injury. Secondly, any surgery, you must all realize, all of us do realize, carries with it the risk of death. Dr. Hatch is not a god among men, a miracle-worker among doctors. He is only a human being. He did his best in the case of Mr. Louis Corti, and we will show this. He did his very best, as he always does for all of his patients. His life is lived as a dedication to his patients. Talk to his wife, talk to his children, find out how little they see of him, how much of his time and energy is spent caring for his patients, and you will realize how dedicated and responsible a man we have now as defendant in this unnecessary suit." He paused now and raised his voice as he moved in front of the defense table, pointing to Dr. Hatch, who in turn looked up at him. "But you must understand that this fine man, as all physicians, is only required by the law to treat a patient with 'the reasonable degree of skill and learning,' and these are legal words so I quote them here, 'the reasonable degree of skill and learning possessed by others in his own or a similar locality.' Only if injury is caused by such lack of care or skill on his part would he be liable to damages. We will show, in the course of this trial, that the defendant, Dr. Matthew Hatch, passes this test easily and unquestionably. Ladies and gentlemen of the jury, I thank you for your attention." There was a stir of comment in the courtroom as Mr. Tolliver sat down.

"Mr. Cousman, will you proceed now?" Judge Fielding asked.

"Your Honor, I had subpoenaed the chief record clerk at the Hatch Hospital along with all the records, both hospital records and Dr. Hatch's own office records, as they are kept together in the same chart there, but the defendant's counsel agreed that they should be introduced without her formal testimony. I would like to offer them in evidence at this time as plaintiff's exhibit of the official business records of the Hatch Hospital, kept in the regular course of business of the hospital."

"Plaintiff's Exhibit One will be the records of the Hatch Hospital, including the outpatient records of Dr. Matthew Hatch," the judge said.

"Your Honor, I want it to be understood that part of the stipulation by the defendant's lawyer, Mr. Tolliver, when we discussed this yesterday in your chambers, was that these are without question the official business records of the hospital, is that right, Mr. Tolliver?"

"You know that is so, Mr. Cousman," the judge answered.

"To be even more sure, we have had an official statement prepared by the hospital record room librarian and duly witnessed and notarized. It is attached to these photostatic copies of all hospital and office records on Mr. Corti by Mrs. Jennie Washburn, the librarian."

"Is all this necesary?" Mr. Tolliver asked.

"Perhaps not," Mr. Cousman said. "Just being cautious."

"Do you have other exhibits now?" the judge asked.

"Yes. Exhibit Two is the file card from the Hatch Hospital and Clinic business office, showing all charges made to Mr. Corti or his estate to a total of two thousand, two hundred and ten dollars and twenty cents. Will it be stipulated by you that this is the charge sheet, Mr. Tolliver?"

"Certainly. No certified and notarized statement with it, Mr. Cousman?"

"Now Exhibit Three of the plaintiff is six, no seven, X-rays taken of the deceased Mr. Corti while hospitalized."

"Stipulated to," Mr. Tolliver said.

"Are these all your exhibits for now?" the judge asked.

"Yes, your Honor," Mr. Cousman answered. "I would like to call as our first witness Mrs. Margaret Corti, the plaintiff."

Peggy Corti stood up, but her four-year-old began whimpering, so she made a face at her, picked her up, kissed her solemnly, and put her in her grandfather's lap, before going to the stand to be sworn in.

"I know that I told you this the other day, but will you try to speak up so all the jurors can hear you?" Mr. Cousman said to her pleasantly.

"Yes, I will."

Mr. Cousman paused and looked at her. Peter felt he knew what the lawyer was thinking. There she was, poised and attractive, nicely dressed, undoubtedly sick at heart and desperate at times, but determined not to show it to the world. She would recover, perhaps even marry again, but she had been through hell, and Mr. Cousman wanted the jury to see it. To expose it, as was his obligation, he would have to hurt her now, even embarrass her, get inside her and disclose some of the despondency and deep sorrow that was there.

He took her through the routine opening questions, and then asked about their life together.

"Were you happily married?"

"Oh, very. We didn't argue at all, except once in a while because he'd never scold the children. I always had to do that."

"He was a good father, then?"

"Yes, he was wonderful. He was always taking the children somewhere, or bringing something home for them."

"Being so busy in recent years with his work, did that leave him little time for home?"

"He always found time for us and for the children. We went out to dinner and dancing or to some friend's house almost every weekend, and he always saved all day Sunday just for the kids."

"Did he work around the house some, or in the garden?"

"Your Honor, I object to this line of questioning as immaterial and irrelevant," Mr. Tolliver said impatiently from his seat.

"Oh, I think we will allow it, Mr. Tolliver, up to a point," Judge Fielding said.

"Mrs. Corti, did your husband work around the house or in the garden a good deal?" Mr. Cousman continued.

"He used to, but of course since he was so busy, and

making so much more money in recent years, we hired a gardener and an—"

"Now I do object to that, your Honor," Mr. Tolliver said.

"Strike that last as indicating the financial position of these people," the judge said.

Mr. Cousman took Mrs. Corti through more details of the pleasant years she had with her husband, her good nature and her happiness at their life together showing through in her testimony. Then he went into the painful matters of the illness, how it started, what she saw and felt going to the hospital, watching Lou there so ill and getting encouraging reports about his condition from Dr. Hatch daily. Next, she told of being suddenly alerted by Dr. de Haan, in the early afternoon Thursday, to the very critical nature of her husband's illness, and then staying with Louis through the rest of the day and night until Friday morning, when he died. She emphasized how much of the time Dr. de Haan had been there with her husband, how little of the time she had seen Dr. Hatch. She repeated Dr. Hatch's conversation after Lou's death, how he had said Lou's death could not have been avoided, but was interrupted by a hearsay objection by Mr. Tolliver, so she continued giving only the gist of what she had understood from Dr. Hatch.

During her description of her husband's last hours she had begun to weep, and Mr. Cousman pushed her through the rest of the questions with a little difficulty. He stepped back when it was over, looking a little shaken himself at her grief. Peter knew he felt he had at least done his duty to her, hard as it was, by revealing as she had tried to hide, the depth and fineness of her feelings for her husband, her lover, the father of her children, as well as the agony at his loss that would persist.

Peggy sat down next to Peter, looking older for her hour on the stand, her eyes no longer bright, her lids puffed with the irritation of crying. Mr. Tolliver had asked her no questions. He had probably wished to get the appealing and attractive widow off the stand as soon as possible, Peter concluded, to give the jury as little as possible to remember about her.

Peggy Corti took the children home at the noon recess, and Mr. Corti went with her. Mr. Cousman wanted to meet with the Corti accountant who was to testify that afternoon, so Peter found himself having lunch alone in the large cafeteria of the courthouse. He was embarrassed there by running into some doctors from town, Richard Caspari, the young urologist, and Al Belcher, radiologist at the Valley Hospital. They were apparently down for the afternoon session, and getting lunch beforehand. Seeing him behind them in line, Dick Caspari turned and stared. "Hello, buddy," he said. Al Belcher simply looked back, and shook his head. Peter blushed and then felt angry at himself for it, and angry at them for their stupid behavior that made him blush.

Eating his meal, he was gloomy, lonely, missing Anne and thinking of her. It had been almost a physical shock, he realized, to see Matthew Hatch in the courtroom. Not just because he had become increasingly more shadowy in Peter's thoughts, like an old portrait on some museum wall, but also because seeing him again, pleasant-looking, in good health, sitting quietly at his defendant's table, Peter had felt for a moment the old original tug of friendliness and attraction toward him. Appearances, appearances. They were damnable.

36

"YOUR Honor, I call Dr. de Haan to the stand as a witness for the plaintiff."

It was the next afternoon. Peter stood up, his palms cold and moist. He crossed the floor, mounted the witness stand, was sworn in, and at once started to relax. He inspected the jury again as Mr. Cousman was arranging papers on his table. The faces in the box seemed frank and even friendly enough. From the new elevation some of them looked different, grayer or fatter, younger or thinner. Mr. Guyton, the foreman, scowled intently at him. The woman next to him in the front row, looking almost too businesslike and self-assured, had knitting in her lap and a notebook too. A south county jeweler, Harrison Brubaker, smiled benignly at him from the middle of the back row. Peter turned his gaze to the defendant's table and saw several medical colleagues leaning over the railing of the enclosure so they could pat Matthew Hatch on the back. Then for a moment Dr. Hatch looked directly at Peter, a smile spread broadly across his face. The bastard.

The two hundred seats of the gallery were filled. Peter saw Dr. Belcher and Dr. Caspari again in the front row, with three or four more from the north county, and several rows back, he recognized Frank Lewicki and Norman Silvana talking with heads bent toward each other. Then Peter realized Al Humphers was right behind Frank with his wife and Herbert Hard's wife, Betty. Quite the social affair, wasn't it? Perhaps better than the local season of the Valley Players.

Judge Fielding, his white hair in disarray, great bags under his huge eyes, rapped his gavel for silence.

After the usual preliminary questions were dispatched, Mr. Cousman asked, "And you were then discharged from the Hatch Medical Clinic on April twenty-third?"

"Yes, I was."

"Was that because of a controversy between you and the defendant, Dr. Matthew Hatch, over the case we are now trying in this court?"

Mr. Tolliver was on his feet at once. "I object to that question as improper. It is leading, and irrelevant and immaterial to the issues here, as well as prejudicial toward my client."

"Objection sustained," Judge Fielding said blandly.

Mr. Cousman sighed and then dug in, reviewing Peter's undergraduate training, his medical school work, and finally his internship. Then his questions turned to the paper Peter had worked on with Dr. Cunningham concerning infection in post-operative patients, since completed and published in the *Surgical Archives*.

Mr. Tolliver stood up again. "Your Honor," he said, "I am not going to stipulate to this young man as an expert witness for this court, in case Mr. Cousman has any such idea. We have here a suit against a doctor of great experience and many years of surgical practice. This young man just out of internship would not accord with my idea of an expert witness for this case."

"Mr. Cousman," Judge Fielding said, after a moment's pause, "I am going to agree there, and I am not going to certify to this young man as an expert witness in the present suit. You have another doctor from Los Angeles coming up to testify and it is assumed that he will be your expert witness, rather than Dr. de Haan."

"Your Honor, you know that the usual course is to presume that any licensed and practicing physician in the state of California is allowed to testify as an expert witness—" Mr. Cousman said.

"This is just ridiculous, your Honor," Mr. Tolliver interrupted.

"Gentlemen, I am going to declare a short recess. We will meet in my chambers at once to settle this before proceeding."

In ten minutes when court reconvened the judge announced, "For the record now I am not going to accept Dr. de Haan as an expert witness for this court. I will review his qualifications later on in the trial if the plaintiff's attorney so wishes."

"Dr. de Haan," Mr. Cousman asked, paler now, "were you employed as a general practitioner of medicine at the Hatch Clinic?"

"Yes, I was," Peter answered, and then continued to describe under questioning the character of his duties, the kinds of cases he had cared for.

"In two different periods you assisted at surgery, both last fall and this spring, then. In how many separate surgical procedures would you estimate you served as assistant to Dr. Matthew Hatch or one of the other surgeons?"

"Between two hundred and fifty and three hundred."

"And you felt that you were able to do an adequate job of assisting through these times?"

"Yes, I believe so."

"During internship at how many procedures did you assist?"

"I'd say approximately one hundred."

"And have you yourself performed any major surgical procedures on patients?"

"During my internship, I did a number of appendectomies and repairs of hernias."

"How many of each?"

"I'd say between six and eight."

Mr. Tolliver stood up with a loud complaint. "I object to this whole line of questioning, your Honor. I think the plaintiff's attorney is still trying to establish the credentials of Dr. de Haan instead of proceeding with evidence pertinent to the suit."

"Your Honor," Mr. Cousman snapped. "I am merely trying to lay a cohesive and understandable background to the significant events of Dr. de Haan's testimony which we'll get to shortly."

"I'm going to allow you to proceed, Mr. Cousman. Objection overruled."

They went ahead with questions about the pre- and post-operative care which he was often responsible for, and shortly they came to the illness of Louis Corti. Mr. Cousman carried Peter carefully through the preliminary details of the hospitalization, and then through the surgery point by point.

"Your Honor," Mr. Cousman said, "I want to submit as Plaintiff's Exhibits Four and Five, a chart of the gallbladder bed with important structures of the area shown on it, and then this general chart of the liver and gallbladder region as seen when exposed at surgery."

The judge inspected the placards, and gave them down to Mr. Tolliver. Mr. Cousman waited. The objection came. "Your Honor, the use of demonstrative evidence I believe brings us so close to employing Dr. de Haan as an expert witness that there would be no practical distinction left as to the difference."

"I understand your point, Mr. Tolliver, and thought you would make it," the judge said in his harsh monotone. "However, I am going to allow this witness to continue to testify with the use of these charts, understanding, Mr. Cousman, that there are to be no hypothetical questions, and no questions for the witness to come to conclusions on matters of opinion, and no questions requiring statements about standards of care."

"I will try to *struggle* along under those provisions, your Honor," Mr. Cousman said, wrinkling his face up at Mr. Tolliver with his back turned to the bench. The jury saw the grimace, and broke into laughter, the first of the trial, and the spectators laughed, too. Judge Fielding pounded his gavel, and turned his wide-open eyes on Mr. Cousman. "There is no need for tricks on your part, sir," he said.

At once solemn again, and with the jury subdued, Mr. Cousman asked the bailiff to set two easels up between the jury box and the witness stand for the charts.

"Now, Dr. de Haan," Mr. Cousman said, "will you let us look at the first large chart there nearest you that illustrates the arrangement of the common bile duct, the cystic duct, the portal vein, and the hepatic artery and so forth, and then use the second diagram to show us about the hepatic artery specifically."

"This picture on the left," Peter said, "indicates the relationship of the various organs in the region of the gallbladder. First there is the liver which normally occupies nearly the whole of the right upper corner of the abdomen. The right side or right lobe of the liver has been pulled up here so that we look at its under surface which shows the gallbladder lying in a fissure of the liver there and attached to it. The fundus or body of the gallbladder hangs down from the lower margin of the liver ordinarily. The neck of the gallbladder passes into the cystic duct, a structure which is about one inch long and which in turn passes into the common hepatic duct. Cystic is an adjective meaning gallbladder here, hepatic is an adjective meaning liver. Cystic duct is the gallbladder duct, common hepatic duct means the ducts from the liver that have joined to form the common drainage channel from the liver."

Peter paused to take a breath and think over what he had just said to see if it made sense. "The gallbladder duct joins the liver duct right here to form the common bile duct which empties into the duodenum."

"The gallbladder then is a reservoir for the storage of bile which can be released down this common bile duct into the intestine when needed for the digestion of foods, particularly fatty foods, is that correct, Doctor?" Mr. Cousman asked.

"Yes, sir. Now this structure, the hepatoduodenal ligament, carries the common bile duct and two very important vessels, the portal vein which brings blood from the intestines to the liver to start the digestive processes, and the hepatic artery, the principal source of blood supply to the tissue of the liver. These three structures, the common bile duct, the portal vein, and the hepatic artery, as they are gathered together here in this ligament, are known as the porta hepatis, meaning the gateway to the liver."

"In other words these structures are the important passageway or gateway, the umbilical cord of the liver in relation to the rest of the body?"

"Yes. Now the second diagram shows the artery circulation to the liver. First, there is the aorta, the great vessel of the abdomen running along the backbone. The celiac artery comes off the front of the aorta, and breaks up almost at once into three branches, an artery to the stomach, an artery to the spleen, and the hepatic artery, the artery to the liver. The hepatic artery runs forward to the top of the duodenum, which is the first part of the small intestine, and then turns up into the hepatoduodenal ligament that we've talked about. As it climbs up into the ligament the hepatic artery gives off the cystic artery or gallbladder artery which usually goes behind the common liver duct and the gallbladder duct to pass to the gallbladder itself."

"This artery, the cystic artery, is routinely cut and tied at the time the gallbladder is removed. Is that right?"

"Yes, but there is a great deal of variation in how the cystic artery comes off the hepatic artery. The main hepatic artery divides into two, a right hepatic artery and a left hepatic artery. Usually the cystic artery comes off the right hepatic artery, that is, in over ninety per cent of people it does. But—"

Mr. Tolliver had been standing again for several minutes and now he spoke. "I'm going to object to this line of questioning again in that I think the information being presented is definitely the type that should come from an expert witness. I mean, how do we know what this young man says is true, whether the cystic artery comes off the right hepatic artery thirty percent of the time, or fifty percent, or ninety percent. This seems to be a subject for expert testimony."

"Your Honor, these charts were prepared by professional medical illustrators from articles in *Surgical Archives* and from classic books such as Gupton's *Regional Anatomy* and Cavendish's *Surgical Anatomy*. I have these books and articles here with me in my assistant's briefcase, and the passages and illustrations dealing with what we are presenting are carefully marked for the defendant's counsel or any member of the jury to inspect and read."

"Mr. Cousman, I will allow you to proceed, but I think that Mr. Tolliver has a point. Cover the rest of the material about these charts quickly, and let your expert witness next week go into more detail if necessary."

"Dr. de Haan, will you finish rapidly then?" Mr. Cousman said.

"Yes. I would like to show these variations on the chart. First, the cystic artery may also arise from the right hepatic artery as two separate trunks. Thus *two* branches of the cystic artery would have to be tied off at surgery. And then the cystic artery may at times arise from the main hepatic artery rather than its right branch."

"Thank you. You may take the stand again. You see this is

complicated anatomy and I think we can all benefit by this first lesson."

Settling himself again in the wooden chair, Peter felt the fabric of his shirt hot and soggy at the collar and over his back. The courtroom had become very warm, and though the cranking whir of the antediluvian fans could be heard above the skylighted ceiling they were obviously no match for the afternoon sun slanting in through the Venetian blinds onto the jam-packed spectators.

Mr. Cousman started in detail through Peter's recollection of the surgical procedure. Peter explained how difficult it was for the assistant to see the surgical field in this operation, and that he was not aware during the surgery of any specific error of cutting or suturing, or of any injury to the vital structures passing through the porta hepatis. He specifically was not aware of any damage to the hepatic artery. He did recall that the gallbladder when removed looked swollen and red, and had several gallstones in it. He remembered clearly that Dr. Hatch seemed to be hurrying through the operation, after saying laughingly at the start that he had to finish this one in thirty minutes because he was due at the South County Auditorium to have a steak dinner and give a talk. Mr. Tolliver had this quickly expunged from the record as hearsay.

Peter then testified that he had directly and bluntly asked Dr. Hatch to slow down several times, but these requests had been greeted with silence and no perceptible diminishing of speed.

As he talked, Peter could see that Dr. Hatch seemed to pay little attention to what he said. He doodled on a pad in front of him, whispered to one of his legal aides, or let his eyes wander around the courtroom. Occasionally he would pour himself some water. With this last exchange, though, he found his eyes directly on him, following his words closely, his features grimly taut. Peter wished one of the jurors might have caught this angry look.

"Dr. de Haan, I wanted you to tell us if you were unable to get Dr. Hatch to come to Mr. Corti's bedside at any time when you felt he should be there."

The judge cleared his throat, and Peter looked over at him, but the magistrate said nothing, simply rolled his large eyes and tipped back his head, then swung his chair away from Peter. "The night of Thursday, April seventh, Louis Corti suddenly got worse when it was obvious he was already desperately ill—"

"Objection. That statement involves a conclusion on the part of the witness," Mr. Tolliver said.

"Sustained. Rephrase your answer, please."

"The night of April seventh, at a time when he already had a high fever and poor blood pressure, Mr. Corti abruptly began vomiting and lost consciousness. We could obtain no pulse at all on him for a few minutes, so I asked the nurse to try to get Dr. Hatch over to see the patient with me."

"What hour was this?"

"About ten at night."

"Did you talk to him yourself?"

"When the nurse said that Dr. Hatch did not see any reason for him to come over, I phoned him and asked him to come. The family wanted him there, for one thing. He said for me to proceed to treat him myself, and tell the family that I'd discussed everything with him, and had received directions."

"Did Dr. Hatch instruct you as to the care of the patient at that time?"

"He did not. He left it all to my own thoughts and methods."

"How long did you stay with the patient?"

"I was in and out all night."

"Did you call Dr. Hatch again about him?"

"Yes, I did, at about two A.M."

"For what reason?"

"About the same thing. He stopped breathing and we could get no pulse on him, and I thought he might be expiring."

"Did you ask him to come over to see the patient?"

"I did, but he declined again. He said there was nothing he could do. He said the family would have to accept the fact that Mr. Corti was going to die. Nothing could be done for him."

"What was Mr. Corti's course after two A.M.?"

"He continued to deteriorate and died about eight thirty in the morning."

"Was Dr. Hatch there at the time of the patient's death?"

"No, he came in a few minutes later on the way to his morning surgery."

"I object," Mr. Tolliver called out. "The last part of that sentence is again a conclusion on the part of the witness."

"Sustained. Strike out the comment about 'on his way to the surgery,' " the judge ordered.

"Dr. Hatch then did not visit the patient's room at all during his last critical night?"

"No, sir, he did not see him from around six o'clock the evening of April seventh, until after his death at eight thirty A.M. the morning of April eighth."

"All right, now, Dr. de Haan, to go back for a moment. Dr. Norman Silvana was called in as a consultant on this case, is that right?"

"Yes, he was. I asked him to see Mr. Corti about noon on Thursday, April seventh."

"And what was Dr. Silvana's impression of Mr. Corti's problem at this point?"

"It is part of the hospital record, his consultation. In it he stated that he thought the patient probably had acute liver failure, or second choice was some overwhelming infection."

"Did Dr. Silvana recommend that Mr. Corti be re-operated?"

"Not on his official, handwritten consultation."

Mr. Cousman read the consultation, and then asked Peter if he would care to amplify.

"There was a long discussion between the two doctors, Norman Silvana and Matthew Hatch, about the patient—"

"I'd like to object to any repetition of the conversation between Dr. Silvana and Dr. Hatch as definitely hearsay, your Honor," Mr. Tolliver immediately said.

"Your Honor," Mr. Cousman returned, "I respectfully submit that this conversation clearly falls into the class of hearsay exceptions as I believe it represents a declaration against interest. I believe also that this conversation is germane to our case and it can be brought before both Dr. Silvana and Dr. Hatch, who will be on this stand in the next week, so they can be questioned and cross-examined as to Dr. de Haan's presentation of it. There is a real necessity for the admission of this conversation, too, because it is the only way we can introduce this particular evidence since there is no written or circumstantial approach to it."

"I am going to overrule you, Mr. Tolliver, at least provisionally, and I am going to allow Dr. de Haan to relate this conversation, holding back the right to strike it."

"I respectfully except, your Honor."

"Exception to you then, Mr. Tolliver."

Peter went ahead to describe the bitter verbal battle between Dr. Silvana and Dr. Hatch, though there were many interspersed comments and frequent objections from Mr.

Tolliver. It was obvious to Peter that this testimony disturbed the lawyer, that he was worried about it and trying to dilute its effect on the jury with diversions.

Finally the judge said to him, "I am not going to tolerate these continuing interruptions from you, Mr. Tolliver. We know that you do not go along with this entire line of questioning, and when this subject is completed, we will decide whether to strike it or not."

Mr. Tolliver clenched his fists and hit them against his thighs, threw his head back to gaze at the ceiling and then shut his eyes. Judge Fielding carefully observed his actions, and then said quietly, "When you are finished we will proceed."

Peter was able to tell how Norman Silvana had said that he felt Louis Corti's trouble could be from a tying off of the hepatic artery, and that surgery should be done to see if this were so, and to correct it if possible. He emphasized Dr. Hatch's complete refusal to consider a re-operation on Louis. His repeated statements that it would be fatal to do so were stressed.

"Then no decision to change the plan of therapy came out of this conversation?"

"No, sir."

"Mr. Cousman, may I interrupt here? How much longer will you be with this witness?" the judge asked.

"I have quite a way to go with him yet, your Honor."

"It's after four thirty. I suggest we recess now until Monday morning. We'll make it ten A.M. as I have other duties earlier that day."

"Fine, your Honor."

"Ladies and gentlemen of the jury, I shall give you the admonition again that you discuss this case with no one, neither among yourselves nor with anyone else. Do not form or express an opinion until the case is finally submitted to you, but rather keep an open mind. Also, I see that some of you have been making notes. This is perfectly all right, but you will kindly seal them in an envelope each time you leave the courtroom, and leave them here with the bailiff for safekeeping."

Peter at that moment saw Rosalie Hatch talking to her husband over the railing, holding his arm with her gloved hand as she smiled at him. In a few moments they left together, as Peter waited for Mr. Cousman who was busy giving his assistant instructions.

"Peter," Mr. Cousman said, coming up to him, "you did all right. You seemed a little nervous at first, but then you settled down and came across fine. You know I was just talking to my associate, Jack Penberthy, here."

"The listening post?"

"Yes, the miraculous ear, whom we have sitting as close to the defendant's table as possible. He says we really got to them with this last testimony, both about the times you tried to get Hatch to come over, and also about the consultation. Of course they'll deny it, at least Hatch will. I don't know what Silvana will do. But it surprised them. You weren't asked about it on your deposition. How could they ask you if Hatch didn't tell them? That's going to be part of their trouble, I can see. Your former employer, as you say, forgets everything he wants to forget, so they can't get the information out of him they need to run an intelligent case."

"Talk about rose-colored glasses."

"Anyway, Jack overheard Tupper, you know, Hatch's local attorney, snap at him, 'How come you never told us about this?' He couldn't hear Hatch's answer. Then later on Tupper said to Houston, 'You'll have to check this all out with Silvana.' Houston came back with something like, 'You can unfasten your seat belt, Tup. We'll work it out.' "

Peter laughed. "I love to hear we're confounding our enemies."

"But we have to do more than confound them. We have to kill them dead," Mr. Cousman said solemnly. "I want you in my office tomorrow morning so we can go over your testimony for Monday. I'll have the sheets from today's testimony by then and we'll look them over, too."

As he left, Peter felt warmer toward the tough old attorney. He saw a kinship developing with A. O. Cousman, who for the first time had called him Peter.

37

"I GUESS I won't have any more trouble getting enough sleep for a while," Peter said as he walked into Mr. Cousman's office the next morning.

"What?"

"I got fired."

"You did?"

"When I went to work last night there was a letter for me from the hospital board saying that they had appreciated my services so far, but that as they understood I only wanted temporary employment they had taken advantage of a chance to hire a permanent night doctor."

"I guess they've been reading the newspapers. I'll be damned."

"I scared them. Funny, I'm not even good enough for a second-class place, now."

"Probably some of their San Marcial brethren passed the word along."

"Maybe even the insurance company suggested they better get rid of me."

"Well, what are we going to do about you?"

"I think I'd better not make any effort for another job until this trial is over. Then I'll look. I want to go back into a residency, anyway. I've decided that definitely. General surgery. The question is where and when. It's awfully late for this year."

"Good, Peter, I'm glad to hear what you're planning. Just to get one thing clear, though, you are all right financially?"

"Yes, really. My dad left a little insurance money for me I can use."

"Fine. That relieves me. Well, here's the transcript from yesterday. You might be interested to read what went on in chambers."

"Oh, that's taken down as part of the regular minutes of the trial? I didn't realize that." Peter finished the section in five minutes. "So the judge thought because of my inexperience, and my possible bias as a recently fired employee, plus the fact we had another man selected as expert witness, that he would not let me be one. It's ironic, because I figured I had to be the expert witness for this case. I thought I would be the most convincing one possible, being so close to Dr. Hatch and all his actions."

"Listen, you're doing fine the way it is as an ordinary witness."

"It doesn't bother me. Nothing bothers me anymore. Getting fired out of three jobs in less than four months doesn't make me feel martyred. Actually, I have more self-confidence than ever. Hell, after this, I figure I can go through anything. And I think that what I'm doing is somehow going to be of value. But even if it isn't, I'll have had the satisfaction of trying."

"That's right," Mr. Cousman said. "Now, sit down again here, and we can plan Monday's session. I'll finish direct with you in the morning, but it will take the whole morning, I think. I want to give you a lot of exposure, so the jury will remember you very well. This was a tragic event of great scale in the Corti family, and I want to give it time according to its size by the one eyewitness to all the events. Then Monday afternoon, I'll throw you to the wolves. Tolliver may take a great deal of time cross-examining you, or he could do just the reverse."

"I don't care what he does."

"Good. Let's go over your testimony then."

"I want to ask you something first. Aren't you surprised there's never been any mention of a settlement?"

"A lot of things affect that. Matthew Hatch might have told them he was completely against it. I let them know at the first deposition that we were not inclined to consider settling our claim. Maybe I didn't tell you I said that to Tupper. The reason is simply that I've found out Dr. Hatch's insurance company never makes a decent settlement offer. Since then I've never had any idea of not going to the jury, unless they surprised me and offered some fabulous sum."

"I'm glad to know that."

"I think today was the first time they've realized what a good case we have. So perhaps they will come up with a try at settlement if we get past non-suit."

"It will be nice to turn them down."

The rest of the weekend went rapidly for Peter. Monday morning, July 25th, started out bright and warm. His alarm unaccountably failed him and he slept late. Leaving his apartment on the run, he sat down on the bench next to Peggy Corti just in time for the opening of court. The judge came in looking more rested, more amenable, the lines on his face not cutting so deeply into his skin.

As Mr. Cousman stood up, Peter looked around the courtroom. No Dr. Hatch there, he saw, and no Mrs. Hatch. So far, as a matter of fact, the gallery was only one-third full, which seemed practically deserted after Friday. Was he such a boring witness?

He stepped quickly to the stand when called, and waited

for Mr. Cousman to walk over. The jurors looked at him pleasantly.

Mr. Cousman bore on with his questioning of Peter, concentrating now on the events at the mortuary: the start of the postmortem, the arrival of Norman Silvana, the progress of the findings, the discovery of the ligature around the hepatic artery. Mr. Tolliver objected strongly to almost every question, trying to get the judge to disallow any testimony by Peter about the conduct or findings of the autopsy. But the judge permitted Mr. Cousman to go on, and let Peter's answer that he was sure he had in fact seen the main hepatic artery tied off stay on the record.

When Mr. Cousman attempted to get a statement from Peter that ligation of a hepatic artery could lead to death, the Tolliver pyrotechnics burst out at their brightest. "This is what we have expert witnesses for," he insisted.

"We are going to allow the witness to answer your question, Mr. Cousman," Judge Fielding ruled. "But we are permitting him to answer no questions relating to the cause of death in the proximate sense, or cause-and-effect manner, as concerns this particular case."

"But that is the unfortunate effect of the answer to the question, your Honor," Mr. Tolliver insisted.

"Now that is what I am deciding, Mr. Tolliver, so let us go on, please."

"I take exception to that ruling for the record, your Honor."

"All right, we have your exception, Mr. Tolliver. Clerk, will you please restate the question for the patient witness?" the judge said.

The clerk did so, and Peter said simply, "Yes, it could."

"That is all the questions I have," Mr. Cousman said briskly. "Thank you very much, Dr. de Haan."

Mr. Tolliver rose then, taking out large, black-rimmed glasses from a case in his inside coat pocket as he did so. He cleaned them with tissue from another pocket, put them on and glanced at a notebook on his table. Then he put the glasses in their case, the notebook down, and advanced rapidly on the witness box, a large, handsome man whose small moustache glistened in the light of the courtroom.

"Mr., I'm sorry, Dr. de Haan, to review your background again, would you state to the jury how many years you have been in active medical practice?" Mr. Tolliver asked.

"Less than a year. About eleven months."

"You were a general practitioner in the private practice of medicine at the Hatch Clinic for barely over nine and a half months, and since then you have been variously employed, is that not correct?"

"Yes," Peter said.

"Are you a member of any learned societies or have you ever served on the faculty of a medical school?"

"No, sir."

"As a private practitioner for nine and a half months were you ever permitted to do any major surgical procedure yourself?"

"No."

"Any minor surgical procedures in the operating room?"

"None, except that I opened several large abscesses in the surgery under anesthesia."

Mr. Cousman stood up now. "Your Honor, we concede that Dr. de Haan is a young physician with only a short experience behind him. I feel this present line of questioning is not material."

"Perhaps you could proceed a little more quickly, Mr. Tolliver?" the judge said.

"How much are you being paid for your testimony in this case, Dr. de Haan?" Mr. Tolliver asked. "Are you getting a set amount, or do you have an arrangement to get money from the plaintiff if she is successful in her suit?"

"No, I have no arrangement to get any payment at all."

"You're doing this all to be helpful, are you?"

The judge swiveled his chair around to look sternly at Mr. Tolliver. "I believe you had better restate that question, counselor," he said.

Mr. Tolliver nodded at the judge, and continued. "We'll just go on, and let me ask you this, then. Do you know a young woman by the name of Anne Alexio?"

Peter was surprised at once by Mr. Cousman on his feet objecting loudly, "I fail to see how bringing up this young woman can have any bearing on a suit against Dr. Hatch, your Honor," Mr. Cousman said. "It seems immaterial to me."

"What point are you trying to make, Mr. Tolliver?" the judge asked, already looking baggy-eyed and prickly-faced though it was not even noon of the first day of the week.

"I'm trying to show bias. If you'll let me proceed I think I *can* show clear bias against Dr. Hatch on the part of this witness, that developed from a relationship with Miss Anne Alexio." The courtroom was getting noisy now.

"All right, Mr. Tolliver, go ahead," Judge Fielding said, pounding his gavel for quiet, and then again swinging his chair completely away from the jury and the lawyers.

Mr. Cousman sat down quickly and Mr. Tolliver went on. "Now, Dr. de Haan, do you know Miss Anne Alexio?"

"Yes, sir."

"As a matter of fact, you have been very well acquainted with this young woman, who formerly lived in San Marcial, but now resides in Berkeley, is that not true?"

"I have been."

"Are you and Miss Alexio engaged to be married?"

"We are not now."

"Were you in the past engaged to be married to Miss Alexio?"

"I was."

"When did your engagement occur?"

"In January of this year."

"Did Dr. Hatch operate on Miss Alexio in December of last year?"

"Yes."

"Was it on December twenty-eighth that he operated on Miss Alexio?"

"Let's see, yes, it was that day."

The shufflings and whisperings had stopped, and between the loud questions and soft answers there was unnatural quiet in the courtroom. "Was the lady operated on for bleeding from her uterus or womb?"

Peter looked at Mr. Cousman before replying, but the lawyer was silent in his chair, staring at his hands on the table. "Yes," Peter said.

"Was she seriously ill at the time she entered the hospital?"

"I was told so. I wasn't there at the time."

"Was her bleeding found to be due to a pregnancy with miscarriage?"

"It was to the best of my understanding." Damned if he would be an evasive witness, Peter thought. He gritted his teeth and waited for the next question.

Mr. Tolliver let the answer sink in with the jury as he pretended to clean his glasses again. Finally he asked, "Were your intimate relations with this woman responsible for her pregnancy?"

Peter paused now—not to shield himself, or Anne, because they were unshieldable now, and to hell with anyone who thought the less of them for it—but to cogitate momentarily on the words for his next answer. He decided on a simple, "Yes, they were."

"Did you have a bad scene with Dr. Hatch subsequent to this operation, over what you felt was an unsatisfactory result to this life-saving surgery?"

"I object to the use of the word 'life-saving.' "

"Do you think the young woman would have lived through this difficulty without prompt surgical intervention?"

"I did not object to the act of surgery but to the character of the surgery done."

Mr. Tolliver exhaled loudly. "I will rephrase the question any way you wish to suit you," he said.

"Dr. Hatch and I did have words, is that what you want to know?"

"You mean, you were angry with him, not he with you, is that correct?"

"I was angry with him first," Peter said, smiling. "Then he got just as angry with me." The whole courtroom laughed in relief.

As if timed for effect, Dr. Hatch just then walked in the courtroom, swung through the gates of the enclosure, and sat down at the defendant's table, looking around to see what caused the hush at his entrance. Peter shook his head. Only Matthew Hatch would come into court with his scrub suit still on under his jacket, the tunic showing below the gray chest hair, the baggy green cotton pants obvious on his legs. Even his face still held the impressions of his cap and mask, a solid red line across his forehead, and other separated lines across the bridge of his nose and cheeks.

Of course, Peter thought, it probably did fascinate a lot of people. Juries are made out of the kind of ordinary folk that Matthew can impress the hell out of, anyway.

"Mr., I mean, Dr. de Haan, may I have your attention, please?" Wasn't Tolliver cute, Peter thought viciously. Always absentmindedly forgetting to call me Doctor.

"Are you now involved as a plaintiff's witness in this suit against our defendant here, because of enmity against Dr. Hatch as a result of his surgery on your former fiancée?"

Mr. Cousman called out an objection from his table, but Judge Fielding, staring at the witness box now, overruled it without looking at the lawyer. "The witness," he said, "will answer the question. The defendant's attorney is within his rights, I believe, trying to show the bias of this witness."

"I believe no is an honest answer," Peter said.

"Did Dr. Hatch say to you during your, shall I call it discussion, that you were responsible for the lady's condition of pregnancy, and that you should be absorbing the blame for the consequences of the necessary surgery done on her, not he?"

"He said something to that effect."

"Do you now at this time believe that statement of Dr. Hatch's to be a true and appropriate one on the matter?"

"I do not, and I can tell you exactly why I don't."

Mr. Tolliver looked at the jury then, his face drawn into an expression of sad despair as he said, "Your Honor, I am not going to ask for impeachment of this witness on the cause of bias. His testimony will stand by itself for the jury to evaluate."

"We do not need any summation at this time, Mr. Tolliver. You may proceed."

Mr. Tolliver's head jerked toward the judge and his body was tense for a moment before he relaxed. "Yes, your Honor," he said, imperturbable again. Then he went on. "Mr. de Haan, that is Dr. de Haan—"

"Your Honor, I protest the continued addressing of this witness as Mr. de Haan. The defendant's lawyer knows his name and title, knows he is a doctor, and should refer to him as such," Mr. Cousman said angrily.

"I agree," the judge said. "The court requests that you be more careful, Mr. Tolliver."

"Of course," Mr. Tolliver replied, under wraps again, cooling off, breeches open in recoil, loading for the next encounter. It was not long coming.

"You stated during your direct examination that it was often difficult, as a matter of fact impossible, to see what was going on in the surgical field as an assistant at surgery? Is that correct?"

"Yes."

"Now to some extent wouldn't this same observation hold true, or hold true even more so, during an autopsy? In an operation you are scrubbed, gloved, and can step right up to the body of the patient, put your hands inside, and examine everything closely, isn't that true?"

"Your Honor, counsel has made two questions out of it.

Which does he want the witness to answer?" Mr. Cousman asked.

Peter said, "I can answer them both. I would say that because there is no need for care about sterility, and because of course there is *complete* exposure of the abdominal contents during autopsy, it is much easier to see abnormalities and pathology at an autopsy, even for the doctor who is not gloved and actually performing the postmortem. Of course, it is standard procedure for the autopsy surgeon to remove, dissect, analyze, and then demonstrate to the other doctors present the exact findings as they appear to him in the gross—"

"Now I did not want a complete dissertation, Doctor—"

"However, Dr. Parmelee, the autopsy surgeon, did not talk much about the findings on Mr. Corti. As a matter of fact he said almost nothing after the gallbladder area was exposed, but the findings were clearly seen by us present, because the abdomen was widely opened."

"Now, I would like to go to the next question, Dr. de Haan, if you don't mind. I want to ask if you feel that you are in a better position to observe and decide on the pathology present at an autopsy, and specifically I will make this question, at this autopsy on Mr. Louis Corti, than the autopsy surgeon?"

"I know what I saw."

"Please answer the question as asked, Dr. de Haan," Judge Fielding said, his voice getting rougher through the day.

"May I have the question read back to me, sir?" Peter asked, and the court reporter complied. "No, I would say not ordinarily," he replied.

"Would you just like to answer it no?" Mr. Tolliver interjected.

"Yes, all right. I will answer just a plain no to that question."

"Now you have claimed that at this autopsy you saw a ligature around the hepatic artery, yet you say that the hepatic artery after breaking up into two branches, right and left hepatic arteries, then gives off the cystic artery to the gallbladder."

"Is that a question?"

"Well, let me go on first. You would agree that in fifty percent of cases, the cystic artery breaks up into two branches before it reaches the gallbladder, and that the cystic artery at times may come off the right hepatic artery in two branches. Now how can you be sure when you are examining this region, and you see these arteries, that you are looking at a common hepatic artery, or a *right* hepatic artery, or a *cystic* artery coming off the right hepatic artery, and then going over or under the common duct, as the case may be, and after this dividing into two cystic artery branches? Especially how can you decide if the gallbladder isn't there and the area is distorted by infection and the scarring following cholecystectomy?"

"In this case with Mr. Louis Corti," Peter answered, "there was the less usual situation, though not at all uncommon, where the right hepatic artery passed posterior, which means behind, the common bile duct, and then gave rise to the cystic artery. The ligature was on the main hepatic artery, though, before the right hepatic artery came off it to pass under the common bile duct, and I can't say right now how I was sure, except that I looked, and traced it out along with Dr. Silvana and Dr. Parmelee."

"Did you actually handle any of the autopsy material yourself; did you actually have any of it in your hands?"

"No, I didn't."

"Did Dr. Silvana?"

"I don't believe so."

"Now, I have a photograph of the autopsy room at the mortuary, which Dr. Parmelee was kind enough to set up exactly as the room was used the night that Mr. Louis Corti had a postmortem exam performed on him. Dr. de Haan, I want you to examine this photograph—"

"Do you want to submit this in evidence for the defendant, Mr. Tolliver?" the judge asked.

"I was about to do that, your Honor."

"All right, clerk, please admit this in evidence and mark it as Defendant's Exhibit A, and return it to Mr. Tolliver." This was done, and Mr. Tolliver took the large blowup, several feet wide and high, to the easel between the witness stand and the jury box.

"Now, I submit that in this room, with the arrangement as shown of the prosecutor's table and the table on which the cadaver lies, there is no really close approach to the visualization of the body that compares with the visualization afforded the autopsy surgeon. You, Dr. de Haan, and Dr. Silvana were on the other side of the table all the time. Do you agree, not speaking of physically handling the material, and not considering here the question of competence to view and analyze autopsy material, that Dr. Parmelee at all times had a closer and better contact with the findings from the autopsy than you did, or Dr. Silvana did?"

"I saw perfectly what I wanted to see, and what I have said I saw."

"The question is, did Dr. Parmelee at all times have a much closer and better visual and physical contact with the autopsy findings on Mr. Louis Corti—for the moment not considering his competence to judge this material—than you or Dr. Silvana had?"

"Yes, is my answer."

"Thank you. Thank you. Now I want to go back to the time of the surgery—"

"Mr. Tolliver," Judge Fielding said, smiling sweetly, "I'm going to interrupt you there. It's almost noon. Shall we continue this cross-examination after lunch? Fine. Ladies and gentlemen of the jury, remember my admonition to you not to discuss this case with anyone."

Peter ate with Mr. Cousman, his assistant, Jack Penberthy, Peggy Corti, and Mr. Corti. Peggy seemed paler, tireder each morning. Still day after day she was always dressed well, made-up carefully, coiffured neatly. Try as he would, though, Mr. Cousman could not make her wear black.

"Maybe she's right," Mr. Cousman told Peter. "Maybe the jury will see her as more genuine doing it her way."

Mr. Corti changed little. He was quieter in the unfamiliar setting of the courtroom, but at their lunches he kidded Mr. Cousman, and told Peter funny stories of things Louis had done when a child. This day, though, he was angry. "What's the matter with that Tolliver? I don't get it. I don't like the way he talk to you there, asking questions. What the hell!"

"It will probably get worse today before it gets better, Mr. Corti," Mr. Cousman said smiling. Peter could tell he liked the old man too.

"This young doctor, he's a fine young man, don't you think, Mr. Cousman?"

"Of course."

"I think someday he's going to be a very important man in medicine."

"I agree," Mr. Cousman replied emphatically, sipping his coffee.

Peter remembered when the photograph was shown of the autopsy room during the morning that Peggy had lowered her eyes, refusing to look, but the old man had stared straight at the picture, holding her hand the while. "The Cortis are looking, if they need to," his demeanor seemed to say. What a tragedy. It was so hard to keep the really bad things of life in focus, but the truth engulfed Peter for a moment as he looked at the older Corti. He returned to the stand that afternoon in a less generous, less cautious frame of mind.

Mr. Tolliver took him through the surgery and the post-operative care again rigorously. Did he know the anatomy of the biliary tract and its vessels or did he not? Was he not Dr. Hatch's paid employee and regular assistant, in charge of handling his patients pre- and post-operatively, and if this were the case, and he was at the patient's bedside, no matter how critically ill the patient, and even if it were in the middle of the night, was there any reason for Dr. Hatch to come to help with care which he had every reason to believe was being appropriately handled by his paid assistant? What could Dr. Hatch have done, anyway, that anyone so far could show would have changed the course of this case of liver failure and body infection?

Objection Mr. Cousman here: No infection or liver failure had been proved yet.

While Judge Fielding stared at the paneled walls of the courtroom and then pointed his blue eyes upward at the ornate patterns in the old ceiling, showing great expanses of white eyeball as the lids clicked open and shut, Mr. Tolliver went on. Just as in the Army chain of command, or in any of the other military forces, wasn't it wrong of an assistant to commit himself to carry out the orders and needs of his superior while he was secretly trying to undermine him? Hadn't young Dr. de Haan taken on unusual prerogatives in ordering consultations and autopsies, changing orders, at every turn showing a wish to subvert the work of Dr. Hatch? Could this have been for the patient's benefit? Did the hospital record have anything recorded to show that there was any mishandling, any failure to respond when really needed, on Dr. Hatch's part, though there was every opportunity for Peter de Haan and nurses to make whatever notes they chose? Did not Dr. Hatch's own notes—and he read from some of them—clearly show how carefully he had followed the patient, and understood the patient's problem? Was it not, in fact, almost criminally wrong for Peter de Haan to disguise himself as a loyal employee to Dr. Hatch when he, for distorted personal reasons, was trying to destroy this fine man of great reputation and deserved honor in the community? Was it not considered grossly unethical for a physician such as Peter to foment a malpractice suit as a personal retributive act of vengeance against another physician?

It was a bitter, wearing attack, a long, abrasive afternoon for Peter, and though there were at first many objections from Mr. Cousman, after a while Peter found that he had only the judge to protect him. Mr. Cousman sat back, letting Mr. Tolliver loose any napalm he wished, with Peter having then to work his own way out of the resulting fire and explosion. By the end of the day, Peter felt as if he had gone fifteen rounds in the ring with a merciless world champion.

Court adjourned and the chamber cleared, and Peter was left with Mr. Cousman and Jack Penberthy. "The Cortis left early," Mr. Cousman said to him.

"I noticed. Was something wrong?"

"The old man had a stomachache and said he better go home. Mrs. Corti went with him. Actually, I think he just got upset at Tolliver, and then at me too for not shooting Hugh down."

"You did rather leave me to my own devices."

"I thought we should."

"How did I come out?"

"Can I read the mind of a jury?"

"I wouldn't be surprised."

"I think you did quite all right. However, I'm sure you realize that Matthew Hatch is a household word in this county, and you must expect a great deal of sympathy for him at every turn."

"I know. Well, I'm going home and have a drink. I'll see you tomorrow."

"Don't forget you'll be back on the stand in the morning."

"I will? Oh, you mean on re-direct."

"Yes, I want to go over a number of things our nasty opponent brought up. Actually, I don't think Hugh did himself that much good, because just as there's sympathy for Dr. Hatch, so inevitably some sympathy will develop for you in the jury."

"Well, at least I'm glad to hear that."

"Our expert is here tomorrow, Dr. Arnold Dunning, so we'll have you on re-direct and re-cross in the morning, then Dr. Dunning in the afternoon, and Wednesday, too, as needed, with Silvana to follow him."

"Do you think Dr. Dunning will be a good witness?" Peter asked.

"Oh, I think so," Mr. Cousman said, packing up his papers. "I used him in a case once before and he was fine. I've talked to him on the phone a lot about this one, and sent him copies of almost everything, including the daily testimony. I think he's showing real interest, and should be well-informed and helpful."

"Are you going to pick him up?" Peter asked, holding the courtroom door open for Mr. Cousman and his paraphernalia: hat, books, briefcase.

"Yes, I'll bring him over from Oakland airport in the morning for the ten A.M. court opening, and we can talk on the way."

"Tolliver," Peter said, watching silent Jack Penberthy push the button for the elevator, "seems very well prepared to me, especially for coming in the case so late. I think he's getting *better* prepared all the time. He must be studying like a beaver every night."

"That's Houston for you. Even if he looks like a floorwalker, he's a worker, he does prepare well. He knows how much it means and is very professional about his cases."

"Maybe it's the moustache, but he seems like a smoothie. I can imagine him out every weekend living it up with three girl friends that his wife doesn't know about."

Mr. Cousman put his hat on and stepped into the elevator. "You know he's almost a teetotaler, sails on the Bay on the weekends, has been impeccably married to a social lady in San Francisco for twenty-five years, with never a breath of scandal, and doesn't even smoke."

"Appearances *are* deceiving," Peter said, as they left the elevator and started down the long corridor to the entrance.

"Don't think that comment doesn't fit juries, too, my boy. Watch them, play to them, stuff them with evidence they can sink their teeth into, and then what happens, they're off on some flight of their own. One thing for us, anyway, we've had such big crowds in court that the jury is afraid to go to sleep."

"Funny, I don't notice the spectators anymore. I'm thinking of the judge and the jury, and you and the other lawyers, and Peggy Corti, and everything inside the enclosure, and I ignore the rest."

"It's always that way in a tough case," Mr. Cousman said,

pushing through the door to the outside, and then holding it open for the younger men. "Come on, Jack. *Arrivederci*, Peter, and Excelsior, which is to say, onward and upward."

38

THE next morning Peter was back on the stand for an hour of re-direct by Mr. Cousman. Surprisingly, the re-cross that followed by Mr. Tolliver was quite gentlemanly.

Dr. Hatch arrived late again, once more with scrub suit garb showing, and he brought Rosalie in with him. She sat by him at the defendant's table, looking poised and very beautiful.

The Cortis went home at noon because Mr. Corti's stomach was still "burning sour," so Peter had lunch alone with Dr. Dunning and Mr. Cousman.

For some reason, Peter had expected to find the doctor from Southern California elderly, dull, and pompous, with dandruff on his collar and an unpressed suit. Instead he was a young-looking man of forty-five with dark hair waving back from his forehead, immaculately but not ceremoniously dressed. He was obviously a person of dash and enthusiasm, alert, quick-talking, *and* he had a sense of humor. He had them both laughing at lunchtime with his anecdotes of the other trials in which he had testified.

On the stand that afternoon he was the same way, very fast with his smooth-flowing answers, at ease, pleasant, almost seeming to be enjoying himself, not unwilling to be a little sly, or even downright humorous, but still knowledgeable and informed, and emphatic on the points he wanted to stress.

The data uncovered by Mr. Cousman as he qualified this young surgeon for expert testimony were surprising. He had just been appointed associate professor of surgery at the University Medical School and Hospital in Los Angeles, for one thing. He had sixty-eight medical papers to his credit, and he had himself written a surgical textbook. He was acting head of the surgical department for the summer while his chief was on a medical mission for the government in the

Far East, and was a senior examiner for the National Surgical Board. He was a member of ten different major societies, including the National Academy of Surgery to which only two hundred members could belong at one time. He had one operative procedure and two surgical instruments carrying his name. ("If you want to know who named them," he said to Mr. Cousman, "I did," with a big smile. The jury laughed.)

"Now, Dr. Dunning, can you tell me how many cholecystectomies, that is operations for gallbladder removal, you have done?"

"Approximately seven hundred."

The jury stopped smiling, and stared quietly, obviously impressed. This was something they could appreciate, the learned societies and honors and prestige appointments meant little to them.

"I would like to ask you if there is considerable hazard in performing a cholecystectomy, that is, in removing a gallbladder surgically?"

"There is certainly a hazard to any procedure involving anesthesia, first, and more in the opening of a body cavity, such as in the opening of the abdomen in a cholecystectomy."

"But in the case of an acute infection of the gallbladder, the risk of cholecystectomy is considered justified, is it not?"

"In general, I would say yes. Though at times there may be reason in acute gallbladder infection to postpone surgery and treat with antibiotics, bacteria-killing drugs that is, until the patient's condition improves. Decisions of this sort are not easy to summarize and involve expert judgment in the individual case."

At Mr. Cousman's request, Dr. Dunning went on to give his own complete discussion of the anatomy of the gallbladder, using the charts, and also of the technique of cholecystectomy.

After a twenty-minute presentation, Mr. Cousman said, "Now, Dr. Dunning, I want to ask you some other things that might not be clear. In the case of the hepatic artery, and its right and left branches, as we've learned, these carry the nourishing, oxygen-rich blood from the heart pump into the liver to supply it with necessary food to function. Am I right there?"

"Exactly."

"And the ligating of the main hepatic artery, or its right or left trunk, may result in death because of damage to the liver through its lack of blood supply?"

"Yes, the liver is a great organ of multiple tasks, with hundreds and perhaps thousands of operations vital to the body. If it is destroyed, the body will die, of course. Now in cases where there is interruption of the hepatic artery, death may not always occur, but generally will. There is not a great deal of experience with these cases in the medical literature, because frankly most of them are never reported. But ordinarily death is rapid, in several days, and it is likely to be unexplained until autopsy if the surgeon does not know he has tied off the hepatic artery, which ordinarily he would not know, or he would not tie it off. This is an obvious point."

"Now Doctor, have you ever tied off a main or right or left hepatic artery branch?"

"No, never."

"And you have done how many cholecystectomies?"

"Over seven hundred."

"And those were not all simple gallbladder removals, but a number of them were re-operations after surgery done elsewhere, with damage to some part of the bile duct system, is that correct?"

"Yes."

"Now in respect to ligating the hepatic artery, you state you have never done this inadvertently. Have you ever seen cases where this was done?"

"Unfortunately, I have seen two cases where this happened, and I am familiar with several others."

"In Southern California?"

"Yes."

"What are the characteristics of these deaths? What is noticed in these people? First of all, did they all die?"

"Yes, they did. The ones I saw had a similar course. Post-operatively there was high fever, and shock of undetermined cause developed. Antibiotics were given, many studies made, everyone involved rushed around trying to discover what was going on. Regardless of treatment though, death occurred four to seven days after surgery."

"So the major characteristics were high fever, shock, chills. Was there jaundice in any of these?"

"Apparently this necrosis, that is, liver tissue death, when it starts, works too fast for jaundice to develop. The cases I'm familiar with did not develop jaundice."

"Now. Doctor, as I have stated, you are acquainted with

the complete record of hospitalization, with all the depositions of the major witnesses before trial, with the report of the autopsy, gross and microscopic, as prepared by Dr. Joseph Parmelee, and with the pathologic report of the surgical specimen, in this case of Mr. Louis Corti, is that correct?"

"Yes."

"I arranged to send you the pathologic slides, after getting this court to subpoena them from Dr. Parmelee and the Hatch Hospital, and you examined them too, did you not?"

"I did."

"Are you competent to examine pathologic slides?"

"As a matter of fact, I have spent a great deal of time doing this. I took two years of training in the surgical pathology laboratory of Michael Weiss Hospital in New York City, but also I had these slides reviewed by Dr. Joseph Litner, a recognized board-certified pathologist, and Associate Professor of Pathology at our University Medical Center in Los Angeles."

"Now, your Honor, I would like to introduce into evidence this interrogatory I received from Dr. Litner regarding these slides as Plaintiff's Exhibit Six."

"The Clerk will so mark it," said the small judge, his face unusually ruddy this afternoon.

"I will read Dr. Litner's interrogatory to the jury before the plaintiff rests, but first, Dr. Dunning, did your interpretation of the pathological slides agree in general with those of Dr. Litner?"

"We agree completely in all details."

"Well, then I would like to ask you, for the record, if you have formed any conclusion as to the cause of death in this patient, Mr. Louis Corti?"

"Now, your Honor," Mr. Tolliver bellowed, "I do not think that is a proper question. The formation of that opinion here by this witness, an expert witness, would be on a topic which is a question the jury is entitled to decide, after hearing the facts, and not to be decided for them by this witness's secondhand, roundabout testimony. We have many witnesses to the actual events, and this witness's conclusions would be strictly—"

"I don't think I'm going to allow that objection, Mr. Tolliver," the judge said low-voiced again, rolling his eyes around dangerously. "You may answer, Doctor."

"I believe that this man in all probability did die from

ligation of the hepatic artery," Dr. Dunning said. "I felt a review of his clinical information tended to corroborate this assumption. I base my judgment on the following facts. To begin with, this man had a cholecystectomy done in extremely rapid time, which would seem to allow for a possibility of error on the part of the surgeon—"

"I object to that conclusion on the part of the witness as being without substance and possibly prejudicially arrived at or inferred without—" Mr. Tolliver put in, still standing and pale.

"I'm going to sustain that and order the last part of that statement after the word 'time' stricken. Please continue, Doctor."

"Well, here we have a cholecystectomy done in rapid fashion," Arnold Dunning went on in good humor, "with unexplained high fever beginning about thirty-six hours after surgery. No corroboration of urinary tract infection, of lung infection, or liver or bloodstream or gallbladder area infection came out of any of the studies done. Even so, the man was adequately treated for a wide spectrum of possible infections that could be causing him trouble. Mr. Corti, presumably in top physical shape before surgery—according to the defendant's own records he had easily passed his examination for health insurance three months earlier—still continued to be intractably ill after the onset of fever, developed severe shock, and ultimately expired in another seventy-two hours. Dr. de Haan has already testified, I understand, as to his noting a ligature around the main hepatic artery at autopsy, though there is supposedly a difference of opinion as to whether or not a tie was there. But Dr. Litner, my pathologist associate, and I felt conclusively after studying the liver sections following death, that the changes present *were* the changes of what we call infarction."

"How do you spell that, Doctor?" Judge Fielding asked.

"Infarction, i-n-f-a-r-c-t-i-o-n."

"Thank you. Proceed."

"Infarction, not to be confused with infection, is the situation where a body tissue suffers death from a cutting off of blood supply to it. The vessel bringing blood to the tissue could have a clot form in it, or could be accidentally cut or tied off. Anything obstructing it or severing it could cause infarction."

Mr. Cousman, quiet now, deferential in tone, allowing this magnificent witness all possible room to clarify, inform, and impress, asked, "In the folder there in your lap, Doctor, is a copy of the autopsy report by Dr. Parmelee. Now this has already been submitted in evidence, though the jury has not examined it yet, but I would like you to review it for us, and comment on it in relation to your diagnosis, which we should all understand was deduced after a careful review of this patient's entire course and his pathologic slides. If you would, please?"

"Certainly. In the description of the gross findings at autopsy, the examiner states, and I quote here: 'The liver is enlarged, extremely soft, necrotic, and friable. Mattress sutures are present at the gallbladder bed. There is a large hematoma occupying the liver bed adjacent to the hepatic artery.' Please note that the examiner himself here used the terms 'necrotic' and 'friable' to refer to the liver. He goes on to say that 'Multiple sections through the liver show that the vascular channels are filled with well-formed thrombi,' in other words, the liver was filled in its blood vessel spaces with clots." Dr. Dunning for the first time raised his voice here, and for a moment it cracked with emotion. Peter saw that the jury, even to the old man on the left in the front row, whom they had figured as a certain Hatch vote, was watching with eyes open wide, more attentive than at any time during the trial.

"To go on from the report: 'A large pseudocyst filled with necrotic debris occupies the upper and middle portions of the right lobe of the liver. The left lobe is approximately twice normal size and also contains a number of thrombi . . .' Please note that it is written here in the official report of the autopsy that it contains a number of thrombi, of clots, that is. Then the report continues, '. . . and there is a uniform infarction with resulting softness and friability in all areas.' The report states there is 'a uniform infarction,' which is a death of tissue with clotting in its tiny vessels from lack of blood supply, ordinarily from a lack of the arterial blood supply. Also it is stated in this report that the liver tissue is noticed to be soft and friable, that latter word means crumbly, which is the classical result of infarction in liver tissue."

Dr. Dunning paused for a moment, silently reading further into the autopsy protocol. "Are there other points, Dr. Dunning?" Mr. Cousman prodded him.

"Yes, a good many, Mr. Cousman. I'll first explain to the jury that ordinarily temporary initial diagnoses are put down after the autopsy is done, then the diagnoses are reviewed, very often altered or added to after the microscopic examination of the tissues is completed several weeks later. The initial diagnosis, in other words, is needed for many causes, the death certificate, the chart records, insurance papers. The final diagnosis, often more formally stated, is reserved for later. But our examiner here comes to the simple conclusion, after all these findings of infarction, and tissue death, and clotting through all the vessel spaces in the liver, merely of, and I read, 'Immediate and principal cause of death: (1) Acute hepatic necrosis. (2) Status post-cholecystectomy.' This means that there was death of liver tissue from some unknown, undescribed, unguessed-at cause, after the man had his gallbladder removed."

"Do you feel that this is an inadequate diagnosis then?" Mr. Cousman asked.

"Yes, of course I do," Dr. Dunning said. "Then there is a simple note below this so-called Gross Diagnosis which only says, 'Microscopic examination confirms gross diagnosis.' A very inadequate rendering, I would say."

"Your Honor," Mr. Tolliver said, leaving his table and actually approaching the bench, his face now flushed, "I want to place an objection."

"I agree," Judge Fielding said, "that there is reason to object there. Strike that last sentence. Witness may proceed."

For the first time on the stand Dr. Dunning looked over at the judge. He seemed to inspect the old jurist's snowy hair, and scarred, tomato-red complexion curiously for a moment, and then turned back to the jury. "As far as the protocol's actual description of the microscopic findings, which follows on the next page, I am not going to bore everyone with analyzing all the details there. I'll simply read Dr. Parmelee's brief summary of the findings on the liver. He writes, 'The essential findings are as indicated in the gross description, a severe degree of hepatic ischemia with foci of frank necrosis and mild generalized fatty infiltration.' The important point here, then, as also came out in the first part of this autopsy report, is the inescapable conclusion that something interfered with the liver to cause it to clot and die, and this something was a lack of blood circulation to it."

Mr. Cousman could barely keep the satisfaction off his face as he asked the next question. "Now, how does Dr. Litner fit into the thoughts you're expressing here?"

"Whatever Dr. Parmelee calls it in his autopsy report, he seems to be talking about the same thing that Dr. Litner, my pathologist associate, and I found from studying the slides, namely *infarction* of the liver from interference with its blood supply. So, analyzing the autopsy report on Mr. Louis Corti prepared for the defendant doctor in this case, a report obviously never intended for the courtroom, a report which doesn't mention, but still leads one directly to the conclusion that the hepatic artery was tied off, one should say—"

"I object to this entire statement as being the witness' personal opinion on non-medical facts, and therefore invalid," Mr. Tolliver put in hastily.

"Sustained," the judge said. "Please rephrase your last answer leaving out any opinions of your own on Dr. Parmelee's motives, or what his report did or did not show, or was intended or not intended to show."

"Yes, sir. Let's see. Analyzing the report, then, that was prepared on the autopsy by Dr. Parmelee, one is definitely led to the conclusion that the hepatic artery *must* have been tied off to produce the pathological picture as described by Dr. Parmelee."

"I object, your Honor, to that unwarranted statement." Mr. Tolliver's characteristic composure was gone. He seemed unaware that his hair had dropped over his forehead, and there was even some ink smeared on his cheek.

"No, I'm going to allow that as now phrased, Mr. Tolliver."

"Your Honor, I believe that this unproved assumption is not a professional medical opinion, but rather a non-professional, non-medical opinion, unsupported by the facts and by the reasoning process he tried to make us follow through with him. I ask that it be stricken from the record."

"I'm not going to sustain you, Mr. Tolliver." Peter continued to be surprised at Judge Fielding, the old San Marcialite, supposedly so tough on malpractice and personal injury plaintiffs, assertedly bound to be on the side of Dr. Hatch, still giving them a fair and just chance so far.

"I respectfully except, your Honor," Mr. Tolliver said, in a soft if stricken tone.

"Your exception is noted, Mr. Tolliver. Will you continue, Mr. Cousman?"

"Dr. Dunning, after examining all records available on Mr. Corti's illness, after going over the pathological slides on Mr. Corti and the autopsy report yourself and with Dr. Litner, after reading all the depositions, and this morning hearing some of the testimony, it is your opinion then from the evidence available that Mr. Corti's death was from inadvertent ligation of the hepatic artery, and further that death ordinarily will follow mistaken ligation of the main hepatic artery at surgery for cholecystectomy. Are these statements correct?"

"Yes, they are."

"Now, I want to ask you if, in your opinion, you know it to be possible or impossible to do a proper removal of a gallbladder for acute cholecystitis, plus an incidental appendectomy, in thirty-three minutes?"

"That is not a difficult question for me to answer, Mr. Cousman. In rare instances there might be extenuating circumstances to change the case, but generally I would say it could never be proper for this sort of operation to be concluded in that brief time. It is too complex and too difficult for proper completion in thirty-three minutes." Dr. Dunning looked over to Mr. Tolliver's table for the objection, but none came, so he continued. "I am acquainted with the abilities of a large number of the best surgeons throughout the country, because we once did what you would call a time-motion study for the National Academy, thinking that with hospital operating rooms crammed all the time, it would be a wonderful help to find a way to get some of the slower surgeons to move faster. We wanted to find out what techniques, skills, natural propensities allowed some of the really fine surgeons of the country to be also speedier in their surgery. The study was essentially unprofitable, but I have the figures here with me that do show, in our survey among the fastest of the fine surgeons of the United States, *no* cholecystectomy was completed in the time of thirty-three minutes, much less one including an incidental appendectomy. As a matter of fact, in seventy-eight cholecystectomies we surveyed, the shortest time recorded was *forty*-three minutes."

After Dr. Dunning's emphatic words there was a whir in the courtroom that took several minutes to die down. Mr. Tolliver did not move from his table, but instead bent over it going through notes out of his briefcase. Mr. Cousman waited for the noise to subside, and then began, "All right, Dr. Dunning, now let me state to you in hypothetical form a question—"

Judge Fielding spun his chair around toward the jury then, smoothing down his hair as he said in his softer voice without the graveliness, "If I may interrupt you there, Mr. Cousman, I would like to explain to the jury the importance of the hypothetical question. Ladies and gentlemen, in such a question the attorney presents a succession of facts already introduced to the jury about the patient involved in the malpractice case, giving symptoms, signs, conversations between principal parties if pertinent, reports of tests, operations and treatments by the defendant and other doctors, and any additional evidence or information that seems needed to frame the question. The lawyer then tries to obtain from the expert witness, in this case Dr. Dunning, a statement to support either the contention of the plaintiff that malpractice occurred, or to support the defendant's side in the opposite view. To prove malpractice, the plaintiff is required to show that the defendant did not exercise reasonable diligence in his care, or did not show good judgment in his care, or that he departed from approved methods of medical care. A physician in practice is ordinarily expected to exercise his own medical skill only to the degree medical skill is possessed and exercised by other physicians in his own or similar communities. By law, he must only do as well as the *average* physician in his own situation would do, then. Now the plaintiff's attorney may go ahead with his question."

"Thank you, Judge Fielding. Now Dr. Dunning, I want you to assume that there is a thirty-two-year-old man who at a time of apparently excellent health suddenly develops the signs and symptoms of acute cholecystitis. . . ." Mr. Cousman proceeded to elaborate all the details of Louis Corti's illness, and then concluded, "So I want to ask you, Doctor, considering these facts, if you can tell whether or not a surgeon who operated on this man and in so doing tied off or ligated the hepatic artery instead of the cystic artery, with the death of the patient resulting, was performing his medical duties in accordance with the usual standards of medical practice?"

"Your Honor, just a moment, now," Mr. Tolliver put in, calmer, cooler, his skin color back to its normal pink. "Before the doctor answers that question, I wish to object to it. It has not been substantiated that the patient involved here in this hypothetical question, Mr. Louis Corti, had his hepatic artery tied off. The plaintiff's attorney and his witnesses have assumed that he did, but as your Honor very well knows from the depositions, we have evidence to present to the contrary."

"Now I disagree strongly, your Honor, in that we have brought out directly through the testimony of Dr. de Haan, and indirectly through the present witness' testimony, that the hepatic artery was occluded. Now what does the lawyer for the defendant expect, that we should have motion pictures showing the defendant executing the act?" Mr. Cousman was standing on his tiptoes talking now.

"Besides," Mr. Tolliver said, walking toward the jury now, "many of the particulars in this case were left out of the question, including the fact that Dr. Hatch, the surgeon and attending physician, made a proper diagnosis, and prescribed and carried out proper surgical therapy."

"Now you know that we have stipulated to all that, Mr. Tolliver," Mr. Cousman said angrily.

"And further," Houston Tolliver went rapidly on, "that the post-operative care had no deficiencies in it. Actually, even the present witness, Dr. Dunning, pointed out how well treatment for infection and shock had been carried out."

"Now really, your Honor, is this Mr. Tolliver's hypothetical question or mine? I take complete exception to that last remark. We have testified to how and why we thought there were deficiencies in the post-operative care, and some of those were mentioned in the hypothetical question."

"All right, Mr. Cousman," the judge put in, "on the matter of this hypothetical question I am going to hold up Mr. Tolliver and ask you to rephrase it. Dr. Dunning's supposition as to the cause of death is largely based on negative evidence and his own deductions, rather than observed and provable facts at this stage. The jury is not only familiar with Dr. de Haan's evidence on the existence of a ligature around the hepatic artery, but they are also fully aware that the pathologist conducting the autopsy *did not* find this. These viewpoints tend to cancel each other out. Additionally, Dr. Dunning's interpretation of events are predicated on the depositions, testimony, and writings of others, especially of Dr. Parmelee, who is an expert witness in this case himself. Now the opinion of an expert witness based on that of another expert witness is incompetent as evidence, and we are obviously close to that here. So I am going to ask you to reframe your question, not the whole thing, but the last part only, which contains the reference to the hepatic artery. That reference shall be stricken and I wish to have you restate your hypothetical question without it."

Peter pursed his lips and whistled through his teeth.

"What's the matter?" Peggy Corti asked him,

"Lord, that's bad news, Peggy. They're really going to hurt our expert testimony there. The judge is allowed to police these questions, to rule on their form and content pretty thoroughly, I understand. I thought the judge was being fair enough before, but now we're in trouble. First, he won't let me be an expert witness, and now he doesn't let Dr. Dunning perform like one. He's chopping our case to pieces."

"Your Honor, I object seriously," Mr. Cousman was saying. "I just can't accept that ruling as proper. Hypothetically I should be allowed to decide if the question itself, regardless of the answer, is based upon preceding evidence which has credibility and weight to it. The jury's province is to determine the facts. The answer to this hypothetical question is an opinion, as you know, and it is assumed the jury and the jury alone must find the evidence on which the opinion is based to be false or true. I cite you Baggoss versus Rensey, in 117 Cal. App., at page 284, and the well-known case of Hoffman versus Leyenquist from 1934. I would be very upset if I could not have my question."

"You're not going to have it here, Mr. Cousman. I shall look up your first citation, however; the second I know."

"I think you'd find Black versus Blackwell here, your Honor, from 153 A.C.A., 502, as precedent here," Mr. Tolliver said.

"No, I disagree," Mr. Cousman said.

"Now gentlemen, that's enough. I'm perfectly capable of running this court, without help from either of you. And, ladies and gentlemen of the jury, I must remind you that everything the attorneys say trying to quote from the evidence or explain the evidence, which in any way departs from the testimony as actually presented here, is of course to be ignored by you. The only evidence you are to use to decide this case is the evidence actually presented from the witnesses themselves, and you and you alone are the ones to analyze this evidence and the witnesses, as to credibility, then to make your final decision as you see fit. Now please go ahead, Mr. Cousman."

"Your Honor, I wish to take exception to your ruling on my hypothetical question."

"That is your privilege, Mr. Cousman," the judge said coolly, gazing down imperiously at the lawyer. "Let the record make note of your wish."

Mr. Cousman walked back to his table, pushing his gray hair forward again in his unique way.

"Now then, let us see . . ." he sighed, letting his displeasure fill the courtroom, soak into the jury, before he resumed his question again with slow speech, a slouch and drooping, enervated lids. "Dr. Dunning, consider the facts in this hypothetical case that I have enumerated to you, where several days after cholecystectomy this young man died from *acute liver failure.*" Mr. Cousman abruptly snapped the last words out. "Can you tell us from these facts whether or not this doctor in your opinion was exercising the degree of care and skill ordinarily exercised in a city such as San Marcial, by a physician who largely specialized in general surgery?"

"Mr. Cousman, I believe that the facts in this hypothetical case do indicate that this doctor was not showing the skill, the care, the competency which would be expected from such a physician in a community like this. I would like to enlarge on my answer if I may."

"Surely."

"To take events in their turn, there is no reason to think that the surgery for gallbladder removal was at fault. On the contrary that was obviously the right thing to do. But then, the speed with which that surgery was done indicates negligence to me—"

"I object, your Honor, on the grounds that this is a conclusion for the jury to come to, not the witness," Mr. Tolliver said.

"Sustained."

"Then, let me say that the speed with which the surgery was done indicates haste to me, as it was faster than competent surgery can be done. Subsequently, the patient was Dr. Hatch's primary responsibility, and if there is evidence he delegated that responsibility partially to someone else, this does not in any sense relieve him of the weight of the primary burden. Then, the doctor refused to accept the strong advice of a qualified surgical consultant to reopen the patient's abdomen with the thought on this consultant's mind that the hepatic artery might have been ligated and that if so, grafting it could save the patient's life. Developments, *I believe*, indicated that this should have been done. Finally, it seems to me, as I have indicated, that there is a strong presumption, a strong air of circumstantial evidence, even if the direct evidence of Dr. de Haan is overlooked, leading to the opinion that hepatic artery occlusion did cause this man's death. If this is the case, and the arterial occlusion did take place by surgical tying and cutting of the artery, then I say that there is no question but that negligent, incompetent, below-par medical and surgical skill did take this young man's life."

From some corner of the chamber loud clapping started up. Peter peered, straining to see who it was clapping as the judge's gavel banged the courtroom into silence.

"There'll be no more outbreaks like that. Any person so doing will be held in contempt. This is my only warning."

"Dr. Dunning," Mr. Cousman went on, "I want to thank you for your courageous statement."

"That's unnecessary, your Honor," Mr. Tolliver said angrily. "Counsel knows that is inappropriate, and unethical, and . . ." he sputtered.

"All right, gentlemen, all right. Let's have a little less of your personalities and more testimony."

"Your Honor, I object to the answer there, anyway," Mr. Tolliver said. "The witness brings in the issue of the hepatic artery again, after the court has clearly indicated that it should be excluded."

The judge sat there for a long moment, eying Dr. Dunning, then bent his neck back to look at the ceiling. Finally he said, "Mr. Tolliver, I am going to leave that up to the jury now. Proceed, Mr. Cousman."

"Then Dr. Dunning, is it your belief, based on this hypothetical case, which you understand relates to this actual case we are trying, that negligence is shown?"

"I do believe that. This sort of operation, cholecystectomy, could result in death, but rarely in a man of this age group, and certainly never from a series of events as depicted here. It should not happen, it is an infrequent, uncommon occurrence, and I truly believe that negligence is shown here."

"Thank you very much, Doctor, that is all."

"Gentlemen, after a short afternoon recess, we shall get to the cross-examination on Dr. Dunning. Ladies and gentlemen, remember my admonition."

The cross-examination by Mr. Tolliver was a harsh one. Peter had thought of Houston Tolliver as essentially a pleasant person, smooth rather than tough, but now he was deadly. He dug in, and meant it. He was rougher in tone and manner, in voice and language than Peter had imagined he could or would be, much rougher than in his own cross-examination.

First the lawyer went through Arnold Dunning's credentials briefly, making negative points for the jury: he was not a full professor, he had written only one book, he was only acting head of his department of surgery which was far different than being permanent head. He was not a specialist in gallbladder surgery, but a specialist in general surgery. He had looked up his published works and found most of his papers dealt with burns, and stomach surgery for ulcers, and methods of bowel resection, which he pointed out.

"Now, when were you first asked to appear in this case, Doctor?"

"About two months ago."

"Would that be in May then?"

"I would guess late April."

"And how did you hear from Mr. Cousman, was it by phone or by letter?"

"By phone."

Mr. Cousman interrupted here. "This is cross-examination, your Honor, I know, but I don't know what is material about this. I would like to object on the basis that this is entirely immaterial."

"I will permit the questions subject to your objection," the judge said.

"Doctor, have you testified for Mr. Cousman before?"

"Your Honor, I'm going to object to that as immaterial, too."

Mr. Tolliver began, "I believe the jury should be allowed to—"

"I will permit the question for the limited basis of showing bias or prejudice though I am not suggesting an opinion on that matter one way or another," Judge Fielding said.

"You did testify for Mr. Cousman before, Dr. Dunning, did you not?" Mr. Tolliver asked.

"Yes, about two years ago."

"It was not in a case involving Dr. Hatch," Mr. Cousman put in.

"Had you ever heard of or met Dr. Hatch prior to testifying here?"

"Never."

"You're sure you never met him or were introduced to him at any of the surgical meetings?"

"Not to my recollection."

"This is still all immaterial, your Honor," Mr. Cousman said.

"I will allow it for the same limited reason though it does not seem very productive."

"All right, your Honor, I'll move on. Have you testified often in malpractice cases before?"

"Possibly five or six times."

"Always for the plaintiff, Dr. Dunning?"

"Not at all, but I believe more often than not. The doctors I know don't need me on the witness stand."

Mr. Fielding rolled his glistening eyes at that. "Strike the last statement. Doctor, that kind of remark does not become you. Incidentally, Mr. Tolliver, we have about an hour left in the day and I know the doctor is from Los Angeles. If you could complete in that time or an hour and a half, I could hold over."

"I have a great many questions, your Honor. I'm not sure I could do so. I believe I'll have to go into tomorrow."

"At the rate he's going, I'm sure he will, your Honor," Mr. Cousman put in softly. The courtroom shuffled in their seats at this. The antiquated fan system was increasingly noisy but still inadequate, so many of the jurors and spectators had been using their handkerchiefs to mop brows and wipe off upper lips.

"Now, Dr. Dunning, you will charge a professional witness fee for your appearance here today, will you not?"

"Yes, I will."

"Is that for a substantial amount?"

"I would say so."

"Is it for a four-figure amount?"

"Not that much."

Mr. Tolliver went through the post-surgical events first, asking about many of the small points of care, as he read orders of Dr. Hatch's from the chart and had the doctor reply if he thought they were reasonable. He agreed with all orders of more than twenty-five that were read, except for one about the use of cascara as a laxative, and one concerning the administration of blood, but admitted there could be questions of judgment here and extenuating circumstances not listed on the chart.

"So, you would say you were in agreement with the general nature of the treatment as exemplified by these orders that we discussed, except in the two instances out of twenty-seven."

"At this point I disagree with the use of the cascara immediately post-op, and with the giving of the blood. I've already indicated that re-surgery was strongly suggested and turned down, so when put together these all make reasons for not agreeing with what you term 'the general nature of the treatment,' sir."

"Now, Dr. Hatch, as you have read in his deposition, Doctor, and as he will later testify, states that he did the surgery—" Mr. Tolliver paused.

"We will stipulate to that, your Honor," Mr. Cousman put in laughing, and for once the judge himself smiled.

"Thank you," Mr. Tolliver said. "Now Dr. Hatch, in doing this surgery, has stated that he carefully identified the hepatic artery and then separated the cystic artery from it before he tied it off. You would admit, would you not, that he was in a better position than anyone else to know what he observed and what he did?"

"Yes."

"And Dr. Hatch, as he will testify, and has stated in his deposition—here let me read it to you." Mr. Tolliver read several pages of the deposition, and then asked his question. "So Dr. Hatch also saw and observed the autopsy tissue and he avers the cystic artery, not the hepatic artery, was tied off. Would you not say that he was in a better position to judge than you as to the state of the circulation in this area, just as you could say better than he about a case you yourself had operated on and followed to the autopsy room?"

"I don't know why you suggest the latter should happen to me," Dr. Dunning responded, but before he could continue the courtroom broke into laughter. "I am sorry, your Honor," Dr. Dunning said in a moment, "I did not mean to make light of a serious question."

"I would like to state," Mr. Cousman said, rising as he spoke, "that I don't think the counsel for the defendant here should expect the witness to state whether or not he believes the defendant would make an admission against interest in the matter of admitting that he did negligently tie off the hepatic artery, which is essentially what would be involved here."

Before the judge could comment, Dr. Dunning went on, "Of course, I have no idea what Dr. Hatch saw at the operation."

Mr. Cousman continued with his objection. "And the witness could never be in a position to tell the court what Dr. Hatch saw or did then."

"I feel, based on the information I have received and extracted about this case, that there must have been interference to the circulation of blood to the liver. I have said before that that is my conviction."

"I think, your Honor, that I should be entitled to an answer to my question," Mr. Tolliver said.

"I thought he had already answered it."

"No. I asked if the witness did not feel Dr. Hatch was in a better position to determine the state of the circulation to the liver, including the hepatic artery, and I would like a yes or no answer."

"Yes, he undoubtedly was in a better position."

"Your Honor, I think I'll delay the rest of my questions until tomorrow."

"All right, we'll adjourn now. Ladies and gentlemen, we expect you back here at ten o'clock in the morning."

Peter felt more sorry for the Cortis each day. The ordeal of the trial, recreating, as it constantly did, the image of their fine young Louis and his illness, was certainly torture for them. The end of the trial, however it turned out, might be difficult for them, too, because Louis would slip a little more away from them when it was over.

Peter walked out of the courtroom with them. "You look so tired, Peggy. And so does Amadeo," he said. "Maybe you both ought to skip tomorrow."

"That's just what I tell her. It's okay with me if *she'll* do it," Mr. Corti said.

"I couldn't stay away. All I think about now is what's happening here. Besides, Mr. Cousman said I *should* come each day. I really don't care about the money. Whether I get it or not, it doesn't matter to me now. But I do care about doing this for Louis. I think Mr. Cousman is such a fine lawyer, and I want to do what he says. I guess today was a bad day for him, too. He's the one who looked tired tonight, I thought. *He* ought to take a day off. He must spend half of every night reading, besides everything else."

"I know he worked a lot last night because when we finish presenting the plaintiff's side the other side will make a motion for non-suit, and he likes to be prepared in advance just in case. So tonight he can rest, and he'll probably look better tomorrow. I hope you do, too. Good night, Peggy."

"Good night, Doctor."

"You still can't call me Peter."

"Maybe when this is over I can. Somehow, you're still on the case and I have to call you Doctor. Do you know what I mean?"

"Yes."

Peter walked on out to the parking lot and opened the door of his Ford. Anne was in the front seat waiting for him.

PART FIVE

39

"HELLO, Peter," she said.

"Anne, how—what are you doing here?"

"I decided I wanted to see you. I've been in the courtroom all afternoon listening."

Peter could not believe he had looked at Rosalie Hatch the other day and thought her beautiful. Anne was twice as beautiful. Her black hair was long again and shining, her eyes were bright and her cheeks flushed, the lovely swoop of her delicate nose was still there to amaze him.

"You were in the courtroom?"

"I called Marsh and he took me in. He clapped loud once and you looked around. I thought sure you'd noticed me then."

"Oh, he was the one who clapped." Peter was so astonished to see her that he found it hard to make sensible conversation. "I'm so surprised. Why are you here, Anne?"

"I came because there's something I want to tell you, but first I have to ask a question."

"What?"

"Are you angry at me, or disgusted with me, or anything?"

"No, of course not. I'm just delighted to see you—so very happy to have you here. What do you ask for?"

"I guess you don't understand why I did what I did, really, so let me try to explain. Nothing was ever so hard on me to accept as the fact that I couldn't have babies. I've always wanted them so. I just knew after my surgery that you couldn't love me as much, that you were confusing love and pity. Besides, you were so difficult to get along with then, so different, at a time when I needed love and attention, you were so absentminded. I realized afterward you were really obsessed. Of course, you were working like a dog, and totally worn out all the time."

"I'm sorry if I was bad then."

"You were just possessed by the idea of getting Dr. Hatch. I guess you'll have that out of your system now. You seem changed already, more as you were at first, relaxed, part of the world. And you've gained weight."

"Fifteen pounds now. I've even got a suntan."

"It looks wonderful."

"What are you trying to say?"

"You know I've been going out some, especially with Stanley Evans, who's an old friend. Yes, I know you're going to ask me, and he has kissed me a few times. I wanted him to. I wanted to see if it meant anything to me. If it meant anything like your kissing me meant. I just couldn't tell. He kisses very well."

"I don't know what you're telling me this for."

"Wait a minute and you'll see. I'm coming to it. A couple of nights ago Stanley tried to make love to me. I can't say I didn't allow him an opportunity—I don't mean I asked him, or anything, but I didn't make the opposition clear, either."

"Do you really want to say all this?"

"Yes. Anyway, as soon as he started being really serious—nothing happened, he just kissed me, told me he wanted to sleep with me, and we talked about it—and I realized that I wasn't interested, how totally uninterested I was in him or anyone else, but you. I do love you. I thought I did, but I had to be sure, and now I am. But what about you?"

"You know I love you. I've been crazy about you since the moment I first saw you. How do I feel? I just get crazier."

Peter pulled her to him and kissed her. Never had he loved her so as at this moment, never had her lips felt so good kissing him. She pulled away to breathe and then he kissed her again, harder and longer. People coming out of the courthouse paused to stare at them before walking on.

"You're so beautiful, Anne," he said, "so soft and warm and delicious. I haven't had a date, haven't looked at another woman, even thought of another woman through all these months. All I've cared about is you, and now I don't have to keep worrying because you're back with me." He kissed her cheeks, kissed the tears on her eyelids.

"Darling, I want to get married," she said. "Can't we get married sometime soon?"

"Of course, we must. Are you here overnight?"
"Yes, Dad's expecting me."
"Look, I want to get your engagement ring. It's at the apartment. So I can give it back to you. And let's go out to dinner, have a celebration, get drunk."
"I'm right at the end of a summer session with tests next week and everything. I can't be too wild. I can't afford to be hungover tomorrow."
"I feel like getting bombed, but we'll be moderate. There are so many things we have to talk about. I've got to find a place to go next. I want to go back into residency, in surgery. You don't know I've decided that."
"I think it's the right thing."
"And you'll go with me anyplace, won't you?"
"Of course."
"That's wonderful. This has turned out to be the most tremendous day."
"Kiss me again, and then I'll go home and wait for you."
"Of course. I am at your service and your mercy."

40

EARLY the next morning, Mr. Cousman was on the phone to Peter.
"After a bad day in court yesterday, Peter, I have worse news today."
"What's that?"
"A witness flew the coop."
"Who?"
"Your friend Norman Silvana. I had my girl call his office yesterday afternoon to remind him that we wanted him today, and they said his mother had gotten sick, that he had flown East to see her and was expected to be gone for several weeks. How about that?"
"For Christ's sake. His mother is old, I know, in her seventies, but I'll be damned."
"You see, I made a mistake. He didn't want to testify, as you know. He made that clear. So now he's popped out on us, and we are left wiping the egg off. It's my fault, too. I

should have subpoenaed him. It's probably hopeless, but I thought you might have an idea how to get in touch with him in the East."

"I really don't. I can't even remember which town his folks live in, except that they're around New York someplace. What will you do in court?"

"After Houston finishes with Dr. Dunning, there'll be a little re-direct, and then I'll have to read Dr. Silvana's deposition to the jury, I guess. Nothing else I can do. That'll finish the plaintiff's case, and of course then we'll have our session over a non-suit motion by the defendant in chambers, which I'm frankly worried about after the judge's attitude yesterday. But anyway, nose around and see what really happened to Silvana."

"I'll call my friend, Marsh, the anesthesiologist. He'll know."

Marshall was in surgery at the Hatch, but could answer the phone. "Sure," he said, "I know what happened. Norman got chicken-shit and took off. His mother's not any sicker than she's been for the last year.

"Hey, listen," Marsh lowered his voice. The phone he was using was evidently in the main surgery vestibule. "Old Hatch is really shook up by this whole thing, do you know that? He's so paranoid now you couldn't believe it. He fired old Steve the janitor the other day who's been here for a hundred years, and he looks at everybody else like they're conniving against him. And eating, he's eating like a horse. Fatter all the time. Have you noticed?"

"He does look like he's gaining weight."

"Hell, he put twenty pounds on the last two weeks. Say, did you see Anne yesterday?"

"Yes."

"Everything all right between you two now?"

"Yes."

"That's more like it. When the trial's finished, you both come over to my place and I'll give you dinner and we'll get drunk together."

In court, Hugh Tolliver started the morning by reading the description of the operation to Dr. Dunning, then asked if it sounded like a proper procedure to him. The surgeon answered that it did, and then the attorney began to question him about surgery speed, and asked if there wasn't much variation in individual cases, and variation between different doctors, to which Dr. Dunning agreed.

The attorney displayed a compendium of cases taken from the Bay Hospital in San Francisco, a large, old-time, private institution there, listing the times elapsed for all cholecystectomies done the previous three years; they had found several done in thirty-eight to forty-one minutes. Would Dr. Dunning comment on that? He merely said he still felt it was too fast to do a proper job, and added, "I notice that even so none of those was done in thirty-three minutes."

There were a dozen questions after that for the expert witness, and then Hugh Tolliver turned him back to Mr. Cousman for a short re-direct, after which he was dismissed. Mr. Cousman then explained to the judge and jury that his next witness, Dr. Norman Silvana, had been called East suddenly and surprisingly by the serious illness of his mother, and was not available for testimony. He planned to be gone for several weeks, he was not under subpoena at the time he left, and he had already given his testimony in the form of a deposition.

"Still, this was quite a blow to me, your Honor," Mr. Cousman explained. "I had expected Dr. Silvana to be here in person. I had kept him informed every day of the progress here so he would have plenty of advance notice of when he should appear, and he left without notifying me in any way of his departure. I feel we needed his further testimony to present this case in the fullest, but failing it, I wonder if you would allow me to read his complete deposition to the jury?"

"Go right ahead."

It took the hour before lunch recess, and forty-five minutes afterward for this to be done. As soon as he had completed it, Mr. Cousman said, "I would like to reserve the right later on to call this doctor to the stand, if the witness should reappear in town before the case goes to the jury."

"Very well," the judge said. "Dr. Hatch, as Dr. Silvana's employer, do you think he's likely to be back in the next week?"

"I don't think so, your Honor, not from the way things sounded."

"We could use his testimony, too, your Honor," Mr. Tolliver said from the table. "You can be sure of that."

"Your Honor, I would like to read into the record now the short interrogatory of Dr. Joseph Litner," Mr. Cousman said quietly.

"Proceed."

In fifteen minutes he finished, put down the paper, took off his glasses, smiled beatifically at the jury, and said to the judge, "Your Honor, the plaintiff will rest her case."

Mr. Tolliver was already standing and at once said, "I have a matter to take up with the Court, your Honor."

"Will it take awhile?"

"Probably so."

"I must say it's time for afternoon recess, and I do have some further duties which need my attention today. If it's all right with counsel, I will dismiss the jury until ten tomorrow morning."

"That's fine," Mr. Cousman said.

"Ladies and gentlemen, please remember my instructions to you about not discussing this case and we'll see you at ten o'clock in the morning. Bailiff, will you clear the courtroom, please?" Mr. Cousman motioned to Peter to stay. "It will be all right," he whispered.

In less than ten minutes they were ready to proceed. "All right, Mr. Tolliver."

"Your Honor, on behalf of the defendant I would like to move for a judgment of non-suit in this case. My motion is based on the ground that there is not sufficient evidence to warrant submission of this case to the jury on the issue of liability of my client for negligence or for malpractice. There is nothing to indicate from the record that anything Dr. Hatch did do or did not do caused the death of this man, and certainly nothing to suggest there was negligence. This man had a death due to acute liver failure, which may arise from toxic or infectious damage. There are many other causes of liver damage, including the concurrent existence of viral hepatitis, as even Dr. Dunning admitted, but there is no proof, and certainly there should be proof—and we have much information on the defendant's side to show just the opposite—but there is not any proof established by the plaintiff here that a ligature was negligently tied around the hepatic artery in this man. The case of Georgeson against Tomlin, or I mean Tomkin, in 14 Cal 2nd, applies here, I am sure."

"I've written that down," Judge Fielding said.

"Yes, at page 272. And the case of Prospect *vs.* Shinn, 116 Cal App. 2d at page 353. Generally these cases indicate that people may die after abdominal surgery, and the latter one is specifically cholecystectomy, without any presumption of negligence. This is a fact almost of common knowledge, actually I would say it definitely was a fact of common knowledge, and I believe there is no basis for any such presumption here."

Mr. Tolliver droned on, smoothly, courteously, but with aplomb, and Peter noticed how carefully he halted after each point for the judge to make his note. In twenty minutes, he had finished his presentation and Mr. Cousman began, a little nervous at first, with even a bit of a shake in his voice as he started, but increasingly assured in his delivery as he went along, finally snapping out his arguments and citations with an impressive authority and speed. Peter wondered at his ability as he took his listeners through a series of intricate paths, in doors and then out of them again, off into other corridors and other rooms, with a continuity and a logical advance of ideas that was amazing. He spoke for nearly forty minutes, before summing up.

"Your Honor, on the question of non-suit then, I believe there was a definite admission against interest by Dr. Hatch himself, when he said in front of Dr. de Haan, talking to Dr. Silvana, that he wasn't going to re-operate this young man, because that would be signing his death warrant, and then said, 'I'm not going to be held responsible for that.' But especially, during this conversation it came out that Dr. Silvana urged him to perform surgery, and told Dr. Hatch that he felt it was possible a ligature had gotten placed around the hepatic artery instead of the cystic artery. Now, on that one point alone, I think this case is entitled to go to the jury, for them to decide if there was or was not a surgical tie placed around the hepatic artery. Whom do they believe, Dr. Dunning and Dr. de Haan, or Dr. Hatch? It is for them to decide on the believability, the credibility of the witnesses and they should have the chance in this case."

"Gentlemen, I'm going to take your discussions under advisement. I will go through the citations listed and then you may meet me in my chambers before court tomorrow."

"What do you think?" Peter asked Mr. Cousman, as they left the court.

The little lawyer shrugged his shoulders. "I don't think he'll grant them a non-suit. He just doesn't quite dare. I believe he'd like to, though, after yesterday, I really do."

The next day the judge talked to the attorneys in chambers. Peter was waiting when the two lawyers entered the court with their assistants, but looking at their faces he was not able to tell anything.

"Well?" Peter asked Mr. Cousman over his shoulder as the lawyer sat down with only a brief nod.

"He refused the motion for non-suit, all right, but then he sent the court reporter out, and Houston too, and talked to me alone. He told me we had better improve our status on the plaintiff's side before the end of the trial or he would be inclined toward encouraging a similar motion from Mr. Tolliver again at the end of the defendant's presentation. He told me he took these cases very seriously, that he was fundamentally cautious about assigning liability to physicians in malpractice cases, and that he wanted to see a first-rate *prima facie* case ordinarily to do so and didn't believe we'd presented one so far. Oh, it was quite a little conversation."

"I wonder why Mr. Tolliver just came in now?"

"He was waiting outside trying to find out what the hell was going on. I didn't give him an inkling."

Dr. Hatch walked in and Mrs. Hatch, too, with Peggy Corti and Mr. Corti behind them. The Hatches ignored the Cortis, and the Cortis the Hatches. Wasn't it funny, Peter thought, after all that had gone before, how people still sat with each other for days in court never seeing one another, never looking across the room, in essence acting as if the others did not exist. Except on the witness stand. Reality was restored when one appeared there. Then scowls and whispers and even louder asides about the other's testimony took place, but as soon as the opponent left the witness stand, he reentered limbo and was lost to notice.

Mr. Cousman leaned back from the table to talk to Peter again. "We've got to dig in on this case, Doctor. We need to study and plan our every move from now on, and analyze theirs as carefully. We'll go over each day's testimony together whenever possible. That might help. I'll get a reporter of our own in here who can type up the proceedings after court, then we'll go over them in the evening."

"You know I've never looked at the photostats of the hospital records. Do you think I should?"

"You could check them over this weekend. This is Thursday. I presume they'll take at least the next three days for their regular witnesses, and Hatch and Parmelee will be up next week."

"I'll look them over."

"I'm also arranging to put my junior partner, Frank Crenna, on this case full-time to prepare our position for the defendant's next petition to the court for dismissal, after his side rests. At noon today, too, let's see if the Cortis wouldn't have lunch with us, so I can explain our new tactics to them."

The defendant's first witnesses were also hospital nurses, this time including Miss West. The afternoon was warm again and the fan in the roof was clattering. Most of the spectators had their coats off. After the nurses, the first expert witness for the Hatch side came on the stand, an elderly and prominent surgeon from San Francisco, former president of the State Medical Society, on the faculty at the University Center in San Francisco. He was relaxed and pleasant, an impressive senior member of the medical community who was firmly on Dr. Hatch's side, and emphatic in his belief that the Corti case had been well handled, that this death had been due to endotoxicity from a gram-negative bacterial organism which had spread from the gallbladder into the bloodstream and taken this young man off. "I've had experience with these, even lost a few myself, and I know that unless you have the most expert bacteriologist working on the case, you won't culture the bug, because most of these lethal, rapidly fatal gram-negative infections are difficult to grow."

"What particular bacterial organisms do you refer to, Doctor?" Mr. Tolliver asked him.

"Oh, some species of *E. coli,* that is *Escherichia coli,* the most common bacterial inhabitant of the intestinal tract, get very pathogenic, and of course there's the *Proteus* species, the *Aerobacter aerogenes* and *Klebsiella* groups, and several others. These are all particular types of what we call gram-negative organisms, bacterial organisms which react to the gram stain with a blue rather than red color."

"Now, Doctor, in this particular case the assertion has been made by the plaintiff that the hepatic artery was inadvertently tied at surgery by Dr. Hatch, resulting in the death of the patient. Would you feel the facts given to you so far are consistent with such a possibility?"

"Not at all. I've seen one or two of those cases. The patients usually develop a severe jaundice. There was no jaundice here at all. That's fairly well agreed, I understand."

The old fogey, Peter thought, he doesn't know anything of the sort. He is a social doctor, a medical politician hopelessly behind the times. Even his use of the outdated term, *Aerobacter aerogenes*, suggests that.

Immersed in the witness's statements and his own thoughts, Peter did not see when Peggy Corti, sitting next to him on their hard bench, slipped off it and fell to the floor. At first he thought there was some purpose in the movement she made, she must be looking for her gloves. Then he realized something was really wrong. Peter jumped off the bench and kneeled down to look at her. She had slumped onto the floor, but with no loud crack to suggest her head had struck in the process. She was out cold on the floor, though, and there was noisy commotion in the courtroom. Peter held up his hand to stop the people who were bending over to help lift her up. "Give her a minute lying down first," he said.

Peter noticed then that the judge was standing up for a better view of the event. "Doctor," he called. "Dr. de Haan?"

"Yes, sir," Peter said.

"Three doors down the corridor on the right is my office. The next door is a large waiting room with a couch. You may take her there. My secretary can help you."

"Thank you."

Peggy Corti stirred then and moved her head. "Thank God we'll be in the new courthouse building by Christmas," Peter heard the judge say as he and Mr. Corti helped her up, then walked her out of the old chamber and down to the judge's waiting room.

"Stay with her, Mr. Corti," Peter said, "and I'll get her some atropine from my bag in the car." The judge's elderly secretary was turning on the room air-conditioner as Peter bounded down the hallway.

Thirty minutes later Peter was insisting to Peggy Corti that she go home, but she was refusing. "I'm staying here. I want to go back into court."

Peter admitted defeat finally, and the three of them marched back in, Peggy Corti not allowing even a hand on her arm as they entered. She sat down in her usual place as the judge nodded at them and interrupted Mr. Cousman's cross-examination of the elderly doctor to say, "I'm glad to see you back, Mrs. Corti."

The rest of the week was repetitious to Peter. There were two more experts taken through the same series of facts, the abdominal pain with tender right upper quadrant and fever, the surgery, the post-operative illness and death. All of them had the hypothetical question put to them. All of them denied that Dr. Hatch had acted against the standards of good medical care. Interestingly, all of them had a different notion of the cause of death. The first elderly gentleman had said gram-negative infection, the second doctor, Harry Hamuth, a highly experienced, older, general practitioner from Oakland, thought portal vein thrombosis was likely as a cause of death ("they're easy to overlook at post"), and the last physician, a university professor from the staid old Madrona Medical School on the Peninsula, believed the "hepatorenal syndrome" was responsible, an enigmatic pathological process, as he explained it, which combined serious liver and kidney abnormalities. "Very hard to know what causes this," the thin but paunchy academician said, "and impossible to treat it. Working with the electrolytes of the body, the salts, is the one big thing that can be done, and I'd say after going over the records that this patient was treated as well as possible."

Looking over to the defendant's table, Peter found it always abuzz now with whispering, scribbling of notes back and forth, couriers from it in and out of the courtroom. Even Matthew Hatch was more attentive, listening to the witnesses closely, often smiling, waving his hands as he explained something in a lawyer's ear.

Before Friday was over, Mr. Cousman got two of the expert witnesses to admit that if the hypothetical question were amended to include the presence of a ligature around the hepatic artery they might possibly consider the standards of good and proper care had not been met. The third man, the Peninsula medical school professor, refused to comment on this possibility and his refusal was upheld by the judge.

Sunday Peter called Mr. Cousman at home. "I've really stumbled onto something here, A. O.," he said excitedly. "The next to the last sheet of progress notes has been completely rewritten. To begin with, this consisted of three notes by Dr. Hatch, one on April sixth and two on April seventh. Then there was a long note in the middle of the page by me the evening of April seventh which stated in essence that the patient's condition was critical, the outlook nearly hopeless, and that I had definitely concurred with Dr. Silvana's position earlier in the day that immediate re-surgery was necessary."

"Did Dr. Silvana write on this page?"

"No, just on his separate consultation sheet."

"But he didn't put it down on paper that strongly, did he?"

"No, not at all. He *said* it strongly but didn't write it. That's why I made this note of mine. Because he didn't write it. Anyway, this sheet of progress notes that has been rewritten is the second of three pages. My note is deleted entirely. Then Hatch's first note of April sixth originally read:

> 4/6: Post-operative course satisfactory to this point but for fever, apparently due to infection above the diaphragm (rales heard in lung base on left), a medical problem and only indirectly related to surgery. Will X-ray chest, antibiotics started by Dr. de Haan. Hatch.

"Now this note was changed to read:

> 4/6: Consideration of damage or clotting in blood vessel supply to liver considered carefully but rejected as entirely unlikely. Patient remains very ill from toxicity secondary to his acute gallbladder infection, and development of hepatorenal syndrome from shock and toxicity is likely with BUN also rising. Wife and rest of family informed of change in patient's status to serious since yesterday. Hatch.

"Then the next note replaces mine plus an earlier one of his and it reads:

> 4/7 A.M.: Patient remains shocky and in poor condition. Family called to bedside. Portal vein thrombosis is possible. No surgical therapy indicated. All-out treatment of shock, toxicity, possible disseminated infection or hepatorenal syndrome is under way. Hatch.

"His last note of April seventh at first read:

> 4/7 P.M.: Patient in better condition tonight. Overwhelming toxicity has possibly been related to bloodstream invasion from lung infection, or toxic reaction to anesthetic agents may be responsible. No evidence of trouble at surgical site or from surgery. Family knows everything is being done and patient will come along in due time. Hatch.

"The note replacing it goes:

> 4/7 P.M.: Patient constantly growing poorer. No signs at

all suggestive of interference with blood supply to liver. Any attempt at re-operating patient discarded yesterday as impractical, dangerous, improbable of any help by Dr. Norman Silvana and me after careful consideration of the clinical facts. Family at bedside. Hatch.

"The next page then carries only the death notes by Dr. Hatch and me on the morning of April eighth, and these weren't disturbed."

"That's very interesting, Peter. We were looking so hard at the trees, we overlooked the ground underneath. We should have had this information before. I suppose their expert witnesses had been reading those notes and thinking how wise Dr. Hatch was during all the troubles that beset his poor patient, and we could have been shaking them up by cross-examining them on this all the time."

"I can't believe Hatch would be so stupid as to change the hospital record. I really had it photostated just to get started on the case. I thought it might be hard to get it out of them without a court order. How are you going to put this into evidence now?"

"I'll wait and cross-examine Hatch on it. No reason at this point to bring it up sooner. It might even turn out better that we didn't find it until now. We can use it this way as a bombshell to throw into the court's lap. You see I'll introduce it into evidence in our rebuttal time after Tolliver finishes. I'll put the Hatch record room girl on, and the girl who photostated it initially for you and have them swear to its accuracy, and then carefully read through the discrepancies. This is terrifically good news and we really need it, believe me."

On the stand the next day Dr. Joseph Parmelee III looked more like an actor from the English stage than a California physician. Toying with his moustache, smoothing the brindle brush of his hair, he told his story rapidly and simply, though. Peter noticed that the jury was unusually attentive to him.

It seemed odd to Peter that the Hatch attorneys had not put Parmelee on before the other experts. His testimony logically seemed to precede theirs and would have been a help to establish the defendant's position of no ligature around the hepatic artery. Probably, Peter decided, Tolliver wanted the full weight of the experts' testimony *before* Parmelee testified to help support *his* position.

"Now we come to the autopsy, Dr. Parmelee," Mr. Tolliver said. "And we should like first to have you summarize your findings for the ladies and gentlemen of the jury."

Dr. Parmelee turned to the jury box with his constant half-smile, a bandbox figure in his narrow-shouldered dark suit with black tie and pocket handkerchief. For all his surface polish his voice frequently leaked nervousness as he explained with surprising brevity the results of his autopsy on Louis Corti. When he concluded, Mr. Tolliver said, "Well, thank you, Doctor, that was fine. I didn't mean it to be quite that short, but we can cover any other points needed with our questions as we go along."

Joe Parmelee now went to their own chart at the easel, and gave a description of Louis Corti's gallbladder area, liver, blood vessels, and bile ducts.

"Now, can you make a specific statement about the cystic artery?" Mr. Tolliver asked him.

"It was definitely tied off all right."

"That you determined at the time of autopsy?"

"Yes, I did."

"And the main hepatic artery, as well as right and left branches, were intact then?"

"They were."

"All right, Doctor, would you please resume the stand? Thank you. Now as to the liver pathology, in your professional opinion what caused it?"

"Liver necrosis, which is liver cell death, resulted here from toxicity, shock, infection, and possibly intravascular clotting—that's clotting inside the blood vessels, occurring in this case in the vessels inside the liver."

"What was the connection of the gallbladder disease to the liver disease, and also to the patient's death, in your opinion?"

"Acute cholecystitis, a term which I assume is familiar to the jury by now, is a serious, shocking illness. Surgery for it carries a five to eight percent mortality, with complications such as bloodstream or liver infection, pneumonia, atelectasis, which is lung collapse, and many other possible conditions. In this case, I presume the shocking toxic effects on the body of this acute, severe ailment, plus blood-borne infection spread from the inflamed gallbladder to affect the delicate, tender, easily damaged cells of the liver, both the sinusoidal and reticulo-endothelial types, interrupted the function of this most important organ, and resulted in death. If the patient could have only survived forty-eight hours more, quite possibly the patient's body, especially the liver, could have made adjustments allowing Mr. Corti to recover and live. Quite a shame."

"Thank you, Doctor, for your natural and well-meant expressions of sympathy. I am through with the direct inquiry, your Honor."

Judge Fielding recessed court for lunch then. Peter saw that Matthew Hatch rose from the defendant's table to grip Joe Parmelee's hand, shake it, and then walk out with his arm around Joe's shoulder.

Mr. Cousman saw where he was looking and said, "Wait until this afternoon, my friend."

At two o'clock Joe Parmelee was back on the stand. Mr. Cousman, wearing a vivid red tie, and intense as ever, stepped snappily up to the witness box.

"Sir, it is my recollection that you stated you graduated approximately twenty-four years ago from Southern Reserve Medical School in Georgia. Is that correct?"

"Yes, sir." There was edginess in Joe's voice again.

"Then you interned at Atlanta, Georgia, and after that went on to practice, was it general practice, in Chicago?"

"Yes, sir. I was in general practice."

"How long was that?"

"Between four and five years."

"You had no military service then?"

"No. I was deferred for—reasons of health."

"Then when did you take your pathology training?"

"I left Chicago and went to San Jose for a residency in pathology."

"That was for three years, I believe you said."

"That's right."

"And that was at what hospital?"

"Santa Prista Hospital."

"Is this hospital affiliated with a medical school?"

"No, it's a large private hospital."

"The residency is an accredited one, though?" Mr. Cousman put his hands back on his hips as he asked this.

"Yes, fully accredited," Dr. Parmelee answered, starting to pick again at his moustache.

"Now, sir, have you engaged in any medical teaching activity?"

"I teach the residents here at San Marcial County General Hospital."

"I mean, sir, any teaching duties in connection with a medical school?"

"No, sir."

"Do you belong to any honorary professional societies?"

"I belong to the National College of Pathologists."

"Is that an honorary society?"

"Well, not exactly."

"Is it, or isn't it, Doctor?"

"No, I'd say, strictly, no."

"Have you won any awards, scholarships, or fellowships in pathology?"

"No."

"And you state you *are* a pathologist certified by the American Board of Pathology?" Cousman's hands were on his hips again.

"Yes, sir." Dr. Parmelee's answers were soft.

"Would you repeat your answer, sir?" Mr. Cousman asked. "I'm afraid the reporter can't hear you."

"Yes, sir."

"How many medical papers have you written and had published?"

"One, sir."

"One, Doctor? What was the title of that paper and when published?"

"That was many years ago."

"You mean you've forgotten?" Cousman could be nasty, too, Peter realized.

"It was about granulomas, chronic infections of the lung."

"All right, sir." Mr. Cousman stood back now, surveying the physician for a moment. "Sir, you are the pathologist for the Hatch Hospital in San Marcial, are you not?"

"Yes."

"And do you do pathological work for any other hospital?"

"For the San Marcial County General Hospital."

"But that is only part-time, is it not?"

"Yes."

"You share that work with the two other pathologists in town, do you not?"

"Yes."

"Then you run a small commercial laboratory for blood testing downtown, do you not?"

"Yes."

"And also run all the biopsy specimens and Papanicolaou smears from the Hatch Clinic?"

"Yes."

"And also at least in name run the Hatch Hospital laboratories?"

Dr. Parmelee hesitated here. Mr. Cousman waited for the answer. The witness looked at the defendant's table, but no objection appeared, so he answered, "Yes."

"Would you estimate that eighty percent of your professional income, or more, is derived directly from the Hatch Hospital and Clinic, sole owner and proprietor of which is Dr. Matthew Hatch?"

"Now, your Honor," an angry-sounding Houston Tolliver was on his feet. "This last question is definitely irrelevant, immaterial, and improper."

"Mr. Cousman?" the judge asked with a sigh.

"Your Honor, this question is for the purpose of attempting to show bias or prejudice."

"We will allow it, then, for the time being and for that purpose."

"Thank you. Will the reporter please read that question back for Dr. Parmelee?" The reporter did so.

"I can't answer that," Dr. Parmelee said softly, bleakly.

"You mean you can't estimate even to a rough degree how much of your income is derived from Dr. Matthew Hatch and his group?"

"It's hard for me to do that."

"Well, now your income from the county hospital, which is available as public information, ran to two thousand nine hundred dollars last year. I shouldn't think that would be too large a share of your income, is that right?"

"No, I mean, yes, that isn't too much. Oh, I guess at least half of my income comes from the Hatch sources."

"Now I have a report here from the Hewson Credit Service of San Marcial, and they estimate your clinical laboratory services, which are incorporated into—"

"I suppose that, when I stop to think of it, three-quarters of my income is from the Hatch services."

"I see, not eighty percent but seventy-five percent of your income is from the Hatch Hospital and Clinic services you perform, is that right?"

"Yes, roughly."

"All right, now, isn't it true that you testified for Dr. Hatch at a previous trial four years ago?"

"Now it is absolutely improper, your Honor, for him to make mention of a previous trial."

"It's for the same purpose, your Honor, to show possible bias."

"I will allow it again, Mr. Cousman, for that limited use."

"Did you testify in behalf of Dr. Hatch in a previous trial four years ago?"

"Yes, I did."

"And was your testimony helpful to him, would you say?"

"It was the truth, and he was acquitted."

"It involved a hysterectomy operation, a procedure for removal of the uterus, did it not?"

"Yes."

"And wasn't it the plaintiff's contention that Dr. Hatch had performed this operation unnecessarily—"

"Now, I object strenuously, your Honor," Mr. Tolliver trumpeted. "The plaintiff's attorney is not giving the witness proper questions, is leading him, and not allowing him to make proper answers. Besides, my original objection remains that this entire line of questioning is immaterial, irrelevant, possibly prejudicial to my client, and improper."

"For the limited purpose of showing bias, we have allowed this testimony," the judge ground out in his pebbly voice. "But we will strike that last question. Please be more careful of your future questions, Mr. Cousman, and I hope you will complete this excursion quickly."

"I might say," Mr. Tolliver inserted, "that Dr. Hatch tells me he certainly did win this case in mention, in fact it never went to the jury, but was dismissed by the judge after the defendant's presentation was over."

"I think Mr. Tolliver at this point might be excused for a little wishful thinking into the future, your Honor, but I certainly trust that the ladies and gentlemen of the jury will not find his remark leading in their own regard." Light laughter powdered the air momentarily. Mr. Cousman was grim again, though, as he turned back to Dr. Parmelee.

"There will be but one more query on this topic, Doctor, so relax. I only want to ask if in this previous trial there was not also contradicting pathological testimony by a Dr. Willicomb of the State University of San Francisco?"

"Now that is indisputably improper, your Honor!" Mr. Tolliver roared.

"Objection sustained. I expect better performance than that from you, Mr. Cousman."

"All right, then, we'll leave this unpleasant line of questioning, Doctor, and go on to something else. Now—"

"Your Honor, the plaintiff's attorney's constant insinuations are most annoying. I wonder if you could not speak to him?" an annoyed Mr. Tolliver asked.

"All I'm going to say is to tell the jury again that counsel's remarks and comments are not evidence. You will judge this case on what the evidence is, what the witnesses say, how credible and believable you find their testimony to be, and nothing else. Counsels' statements are not evidence, and you will not use them to make your judgment. Now Mr. Cousman, please continue."

"Dr. Parmelee, do you think Dr. Peter de Haan is a liar?"

Dr. Parmelee looked Mr. Tolliver's way again. "I wouldn't say so."

"Do you think he is mentally incompetent or insane?"

"No."

"He testified here that he saw the autopsy you performed and that there *was* a ligature around the hepatic artery. Do you still insist that there was no ligature around the hepatic artery?"

"Yes, of course."

"How do you explain the difference in testimony?"

"Dr. de Haan is young and inexperienced. He didn't know what he saw."

"Do you know Dr. Norman Silvana?"

"Certainly."

"Do you think he is a liar?"

"No, of course not."

"Do you think he is insane?"

"No."

"Unfortunately, he has been a most reluctant witness to testify, so reluctant that he did not show up here at all—"

"Now, your Honor—" said Mr. Tolliver.

"All right, Mr. Tolliver. Strike that last from the record. Start your question again, Mr. Cousman, with my same injunctions if you don't mind."

"Dr. Silvana, whom you said was not dishonest and not incompetent, gave us a deposition which I have read to the jury. I do want to say that we considered him definitely uncooperative, unfriendly, in other words hostile, so he was therefore interrogated by us as an adverse witness, and our questioning was labeled cross-examination. Still he said, and I quote, 'COUSMAN: Was there or was there not a tie around the hepatic artery? SILVANA: I believe there was. I have to repeat that I did not perform the autopsy, and I did not actually handle the material. COUSMAN: You would say that there was a tie around the hepatic artery, then? SILVANA: I believe there was. I may have been mistaken. COUSMAN: You would say then that when you left the autopsy room you thought that you had seen a ligature around the hepatic artery? SILVANA: That was my impression, at least, though I would not and do not feel right about testifying positively to it in court, because I could have been mistaken.' " Mr. Cousman stopped then, went back to his table and threw the transcript down, and came back to the witness stand. "Now, that is taken right from Dr. Silvana's testimony about the autopsy, and do you consider him young and inexperienced?"

"No."

"Would you like to change your testimony about your findings in regard to the presence or absence of a ligature around the hepatic artery?" Mr. Cousman's questions were loud and forceful, delivered directly in front of the witness, in fast sequence with scant time allowed for answers.

The witness shook his head.

"Speak up, please. What is your answer?"

"No."

"You don't feel that Dr. Silvana is lying, insane, blind, or inexperienced. Then why should he say that he *believed* there was a ligature around the hepatic artery?"

"He was mistaken," Joe Parmelee answered weakly. He was visibly trembling now, pale and sweating so intensely his collar was wilting, his voice a croak.

"Dr. Arnold Dunning, an eminent medical authority from Los Angeles who testified for us earlier, a general surgeon of national repute, and at this moment temporary chairman of the Department of Surgery at University Medical School in Los Angeles, stated here before this court and jury that he felt sure the pathological changes seen by him in the slides made available through court order resulted from ligation of the hepatic artery. Would you disagree with him?"

"I would have to."

"What was your answer?"

Dr. Parmelee cleared his throat, and croaked louder, "I would have to."

"Dr. Dunning also testified that he felt in general the diagnostic conclusions arrived at by you were inadequate. I quote his testimony here: 'Analyzing the report that was prepared by the pathologist, Dr. Parmelee, for the defendant doctor on this patient, Mr. Louis Corti, a report which never states directly that the hepatic artery was tied off, one is led to the unmistakable conclusion that the artery *must* have been tied off to produce the pathological picture as described by Dr. Parmelee.' Do you agree with him?"

"No."

"We have an interrogatory here from a highly qualified and able pathologist in Southern California, Dr. Joseph Litner. He is a member of the National Association of Pathologists, an honorary society of top pathologists chosen by invitation only. He is associate professor of pathology at the University Medical School in Los Angeles, and the author of ninety-two papers, including ten on various diseases of the liver."

"We have stipulated to Dr. Litner's qualifications. Counsel knows that," Mr. Tolliver said.

"In his interrogatory, he states positively, and now I quote from his testimony: 'The liver slides in this case are representative of coagulation necrosis due to ischemic infarction such as would be caused by total interruption of the blood flow through the hepatic artery.' Doctor, do you dispute this authority?"

Mr. Cousman went on without waiting for answers. "His interrogatory goes on: 'QUESTION: What are the possible causes of this pathologic picture? ANSWER: Anything interfering with hepatic artery blood flow. Inadvertent ligation of the hepatic artery at surgery would be the most common and most likely. Thrombosis or embolism of the hepatic artery would be much less likely.' Do you dispute these comments?"

Dr. Parmelee after a pause, nodded.

"What is your answer?"

"Yes." It was a voice from a well.

"Tell me, Doctor, isn't it true that you in fact did find the hepatic artery to be tied off at the time of autopsy and that from a natural wish to protect your employer, Dr. Hatch, you have refused to admit this?"

"Now I vigorously protest the form and implication of that question which is leading and improper, and the whole insulting, abusive approach of the plaintiff's counsel. I am shocked at counsel's conduct and wish to register a strong complaint to the court, and a request for reprimand of counsel." Mr. Tolliver's words got choked on his own rage.

"Please rephrase that question, Mr. Cousman, into a proper form. And I think Mr. Tolliver's points are well taken. A vigorous cross-examination is your prerogative, but you are pushing it. If you do not restrain yourself, I will take measures to restrain you." Judge Fielding's comments were in an acidic monotone.

"No, I don't care to rephrase that question. My cross-examination is completed." Mr. Cousman let the shocked, silent jury see a look of disgust on his face and then stalked back to his table.

Mr. Tolliver, seemingly afraid to extend further his suffering witness's exposure, asked Dr. Parmelee only one brief question. "Doctor, you then affirmatively state that you did not find a ligature around the hepatic artery at autopsy. Is that true?"

The ghostly voice murmured, "Yes, sir."

"That is all I wanted to ask, your Honor."

"Mr. Cousman?"

"No more questions."

"You may step down, Doctor. Gentlemen, this court will adjourn until tomorrow at ten A.M."

Dr. Parmelee sat for a moment as if gathering strength in his legs before disengaging himself from the witness chair and shambling across the courtroom floor to his seat. Peter wickedly flashed a big smile at him as he went by.

41

THAT night Peter slept poorly. The judge, Mr. Tolliver, the court reporter, and the sharp-nosed bailiff were in his dreams, and Mr. Cousman was threaded through the vignettes, at times traitorous himself, at other times marshaling resources and outlining defenses against the forces of evil. The next morning his coffee greeted his jumpy stomach unpleasantly. He drove to the San Marcial County Courthouse parking lot, thinking he was probably more nervous than the day he had testified himself.

Mr. Cousman greeted him pleasantly from his chair. "We're all set, Doctor. Those two ladies have been subpoenaed and will testify as soon as Dr. Hatch is done. I imagine he'll take all of today and tomorrow, though."

Peter sat down on the hard surface of the wooden bench next to Peggy Corti and smiled at her. "Ready for the big day?"

"I guess so. I'm pretty tired. I didn't sleep too well. I suppose because I was thinking about today."

"Me too. Say, hasn't Dr. Hatch come yet? It would be just like him not to show up."

"There he is now, Dr. de Haan," she said.

"At least he isn't in that damned scrub suit," Peter said, looking over at the defendant's table. Matthew Hatch was still annoying, though, standing with a smile on his face talking to Mr. Tupper, too composed, too relaxed in his manner.

Shortly the bailiff had them all on their feet again, and crusty Judge Fielding was on his bench rapping the gavel, red-faced and red-eyed, his white hair already disheveled. Must have had a bad night again, Peter thought.

Mr. Tolliver announced at once, "I would like to call Dr. Matthew Hatch to the stand." There had been a prominent story in the newspaper the night before headlined, "Dr. Hatch Takes Stand in Malpractice Trial Tomorrow," and the courtroom was once again full. Peter watched Dr. Hatch, stouter now than he had ever seen him, gracefully lower himself into the witness chair after nodding politely to the judge.

During the first hour of his testimony he was the quiet, soft-spoken, impressively direct person of Peter's first meetings with him. The jury responded with attention and interest to the humility and reasonableness he presented to them. The tension drained out of Peter and was replaced by anger and disgust. After the morning recess, though, a subtle change came over Matthew Hatch and through the day this change grew more obvious. It was as if a rheostat were gradually being turned up. Dr. Hatch grew steadily more self-assured. His normal swagger began to show through. How foolish of him to allow the change, Peter thought. He seemed most appealing, most believable, when a little frightened and unsure of himself, but as soon as he felt he was getting in charge of a situation, he was off and running, impossible to manage and much less pleasant. On several jurors' faces, especially two of the women, Peter thought he could see skepticism beginning to replace initial sympathy.

By late morning he was speaking vividly, even carelessly, at times allowing some of his own anger to spill over into view and sizzle there on the floor between him and the jury.

At first Mr. Tolliver had questioned Dr. Hatch at length about his training, his large surgical experience including hundreds of gastrectomies, appendectomies, cholecystectomies, and herniorrhaphies. Then equal time was spent putting into the record the details of the past care Matthew Hatch had given young Louis Corti over a fifteen-year period.

"He was still in high-school when you first saw him, is that right, Dr. Hatch?"

"Yes."

"And what was the occasion of his visiting you then?"

"He had a charley horse, which is a painful bruise of a thigh muscle, following a football injury. He was a halfback for the Jefferson High School team here."

Then there were colds, sore throats, a back sprain on a job once, another time a hand laceration. He had had chest pain three years before which turned out to be from a sore muscle aggravated by overwork and tension. There were insurance examinations through the next few years, and then a severe cold six months before his death. Mr. Tolliver was trying to sketch out the picture of the faithful, sympathetic, and trustworthy family physician.

In the early afternoon they got into the first details of the case itself, and by late afternoon they were through the surgery itself, and into the post-operative care.

"You see it wasn't really infection that was responsible for this man's problems after surgery, I mean not directly," Dr. Hatch testified confidently. "Toxicity was his problem, toxicity from the infection, and from everything, the whole course. Overwhelming toxicity."

"Did you consider this man a good risk before surgery, Doctor?" Mr. Tolliver asked.

"No, I didn't, I didn't think he was a good risk even before surgery. By now, in my practice I can tell very quickly by looking at someone whether they're a good risk." He was talking much more rapidly than at first, and Mr. Tolliver was spacing his questions, asking them slowly, trying to keep out extraneous remarks, but he could not always hold him back. "There was something wrong about Louis that struck me. I've always found that when I had that feeling, I needed to be careful. I always try to do my surgery especially fast when I think toxicity or poor risk is a feature of the case. The longer the surgery, the more the anesthesia, the more the toxicity."

"I see, Doctor. Now, could you tell us more specifically what you suspected when it appeared after your history-taking and examination that you had a poor-risk case in Mr. Corti, although still demanding immediate surgical care? What did you suspect you might be dealing with here?" Another unnecessarily long question.

"I suspected a malignancy might be playing a part in the features we were seeing, frankly, a cancer or some serious disease of the blood. We had a leukemia a short time ago that presented as an acute cholecystitis. I thought of that. I, of course, felt surgery might give some clue to the trouble. I didn't find malignancy, but at operation his liver was definitely not normal." After a long day of testimony the jury was still very attentive to Dr. Hatch.

"Now in your operative report, Doctor," Mr. Tolliver went on, "you don't mention the liver as being especially abnormal. In one brief statement you do say that its border was rounded, though. Would you like to comment on that?"

"Well, sir, I do so much surgery that I can't always make the most comprehensive description of every procedure. It would just mean interfering with my proper service to my patients if for each of my daily operations I spent fifteen minutes dictating a report. You can see what I mean?"

"I certainly can, Doctor, but did you want to comment on the statement in your note that the liver border was rounded?"

"Oh, yes. This is definitely pathologic to me, and means liver disease is present. A liver border should not be rounded but sharp. This was the clear way I indicated in my surgical report that I had found definite liver disease." Sometimes when Matthew began answering a question he would turn his magnificent head with its waving hair directly toward the jury box and focus his intense gaze on the members there. He did this now. "Some of the things I didn't include in my note about the operation are these," Matthew Hatch went on. "The liver color was poor. I suspected some congenital abnormality, and looking at the case retrospectively now, I believe there was some congenital or preexisting abnormality of the liver which these other circumstances affected badly. I mean by other circumstances the acute cholecystitis and the operation for it, the anesthetic, the bloodstream infection, and the shock following surgery." He gestured with his large and dextrous hands, his voice full now and almost eloquent. The jury was enthralled.

"But there was more, too, in the surgery that wasn't included in the operative note. The boy's tissues cut oddly, they were gritty, there was grittiness to them indicating disease."

It might all be convincing, Peter realized, to a layman. It had even convinced him the first time or two. "I didn't kill this patient," Dr. Hatch might say, "Mother Nature did, or the anesthesiologist, the internist, incipient cancer, some strange biochemical factor, an abnormal bleeding tendency, congenital liver disease, toxicity, mysterious and unfindable bloodstream infection, one or all of these factors were the death-dealing ones. The fact I took out four-fifths of a normal colon in a sixty-nine-year-old woman with emphysema, asthma, and arteriosclerotic heart disease had nothing to do with her death." This was the kind of logic Dr. Hatch used to clear his sanguine decks for new intrigue and new income.

"This was a fine boy," he told the jury, and Mr. Tolliver let him talk now. "I'd known him for years, taken care of him for years. He was like my own son. I wanted to give him only the best care, but from the start I was worried. Then at surgery we came on that liver, I believe congenitally diseased. The anesthesiologist is probably sorry now for using the Demerol-scopolamine-Thorazine mixture as pre-op anesthesia. This abnormal liver could have been damaged more by those drugs, too, especially the Thorazine, thereby reducing the normal body defenses that this great organ routinely provides. But we all did our best." He even gulped here for the wide-eyed jurors. "This boy didn't bleed right, either. At some tissue levels he bled more than a normal person should have, at other levels less. It was very strange. I've never seen anything just like it." This was the Hatch line again. Everything was always *very* strange, *very* unusual, the biggest he'd ever seen, the hardest operation he'd ever done. He was throwing it all in today, wasn't he?

"Now a major contention of the plaintiff's, of which you are aware, Dr. Hatch, has been that Mr. Corti's hepatic artery was inadvertently and negligently tied off by you at surgery. What is your comment on this matter?"

"Absolutely no. I can state positively, regardless of the pronouncements of the other side, that I did not do that. I clearly recall identifying the hepatic artery and the cystic artery, and tying off the latter. Furthermore, I myself examined the autopsy specimens, and found no evidence that an improper vessel had been tied off."

"Do you think this patient's death was consistent with hepatic failure from death of its cells after tying off of the hepatic artery?" Mr. Tolliver asked.

"No, I don't think so. There was no jaundice, and the course wasn't that of the usual hepatic failure. They're slower. This was more that of acute toxicity related to acute bloodstream infection with gram-negative bacteria, plus the burden of the surgery and all placed against an abnormal liver."

Mr. Tolliver then went through a number of questions about the post-operative course, including some about the Silvana consultation, before returning to the surgery itself at the end, to ask, "All right, Doctor, now we come to the question of excessive speed. It has been alleged that you performed this operation with excessive speed, which was in and of itself evidence of negligence, or contributed to the occurrence of negligence. What are your comments on this point?"

"I am what is called a fast surgeon. I work rapidly and always have. I do a great deal of surgery and, of course, speed allows me to do more. Throughout my professional life I have cultivated speed, but always with accuracy. I have worked as fast as I could, still working properly, carefully, and achieving good results for my patients. The facts are these. It means a lot to patients to do your surgery speedily. It shortens the time of stress on them, reduces shock therefore, shortens anesthesia time. It saves them money, too, because there are less operating room charges, lower assistant's fees, lower fees by the anesthesiologists. I charge a little less than the average surgeon in my locality, too, because I know I work faster than the average, quite a bit faster, and it seems only fair to me that I should. But this boy seemed sick to me before the operation, and I had already decided to do it as fast as possible before we began. After seeing that liver, I wanted to get in and out even faster. I've done gallbladders before in thirty-five minutes, and not infrequently I do them in forty-five or fifty minutes. As a matter of fact, usually."

"So there was no consideration of a speaking engagement, or anything else involved in the fact that you completed this surgery in thirty-three minutes?"

"Absolutely not. I didn't consider any engagement afterward and I never would. I've always found that if a doctor considers the patient first, last and always, and himself, his family, his own time, his own plans, secondarily, he'll practice good medicine. Money and one's personal life should never be a consideration, and never have been with me."

At the end of the day Mr. Tolliver turned Dr. Hatch over for cross-examination to start the next morning. By now, Peter almost expected the entranced jury to clap; it had turned into that kind of an afternoon for the surgeon. His cockiness had not seemed to hurt him after all. He had ensnared the jury, instead, with his quick, confident replies.

After court, Mr. Cousman took his group into a nearby waiting room and sat down with them. "We have to talk. Dr. Hatch was bad for us today. I guess you all realize that. So we need a pow-wow. Now, Mrs. Corti, first, do all of those statements about the small things Dr. Hatch treated your husband for seem right?"

"I think so. That last illness, the cold six months ago, Dr. George Carr treated him for instead of Dr. Hatch. I remember because he gave him a whole bunch of pills which are still sitting in our bathroom cupboard with Dr. Carr's name on them."

"Well, that's a small point, but I'll remember it. And Peter, what comments do you have to make?"

"Well, I probably think about the same things you do. The jury seemed to eat him up at first, then had a few reservations as he blossomed out and became more natural, fast-talking, and smarty-pants. But by the end of the day, I think he recaptured them all, and put us right on the spot. That's the way it looked to me."

"I watched that jury all day. You notice I scarcely objected to anything. I just looked at their faces, and tried to remember when they found something in his testimony that was weak. I'm going to pound on those things tomorrow."

"He threw in everything but the kitchen sink in his analysis of Louis' troubles," Peter said. "All the same kind of crap—excuse me, Peggy—all the same kind of stuff I've heard time and time. It's meaningless, but the jury doesn't realize that."

"I agree with you, Peter. Now Mrs. Corti, and Mr. Corti," Mr. Cousman went on, "there is something else you should know." He proceeded to tell them about the uncovering of the altered record, and the hope he had it might help. "At this stage, I'm worried about everything, believe me. I was much more confident about our chances even a week ago, than I am now, so prayers are in order. That's all, then. See you folks in the morning, and you tonight at the office, Peter." He grabbed his paraphernalia and literally ran from the room.

Peggy smiled after the lawyer, and said to Peter, "Well, as we've told you, we think we're doing the right thing, win or lose."

"I say the same thing, too, Doctor," Mr. Corti put in. "We stay very grateful to you. We lose, well, we lose, but you know, we still could win, too."

In the mail at Peter's apartment that night was a long letter from his mother, which Peter sat down and read quickly before picking up his other envelope, which had the San Marcial County Medical Society as its return address. After slitting its top, Peter extracted the stiff single sheet inside and read:

> DEAR DR. DE HAAN:
>
> At a meeting of the Executive Committee of the San Marcial County Medical Society the evening of Thursday, July 28, it was unanimously passed by the Committee to submit your name at the next regular society meeting on the 20th of September for removal from membership in this society and from all privileges pertaining thereto. As you doubtless realize, this move is not taken lightly, but after long consideration of your recent actions in this community. If the society acts favorably on our recommendation, you should be informed that this would suspend you from all rights as a member of this County Medical Society, which in turn could affect your right to be a continuing member of the State and National Medical Societies.
>
> We have taken this preliminary disciplinary action for good cause, we feel. According to the rules of our constitution, it is your right to appear before the Executive Committee with any friend, representative or counsel you choose, to permit us to reconsider our present initial action. The reasons we took this action will be presented to you at this time.
>
> Expulsion from the society must be taken up at a regular meeting, and the vote in favor of it must be by a majority of active members present, for this matter a quorum being re-

quired according to the constitution. You also have a right to appear at the September 20th meeting, therefore, to present any comments you wish to the membership before they vote on this action to expel you.

Yours,
ALBERT HUMPHERS, Secretary
for the Executive Committee
San Marcial County Medical Society

42

MR. COUSMAN stared at the pale, unusually clear blue of Dr. Hatch's eyes the next morning at ten fifteen A.M. "Doctor," he said, "please answer my question directly. You are not a board-certified surgeon, you are not a specialist certified as qualified by the American Board of Surgery, is that correct? Yes or no?"

"I'm a highly trained doctor who is eligible to take the qualifying boards for general surgey."

"Doctor, yes or no, are you a board-certified surgeon, a member of the American Board of Surgery?"

"I've tried to explain this to you."

"Explanation is not needed. An answer is all I'm asking for." Mr. Cousman had been going over the surgeon's qualifications, but Dr. Hatch had been evasive, refusing to admit to any lack of the important stamps of approval. In answer to the question if he was a member of the American College of Surgeons, he said that he had never applied, but that he was a member of the National College of Abdominal Surgeons. When Mr. Cousman had pointed out that this group had little prestige attached to it, and that almost any practitioner could gain membership simply by applying, Dr. Hatch had refuted him, insisting that the members were carefully selected. And so it had gone.

"All right, Doctor," Mr. Cousman said now, "I don't care if you answer that question or not. I'm not going to go over every last detail of your testimony. We've had a good many days of trial here, and we're all tired. We're interested in fundamentals. Now, Dr. Hatch, let's get right into the surgery itself."

"Thank you, Mr. Cousman," Mr. Tolliver said, "I was

going to suggest that we weren't interested in learned counsel's speeches, either."

"Perhaps you'll be more interested in my summation, Mr. Tolliver. All right, Doctor, to start with we have stipulated that the decision for the surgery on Mr. Corti is not contested."

Dr. Hatch's prominent frame, visibly ballooning during the trial, dwarfed the witness box. "Thank you," he said, crossing his legs carefully and looking down at his neatly polished shoes as Mr. Cousman went on with the next question.

"Doctor, to come to the surgery itself, Dr. de Haan has testified that in the early stages of the surgery, perhaps three or four minutes after the initial incision, he asked you to slow down in your surgical speed because he could not catch all the bleeders. Is that correct? Did he do this?"

"No, he did not."

"He did not ask you to go slower?"

"He certainly did not," Dr. Hatch said strongly.

"Let me then carry this point a little further. None of us recalls every event of every day, every word spoken to us, everything that happened to us. As a matter of fact, in a busy professional life, a great many of the minutiae that fill each day are quickly forgotten. Now when you say no to my question, do you mean, no, I am positive that Dr. de Haan never said any such thing at that time in the surgery, or no, I don't definitely recall such a comment?"

"No, he did not ever say anything to me about slowing up. A comment like that I would never forget."

"Now, later on in the surgery, according to Dr. de Haan's testimony, he again asked you to, as he put it, 'take it easy.' This was when you were working in the gallbladder bed and he was unable to retract tissues properly for you, to give you adequate visibility. Do you recall this remark?"

"Again, he did not ever say such a thing to me. I'm positive. I would certainly remember any such comment."

"The scrub nurse for that day, Miss Masters, stated she remembered that Dr. de Haan asked you to slow up during some operation, but she has no recollection which one it might be. Do you recall a remark like this during a different operation?"

"He never said anything of the sort to me at any time. That's definite." Dr. Hatch's tone was one of impatience and pique.

"Then you believe Miss Masters is mistaken in her recollection?"

"Apparently she is, yes."

"Reading to you here from the National Conjoint Committee of Hospital Accreditation, and your hospital operates under the approval of this committee, and is supposed to follow its rules, I find its instructions say, 'Surgical reports shall be dictated or written out the day of surgery and they should include all pertinent information concerning every detail of the surgery done, and especially include all needed details about the findings at operation, normal as well as abnormal. Too much stress cannot be made about the required proper completeness of operative reports.' Still you say, owner and operator of the Hatch Hospital, that you cannot take time to dictate properly complete reports on surgeries done. Why is that?"

"Your statement misuses my words. I merely said that I am often rushed and so do not have the time to put in all the details I would wish." Dr. Hatch seemed angry now in his quiet, pale, staring way.

"But you feel here too, in dictating operative reports, that you should work faster than the other doctors?"

"Now, I think that is not to the issues, your Honor," Mr. Tolliver said.

"Objection sustained. Strike that last question from the record. Proceed, Mr. Cousman."

"Do you feel that you should be an exception to the working rules of the Conjoint Commission on the character and thoroughness of surgical reports, as exemplified in the official rules of that commission under which your hospital, the Hatch Hospital, operates?"

"I object on the grounds that the question is misleading and not to the issues," Mr. Tolliver insisted.

"Sustained," said the judge.

"Do you admit that your surgical report in the case of Louis Corti was sketchy and incomplete, or inaccurate?"

Dr. Hatch looked at Mr. Tolliver, and then at the judge. When no objection was forthcoming, no comment from the judge, his right hand dug under his coat toward his left breast.

"Would you repeat that question, please?" he asked.

"Is there something wrong, Doctor?"

"No. I simply asked that the question be repeated."

"I see your hand is under your coat there. Are you not

feeling well?" The jury abruptly leaned forward to stare at Dr. Hatch after this question.

"I'm fine." He rapidly withdrew his hand and the jury settled back.

"Will the court reporter please read my last question back?" Mr. Cousman asked, and the reporter complied.

"I won't say yes, and I won't say no," Dr. Hatch answered, looking at Mr. Tolliver, who did not stand up, and did not even look up.

"Now, that's not a satisfactory reply, Doctor, you know that," Mr. Cousman said, frowning.

"Well, that's obviously a trick question."

"Nevertheless, I insist on an answer. Do you consider your surgical report on the patient, Louis Corti, sketchy and incomplete, or inaccurate, or do you not?"

"No, I don't. It recalls to me all I need to know about the case."

"May I point out to you then that in your previous testimony here yesterday you said that this patient, Mr. Louis Corti, was a poor risk before surgery, that you found a rounded liver edge indicating definite liver disease, that the liver color was poor, that you suspected congenital preexisting abnormality of the liver on visualizing and palpating this organ, that the patient's tissues cut oddly, were gritty, indicating serious abnormality or illness to you, that at some tissue levels, as you put it, the patient bled more than a normal person should, at other tissue levels he bled less, a very unusual finding in your opinion, you stated, and that because of the young man's poor state before surgery, and his bad liver found at surgery, that the preanesthetic and general anesthetic agents were suspect by you of advancing the serious state of his condition, and yet not in your operative report, nor in your verbal comments during surgery as we have been able to elicit them, nor in your history and physical written on the chart, nor in the first day's notes after surgery, have you indicated any of these findings except for a scant mention of a rounded liver edge, which did not in any way state your concept of the significance of this finding. Now in view of these facts do you still maintain that you were making a properly complete, accurate, and descriptive surgery report, and generally keeping good records on this case?"

"Everything that happens to a patient can't be written

down on the chart or be dictated into the record, and it never will."

"Sir, will you answer my question?" Mr. Cousman was quite sharp in his tone.

"Your Honor," Dr. Hatch said, "I want this man to speak more civilly to me."

"I think you should reply, Doctor. If you will answer his questions more directly I believe there will not be any trouble." A noise of voices arose in the courtroom, while the jury moved and twisted in their seats.

"Now do you want my question reread to you, Doctor?" Mr. Cousman asked, sighing.

"No, sir, I do not, and I do say my records are satisfactory. After all, they were inspected and found to be good ones by the National Conjoint Committee when they passed us."

The judge even flushed now as he bent forward toward Dr. Hatch. "The witness is not permitted to continue to make extraneous remarks. Please answer the questions as directly as possible. Do not comment on the questions, Doctor."

Dr. Hatch looked back and forth, from jury box to defendant's table, sniffing through his nose, rubbing his chin in his hand, moving his jumbo frame around in his chair, and then settling down as the aggravation he appeared to feel wore off. "Yes, your Honor, I will certainly follow your instructions."

"Thank you, Doctor."

"Now, Dr. Hatch, in your deposition before this trial I asked you what had been found in the abdomen of Mr. Corti besides the acute cholecystitis, and you stated only that the liver border was rounded. Doesn't it seem to you that there is some inconsistency in your testimony when yesterday you added all these other abnormalities?"

"No."

"Did you forget to mention these other problems previously?"

"No, you didn't ask me about them."

"I didn't know about them. Why didn't you tell us about them?"

"It must have been the manner of your questioning, because I certainly knew about them."

"All right, Doctor, let me ask you this: In your deposition when I asked you about what the patient's pre-operative condition was, you replied, and I quote here, 'It wasn't too bad.' Now you state in your testimony yesterday, 'It was very poor,' and again I quote the words you used. How do you reconcile these two different statements?"

"The question you asked me then was put in a different way, as I recall it."

"Here's the question, I'll repeat it to you verbatim. 'COUSMAN: Doctor, what condition did you consider the patient, Mr. Louis Corti, to be in when you saw him before surgery?'. Your reply, 'It wasn't too bad.' "

"Well, it wasn't too bad in some ways, not grossly and externally, but as I told you, I had this intuition or premonition about this fellow, developed from years of experience, that he was going to get into trouble, that something was wrong, not something you could definitely put your finger on like high blood pressure or a fever of a hundred and four, but still there was something there."

"You mean because you only had a sort of hunch before surgery that this man wasn't in good condition you didn't mention it previously?"

"Something like that."

"Now I want to know, Dr. Hatch, about this surgery, how you can really justify the speed with which Mr. Corti was operated on as being reasonable when I read you these statistics? This paper I hold I had prepared for me from the four private hospitals in Oakland, California, by the record room librarian from each of these institutions, listing the elapsed operating time of all gallbladder operations done in their hospitals over the last four years. I'll present this as a plaintiff's exhibit on rebuttal time, your Honor."

"I'd prefer you not proceed with this now, Mr. Cousman, unless defendant's lawyer would stipulate to its use now."

"May I see the papers, Mr. Cousman?" Mr. Tolliver said. He examined them, and reported in a minute, "No, I will not stipulate to that. I would want to have the librarians here themselves to cross-examine on these charts."

"All right, that's all right," Mr. Cousman said. "We'll read instead from Dr. Dunning's testimony for a moment." He reread the sections in which the Los Angeles professor had so thoroughly denounced the time of thirty-three minutes for a gallbladder as scandalously fast, as a setting in which negligence could easily occur.

"Do you agree with Dr. Dunning that thirty-three minutes is much too fast to perform a proper gallbladder removal, especially in a patient with acute cholecystitis where more care is needed to remove the inflamed, fragile gallbladder which is often so hard to chisel loose and so easy to perforate?"

"No, not for me. As I've said, I've done them that fast before myself."

"What is too fast, thirty-two minutes, twenty-nine minutes, twenty-seven minutes? Do you recognize any time as being too fast?"

"Of course I do. Ordinarily thirty-three minutes would have been thought fast, I understand that, but the circumstances in this case changed things. I think that forty-five minutes or more would usually be required for the rapid operator in the ordinary situation."

"All right, Dr. Hatch, to go on to some questions about the anatomy of the patient's gallbladder bed, especially in reference to the blood circulation there. Do you remember the structure of this patient's blood supply to the liver area?"

"Of course I do."

"Then in Mr. Corti's case, did the cystic artery to the gallbladder, coming off the hepatic artery, divide then into superior and inferior branches before reaching the gallbladder?"

"It did not."

"Did the right hepatic artery pass under or over the common duct?"

"It passed under the common duct."

"And you feel that you carefully identified the cystic artery coming off the right hepatic artery after it passed under the common duct, and then ligated it?"

"I know I did."

"Yet in your deposition you stated, and I quote, 'The right hepatic artery went in front of the common duct, before giving off the cystic artery,' and again you said 'I believe that the cystic artery did divide into two branches.' Now which testimony of yours is correct, did the hepatic artery go under or over the common duct—it can't have done both—and did the cystic artery divide into branches or did it not before reaching the gallbladder?"

"These are small structures and it's difficult to visualize them perfectly at surgery, you should understand that, Mr. Cousman, if you're going to question me about them."

"All I ask is that you give me a correct answer to the best of your ability, Dr. Hatch. If you don't know the answer to *any* question, please say so."

Mr. Tolliver was on his feet now. "Your Honor, I believe

you should ask the plaintiff's attorney to stop badgering my client." The lawyer's booming voice circled through the reaches of the large chamber like buckshot fired in every direction, shaking up the dozers, and rattling the windows. Talk about Caruso, Peter thought. The man was a singer and an actor. Cousman had said he could even cry during a summation. "As any witness might be, Dr. Hatch is upset by the rapid, unclear questions, and the obvious hostility of the examiner. We're trying to get at facts here in this courtroom, I believe, not trying to third-degree people."

"I agree with Mr. Tolliver entirely," Mr. Cousman said, "and we could make much faster progress here if Mr. Tolliver's client would simply answer yes, no, or I don't know, or explain briefly *when necessary* instead of qualifying every answer with—"

"All right, gentlemen, that is enough. I would like to remind the jury to place their attention on the testimony of witnesses and not on counsels' remarks. Sit down, Mr. Tolliver, and go ahead, Mr. Cousman."

"Now, Dr. Hatch, Dr. de Haan reported the substance of a conversation between you and Dr. Silvana when Dr. Silvana was called in as a consultant for the case of Mr. Louis Corti and advised further exploratory surgery. Dr. Silvana in his deposition, which has previously been read to the jury, admitted also that he had advised further surgical intervention, a re-operation. Your direct testimony said that this was not so. What is your comment now on this?"

"Those statements are not correct. Dr. Silvana suggested that surgery might be considered, but he did not ever urge it. His consultation note in the chart does not even mention more surgery, much less insist that it be done."

"All right, now let me read your testimony of yesterday, Dr. Hatch. 'TOLLIVER: Did Dr. Silvana at any time, then, advise you to re-operate Mr. Corti? HATCH: No, he did not feel it was necessary.' In view of your present testimony, how is your answer today reconciled with that of yesterday? In other words, yesterday you stated Dr. Silvana never insisted surgery be done. Now both Dr. de Haan, and Dr. Silvana in his deposition, have stated that he did advise re-operating Mr. Corti. Did he or did he not give as his advice that Mr. Corti should be opened up again and his abdomen explored for possible ligature around the hepatic artery?"

"Objection, your Honor." The Tolliver cannon roared again.

"Mr. Cousman, please rephrase the last sentence of that question."

"Dr. Hatch, did Dr. Silvana give as his advice to you on April seventh that Mr. Corti should be opened up again and his abdomen re-explored?"

"I said that he suggested this be considered, but I told him I rejected the idea, and I believe he understood my viewpoint and the wisdom and experience behind it."

"Dr. de Haan testified that on the contrary Dr. Silvana became very upset at your rejection of his proposal to operate and argued vehemently with you on the subject. Is that true?"

"No, of course not."

"Now again, Dr. de Haan has stated, and Mrs. Corti has testified, that the Corti family was in no way apprized by you of the seriousness of Mr. Corti's illness until the day before he died, although you testify now that you found his condition grave even before surgery, and certainly after surgery. Is it true that you did not notify the Corti family of the extreme danger of Mr. Louis Corti's condition until the last hours of his life?"

"The hospital record will prove me right or wrong."

"We will come to the hospital record later on. What is your answer to my question?"

"The Corti family was well informed of Mr. Corti's condition and all significant changes therein while he was hospitalized."

"You then maintain that Mrs. Corti's and Dr. de Haan's testimony on this point is inaccurate?"

"I do."

"The official records of the hospital the morning of April fifth show that Mr. Louis Corti's blood count was obtained then with the following resultant figures: hemoglobin was fourteen grams, red blood count was four point five million, hematocrit was forty volumes percent. Now Dr. de Haan, Dr. Dunning, and indeed even your own experts have decided that these were close to normal figures. Do you consider them near normal or normal figures for a blood count?"

"Of course the blood tests from the laboratory are just part of assaying the picture of any patient."

"I realize that. And I'm not asking that. Do you consider these figures normal or near normal for the red blood cell series?"

"I would say yes, but—"

"All right, then, let me ask you this in another way. Do these figures indicate anemia?"

Matthew Hatch's hand suddenly sneaked under his left lapel again and began rubbing his breast there. "No, but there is another consideration."

"Then, the record of this day goes on to indicate that in the afternoon you ordered two pints of blood for transfusion. Transfusions are given for anemia, are they not?"

"At times."

"After the first pint of blood had been given, and the second pint started, Dr. de Haan ordered the transfusion stopped. Is that correct?"

"Yes."

"And there was a discussion between you and him concerning why he had done this?"

"Yes, although it was brief and I made no trouble about it."

"All right, then the blood count the next day showed the hemoglobin was fifteen point eight grams, the red count five point four million, and the hematocrit fifty-one volumes percent, all of which are *above* the standard of normal according to the slips themselves, which list normal values for each item on them. Is that correct?"

"Roughly, yes."

"It is generally considered a clinical error in medicine to give too much blood when a patient is in shock or seriously ill and having trouble supporting his vital processes, is it not?"

"Circumstances vary. May I say a few words here other than yes or no?"

"I would like to have you explain why you ordered blood when you did, Doctor."

"I've taken care of so many cases like this that I know when blood is needed regardless of what the tests on the patient may show. I know the blood loss at surgery, I know the support which extra, fresh blood can give a patient and which he may need. It's often helpful in shock with people who have blood pressures dropping. The blood count itself can give you a misleading picture, too, with these very ill patients."

"You are also aware, Doctor, are you not, that blood transfusions, even properly cross-matched and given, can result in severe reactions, including fever and allergic responses that may lead to difficulty in breathing or sudden added shock and even death. Also there is a high incidence of liver infection later on from blood transfusion that may cause a serious illness or even death."

"I know all those things, certainly. I have to use my judgment."

"All right, Doctor, now for two days after surgery, Mr. Corti did fairly well, and then, according to the records, he obviously became very ill. Is that a true statement of the situation?"

"Let's see, we operated on him Monday afternoon, and late Wednesday he was having high fever and seemed poor. Yes, that's true."

"And you maintain you followed him closely all this time to his death Friday morning?"

"I did."

"And you have stated that his manifestations of fever and circulatory shock, accompanied by elevation of the blood transaminase, an enzyme which is released into the bloodstream in abnormal amounts when the liver is damaged, are not consistent with ligation of the hepatic artery?"

"They may or may not be partly consistent with a great number of things. His condition was most clearly consistent to me with toxicity and the development of bloodstream infection from the infected gallbladder, difficulties which can best be treated by medicines, antibiotics, and other drugs, not surgery."

"But how can you now say that Mr. Corti's post-operative course was most consistent with toxicity and bloodstream infection, when previously on deposition you stated that you knew very little about the problems associated with hepatic artery ligation, which we are strongly suggesting may have been the cause of his post-operative trouble?"

"I know the findings of hepatic artery ligation. I am very familiar with them, and there was no clinical evidence to suggest that such an event had occurred."

"May I read to you from your deposition of May fifteenth. One moment, yes, here it is. 'COUSMAN: I wonder if you would mind confining your statements to simple answers to my questions, Doctor. I'm trying to get at some understanding of this business of the hepatic artery. HATCH: I'm not here to help you do anything, Mr. Cousman. You might as well get that straight. COUSMAN: Be that as it may, isn't it true that when the hepatic artery is mistakenly ligated at surgery the patient dies rapidly of high fever and toxemia with signs of liver failure? HATCH: I don't know anything about the condition. I've had no experience with it. COUSMAN: You mean to say that you are a surgeon who has done hundreds of cholecystectomies during your professional life, and you have no knowledge of the papers or literature on the subject of this possible calamity arising out of improper gallbladder surgery? HATCH: Of course I am familiar with the printed matter and I've talked to others who knew of this condition. I just mean I knew nothing of it from my own personal experience.' Now do you still say you are very familiar with the findings of hepatic artery ligation? To put it another way, can any doctor be very familiar with the clinical findings of any ailment he has never seen?"

"I know what the condition is and I feel I would recognize it if I was ever presented with it. You seem to pick up all these minor points which don't have anything to do with the facts of this case."

"Well, I think, if you don't mind, Dr. Hatch, I'll continue to conduct this cross-examination in the way I choose, and we will allow the jury to decide on what points are minor and what major."

The judge interrupted with a pound of his gavel and a huge sigh. "Let's take our noon recess now, ladies and gentlemen."

Peter had lunch with the Cortis. Mr. Cousman had disappeared with his briefcase. "I've got to go hide away and work," he had said, rushing out of the courtroom.

Just before court reconvened, Peter saw him put out a cigarette at the door and come strolling in, his hair wetted down for once and combed carefully forward, his face looking scrubbed and fresh. "I thought you didn't smoke cigarettes," Peter said to him.

"Now and then," he murmured back to him casually. "Mostly when I feel mean. If I feel too mean," he said, "it seems to calm me down." He smiled slyly at Peter and whispered in his ear. "He's on the run, have you noticed?" Then he became very serious as the jury started to file in.

The judge was seated and the afternoon began. This was the hottest day so far and Mr. Cousman had shed his vest at lunchtime, but was otherwise fully garbed. His shoulders back, his short legs firm, he quickly dug in again at his post by the witness box for the afternoon's battles.

Before Dr. Hatch ascended to the stand, Mr. Tolliver had talked earnestly and steadily to him for ten minutes at the defense table. Now the doctor sat quietly and pensively in the box.

"Are you ready, Dr. Hatch and counsel?" the judge asked, and everyone nodded. "All right, you may begin, Mr. Cousman."

"Dr. Hatch, you've heard almost all the testimony in this trial so you know that we have already established that Dr. Parmelee, the pathologist for your hospital and clinic and the doctor who did the autopsy on Mr. Louis Corti, did not believe Dr. Dunning, the expert witness for the plaintiff, was insane or a liar. His opinion was the same regarding Dr. de Haan. He disagreed with both these doctors in their interpretation of the autopsy findings, though. Now Dr. Hatch, since there were so many events important to this trial where you and Dr. de Haan were both present, and since so far your testimony and Dr. de Haan's on these events have been so inconsistent, I would like to ask you these two questions about Dr. de Haan. First, do you think he was or is insane?"

"No, I don't think so."

"You answer that with some hesitancy, Doctor."

"I am reasonably sure that he has not been nor is insane."

"That is all we asked you to state. Now, do you think he is a liar?"

"I don't like to answer that question."

"Do you think Dr. de Haan is a liar, then?"

"He must be, to say some of the things he's said here, and make some of the nonsensical and totally untrue statements."

"How long have you felt that he was definitely untruthful?"

"I've been watching this young man ever since he came with me, and I've had a number of doubts about him."

"In general he did good service for you though, would you say?"

"Adequate. He was average, no more than that in his services."

"When did you first suspect he might be untruthful?"

"It's hard to say exactly. There were many small things that came up, for instance in chart orders, that made me wonder. I might leave a certain order, and he would change it. The patient would get in difficulty, and he would back out of the situation, and say that it was something else I had done that was causing the trouble, instead of admitting it was his order that gave us a problem with the patient."

"That's not exactly lying, Doctor, and you have said Dr. de

Haan was a liar. Presumably you mean about the events he's testifying to in this trial. Now you consider yourself an excellent judge of people, I'm sure, after your years in practice. Do you feel going back in your association with Dr. de Haan that you could perceive any pattern there to indicate that his personality when stressed might indulge in a campaign of vicious lying against someone such as you, toward whom he had become hostile?"

Everyone in the courtroom listened carefully now to Mr. Cousman, soft-voiced and friendly, cool and coaxing. They all realized some disclosure was imminent—perhaps many suspected a trap was being laid and would be sprung. Possibly even Dr. Hatch, deliberating a moment, might have thought so, too, but instead he went on, seemingly happy for a chance to talk personally about Peter.

"I hesitated to mention this, but last November young de Haan came to me to ask for three days off. He said he wanted to make a tour of the hospitals in San Francisco, perhaps attend a few classes in one of the medical schools. I found out subsequently in quite a roundabout way, and he's never known this, that instead he spent the weekend with a young woman at a beach resort near Santa Cruz. Now he begged me to let him back on the staff after our serious argument at the end of December following surgery on this girl friend for a bleeding miscarriage, and against my better judgment I did allow him to return. I'd found he was untrustworthy, and in my mind incompetent by this time, and I only planned for him to stay until his year was up. In many small ways he couldn't keep up with the pace and quality of medical practice I require at my clinic and hospital, and I knew I would have to let him go, but I wanted to be kind to him—he'd just lost his father and gotten into this scrape with the girl friend—so you can see how my kindness was repaid. Now, of course, we all realize he was lying about wanting to come back, and was just trying to frame me because he was angry at me about the girl friend, not only at finding out about her, but angry I couldn't fix the whole dirty mess up, making everything disappear. It was an unreasonable anger, undoubtedly, and yet I suppose he felt so guilty himself he had to turn that feeling against someone else, and I was the one. That's the only way I can explain it. Insane, no, but certainly pretty mixed up. Realize, I'm no psychiatrist, but this is the way he seemed to me."

Dr. Hatch was leaning forward as he spoke now, gesticulating with his hands, obviously intense about his words.

"Dr. Hatch," and Mr. Cousman's voice was very soft now, drawn into himself as the jury was still, the spectators hushed, only the whir of the fan overhead audible during Mr. Cousman's pause, "Dr. Hatch, I have a letter here which you wrote on January eighteenth of this year to the County Medical Society concerning Dr. de Haan. I have given a copy of it to the clerk, and I would like to read it now, if the defendant's attorney will allow me. My associate there will give you a copy, Mr. Tolliver, and also the judge."

Mr. Tolliver stood, reaching for the copy, then frowning as he read it. "Your Honor, I will certainly object to this being introduced in evidence. We are not dealing here in the issues this letter brings up. The plaintiff has had plenty of chance to go into whatever subjects he wished while he was presenting his case, and this matter was not brought up on direct examination, so it cannot be gone into on cross-examination."

The judge looked up from reading the letter. "Mr. Cousman, what explanation do you have for introducing this now?"

"Your Honor, the most important thing I can do as a representative of the plaintiff, and also as an officer of this court actively involved in this trial, is to try to test the credibility of all witnesses as far as I can. More and more this trial has become a question of divided testimony with the issue of credibility of witnesses a crucial matter for the jury. I am now trying to develop information having to do with the credibility of the defendant's witnesses, or at the moment, the defendant himself, and I think I have the right and the obligation to do this."

"All right, Mr. Cousman, I will allow you to continue, and overrule the objection to the admission of this evidence. Clerk, please mark this Plaintiff's Exhibit Seven."

"I respectfully except, your Honor," Mr. Tolliver said.

"Exception to you, Mr. Tolliver. Proceed, Mr. Cousman."

"Dr. Hatch, this letter is signed by you and was received at the office of the San Marcial County Medical Society on January twentieth, according to their files, and I got it from their files. It reads:

DEAR SIRS:

I am most happy at this time to accept sponsorship into

the Medical Society of my young associate, Dr. Peter de Haan. He is a fine young man, devoted to all medical principles, and should be an asset and addition to our medical community now and for many years to come.

Signed, MATTHEW HATCH, M.D.

Have you any comment, Dr. Hatch?"

"This is just a routine statement, and has no direct meaning whatsoever. It's a sort of blanket endorsement just for county medical society purposes."

"Then you deny that this letter of yours of recommendation and profuse praise on Dr. de Haan's behalf in late January of this year has any truth to it whatsoever, and instead say that these words are meaningless ones, is that correct?" Mr. Cousman's voice became loud as he continued, "And will you sign anything put in front of you regardless of your honest beliefs?"

"Now, that's not the case," Dr. Hatch spluttered, but Mr. Cousman overrode him and went on at the same angry intensity.

"I submit that instead it's true that you found this young doctor to be a good doctor, that he knew what he was doing, that he helped you and helped your patients in an exceptional way and with unusual devotion, that only now that he has attacked you do you decide that there was something wrong with him in the past, something wrong always. I submit that what you have just said is another example of your inconsistent, evasive, unreliable testimony." Dr. Hatch cleared his throat to speak, his hand inside his coat, grabbing at his breast. "And if it is not, then do you not agree, Dr. Hatch—now think on this because I want an answer—do you not agree that it was wrong of you as a principled practitioner of medicine, wrong to the highest degree, to allow a young man you felt to be incompetent, dishonest, and untrustworthy to work with you, handle your patients, operate with you? That surely is a professional disgrace, don't you admit?"

Mr. Cousman was talking now with Mr. Tolliver's strength and inflection—it was amazing, Peter thought, how much he could sound like him. It was deliberate, he realized then, because when Mr. Tolliver rose to blast out objections, he only matched the intensity and the tone of A. O.'s voice, but could not override it. Mr. Cousman continued, "Now I ask you, Dr. Hatch, in the most telling point of all, did you not state that Dr. de Haan was taking care of your critically ill patient, Mr. Corti, *through the worst moments of those two last critical nights and that you were not needed when your help was begged for because Dr. de Haan could take care of everything as well as you?* Now how can you expect us to believe in you as a doctor of conscience and quality and to believe at the same time you would allow a person you state so clearly to be untrustworthy and dishonest *and incompetent* to take care of your moribund patient? Can you make any sense for the jury out of the hash you present to us as testimony on this point, Doctor?"

"Your Honor, your Honor, your Honor," Mr. Tolliver was shouting now as Judge Fielding pounded his gavel wildly trying to calm down the courtroom. "Quiet," Judge Fielding called, and the bailiff took up the cry in echo. In a few moments the flurry had subsided, and Peter found Mr. Cousman at the plaintiff's table in front of him, his back to the judge and the jury, making a small boy's face of contrite obeisance at Peter and then winking at him as Mr. Tolliver began to speak.

"Judge," Mr. Tolliver said, "this is outrageous. I've never seen such behavior toward a witness, the plaintiff's attorney allowing him to answer no questions and making unbelievably outrageous and leading statements which are also irrelevant, conjectural, unproved and not provable, and defamatory. I think this borders on mistrial. This is not summation, this is cross-examination, or supposed to be cross-examination, but I never saw anything like this before that was called cross-examination."

Dr. Hatch sat on the stand, shaking with rage and tension still, his hand firmly inside his coat.

"I agree with you this time, Mr. Tolliver," Judge Fielding said in his hoarsest voice. "That was shocking, and I promise you here and now if there is one more such outburst from either counsel it shall be considered contempt of this court, and shall make me seriously consider a mistrial action if one is put before me."

Mr. Cousman turned around now and walked toward the judge. "I'm sorry, your Honor, and I humbly apologize. In thirty-four years before the bar I have never felt more deeply involved in a case, and that is why I was carried away. Some of the questions I brought up I really do want to ask Dr. Hatch. May I be allowed to proceed?"

"We'll permit you three or four questions now. We'd better take afternoon recess in ten minutes at the most."

"Thank you, your Honor. I'm sorry, Mr. Tolliver, for my behavior. It won't happen again." Dr. Hatch looked nervously up as Mr. Cousman approached the stand.

"Dr. Hatch, I see you have your hand over your heart again. Once more I'm led to ask if there is something wrong?" Mr. Cousman was not going to let that tic alone.

Mr. Tolliver rose again. "I will not permit Mr. Cousman to keep mentioning this point. There is nothing wrong with Dr. Hatch physically or mentally. He has a habit, a custom of putting his hand inside his coat. It has no meaning, and it does not signify that he is not feeling well. We all have our own idiosyncrasies of movement and this is Dr. Hatch's. I squeeze my left elbow, and Mr. Cousman rubs his hair forward with his hand—" This brought forth a loud laugh and the lawyer could not finish his sentence. The tension in the courtroom vaporized.

"I am sorry, I did not understand. I shan't mention it again," Mr. Cousman said, again in his soft range. "Just two questions, Doctor. First, did you in fact write that letter of recommendation for Dr. de Haan to the County Medical Society?"

Dr. Hatch was no longer the figure of confidence, but rather of caution. He showed it clearly in the way he thought about the question now, and the careful way he answered it showed he knew he had better be damned slow and easy with this pipsqueak of an Oakland lawyer he'd never heard of before, funny little guy with ridiculous clothes and laughable hair. Finish up and get the hell off the stand, was the idea.

"Yes, I did, Mr. Cousman," Dr. Hatch answered, reluctantly pulling his hand out from under his coat and putting it in his lap.

"Do you feel that you should have let Dr. de Haan stay with and follow Mr. Louis Corti through his last two nights of critical illness as you did, without coming over to help as you were asked to do? Or do you believe now, after reflection, that you might have been mistaken in not giving your own aid?"

In a split second Peter saw Dr. Hatch's egoism reconstituted. A small smile crossed his face at Mr. Cousman's question. He straightened up and said forcefully, "No, sir. To my dying day I'll know I did everything humanly possible for that Corti boy."

"You affirm then, Doctor, that you made *no* mistakes in the treatment of Mr. Louis Corti, is that correct?"

"Yes, sir, I believe that to be correct."

"Do you ever make any mistakes in your medical practice, Dr. Hatch?"

A moment of suspicion appeared on his face, and his answer was not quite so ready, but still forceful when it came. "Rarely. Almost never. A good doctor after proper experience doesn't make mistakes."

"Have you ever had a patient die after surgery from a mistake you made?" Peter waited for the objection, but then he heard none and looked at the defendant's table. Mr. Tolliver was busily talking to Mr. Tupper and apparently had missed the point.

"Never. I don't make mistakes like that. If I operated my business the way some people do, I'm thinking of some automobile manufacturers who have been selling me lemons year after year, I'd have been closed down the first six months I was in practice." There was a laugh in the court from this, and the judge took the opportunity to recess for the afternoon break.

Mr. Cousman began questioning Dr. Hatch again immediately after reconvening. "You have heard of W. Y. Van Doren's *Textbook of Ideal Surgery*?" he asked.

"Yes, of course."

"Would you say that Dr. Van Doren of Harvard was an outstanding surgical authority in the United States?"

"Of course."

"I quote his book here: 'Anomalies of the hepatic artery are common. The general surgeon, young or old, should always (and the word "always" is underlined), should *always* recognize and know the entire course of the hepatic artery in any patient on whom he is doing gallbladder surgery. This major artery to the liver can usually be felt in the hepatoduodenal ligament. Inability to palpate a vigorous artery pulse at the right border of this ligament should always start a careful search for possible unusual anatomy of the hepatic artery and its branches.' Now, do you always attempt to palpate the artery in the hepatoduodenal ligament, Doctor?"

"Oh," Dr. Hatch said, "I usually do. Ordinarily, you can find these things pretty well when you're in there. It's not that difficult for the experienced surgeon."

"Continuing the quote from this book of W. Y. Van Doren's, he writes: 'The gravest error a surgeon can make during gallbladder surgery is to injure the hepatic artery. For obvious reasons these cases are almost never reported in the literature, so statistics on them are few and far between. It is known from Pruner's review that death follows almost invariably within a few hours or days, though, after the main hepatic artery is tied off, and often in a somewhat longer time after the right hepatic artery is ligated. The probability of death of hepatic tissue increases the closer one is to the liver.' Would you agree with these comments?"

"Surely."

"Now we come to a most serious part of our questioning of you, Dr. Hatch, and I advise you to consider your answers most carefully," the small lawyer said, stepping perkily around to the other side of the witness box.

"I think that's an unnecessary comment, Mr. Cousman," Matthew Hatch said under his breath.

"What was that last remark of the witness?" the court reporter asked, coming up out of his stenotype machine for a moment to stare at Dr. Hatch. Mr. Tolliver shook a hand toward him, waving off the question. Dr. Hatch made the same motion to the reporter.

"At this point I want to introduce into evidence an exhibit for the plaintiff," Mr. Cousman said briskly, looking as bright and sounding as chipper as he had the first moment of the first day of the trial. "Because of the unusual nature of my request, I would like to approach the bench to discuss it with you, your Honor."

Judge Fielding raised his hairy white eyebrows, and rolled his giant eyes at the lawyer's words, but said, "Come over then." They talked for a moment, and the judge pounded his gavel and called out "Bailiff, take the ladies and gentlemen of the jury to the jury room, please."

Soon they had marched out, and Judge Fielding nodded to Mr. Cousman. "Learned counsel will continue his remarks now, for all of us to hear."

"Yes, your Honor. As I told you, at the time of Mr. Corti's death, Dr. Peter de Haan took the precaution of having a photostatic copy of the patient's chart made by the night bookkeeper at the Hatch Hospital. This was done the evening of Mr. Corti's death, as a matter of fact. The past weekend going over the photostated record submitted by the Hatch Hospital, we happened to notice an alteration had been made in the progress notes in this patient's chart. Progress notes are the portion of the chart where the doctors keep serial records about the day-to-day condition, including the setbacks as well as the points of improvement. There were three such sheets on Mr. Corti and the second one covers events of April sixth and April seventh, with two notes for each day. We want to introduce into evidence the original page as our copy of the records obtained by Dr. de Haan shows it to read, and then a copy of the way this page reads in the official transcript of the trial as submitted by the Hatch Hospital record room."

"I wish to see that, Mr. Cousman," Mr. Tolliver said at once in a voice of vigorous disbelief.

"Of course, sir."

Houston Tolliver read through the exhibit rapidly, and asked for the official transcript from the clerk. He turned to the page involved and read there too. "Your Honor, I am going to object strongly to the admission of this evidence. We don't know where or how they got this photostated sheet they claim to be an original progress note, but we are certainly not going to accept it. They have had plenty of time to introduce any such evidence, and this is clearly the wrong way and the wrong time to do such a thing."

Judge Fielding said, "Please, let me see the exhibit." He read the two pages, and then also asked for the official transcript. "I see. Well, Mr. Cousman, you do know that this is an improper exhibit under the circumstances."

"Your Honor, I have outside the courtroom the young lady who obtained this first transcript for us. She can testify as to the events then, and I would like to put her on the stand. I also have waiting outside a lady from the Hatch Hospital who photostated the hospital record which has been used as the official one."

"I'm going to protest strongly the admission of this photostatic copy, your Honor. From what Mr. Cousman says, and what I see looking at it, there is no certainty that it represents an actual copy from the chart of Louis Corti, and also from what he says, I don't see how it could ever be established as such at this time. Additionally, from what he tells us, if it were obtained in the way he states, it would be illegally obtained and therefore could not be submitted as valid evidence."

"Mr. Cousman, what do you have to say?" the judge asked.

"Your Honor," the lawyer answered, "I think you can see how terribly important it might be to resolve this question. We deserve the chance to explore this point fully, because of the possibly different construction it puts on the motives and actions of the defendant. Additionally, I should mention that it is common practice to photostat parts of a chart for any doctor directly involved in the care of a patient. If Dr. de Haan had asked for a photostat of a patient he had no hand in caring for, this would be entirely different. Here, as one of this man's constant medical attendants, I insist he had a perfect right to a copy of any portion of the chart he wished, or the chart as a whole. I believe we can establish the fact of the page substitution through the testimony of the girl who photostated everything for Dr. de Haan, and by the visual evidence which any of us, or any of the jury, can see by inspection, that Dr. Hatch's very distinctive handwriting clearly appears on this second page of progress notes which we are submitting as the real, first and subsequently substituted-for page. How we could have forged Dr. Hatch's unusual calligraphy would be beyond me. Believe me, we didn't."

"Your Honor, I think Weber versus Martinez Key Company has a precedent here which would be—"

"All right, Mr. Tolliver. We don't want any citations now. I am going to allow Mr. Cousman to have these two ladies testify here before the jury. It seems vitally important to me to settle such a question. After the testimony, I will decide if the document involved will be allowed in evidence. So you may take your exception, Mr. Tolliver."

"I do, your Honor."

"Bailiff, call the jury back in here, and Mr. Cousman, we will have your lady of the front office testify first, I believe. So call her up here. Dr. Hatch, you may step down for the moment, but remember you are under oath, and will be recalled."

The jury was quickly back, looking puzzled at their rapid shuffle, and then Mrs. Mary Smead was on the stand, a nervous thirty-year-old with blond, teased hair, and pale lipstick.

She was sworn in by the clerk, and then Mr. Cousman began his questioning. "Your full name again, please?"

"Mrs. Mary Smead."

"And you're a resident of San Marcial?"

"Yes."

"You formerly worked as night bookkeeper for the Hatch Hospital, is that correct?"

"Yes."

"And you were working there in April of this year?"

"Yes, I left in the middle of May."

"What do you do now?"

"I'm working at Crocker's Department Store as a bookkeeper."

"Did you have any special reason for leaving the Hatch Hospital?"

"I didn't want to continue working nights."

"How long were you at the Hatch Hospital?"

"Two years."

"Was your work there satisfactory?"

"So far as I know. No one ever complained to me."

"Do you recall Dr. de Haan asking you to photostat an entire hospital chart one night?"

"Yes, very well."

"On what patient was that?"

"Mr. Louis Corti."

"How do you recall that?"

"I remember for two reasons, first, because I knew him a little when we went to school together. And of course because there's been so much disturbance about the whole case since."

"I see. Now, I have here two photostatic records of the hospital chart of Mr. Corti. Can you examine them and tell us which one you made?" Mr. Cousman handed over the two small volumes of photostats. Mrs. Smead looked at them carefully.

"The ones in my right hand are the photostats I made."

"How do you know that, Mrs. Smead?"

"First of all, most of the photostating at the hospital is done in the record room out in back. They have a Hardman machine there that makes the copies come out this brownish black color. The only place in the hospital or clinic there's a Sterox machine is the front office, and the photostats from it come out clearer, with the print darker, and then a sort of gray haze in between. When you put papers in the Sterox, you put them under clips at the ends to hold them, and on all these pages in my right hand here you can see the clips from that machine on the photostat. The machine is real good, and picks up everything, and you can even see the paper clips."

"Fine. Now, we can in general state that you did photostat the chart, that it was done for Dr. de Haan, that you believe pretty surely that the sheets photostated for Dr. de Haan are being held there on your right knee. These are the ones that we do assert that Dr. de Haan had photostated, though only those from the hospital on your left knee have been officially introduced into evidence. But now we have found that there is a difference between progress sheet number two, in the set of papers we got from you, and the progress sheet number two that the Hatch Hospital submitted to this court on subpoena as a veritable copy of the actual chart in the files at the Hatch Hospital. We need to know if the sheet we were holding is the actual progress sheet number two, or if the one the hospital submitted is the true one. There are important differences in the writings between the two. Can you inspect these two pages here and tell us if one of them is the exact one that you photostated for Dr. de Haan?"

Mrs. Smead was flushed with self-consciousness. Her color deepened further as she stared at the two sheets without saying anything. Mr. Cousman finally asked, "Did you understand my question, Mrs. Smead?"

"Oh, yes, sir, I guess I'm just scared. I've never been in a court before." Her voice shook badly and there were tears coming into her eyes.

"My goodness, dear lady, you just sit there and compose yourself for a minute." Mr. Cousman was all soft-keyed understanding.

"I know that this one in my right hand is the sheet I photostated."

"That is the one that we are maintaining is the actual progress sheet number two," Mr. Cousman said carefully, looking at her.

"Yes," she said, her voice very shaky. "You see it has the same clear print, and grayness in between, and here at the top and bottom are the marks of the clips from the Sterox machine."

"That's fine. Now, the sheet you identify as the one you photostated has three notes on it by Dr. Hatch, and one by Dr. de Haan. From your years at the Hatch Clinic, would you be able to recognize or identify the handwriting of either of these doctors as being the handwriting on this photostated sheet?"

"Objection, Mrs. Smead is not a handwriting expert."

"Now, your Honor, I am not asking her as such to state this, but just out of her own knowledge, as I might ask anyone out of their own knowledge about a handwriting they were very familiar with."

"Within those bounds, I think I'll allow that question, Mr.

Cousman," Judge Fielding said, sitting up to watch and listen with an unusual alertness for him.

"Dr. Hatch's handwriting is so different from everyone else's, big, you know, with sweeps and flourishes and solid black capital letters. He uses pens with broad points, and makes those big flat crosses on the T's. This handwriting on this page, well on both pages, it must be his."

"Then you would say that the handwriting on the paper in your right hand there, which you believe is from the machine in the Hatch Hospital business office, and which we therefore might reasonably infer was produced by you that night in April when Dr. de Haan asked you for a complete copy of Mr. Louis Corti's chart, is that of Dr. Hatch in the three separate notes there signed by his name?"

"Yes, sir."

"As to the fourth entry there, signed de Haan, would you say that that was Dr. de Haan's handwriting?"

"I guess so. I don't know Dr. de Haan's handwriting well at all, and it wasn't too different like Dr. Hatch's."

"You don't believe you could say for sure, or positively then, that that was Dr. de Haan's handwriting?"

"No, I couldn't, Doctor."

"In any other way could you be sure that this photostated sheet of the second page of progress notes on Louis Corti is the actual one that you photostated?"

"There is one other way, Doctor."

"I'm only a plain mister, Mrs. Smead."

"I'm sorry, I mean *Mr.* Hoosman."

"Cousman." The courtroom tittered. "What is this other way, Mrs. Smead?"

"Well, Mrs. Sears, who is the office manager for the hospital, is a real stickler about many things. And one of the things she insisted on was for us to initial all the work we handled. If there was an insurance paper that one of us photostated before sending it in, we were to initial it so if anything ever came up about it, we'd know who had done it, and they could say they did it, in court if necessary, as Mrs. Sears used to tell us. You see, if it was made out wrong, she'd know who'd done that, too. Well, I was trained to initial everything I did, and I suppose you wouldn't need to do it for a hospital transcript, but I guess I must have done it anyway, because I see my initial there on the bottom of this page, M. S., for Mary Smead."

"Then you mean," Mr. Cousman said loudly, with obvious

surprise and pleasure, "that this little initial M. S. at the bottom of this page is yours?"

"Yes, sir, it looks just like mine."

"That's very helpful." Mr. Cousman looked at the page himself. "It looks as if that M. S. is put here with a black ball-point pen. It doesn't seem to have been put first on the copy and then photostated. Is that correct?"

"Yes, I would ordinarily have used a Lindy ball-point pen."

"Thank you very much," Mr. Cousman said. "You have been most helpful. Mr. Tolliver, do you have any questions?"

"Yes, I certainly do. Mrs. Smead, do you mean to say that you can state absolutely that this paper, so suddenly and dramatically produced by the plaintiff at the eleventh hour, is unquestionably one that you photostated four months ago? How can we believe that you can be sure? Are you positive, or are you just nervous, as you said, frightened by being on the stand, and trying to please, saying what first comes into your mind?"

Even with the tremor in her voice, Mrs. Smead managed to sound indignant. "I'm quite sure of what I said."

"Would you concede the possibility, for instance, that someone might have fraudulently written out a sheet of this sort, forging Dr. Hatch's handwriting on it—it's big, bold, I would imagine easy to copy—and then it could have been copied off some other Sterox machine, any Sterox machine, since there are hundreds of them in the state. All of them have these same little clips showing, you know. So you can't really say this is a copy of an authentic document, can you, not even that the photostating was done by you on your machine? Am I not right?"

"Well, I don't know. I can't say for sure."

"I have no other questions, your Honor," Mr. Tolliver said and moved quickly back to his table.

The witness was excused and Mr. Cousman called Miss Alison Kent, a senior record room clerk at the Hatch Hospital. After she was sworn in, he asked her if she had examined the two different photostats in question.

"Yes, sir."

"The two sheets are totally different, are they not?"

"Yes, sir."

"Do you recognize Dr. Hatch's handwriting on each?"

"Yes."

"In the normal course of events, after a patient leaves the

hospital, what happens to his or her chart? How is it processed for completeness before it is filed away?"

"We go through it in the record room," the middle-aged, hook-nosed lady answered gravely, "and find out if there are any deficiencies, missing reports, absent nurses' notes, incomplete diagnoses, and then it is sent to the doctor responsible for final summary and signature before the tissue and record committee reviews it and okays it for filing."

"So in the case of Mr. Louis Corti, the chart after his death would have been reviewed by your office, and then sent to Dr. Hatch to look over and sign out, is that correct?"

"Yes."

"And how long would Dr. Hatch have had the entire record in his personal possession?"

"It usually takes several weeks for the doctors to get through the records."

"Several weeks," Mr. Cousman said, ruminating for a moment. "All right, now did you in fact check this particular record, the record of Mr. Louis Corti, before it went to Dr. Hatch?"

"Yes, I did."

"Did you check it after it came back from Dr. Hatch?"

"I believe so. I'm not entirely sure."

"Do you have any opinion as to which of those two sheets is the authentic one?"

"I don't remember the progress notes on this patient well enough to say."

"You don't recall reading the page on which Dr. de Haan has the single note with three of Dr. Hatch's before you sent Louis Corti's chart to Dr. Hatch for final signature?"

"I do not."

"It is possible, though, is it not, quite easily possible, that substitution of a progress note could be made by the physician holding the chart for sign-out?"

"It is possible," she said, but by her intonation making it clear that she thought such a happening highly improbable.

"It is our understanding that you were the person who photostated all the records on Louis Corti for this trial, is that correct?"

"Yes."

"In so doing, the chart had to be taken apart, did it not? That is, the staples which hold the pages together must be removed and the sheets put through the copying machine individually, is that correct?"

"Yes."

"At the time you photostated the record we're concerned with, do you recall any evidence that it had been tampered with?"

"No, I don't."

"But substitution of one or more sheets of the record could easily have been made without your being aware of it, is that so?"

"Yes, I suppose so, though it doesn't seem very likely."

"I did not ask for your opinion, Miss Kent. That is all I have," Mr. Cousman said abruptly, turning on his heel.

Mr. Tolliver rose and walked slowly over to the witness. "Miss Kent, do you have any reason to believe that any substitution was made in the record of Mr. Louis Corti?"

"I don't really. For one thing, about the middle of April we changed the color of the progress sheets at the hospital from red to green, and the printing was changed slightly, but both of these sheets that were photostated have the old printing."

"Do you believe it would be easy or hard to duplicate Dr. Hatch's handwriting?"

Surprisingly, the witness smiled foolishly and blushed. "I don't think it's too hard."

"Have you done it?" Mr. Tolliver asked, smiling back at her.

"Sometimes we practice it in the record room. Actually, when it's nothing important, we'll sign Dr. Hatch's name to some of the papers." She blushed even deeper.

"Well, thank you, Miss Kent. Thank you for your frank testimony." Mr. Tolliver turned toward the irascible countenance of Judge Fielding. "Your Honor, I think the plaintiff has not satisfactorily shown that this so-called substitution ever took place. I believe that there is not good evidence that this photostat of what he calls the original or actual sheet of progress notes is veritable. If it were an original copy, it seems to me there would be a stronger case for allowing the jury to look at it. But presenting a *photostatic* copy of a *purported* progress note sheet and trying to establish it as the initial, the real sheet, seems a little too much, your Honor. I would like to say that we are glad at any time to bring to this courtroom, not the photostatic copies of records, but the actual records themselves, and we defy the plaintiff or anyone to prove them not to be the true records."

"Thank you, Miss Kent, you may step down," the judge said.

Mr. Cousman recalled Peter then, who was surprised to find himself on the stand again. The questions were few, though. Did the page in their copy of the chart contain the actual progress notes? It did. Did he recall writing the note on April seventh about Louis Corti? He definitely did. Did he feel a substitution had been made for the original progress note? Yes, there was no question about it in his mind.

Mr. Tolliver refused to question him, so he stepped down as the judge sat rubbing the scarred red skin of his face, his chair turned away from the courtroom for the moment. Then he swiveled toward the jury and said, "Ladies and gentlemen, at times it is difficult for a judge to decide what evidence is admissable, what material should be presented to you. I believe, though, that I will let Mr. Cousman go ahead and present this material to you and allow him to question Dr. Hatch on it. Remember that you are the ones who are required to listen to the evidence and decide what is valid and what is not, whose testimony you can believe and whose you can't. My admission of this present exhibit of the plaintiff's does not mean that I recommend it to you as factual." His voice got increasingly croaky as he talked. "That is for you to decide," he finally finished. "Call Dr. Hatch back to the stand, please." He gulped down a glass of water after his last word, and leaned back, the spotted whites of his eyes showing like a scene in a movie chiller as he looked toward the ceiling.

Matthew Hatch stepped quickly up to the witness box, folded his legs and waited, staring at Mr. Cousman, who was madly scribbling in his black book on the table. Finally he threw his book down, spun around, and said, "Yes, Dr. Hatch."

He strode carefully up to the stand, his hair wispily awry again. "Dr. Hatch, we have presented evidence here suggesting that there was a substitution made of the second progress sheet on Mr. Louis Corti's chart. I am going to read the sheet which has been so far a part of the official record of this court, and then read the sheet which Dr. de Haan brought to my office initially." When he had finished reading the two pages, handling the medical terms without hesitation, a buzz of interest was heard through the courtroom. Mr. Cousman continued, "Dr. Hatch, you realize that the first, the one from your own photostatic record of the chart, carries notes only by you. The second sheet I read carried three notations by you and one by Dr. de Haan. Do you admit the authenticity of either of them or both of them or neither of them?"

"The authentic one is the one submitted through my record room girl as the official copy of the total chart. The other one you present now with Dr. de Haan's note on it isn't. That's all I can say."

"Well, let's examine the one you say is not authentic. It first of all has a note in Dr. de Haan's handwriting—Dr. de Haan says it's his handwriting—which states that the patient's condition is hopelessly bad and that Dr. de Haan definitely concurred with Dr. Norman Silvana that immediate re-exploration of the abdomen was vitally necessary if this man's life would have a chance to be saved. Does it not seem to you that the excision of this note is helpful to your side, the defendant's side, in this case?"

"I wouldn't say that. Truth is truth, and we don't need help or hindrance."

"All right, then. Now, you have claimed that Dr. Silvana and Dr. de Haan were happy with your decision not to operate again. Here is a note which I say is a real note, which refutes your statement. Do you agree that it would tend to do this?"

"No, that's not so. First of all, I said Dr. Silvana wasn't necessarily pushing re-operation, but what Dr. de Haan's attitude might have been I didn't know and I didn't say. It could certainly change from moment to moment unpredictably, but besides that, if Dr. Silvana felt the way you keep implying he did, why doesn't his own note say that? Why are we trying to find out from Dr. de Haan's note what Dr. Silvana felt?"

"Thank you for the logical exercise, Doctor," Mr. Cousman said with a mock bow. "And to answer you, I'm sure Dr. Silvana had his reasons for writing his note as he did. Now your first entry on our records has you writing, in part, on April sixth: 'Post-operative course satisfactory to this point but for fever, apparently due to infection above the diaphragm . . . a medical problem only indirectly related to surgery.' The note on the photostat from your own record room on the other hand has you writing in part: '. . . Patient remains very ill from toxicity secondary to his acute gallbladder infection, and development of hepatorenal syndrome from shock and toxicity is likely . . .' Now would you not say that this latter note improves your position, is a more sensible and logical note for you to have written in the light of our understanding here in this court of what this man's difficulty actually was at the time?"

"I suppose so. It also happens to be the note I actually wrote."

"You insist on that?"

"Yes, of course I do."

"About the note being more sensible and logical, I mean that the first note has you saying everything is all right, when all subsequent events proved everything was far from all right, everything was really all wrong. Do you follow what I mean?"

"Believe me, I'm ahead of you, Mr. Cousman."

"No comment. All right. Now, let's go on to the two notes of April seventh. One is from the morning, the other the evening."

"Yes."

"There is no question yet. Give me a minute. Now the first note read in our version: 'Patient somewhat better. Improving under full antibiotic coverage.' The version officially presented to this court goes: 'Patient remains shocky.... Family called to bedside. Portal vein thrombosis . . . possible. No surgical therapy indicated. All-out treatment of shock, toxicity, possible disseminated infection or hepatorenal syndrome is under way.' Do you see the difference in the tone and implication of the two, Dr. Hatch?"

"Are you asking me, or telling me, sir?"

"That's sufficient answer for my purposes, Doctor. I'll just go on."

"The final note on our sheet read: 'Patient in better condition tonight. Overwhelming toxicity has possibly been related to bloodstream invasion from lung infection. . . .' For the ladies and gentlemen of the jury, I want to repeat this last sentence: 'Overwhelming toxicity is possibly related to bloodstream invasion from *lung* infection.' Not liver but still *lung* infection, and the patient is in *better condition* the night before he died. This note continues: 'or toxic reaction to anesthetic agents may be responsible. No evidence of trouble at surgical site or from surgery. Family knows . . .' Now the substituted note says—"

"Objection, counsel has not proved substitution occurred. That is only his speculation."

"Objection sustained."

"All right, the note as it reads from the Hatch Hospital record room version (the official court version until now), goes: 'Patient constantly growing poorer. No signs at all suggestive of interference with blood supply to liver. Any attempt at re-operating patient discarded yesterday as impractical, dangerous, improbable of any help by Dr. Norman Silvana and me after careful consideration of the clinical facts. Family at bedside.' Now there they are. You see the one note the evening before death pointing only to lung infection as the cause of death. The note brought to this court, though, almost seems designed for this trial, don't you think, Dr. Hatch, refuting suggestions that you had not thought of hepatic artery ligation with the second sentence, and with the third bolstering the fact that the unfortunately missing Dr. Silvana, not here to testify to this statement, or any other involving him, was at your side through the whole sticky affair, holding your hand high in victory, clapping you soundly on the shoulder for good work well done."

"Are you asking me that?"

"What I'm asking you, Doctor, frankly, plainly, squarely, point-blank, is this: Did you or did you not *forge* a new set of progress notes for this most critical part of the patient's hospital course to help you look good for the purposes of this trial?"

"I did not," Dr. Hatch replied, flushing. Again his right hand sought the solace of his breast.

"Can you give me any other rational, logical explanation for the fact that we have established here clearly and irrefutably, I believe, that there are two sets of progress notes, sheet number two, for this man's case, and that the only handwriting common to both of them is yours?"

"I can't—why, you must have forged them, sir, that's the only way I can see it."

"Doctor, be careful, please, that is an accusation of a criminal act, and a slander of the most vicious and blatant sort, and I will not permit it."

"Well, well—I'm not saying you, I mean by you, I don't mean *you*, but someone, someone else, I don't know how, or who, but someone made it up. I know nothing about two different sets of notes, and I deny vehemently any implication that I do."

"Look at this sheet here, please, which is the photostat that Dr. de Haan obtained. Do you deny that this is a photostatic copy of a page containing your handwriting?"

"Of course I do. I know the sheet I wrote on and what I wrote, and it isn't the one you showed me. Dr. de Haan finagled that photostat he gave you illicitly and illegally some way. You know he's out to get me and I know he is, but there's little of that mentioned here." Dr. Hatch's voice was loud now, and shaky.

"Sir, you are implying, you are virtually stating that Dr. de Haan, then, instead of me, forged the page of progress notes he brought to me when I undertook to support Mrs. Corti's case. That again is an accusation of a criminal act, and in itself an act of public slander. I demand an immediate retraction, and I demand your answer be stricken from the record of this trial." The lawyer looked small indeed before the enraged physician, but his voice was firmer and clearer.

"Mr. Cousman, Dr. Hatch! As presiding justice of this trial, I am interrupting you both and command your attention." Dr. Hatch slowly sat back in the chair, and Mr. Cousman, flushed himself now, backed away from the witness stand. "Now, we will stop these infantile perorations." The judge pronounced the last word as if it were three, his speech crackling with phlegm. "All comments after Mr. Cousman's last question are to be struck by the reporter, and the jury will disregard them. There will be no more such outbreaks from you gentlemen or citations for contempt will be issued. Is that clear?" he said. "Mr. Cousman's last question will be repeated for the witness."

The court reporter, smiling with open-eyed delight at the events of the afternoon, read: "'COUSMAN: Look at this sheet here, please, which is the photostat that Dr. de Haan obtained. Do you deny that this is a photostatic copy of a page containing your handwriting?'"

"Yes, I do," Dr. Hatch responded.

Mr. Cousman stood looking at Dr. Hatch, and the physician looked back at him. "Dr. Hatch," he said, musing, "a minute ago you said that you knew and I knew why Dr. de Haan was trying, as you put it, to get you, but that there was scant mention of it here. I would like to have you give us any other information than that developed already as to why this trial is being held, if you have some. I don't like to leave a comment of that sort alone even if it was stricken from the record. You told us about the surgery on Dr. de Haan's fiancée. Is there something else you'd like to have the jury hear about all this?"

"Your Honor," Mr. Tolliver called out, "I think the

plaintiff's attorney is trying to harass my client into an admission or disclosure which is against his best interest. I object to the question and request it be withdrawn."

"Oh, I think I'm going to allow him to answer that question, Mr. Tolliver. Dr. Hatch, go ahead," Judge Fielding said in a voice that was almost normal again.

"I don't mind saying that I believe this whole trial is a paper tiger, a tissue of misrepresentations without substance created by this young doctor from the East because of anger at me for reasons, as Mr. Cousman reminds me, that I've already disclosed. Somehow this man's guilt for the situation with his girl friend got converted into anger at me, and this entire suit is the result."

"Now I wanted to get this out in the open again. Perhaps you were not in court at the time, Dr. Hatch, I remember you came in late that morning, but Dr. de Haan has even been cross-examined by Mr. Tolliver on this point, and denied all implications that there was a relationship between his problems and this case. However, I would like to ask you two questions on this matter. The lady in question—we'll just call her Miss X—whom you operated on in December, was at that time a patient of yours, was she not?"

"Of course."

"Then I would consider it a breach of the personal and confidential medical relationship for you to bring her up here, wouldn't you? Never mind. Something else. Do you consider the surgery on her to have had a satisfactory outcome?"

"She's alive, isn't she?"

"That's not an answer. Just yes or no this time, please."

"Yes."

"All right, now how often do you find it necessary in caring for a miscarriage, which after all is a very common situation, to do a complete hysterectomy, to take out the entire uterus and render the woman incapable of having any children?"

"Well, not too often, but—"

"Wouldn't you say it would be necessary about one in a million times when proper medical care was being exercised?"

"The circumstances of any case can't be—"

"Doctor, I'm going to withdraw that question, and save you the trouble of answering it. I have no future questions of this witness."

"It's after four thirty, gentlemen, so I'm going to adjourn for today, and we'll see you all tomorrow at nine thirty. I want to start early with the hope that we can finish in the morning, and go into summations in the afternoon. Ladies and gentlemen of the jury, remember the admonition."

Awhile later, going down with Mr. Cousman to his car, Peter found him concerned.

"Didn't you think things went well today, then? This business of the counterfeit page I would expect to weigh very heavily against him."

"Yes, it's a good point. Juries are so funny. I told you that you do have to be careful about doctor defendants. What they think of me isn't important. That I'm hard-boiled, outspoken, that I'll chisel away at anyone's reputation for a buck, or whatever, it doesn't matter, if they'll believe our case. I shocked some of them—two of the women and one of the men, I'm pretty sure—with how rough I was on Dr. Hatch in the morning. I tried to take it easier this afternoon, to change the pace, shift the emphasis, make it more a matter of factual information, but then I actually got angry. I've grown to hate that slippery s.o.b."

"I can certainly appreciate that."

"I don't really think I can do the summation without a little emotion. I imagine they expect it of me now. So I am concerned about the verdict. I have to push hard enough on Hatch to make a strong believable case—but I have to be careful not to push too hard and alienate the jury too much. It's a fine line," Mr. Cousman said, sucking on a cigar again as he stood by his car.

"Well, I'll spend the evening lighting candles, burning incense, and wrapping all my books in red paper, for good luck tomorrow," Peter said. "Oh, by the way, Anne's all through with her work at Berkeley today, and she wanted to come and sit with me tomorrow in the courtroom. When we were talking about it she began to wonder if she should, though. What do you think?"

"If she could come, and didn't mind coming, considering all the circumstances, I think it would be wonderful."

"Swell. I'll phone her tonight."

"Excellent. You know something, I'm very anxious to meet her. I mean that. Good night." The lawyer drove off with his Lincoln at full throttle, leaving at Peter's feet dust, wind, and flying gravel.

43

PETER met Anne in front of the courthouse the next morning. She had on a camel's hair coat with a blue dress underneath and looked fresh and lovely.

Peter kissed her, noticing that she smelled good, too, as her soft hair pressed against his neck for a moment. "What kind of perfume do you have on?"

"Estée Lauder, do you like it?"

"I do. Very much. Just right. Let's go inside. We're almost late."

Riding up in the elevator he asked her, "Are you all through now?"

"Yes, I've finished everything. Turned my last paper in at five yesterday. I'm so happy to have it done."

"Good. Here's where we get off."

As they walked into the courtroom, Peter saw that everyone was there and waiting for the judge. He slipped Anne through the gate to the enclosure, conscious that all eyes in the courtroom were on them. The jury watched him introduce Anne to the Cortis and Peter could see their interest and what he felt was their pleasure, to look at such an attractive girl, to have him bring her into their world.

Mr. Cousman noticed them, and came rushing over from the clerk's desk to greet Anne warmly. "It's so nice to meet you, Anne. I'm so very pleased. I must start off by congratulating you on your ability to pick men. You have the finest young doctor that I have ever known."

"Thank you, Mr. Cousman, I've also heard lots about you, and I know how much Peter thinks of you."

The bailiff stood up then and Mr. Cousman said, "I'll see you later, young lady."

The rest of the morning went by whirringly fast.

Dr. Hatch got back up on the stand, wearing a dark suit and black tie, looking tired, but controlled. (Peter could hear Matthew Hatch in his locker room at the country club talking to some of his medical buddies. "Sure, you're damned right I rewrote that page. I'm going to defend myself any way I can. When you get among the goddam Communists our universities are spawning these days you've got to get right down to basics, guerrilla warfare, fight fire with fire. That's the only way you can keep ahead of these young punks who want to ruin everything, our country, its institutions, our way of life.")

Mr. Tolliver asked Dr. Hatch some questions rapidly, without fuss or histrionics.

"Doctor, I want you to tell this jury frankly, do you feel that at all times you gave this young man, Mr. Louis Corti, the benefit of your best medical and surgical care?"

"Yes, very definitely."

The defense now had Dr. Hatch firmly and briefly refute the major points of the Cousman-Corti case. When they had finished, Judge Fielding, baggy-eyed this morning and not even looking clean-shaven, asked huskily, "Mr. Cousman, have you further questions for Dr. Hatch?"

"No, sir."

"Are there any more witnesses for the defendant, then, Mr. Tolliver?"

"No, sir, there are not."

Mr. Cousman then called Peter as a rebuttal witness.

When Peter was back on the stand, Mr. Cousman asked him, "Dr. de Haan, did you obtain the photostatic copy of the hospital chart of Mr. Louis Corti on Friday night, April eighth, through the efforts of Mrs. Smead who testified in this courtroom yesterday?"

"I did."

"Did you bring that same photostatic copy to my office without any substitutions or alterations, on May nineteenth when we first discussed this case together?"

"Yes, I did."

"Do you swear that the second sheet of the progress notes as delivered to my office and read here in this courtroom yesterday is the actual sheet as it was in the chart at the time of Mr. Louis Corti's death?"

"I do."

"Do you swear that you saw the hepatic artery ligated at the time of autopsy on Mr. Louis Corti?"

"Yes, I do."

"That is all I wish to ask."

"Mr. Tolliver?"

"Just one or two questions. Dr. de Haan, are you now a member of the San Marcial County Medical Society?"

"No, I am not. That is I am probably not."

"What do you mean by that?"

"Well, I received notice the first of this week that the board of directors had voted to dismiss me from the San Marcial County Society. I have the right to attend the next meeting of the Society and present evidence as to why I should not be voted out. I don't plan to do so, though."

"At the start of the trial you told this court you were employed at the Fabiola Hospital in Oakland. Are you still employed there?"

"No, I was discharged."

"What was the reason for your discharge?"

"Supposedly, because I had been on a short-term, essentially part-time basis, and they stated they had found a full-time man."

"Your Honor, this questioning has nothing to do with the evidence Dr. de Haan just presented," Mr. Cousman pointed out.

"I have no more questions," Mr. Tolliver said.

"Mr. Cousman?"

"No more questions. The plaintiff rests, your Honor."

"Do you have any surrebuttal witnesses, Mr. Tolliver?" the judge asked.

"None, your Honor. The defendant rests."

"All right, gentlemen. I think we'll have an early recess this morning, and go into summation immediately after it. As you know, you gentlemen agreed to restrict summation to thirty minutes each, so in one hour we should be completed."

"Your Honor, I have a matter I'd like to bring before you."

"Will it take long, Mr. Tolliver?"

"Possibly an hour."

"All right then, let's dismiss the jury until one P.M. You gentlemen can meet me in my chambers. At one P.M. sharp court will reconvene."

Mr. Cousman winked at Anne as he walked out, leaning over to whisper to all of them, "He can't get a dismissal, anyway."

"Ladies and gentlemen of the jury," the judge began, looking brighter and happier than he had in the morning, "I wish to report to you that the defendant's attorney presented me a motion for dismissal of this suit, which was denied. The defendant's attorney and then the plaintiff's attorney will give their summations of the trial to you, after which I will instruct you in the law regarding this case. Following these events, you will be taken into the jury room where your deliberations will begin on the verdict. With that explanation, we will ask Mr. Tolliver to begin his summation."

Mr. Tolliver stood up, tall, just on the stout side, his luxuriant black hair carefully combed, his moustache meticulously groomed. He moved easily and gracefully to stand in front of the jury box, where he stared earnestly at the nine men and four women there, his eyes falling on one after another in turn, like a movie camera recording their faces, before he began his speech in that silky, low-pitched, reverberating voice.

"Ladies and gentlemen, I believe in the last two and a half weeks we have shown you conclusively that Dr. Matthew Hatch is a fine doctor who has always put the care of his patients above his personal life, above any consideration of money or position. I wonder if each of you can realize the agony it causes a fine professional man to go through an ordeal such as this, what strain and worry it is to him to see his reputation placed in jeopardy in a trial like the present one. As with each of his patients, Dr. Hatch gave his closest attention and his best possible care at all times to Mr. Louis Corti. I believe we have shown that in this courtroom, and I believe each of you has had a chance to see Dr. Hatch through a time of fierce personal attack here, demonstrate his courage and the strength of his belief in himself and in his practice of good medicine.

"Dr. Hatch's reputation in San Marcial is of the highest. He has not just hundreds, but thousands of loyal patients, loyal because he has served them promptly, carefully, and well, with full devotion through the years. He is a well-trained, highly competent surgeon with a tremendous amount of experience in the field of practical medicine, and his words tell you this. His instincts are highly developed and they are good ones. Sometimes, as with blood transfusion, he cannot tell you exactly why he does something. The highest level at which man can function is that of intuition. 'I know this is the right thing for this man now,' a good doctor can often say, and he will be right, though you can't pin him down as to just how he reached this conclusion. Here you have seen a good doctor at the peak of his profession, working at times *intuitively*, in a vain effort to save the life of a young man whose time had run out."

Mr. Tolliver drank half a glass of water at his table, and went back to the jury. "The experience of getting to know this man, through helping with his defense, has been one of the most stimulating and rewarding of my life," he said. "This doctor, whose whole life has been one of devotion to others, exemplifies what a physician should be. He is the kind of doctor we all hope we can have to serve us when trouble strikes, when disease or injury affects us. His life is a model of organization and productivity. Every moment of his day, of each day, is planned and occupied. He subscribes to and *reads* every important medical and surgical journal in his field. His car is equipped with a phonograph so even driving to the hospital or on a house call he can listen to the tape-recorded reports of the latest developments from top medical meetings throughout the country."

Mr. Tolliver cleaned his glasses again, only to return them to his breast pocket, and then continued mellifluously. "You have been through the problem of one man who did not survive, who would not have survived if every doctor in the United States had been at his bedside. What you do not see and know is the great army of successes, the great brilliance with which Dr. Hatch has operated to save dozens, hundreds, perhaps thousands of lives. He has no real hobby or leisure-time activities, as nearly all of us have. His consuming interest, his work, his avocation, his entertainment, his relaxation, are all one and the same thing, the practice of medicine. To be in this courtroom today he arose at five A.M., and started operating at six A.M. One of these operations was a gallbladder removal. That patient had read every day's account of this trial in the paper, every word of it, and she would have no other doctor in the world take out her gallbladder but Dr. Matthew Hatch. This is the kind of trust he breeds in his patients and rightfully, for he deserves it."

Mr. Tolliver went on to explain how wrong it would be to have this good physician marked with the black smear, the heartbreaking blemish on his career, of a judgment against him in this case of Louis Corti. "Are we reaching a point in the law where the doctor can be challenged for any and every poor result? This should not be and cannot be." He pounded his fist on the jury rail and then shook his head sadly.

"Mr. Louis Corti was brought in to see Matthew Hatch at two o'clock the afternoon of April fourth, this year. Dr. Hatch examined him immediately, determined the nature of his problem accurately, and scheduled him at once for an operation on his gallbladder. Dr. Hatch is an exceptionally fast surgeon, and he felt that Mr. Corti was a very ill young man, so he worked even faster than usual in an effort to bring this man through the procedure in as good shape as possible. Dr. Hatch found evidence at surgery that Mr. Corti's liver was not normal, and then when four days of heroic attempts to save young Mr. Corti's life were unavailing, the postmortem examination showed that there were indeed abnormal findings in the liver. Dr. Hatch has insisted that toxicity, infection of the bloodstream, and finally poor liver function resulting in liver and kidney damage, a condition long known to surgeons as the hepatorenal syndrome, caused this young man's death. Dr. Joseph Parmelee was the autopsy surgeon, and he stated here on the stand that Mr. Corti's death was in fact from liver failure, and that as a result of his examination of the body of Louis Corti he felt there was no evidence of negligent action in this case. Three eminent expert witnesses, men of high distinction in the medical field, went over the facts of this case carefully, too, and concluded that Dr. Hatch had not performed negligently, but rather that he had in fact performed *properly* as Mr. Corti's doctor."

Mr. Tolliver stopped gesturing now, dropped his hands to his sides, lowered his voice. "The jury should remember that the physician need do no more than render medical care with the same reasonable degree of skill and ability possessed by other doctors in his locality. Dr. Hatch obviously conducted the care of Mr. Corti with far more than average or reasonable skill, because for one thing he is a far better than average doctor. His great professional success attests to this, the great esteem in which he is held by his own medical colleagues attests to this. The San Marcial County Medical Society as a body has sent him official word of their stand behind him in this time of his trouble, and fully a quarter of the crowded courtroom right now, on the last day of our trial, is I am sure composed of friends of his, physicians, laboratory workers, X-ray technicians, nurses, and aides, who are sitting here quietly plugging for him, silent members on his team.

"On the other hand, the County Society responded to Dr. de Haan's questionable motives and his lack of professional ethics by starting proceedings to dismiss him from their group. For this has been a personal vendetta, a very unfortunate attempt at revenge, by a confused, vindictive, immature, and irresponsible young man who blackens the good name of physicians by being in their ranks. It is the old case of the apple barrel, and the one rotten fruit, and at least the County Medical Society is taking steps to prevent any spread in its barrel." Mr. Tolliver had walked over toward the plaintiff's table to look directly at Peter as he talked about him. Now he went back to the jury railing.

"I think Mrs. Corti is a pawn here," he said. "I feel that her motives are pure and that she has been led into this thing by misrepresentation, mistaken understanding of the facts of the situation. But Dr. de Haan is the ringleader here, and the case he's been responsible for bringing into court, as every case, comes down ultimately to credibility, believability. Do you believe the testimony of the de Haan witnesses, or do you believe Dr. Parmelee, our outstanding experts, Dr. Namuth, Dr. Wilmar and Dr. Merriott, and especially Dr. Hatch himself? Do you believe the testimony of an angry, disturbed young man whose moral quality is displayed by the December episode involving surgery on his girl friend?" Peter glanced at Anne and saw that she was blushing, which depressed him and angered him. "Can you trust what a man says who, like Judas Iscariot, ingratiated himself into a position of confidence and responsibility with a fine physician in order to find a way to destroy him? What kind of truth can you expect from a man who entered into a monstrous betrayal like that? On the other hand would you not rather believe the words and facts presented here by Dr. Matthew Hatch, a non-smoking, non-drinking, religiously oriented doctor filled with Christian ideals, a man of great prestige and high character who has served this community devotedly for twenty years?"

Houston Tolliver's giant voice bellowed now, causing every light fixture in the room to tremble. With grand flourishes of his hands and recurring choked noises from his throat, his wrath was magnificent to behold. Peter felt a sick sweat on his body, a nauseating queasiness in his stomach pit. Tolliver and Hatch could win, couldn't they? With a lawyer who could talk like this, could argue with such fire and persuasiveness, a jury could be swayed, couldn't they, a case could be won, couldn't it?

"Don't, I plead with you," he roared on, "destroy this man of action, this Christ-like doctor with his life of dedication, don't slap justice in the face, don't let the knowledge of his integrity and fidelity and ability slip away from you and float out these windows. I implore you—" And now Peter thought he could see the Tolliver tears. "I implore you to consider this case carefully, fairly, and then if you do, I suggest that you will come to the only reasonable conclusion, the only possible conclusion, that Dr. Matthew Hatch is totally, not partially but *totally*, innocent of any shortcoming in the medical service he rendered Mr. Louis Corti, and therefore not one cent of damages is due this family. But more than that, since money is far from the only consideration here, a verdict for the defendant will restore in the heart of this fine man, Dr. Hatch, the defendant, a belief in this jury, this court, our American justice, in the existence of morality and right in this community, which is his world. It will vindicate him and allow him to leave this courtroom and go back to his medical practice with warmth in his soul; it will sustain him as with God's help he continues his task of saving the lives of your friends and of other young men and women more fortunate than Louis Corti. Thank you, ladies and gentlemen of the jury, for your kind attention, and for your just consideration of the facts and issues we have brought to you here."

It was discouraging, Peter thought, that Matthew Hatch should have found such a convincing advocate for his side. Peter felt his stomach burning suddenly and plunged several antacid tablets into his mouth as he heard the judge say, "All right, Mr. Cousman," and the small lawyer arose, elegant today in a suit of luxurious black cloth with a matching silk waistcoat. A loose-knotted navy tie showed at his neck with small scattered scarlet fleur-de-lis on it. His hair was as neatly combed as possible with his odd coiffure, and he began his words to the jury in the most carefully modulated, yet confident tone imaginable. He also dispensed an air of apology, as if implying: I'm sorry we've beaten them so badly, I am sorry we had to be so savage and cruel in the way we showed you the odiousness of the defendant. We are required now to present you the facts of the case in a simple and concise way, and the facts are such that they will overwhelm you. The facts in this case are ours. Even if you don't want to agree, I know of course you will have to.

All these subtleties and more were implicit in his presentation, in his use of the mannered voice, the excelling verbal skill, in his display of a rational, clear mind at work. Peter continued to be awed at the talent of the physically unimpressive but still luminescent man.

"Mr. Tolliver said that Dr. Peter de Haan brought us all into this room. That is not true. There is a man, though, who did cause our gathering here. That man is, or was, Louis Corti. His death brought about this trial as directly and surely as God created the world."

Mr. Cousman, standing ten feet away from the jury box, spoke in a gentle tone.

"And, ladies and gentlemen of the jury, I bring you a much different picture of Dr. Peter de Haan than that presented by Mr. Tolliver. On my part, I have come to know this *young* physician very well. I've found him to be a fine young man of grit, of principle and character. He decided on his own that the Corti case involved an error so gross that he must disclose it, must do something to make up for it, regardless of the effect it might have on him personally. This took pure courage. It required going against the unwritten law of his own guild, the medical society, to denounce a fellow member of his profession. This is an action all too rare, believe me, ladies and gentlemen. In spite of years of experience with malpractice cases, the present case has opened my own eyes to the distressing way the medical societies of our state and our counties protect their bad seed with a steel sheet of silence. It is a national disgrace, I believe, and I have unqualified admiration for Dr. de Haan as the first physician I know to initiate directly a malpractice action. I believe that in the years to come you will hear many times about this young man. I have wholeheartedly admired the strength of will and the resolute heart he has shown, and believe me they have been tested. His friends and colleagues have insulted him or shunned him completely. He has been unable to keep any employment. He has been fired for vague reasons from two hospital jobs since he left the Hatch employ. He would be destitute if it were not for a small inheritance his father, a fine proud physician in Maryland, left him at his death late last year. This money was designed for his future training though, and instead is being rapidly eaten up so he can be available for this trial. He is receiving *no money* for his days and weeks of devoted help in the preparation of the plaintiff's case, nor for his testimony here. Now, as you have heard, the San Marcial County Medical Society is dismissing him, an action this society has never previously taken against any physician in its history. As a result of this dismissal, it becomes unlikely that any other county medical society in this state would accept him as a member, which means no hospital privileges will be available to him anyplace, since almost all hospital staffs have county society membership as a condition for staff appointments. So this in turn means he could scarcely afford to practice medicine anyplace in this state."

Mr. Cousman paused, took two steps toward the jury box, and raised his voice a notch in tone and volume. "Even Dr. de Haan's fiancée decided they shouldn't see each other for a while before this trial, because he could think of nothing and talk of nothing but this case. I suppose she felt rather left out, and I can't say I blame her. I was happy to learn last week, though, that they are back together again, and as you have noticed she is here in the courtroom today at Dr. de Haan's side." A small gush of feminine whispering in the spectators animated the courtroom for a moment.

"I want you to know how difficult it is to get a malpractice case together. The information needed is all under the control of doctors in their offices and hospitals. It is extremely hard to get an expert witness for a plaintiff. Doctors don't want to testify against each other. That is one reason we had only one expert witness, although a top-notch one, while the other side had three, and could easily have had five or ten if they had wanted. Yet I believe we made our points, proved our case. You know we are only required in this kind of case to have the *preponderance* of evidence on our side. We merely have to make our charges seem *more* plausible and *more* likely to you than the defendant's attempts to refute them." Mr. Cousman nodded his head several times as he looked at his shoes now, preparing his thoughts, it appeared.

"I think we showed a great deal more than required. Dr. de Haan stated strongly and surely to you that he *saw* the ligature around Mr. Louis Corti's artery at the postmortem. He stated that Dr. Norman Silvana found it first and then pointed it out to him and to Dr. Parmelee. Dr. Silvana, a most reluctant witness, still *never directly denied in his deposition read to you that he had found the ligature around the hepatic artery*. A most important point. Dr. Silvana testified, and I quote: 'The ligature appeared to be around the hepatic artery. It might not have been. I could have been mistaken. I can't swear that it was.' He was a hostile and reluctant witness, and believe me, ladies and gentlemen, he would have said that tie *wasn't* around the hepatic artery if he could have. He hedged as best he could.

"Then Dr. Arnold Dunning, our expert surgeon witness

from Los Angeles and a most distinguished doctor, sat in that witness stand right over there and told you that he felt definitely there must have been a ligature around the hepatic artery to present Mr. Corti's clinical picture and to produce the pathological changes found in his liver. His eminent pathologist friend, Dr. Joseph Litner, agreed with and reinforced his opinions. And Dr. Dunning, a nationally respected surgeon, told you thirty-three minutes was too fast for *anyone*, for the finest surgeon in the world under ideal conditions, to do a cholecystectomy in the case of an infected gallbladder. I believe he proved our suit for us when he went on to tell you that placing a tie around a hepatic artery was clear negligence, undeniable malpractice. He also told you how the defendant's pathologist employee, Dr. Joseph Parmelee, in *his own* descriptions of the changes in the liver accurately and effectively set down the exact picture that could have been caused in no other way than by an obstruction of the hepatic artery such as placing a ligature around it would produce."

Mr. Cousman added emphasis to his inflections, with descriptive, graphic, amplifying movements of his hands, but he was still not speaking loudly as he continued. "Believe me, it is true when I say the doctor defendant in a case such as this has any medical testimony available to him that he wants. But did you notice the defendant did not have a liver man, an expert on the liver, testifying? Why not? The liver problem is obvious here, the kind of liver damage present and its cause. No liver expert could have called it other than it was. It is a point of law that if information is available to a side in a case, and this information is not brought in, it *must* be presumed against them. That would be the situation here. The fact the defendant's side could have brought in a liver man and didn't means that any information a liver expert could have given here to clarify the case *must* be presumed by you the jury, to be against the defendant."

Mr. Cousman rubbed his face for a moment, and then destroyed the neatness of his last-day's coiffure with one stroke of his hand to his head. "Now, to a major point. The case of the rewritten sheet. Believe me, we would have brought it into evidence earlier if we had known about it. We never dreamed of any such substitution. We were checking the two transcripts together on the weekend without knowing what we were looking for when Dr. de Haan stumbled onto the difference. The defendant and his counsel muttered this and that about it, but I don't think they convinced any of you. The defendant didn't know we had our own photostat of the chart. We had never told him. So that second page of progress notes got rewritten by him. And if it was rewritten, it was rewritten for a purpose, wasn't it? To improve the defendant's position legally, that would be the purpose. An innocent person, an honorable person, wouldn't use such a method, would he? A frightened and guilty person would. The defendant reread those notes of his from the sixth and seventh of April, along with Dr. de Haan's note, and I would imagine they sounded pretty bad to him, so he changed them. For shame, but he did. I'm sure he had some rationalization in his mind for the act, ladies and gentlemen, but believe me, I still find falsifying records the desperation effort of a guilty person."

Mr. Cousman stepped even closer to the jury box and began to expound on the conflicts in testimony of Dr. Parmelee and especially Dr. Hatch between deposition time and trial time. He quoted from the testimony in a number of places, and after this went back to Dr. Hatch's complete lack of defense to or explanation for the new false progress notes.

Then he assumed a different voice, earnest, friendly, very serious. "The damages we're asking are large, ladies and gentlemen. We have explained why they are so large. This fine young mother, so devoted to her family and husband, so stoic in her daily attendance at our sessions during the fearful summer weather, is now widowed, and she and her children are permanently deprived of the love and attention of their husband and father. All of us recognize that money itself cannot assuage the inconsolable loss in such a situation, but believe me, it will help buy clothes for these children, help make the house payments, send them to summer camps and colleges eventually, allow them to hold their heads high with their friends and playmates, and to meet the inevitable buffets of a competitive and difficult world more successfully. Remember Mr. Corti is gone *forever*, and remember we gave you strong evidence that he was on his way to becoming outstandingly successful. If his life had been spared, we have every reason to believe he would have made a great deal of money, and instead, with him gone, there is no breadwinner at all for his family. Of course, Mrs. Corti can go to work and probably will, but she has no special training for the business world and cannot hope to achieve in the near future any substantial income. Still, if you feel as a jury the damages we ask for are excessive, it is within your province to alter them, should you find for the plaintiff, to an amount you consider reasonable. We would listen with respect to your position in the matter."

Mr. Cousman moved directly in front of the jury box now, and smiled indulgently back over his shoulder at the defendant's table. "Finally, let me scotch an old wives' tale brought up by my learned opponent, the defendant's counsel, Mr. Houston Tolliver. He implored you not to find for the plaintiff if for no other reason than that so doing would ruin his client, Dr. Matthew Hatch, professionally, and he would lead you to believe, financially and socially also. I've seen too many doctors through too many of these kinds of cases to swallow that. The result of losing a malpractice action is surprisingly little, almost nothing. Dr. Hatch will go right on practicing medicine as head of his Hatch Clinic and Hospital, keeping very busy, doing just what he is best fitted to do as he always has, and undoubtedly performing some good works, helping some people to a better life. He made a mistake here in our case, a bad one, we maintain, but I'm sure there is much good in him, that he is a good doctor fundamentally and has much to offer."

Peter bit his lip now, finding it hard to get down this necessary but hypocritical mouthful. Cousman had told him before he had to make some concession of this sort, so as to leave the members of the jury who were sympathetic to the doctor an out, a graceful way to vote a verdict for the plaintiff without feeling they were destroying the doctor. But he did seem to be putting it on a bit thick.

"I hope he'll go back to his practice with a bit more humility after this enterprise of ours—believe me, humility is a wonderful thing for any of us to possess, for all of us to cultivate—but I can tell you with assurance there won't be much difference otherwise in his life."

Peter sat straight up in his chair then suddenly, uncertain now as to Mr. Cousman's real meaning. He had never expressed himself exactly like this before. If he had implied before what he was saying now distinctly, Peter had never made the inference. Could he *really* mean that from Peter's standpoint a victory for their side might amount to just nothing?

"Dr. Hatch's practice will continue large, his income handsome. He might lose a few patients, but there will be others to replace them. Dr. Hatch won't lose membership in any organization or society, his colleagues will still speak to him and be friendly with him, his children will continue to respect their father, even if they learn to hate Dr. de Haan, Mrs. Corti and me."

Peter realized abruptly and blindingly that the lawyer did mean exactly what he was saying, that he had never thought Peter was really going to accomplish anything for medicine or against Dr. Hatch through this trial. Had he then used Peter's energy unfairly, harnessing it to help his case and his client? Peter felt a painful tension crease the back of his neck.

"Let me emphasize to you that Dr. Hatch will stand no further trials, that he will not be blacklisted in his profession in any way if you do find for the plaintiff, and that a verdict for the plaintiff does not in any way open him to criminal charges."

Mr. Cousman paused now, and drew away from the jury box, standing and surveying them all amiably, never once having spoken angrily or loudly, "Do right by your consciences, do right by Mrs. Corti and her children, do right by the memory of Louis Corti. I thank you for your attention."

44

FROM two thirty to three thirty Judge Fielding charged the jury with the law. He told them again that they must feel the defendant had been proved negligent preponderantly, and that the burden of preponderant proof was on the plaintiff. He added that they, the jury, were the sole judges of the facts, and must decide all disputed facts. He reminded them the defendant did not have to disprove the assertion of the suit. If his charge was long, it was clear. At the end he told the jury to favor neither side, and said they should not be influenced to think by his words or actions during the trial that *he* favored either side. "If the evidence balances evenly, ladies and gentlemen, then you should find for the defendant, but if in your judgment it preponderates for the plaintiff, then you must fix damages at what you consider a fair amount for the expenses incurred by the plaintiff's deceased husband, for his pain and suffering, and for loss of income to the plaintiff and her children as the result of his demise. I know that you will not allow personal bias, sympathy for any person on one side or the other, or similar hostility to affect your judgment. You may now retire."

Peter wandered through the corridors of the courthouse, holding hands with Anne and whispering to her. At times they walked back into the courtroom and talked to the Cortis and Mr. Cousman. The lawyer, anxious himself and restless, told Peter, "I think several things in this case represent possible reversible error for our side, such as not allowing you to be an expert witness."

"Does that mean you're looking for a verdict for the defendant?" Peter asked him, still fiercely troubled and depressed by the lawyer's summation, but not telling him so.

"Not necessarily. I think we have a chance all right. I know Dr. Hatch got to several members of the jury with his testimony, though. He's personable, and you know, they've all heard of him. I'm still afraid I was too hard on him on cross. I got carried away."

"What about a hung jury?"

"Oh, I think it is going to be hung. That's the most likely thing. I feel a verdict for the plaintiff is less likely, and that a verdict for the defendant is least likely, but believe me it's always possible in one of these cases. Get a lead juror pushing strongly one way or the other, and that can do it."

At five o'clock the jury asked for the pre-trial depositions to be brought to them. At six o'clock, dinner was taken in, and the Cortis, Mr. Cousman, his associate, Jack Penberthy, Peter and Anne went to a small restaurant close by and toyed with club steaks while they listened to Mr. Cousman's stories of his year in Egypt as a young man in the consulate in Cairo. As they finished eating, the telephone rang with the word that the jury had reached a verdict and would be coming back to the courtroom.

They all turned silent, even Mr. Cousman, and Peggy Corti's already noticeable pallor turned a deadlier white. Peter drove them back to the courthouse rapidly. As soon as they took their places in the courtroom, the bailiff announced the judge was coming in. Peter saw a solemn Mr. Tolliver and Mr. Tupper, with their other lawyers and assistants, at the defendant's table, with Rosalie Hatch in a chair at the side, but Dr. Hatch was not there. Chickenshit again, Peter thought. Some convenient emergency, something *he* had decided represented an emergency, that only he, the Great God Brown, could handle, got him out of hearing the outcome of the trial. He was so transparent. He was doing really important things, and this whole trial was beneath him, that was the line, wasn't it, but still how he would rub it in if he won, and how it would simply not be mentioned, not exist in his world, if he lost.

The foreman of the jury, Mr. Louis Guyton, stood.

"Ladies and gentlemen, have you reached a verdict?" Judge Fielding asked.

"We have, your Honor," Mr. Guyton replied.

He handed a piece of paper to the court clerk, who had stepped over to the jury box, and she took it to the judge, who looked at it and gave it back to her. She read it loudly and distinctly. "Title of Court and Cause. We, the jury in the above entitled cause find a verdict in favor of the plaintiff, Mrs. Margaret Corti, and against the defendant, Dr. Matthew Hatch, and assess damages in the sum of two hundred and fifty thousand dollars. Signed, Louis I. Guyton, Foreman." She paused and then asked, "Ladies and Gentlemen, is that your verdict?" The jurors nodded and mumbled affirmatively. Anne squeezed Peter's hand hard, and delightedly squeaked in his ear like a mouse. He smiled at her.

Mr. Tolliver was on his feet at once calling out. "I am shocked, shocked," he said, then lower, "truly shocked."

"Did you want to say something, Mr. Tolliver?"

"Your Honor, I would like to have the jury polled."

"All right, the clerk will. Miss Hanrahan, go ahead."

She went down the list, asking each juror to respond as to his or her verdict. There were ten ayes. The two no's were the florist's wife in the back row, and the young cattle rancher, also in the back.

Mr. Cousman turned around now and hugged Peggy Corti, who smiled at Peter over the attorney's shoulder. Peter squeezed her hand, too, as she drew it away and reached for her handkerchief. The few dozen spectators there for the verdict stood now, talking to each other. The chattering newsmen came inside the railing ready to get statements from the lawyers and viewpoints from the jurors.

The judge pounded his gavel. "Quiet, please, quiet. Ladies and gentlemen, I wish to thank you for your services. You are dismissed now. I hope the remainder of your summer is a pleasant one."

The jurors stood up, shaking hands and talking with each other. Mr. Corti and Peggy went over to thank them. Peter saw that the court clock said seven thirty as the judge, nose and chin high in the air, disappeared through the door to his chambers. The defendant's lawyers, having packed up their briefcases with unusual speed, were disappearing out the swinging mahogany doors with Rosalie Hatch in their midst, talking earnestly.

"I think that is probably quite the right amount, Mr. Cousman," Peggy said to him. "I'm so proud of you.. You were great. Your final speech was perfect, I thought. Louis would have approved of what we did." She began crying violent tears now, and Mr. Cousman put his arms around her, and comforted her as he might have a child. At last she stopped and gave Mr. Cousman a small kiss on his cheek, while she hugged Peter around his waist. "Good-bye." She kissed Anne, too. "I've got to go home. I'll call you next week, Mr. Cousman. And Peter, you promised, so please come and bring Anne to dinner soon."

Peter nodded, his own eyes full, and then shook hands solemnly with Mr. Corti, who embraced the young doctor, but could not talk. Mr. Corti pounded Mr. Cousman on the shoulder blade again, before he walked out arm in arm with Peggy.

"Wonderful people," Mr. Cousman said, picking up his briefcase. "We better get out of here, Peter, before they throw us out." The bailiff was turning out lights in the now silent and evacuated chamber. Peter glanced around once more before the ancient swinging doors squeaked shut behind them.

As they walked along, Peter was at first silent, and then said to Mr. Cousman, "Ever since the end of your summation, I've been wondering just what I've been doing with all my time on this case. I thought I'd be accomplishing something with Matthew Hatch if we won the case, and then I realized you don't think so at all, and now I'm completely unsure myself."

"Possibly if you had two or three more malpractice cases won against him in the next few years things would really happen. I mean, from what you say, the medical societies probably wouldn't do much even then, but he'd have trouble getting insured. Even some of his faithful patients would begin to wonder about him, I imagine."

"I could never get anything against him again. He wouldn't let me within four blocks of the Hatch Hospital."

Mr. Cousman stopped at the elevator door then and stared straight up at Peter. "I think your thoughts and actions have been right, my boy, throughout this affair. I believe you've come to a better understanding of the problem affecting your whole profession because of it. Believe me, I have too. Besides, I think you're going to do something about it yet. Keep in your mind what you've learned as you go on with your education, decide what to do, when, how to do it. You've got a problem by the tail, and you're hanging on. You have to figure out how to get it by the *neck*. Don't stop now."

An elevator came and went as Mr. Cousman talked. Peter nodded as he stood listening. He realized Mr. Cousman's words were not uttered casually, but rather were carefullly put and totally meant. He absorbed them, stored them for contemplation, happier now that they'd been said, as he asked Mr. Cousman, "Will you have a cocktail with us here, or would you meet us later on in Oakland for a small celebration? Anne and I would love that. It would be a real pleasure for us."

"I appreciate the offer, Peter, but a new case came in my office last week which is a real toughie. We go to court the middle of next week for our first hearing. I've got to get a night's rest and dig in tomorrow, and probably work the whole weekend. Sometime soon though, we will get together. I still want to take you to the restaurant in San Francisco I mentioned, so I'll call you. I want Mrs. de Vega to meet Anne. We'll do it soon. Within a few weekends." He paused and looked wistfully over at Anne, and then shepherded them both into the elevator which had returned. "Peter, I want to know all the time what you are doing, where you are going. Please keep in touch with me and keep me informed. Is there any latest news now?"

"I haven't heard much from my residency applications yet. I guess they're trying to see what they can find for me. Actually, Dr. Dunning did write from Los Angeles and tell me just that, but I haven't gotten any word since."

"Dunning seemed very interested in you when he was here. He asked enough questions about you. I imagine he will try to be of help."

"I hope so, but I wouldn't mind going back to Baltimore either, at this point."

They were at the courthouse door now, and Peter shook hands with Mr. Cousman. At the last moment they were suddenly shy with each other.

"Thanks a million for everything, Peter," the lawyer said. "I can't tell you how pleasant it's been to work with you, and how very much I hope good things will happen for you now."

"I'll call next week, and let you know what's going on."

"Good-bye, Anne," Mr. Cousman said, bending forward to kiss her on the cheek. "Take care of this fellow. And yourself."

"Good-bye, Mr. Cousman," she said.

Peter opened the car door for Anne, and then got in on his side, fussing with the mechanics of starting up the Ford to cover his confusion and sadness at the end of this day.

"What's the matter, Peter?" Anne asked him.

"Oh, it's just hard to put so much of myself into something, and then feel it didn't work out or come to anything."

"Is that what you think?"

"I guess so."

"You're probably wrong."

"Maybe so. I hope so. I suppose it will take some time to tell."

"At least you have me."

"At least? That's not any 'at least.'"

"Thank you, darling, for saying that."

"You know what we have to do next?"

"What?"

"Get a wedding license."

"If you say so."

"You shouldn't kid me. You don't want to hurt the one you love."

"I know it," she said, hugging his arm.

45

PETER'S call the next morning to Dr. Cunningham in Baltimore was completed just as Marshall Wormser came in his apartment and slumped on the couch.

"Did you get my letter, sir?" Peter asked Dr. Cunningham.

"Yes, Peter, but I haven't answered it yet, because I was trying to get some information. I just did find out what I wanted to know this morning, and I was going to write you this afternoon."

"Any good news?"

"As a matter of fact, yes, I think so. One of our second-year residents here in surgery, Philip Merenbach, has been sick for a month now with hepatitis. I was talking to the medical people today, and they say he's going to be on the shelf for several months more. He's been really ill. Well, we talked it over in the surgery department, and we decided we couldn't get a second-year resident this time of the year, but we could take you on as a first-year resident, and have you, with the other first-year men, help to take up the slack with Merenbach out. Of course, none of you can do second-year work, but you can help the second-year residents with some of their routine stuff, so they can stretch themselves over their schedules until Merenbach gets back, whenever that may be."

"That sounds wonderful."

"Are you ready to leave there?"

"Yes, the trial's over. I didn't tell you all about it, but I've been involved in a trial—"

"We've heard about it back here."

"Have you really?"

"Yes, the medical papers carried news about the suit, and a couple of alumni from Oakland noticed you were from Biddle and let us know about it, kept us informed. They seemed to think this fellow, Hatch, was that his name, was a bad actor, and weren't too surprised at his trouble. Felt you were doing the right thing, and I must say I tend to agree."

"I'm not sorry I did it."

"I'm sure you aren't."

"But I don't know that I accomplished anything."

"It's hard to tell often, on something like that. How did it come out, anyway? Did you win or lose?"

"We won. Got a two hundred and fifty thousand dollar judgment."

"That's all right. That's good. Well, you heard my proposal. Are you interested?"

"Definitely. I want to come, and I certainly accept."

"Splendid. When can you be here, Peter?"

"Let me think. I'd have to have at least ten days."

"That's fine. Ten days is fine. Take two weeks if you need to. If you could be here to go to work by Monday, August twenty second, for sure, we'd be satisfied."

"No question about that, and I might be able to get there sooner."

Peter hung the receiver back up slowly. "What was that all about, Peter?" Marsh asked, his feet up on the cocktail table.

"It was Dr. Cunningham, my old teacher back at Biddle in Baltimore. He tells me that they have an opening for me right now as a first-year resident in surgery. This is really great. It all sort of stuns me. I thought maybe he could find some corner in pathology to stick me into, if I was lucky, and then next July first start me off in surgery, so to get right into a residency is a tremendous break."

"Hey, that's all right. Look, I came over here to bring you this letter. I thought it looked important. It's from University Medical School in Los Angeles, and somehow it got sent over to the Hatch."

"Thanks, Marsh. About a quarter of my mail still goes over there no matter how hard I try to have it sent here." Peter opened the letter. It was from Arnold Dunning, a very nice and rather long letter, which said they had no openings now, and would not have until the following July 1st, but would be glad to accept his application for residency in surgery for that time. "Nothing great, Marsh. They won't have any openings at University Medical Center in L.A. until next summer, but would be delighted to consider me for then."

"Well, sit down, buddy," Marsh said, " 'cause *I've* got some other news for you, too, and I don't want you to pass out when I hand it on."

"Now, don't talk like that. I'm not in the mood for any more suspense. Tell me what you're going to say."

"Sit down, and I will."

"Okay, now tell me, you bastard."

"Did you hear that Hatch had another suit filed against him yesterday?"

"No kidding?"

"Yes, a good-sized one, too. I hear it's for four hundred thousand. It will probably be in tonight's paper. A Redfield boy he treated for burns. A teen-ager. Matthew left the pressure dressings on too long, the wound got infected, and there was a very bad cosmetic result. I remember at the time the family was really upset."

"I don't recall the case at all."

"It was before you came."

"Well, personally, I'm glad to hear it. I hope he gets sued ten times more in the next year."

"I'm with you. Well, you're going to Baltimore, are you?"

"Yes, and they'd like me there soon. Anne and I want to get married right away, too. I thought we would here, but maybe we should get married in Reno."

"Why don't you do that? My wife and I would love to have an excuse to fly over there and be your witnesses."

"We could pack up in the next two days and take off Sunday morning, say, and get married in the afternoon, so that wouldn't interfere with you too much. Of course her father should come, too. And if we get my car all filled with our things, there wouldn't be any room for anyone to go with us, I'm afraid."

"So what's the problem? He could fly over with us."

"I suppose so. I'm going to call Anne right now and talk to her."

"Well, I've got to get on my horse. Phone me at home and let me know what's doing. Better yet, come over for dinner and tell me in person. We can all get stinking and celebrate, and talk over everything at the same time."

They went to Marsh's that night, and with great effort kept him, as their too generous host, from getting them so tight they'd be hung-over the next day. Saturday they worked and Sunday morning they were up early, sweeping out Peter's apartment, taking Anne's final small items out of her father's house and putting them in the car.

"Is that everything?" Mr. Alexio asked as he stood on the sidewalk by the car and bent over to look anxiously in the rear window.

"That's enough," Peter said. "Now if we somehow can get Anne's stuff in Berkeley packed in the trunk, we'll be all set."

"Well, good luck, you two," Mr. Alexio said, "and I'll see you in the afternoon in Reno."

"Good-bye, Dad," Anne said, kissing her father on the lips. "Thanks for everything."

"Yes, my doll."

"Good-bye, sir," Peter said, smiling at Mr. Alexio, and realizing at the same time that there was nothing so much in the world he wanted to do now as to get out of San Marcial. But after U-turning on Valleyview and then waving again to

Mr. Alexio, he went only several blocks into town, before he pulled over to the curb and stopped.

"What's the matter?" Anne asked. "Is it a tire?"

"I want you to give me a kiss," he said to her.

She looked at him at first curiously, asking "Why?" as she moved close beside him.

"For good luck. Just because I want to. Because I love you."

"Don't misunderstand me," she said, "I'm all in favor." She kissed him long and fully, holding on to him tightly.

"That's all I need, now, to make me a happy man," Peter said, whistling as he went into downtown San Marcial, then angled out of it through the southern part of town, past the intersection where the truck had snagged Rosalie Hatch's car and brought him into this city unconscious, past the fields and the hills and the tiny towns of the Cima Valley, and onto the open road, heading for Oakland, Berkeley, Highway 40, Reno, Nevada, for Baltimore and Biddle Medical Center, looking optimistically ahead to a future for himself and the profession he had chosen.